LOCKOUT

New York Times Bestseller

John J. Nance

WildBluePress.com

This is a work of fiction. Names, characters, businesses, places, events and incidents are either the products of the author's imagination or used in a fictitious manner. Any resemblance to actual persons, living or dead, or actual events is purely coincidental.

LOCKOUT published by:
WILDBLUE PRESS

P.O. Box 102440
Denver, Colorado 80250

Publisher Disclaimer: Any opinions, statements of fact or fiction, descriptions, dialogue, and citations found in this book were provided by the author, and are solely those of the author. The publisher makes no claim as to their veracity or accuracy, and assumes no liability for the content.

978-1-942266-60-0 *Trade Paperback ISBN*
978-1-942266-61-7 *eBook ISBN*

Interior Formatting by Elijah Toten
www.totencreative.com

"John Nance has added another intriguing volume to his body of work. This fascinating story of technology gone awry, rich with accurate detail, satisfies and terrifies as it takes the reader on a wild ride through the night sky on an airliner no one on board can control."

—**Captain Sully Sullenberger**, author of #1 New York Times Bestseller **SULLY**, and **MAKING A DIFFERENCE:** ***Stories of Vision and Courage from America's Leaders***; pilot of US Airways 1549, "**Miracle on the Hudson**"

"Once again, John Nance has provided a Mach-speed, high altitude page-turner in the form of a modern-day aviation thriller. Packed into the flight plan of "Lockout" are very real challenges faced by today's airline pilot. Captain Nance has done his homework. Both pilots and passengers will enjoy the suspense. Pay attention to the seat belt sign and buckle in!"

—**Les Abend**, Contributing Editor/**FLYING MAGAZINE**, Contributor/**CNN.com**, On-air Aviation Analyst/**CNN**

To Kathleen, with endless love and appreciation!

PROLOGUE

October 2012

On approach to Anchorage International Airport, Alaska

Dan Horneman tried to relax his death grip on the control yoke, but the turbulence buffeting the Boeing 737 was alarming, and with every lurch his right hand squeezed harder.

There was no time to enjoy, or even look at, the snow-covered Chugash Mountains, a framed wonderland off to the right. He was barely hanging on.

Friggin' testosterone test! Dan growled to himself. This flight wasn't a formal checkride, but obviously Captain Tollefson had decided to see what the new guy was made of and whether he could hold his own against the always flawless airmanship of the Arctic Eagles—the name the airline's experienced, Anchorage-based pilots called themselves. Dan had been warned about their superior attitude, a special self-appointed elite among Pangia World Airways pilots, and so far Tollefson was living the image precisely

And I had to pick one of the worst weather days of the year!

It wasn't as if the whole hazing experience was a surprise—Jerry Tollefson had asked enough ridiculously overbearing technical questions before departure from Salt Lake to tip his hand. Slightly younger than Dan's thirty-eight years and slightly shorter at five nine, Tollefson seemed like a decent sort, if a bit too sure of himself. But Dan fully expected to be grilled further during their layover. Clearly Tollefson had heard the rumors about Dan Horneman.

For that matter, who hadn't?

From his left seat position, the captain was glancing

over at Dan now with a smile, clearly enjoying the grim, determined look on his first officer's face, and the arrogance riled Dan even further.

"It's a mite breezy today, to say the least," Jerry Tollefson said.

"No problem," Dan managed, trying to force a smile, his throat feeling like cotton. It was his turn to land, and there was no question that any competent Pangia Airways copilot should be able to take any weather conditions in stride.

Yet …

Tollefson was leaning forward importantly, reading something on his forward computer screen as Dan reached to the glareshield and adjusted the airspeed selector, dialing in 160 knots, an electronic order to the autothrottles to maintain that speed. The landing gear was already down and locked and the flaps extended to thirty degrees—the final setting for landing. He was fighting to keep the Boeing 737 under control, the jet's flight path moving them steadily toward the runway even though the nose of the jet was pointing almost twenty degrees to the left, crabbing into the wind. Their destination, Anchorage runway 7R—one of two parallel runways aligned with compass heading 070—lay three miles ahead, the threshold of the runway beginning on a small cliff some 300 feet above sea level. All afternoon it had been swept by a vicious wind from the north propelling snowdrifts across its 12,000-foot length. To make matters worse, the tower had reported poor braking on 7R, the only runway open and plowed. He might need every inch of the ice-covered surface to fight the airplane safely to the ground and slow her down.

"Winds are three-five-zero at twenty-two, gusts to thirty …" Captain Tollefson said, repeating the latest information from the tower. "That's about a twenty-five knot crosswind component, and … our limits."

"Got it," Dan managed in a low croak.

The tower controller cut through his concentration with the final landing clearance, and Jerry responded in a routine tone of voice. "Pangia 113 cleared to land Seven-Right."

The jet seemed to be settling, but its motion felt a bit strange, and Dan glanced at the airspeed indicator without registering the value. They were bouncing so severely it was hard to read any of the instruments.

He was behind the airplane, barely hanging onto her, like a terrified rider trying to stay on a runaway horse.

An interphone call chime from the flight attendants had reverberated through the cockpit moments before, and Dan's brain was only now registering the fact that the captain had already pulled the interphone handset to his ear, his attention suddenly diverted.

"Smoke in the cabin? Where's it coming from?" Tollefson asked.

From what Dan could hear of the exchange, smoke was curling from one of the restrooms in the back, and it was getting worse, which could mean a real emergency. Whatever the cause, it was now completely distracting the captain.

Dan doubled his concentration on the flight instruments, looking in momentary panic for the ILS, the Instrument Landing System indications, before remembering that the captain had turned it off.

"Dan, you don't need the ILS or the flight director," Jerry had said moments before, breezily playing the instructor. "Your runway is in sight and we're cleared for a visual approach. Real simple, partner. There it is. Go land on it."

For some reason, being cleared for a so-called "visual approach" hadn't struck fear in his heart. At least not like it had before. He'd had almost no flight time in a real 737 since passing his rather pro forma checkride, and even that had been administered in a flight simulator safely bolted to a concrete floor. Not that he couldn't fly manually, but what *was* upsetting him was the unnecessary loss of the Instrument Landing System's guidance. He wasn't used to flying a big jet visually, without the step-by-step procedures of what pilots called an instrument approach.

Dan glanced quickly at the captain. Mr. Macho over there seemed to love seat-of-your-pants flying. He half expected Jerry to turn around and snap off the autothrottles as well, which would force Dan to ride the throttles manually with his left hand to maintain airspeed. He was barely hanging onto the beast as it was!

The fleeting thought that he should make absolutely sure the autothrottles were, indeed, engaged crossed his mind. But the thought instantly fell victim to the avalanche of other stimuli cascading through his consciousness. Trying to figure out why the big Boeing seemed so sluggish and slow was taking center stage.

To Dan's left, Jerry was still hunched over the center console with the interphone handset, trying to guide the flight attendants through the specific steps needed to isolate a cabin fire. Whatever was happening back there wasn't getting any better, and Jerry was violating the sterile cockpit rule talking about other matters during a difficult approach—not that Dan wanted to challenge him on protocol. They might have to declare an emergency any second and ask for the fire trucks, but the immediate plan would still be the same: Land as expeditiously as possible on the runway just ahead.

There it was again, that same feeling they were sinking too much. It shuddered through Dan, prompting him to pull more back pressure on the yoke as he ran the pitch trim nose up to compensate. He had to be missing something. Nothing felt right!

Still more back pressure and more nose up trim. *Definitely not right!*

"Get out the fire extinguishers and check the trash bins in the restrooms and turn off the circuit breakers in the galley," Jerry barked the order into the phone.

"Should we declare an emergency?" Dan asked, glancing at Jerry in time to see him shake his head.

Dan glanced back up at the glareshield, confirming the 160-knot speed he'd dialed into the speed selection window. But his confusion was growing over what the wallowing of the 737 was trying to tell him. He stole another glance at the real airspeed indicator with such a firm expectation of seeing the same 160-knot reading that his brain refused to contradict him with the fact that it read only 130 knots.

The jet was descending through an altitude of 600 feet above the snow-covered surface of Turnigan Arm, the body of shallow seawater that alternately became a vast mudflat at low tide, the scope of it extending from the western end of the runway several miles across the channel.

"You're kidding! A cigarette in the trashcan?" The captain was shaking his head, still on the interphone.

Once more Dan ran the pitch trim nose up and increased his pull on the control yoke to get them back up on the glide path, but as the nose seemed to respond, a sudden, massive, audible vibration coursed through the control column, refusing to stop, the vibrations buzzing through Dan's consciousness, confusing him, paralyzing him, the shaking making no more sense than the sudden blur of motion in his peripheral vision as the captain loosed a guttural cry and lunged forward, flinging the handset away.

"JESUS!"

Tollefson jammed the throttles to the stops and shoved the control yoke forward. The engines wound up to full power, accelerating and buzzing at full takeoff setting, as Dan moved his left hand to back up the captain's on the throttles, but the captain angrily waved him away.

"I'VE GOT IT! MY AIRPLANE!"

The seismic shaking of the control column stopped, but Tollefson's eyes were aflame as he glanced toward his copilot.

With the airspeed rapidly increasing and the nose down, they sank below the 300-foot threshold of the runway as the four blood-red VASI lights ahead disappeared.

Dan was already folding up with embarrassment. He'd failed to recognize the so-called stick shaker, the most basic emergency warning in the cockpit—the 737's way of telling its pilots that the plane was a mere three knots away from not having enough airspeed to stay in the air. He'd all but stalled them, and now Jerry was fighting to keep them in the air.

Tollefson pulled gingerly, carefully, the big 737 too low to get over the embankment less than a quarter mile ahead without more altitude, the airspeed accelerating slowly now above 130 knots. He arrested their overall descent less than 150 feet above the muddy bay, the engines screaming, the Boeing gaining airspeed, the captain careful not to re-enter the event horizon of a stall as they began climbing again, struggling to nurse the jet back above the altitude of the runway threshold.

And just as quickly they were high enough and the runway surface reappeared, the aircraft now climbing, the airspeed coming up through 165 knots, flashing over the threshold embankment at the end without shearing off the landing gear, but with little more than thirty feet to spare.

Jerry swept the throttles back to idle, fighting too much airspeed as well as the vicious, gusting crosswind. He wrestled the 737 toward the concrete, the yoke continuously in motion, using the rudder to kick out the twenty-degree crab into a sideslip as he set the jet down on the left main gear about halfway down the runway. He let her roll to the right enough to settle the right main gear and nose gear and in a blur of movement yanked the spoilers out and the thrust reversers into operation, struggling to keep her on centerline, listening to the chattering of the anti-skid system as they slowly decelerated on the slick surface through a hundred knots, then eighty, then sixty, the end of the runway coming up too fast, his stomach in a knot.

With agonizing slowness the speed decreased until at last it dropped below twenty, and Jerry Tollefson gingerly steered the 737 to the left and off the end of the runway, where he came to a complete stop on the runup apron.

The captain took a deep breath and looked over at Dan Horneman, as if an alien had suddenly plopped down in the copilot's seat.

"What in holy hell was THAT, Dan?"

"I ..."

"You almost killed us!"

"I ... I don't know, Jerry, I ..."

"Where the hell was your airspeed control?"

"I had the autothrottles on ..."

"You WHAT?"

"The autothrottles, I had them on and ..."

"No you didn't...they weren't even armed! I turned them off when I killed the ILS and told you to fly the damned approach manually. You were supposed to be flying this mother, not programming her!"

"I don't know what to say, Jerry, other than I humbly apologize, and I recognize that you saved us."

Tollefson was shaking his head in utter amazement, his left hand still on the yoke and shaking slightly as he tried to get a handle on what to say and how to answer the tower controller who was waiting for them to change to Ground Control.

"Where in the hell did you learn to fly, Horneman? Microsoft?"

CHAPTER ONE

Three Years Later

National Security Agency, Ft. Meade, Maryland (9:05 a.m. EST / 1405 Zulu)

Jenny Reynolds sighed and let her mind refocus as she forced herself to stop tapping out a desktop drum solo with her pencil. Two hours trying to unravel a mystery message had passed her personal breaking point.

Jenny shook her head in a gesture no one noticed and forced herself to disconnect from the puzzle. An hour ago she'd yanked off her iPod headset to concentrate, but the challenge of an uncracked code would not stop chewing on her. Why had a simple unidentified satellite burst managed to offend her so profoundly?

NSA's satellites and computers picked up endless bursts every hour that she couldn't translate, at least at first—transmissions with no known syntax, no known purpose, and no recognized source. Of course, there were also sophisticated communication "gamers" all over the planet who loved to stick a finger in the NSA's eye from time to time with sequences which were exactly what they appeared to be: garbage. Gobbledygook uplinked just to worry Washington and give Ivan, Ahmed, or Chan a good laugh, especially since that scumbag Snowden defected.

But this transmission was different somehow. Not a game. Wrong point of origin, wrong frequency, wrong everything. It was there, just out of reach, teasing her to recognize something in the encoding.

And, there was that other disturbing reality: People didn't waste time encoding messages hidden in frequency harmonics and piggybacked on routine transmissions unless there was a very specific purpose to be served.

I'm trying to be the perfectionist again! she thought, well aware that her penchant for being perfect tended to irritate her geeky coworkers—as did the fact that she liked to dress well. "Learn to call for help every now and then," she'd been told in her recent job review. It was a slap in the face that still stung.

Jenny slipped her feet back into the black pumps that gave her a fighting chance of seeming taller than her petite five feet, and she force-marched herself through the labyrinth of cubicles to her boss's corner office.

As usual, Seth Zieglar's lanky six-foot frame was pretzeled nose-down in his computer, yet he was acutely aware of the skirt leaning into his doorway.

"You clattered?" he asked without looking up.

"Sorry?"

"Your stilettos," he explained, looking over and smiling. "They're like your signature. Along with your Georgia accent, that is."

"They're called pumps, Seth."

He pulled off his glasses, his voice characteristically laconic as his eyes took in her black skirt and tailored, slightly frilly white blouse. "Whatever they are, may I say without fear of receiving sexual harassment charges, that they become you?"

"As long as you don't call them FM boots again. That wasn't even subtle."

"Never! I've been appropriately reeducated. Although … now that you've once again voluntarily instilled the image of hooker boots in my head …"

"Seth!"

He raised his hands in surrender. "Sorry!"

"I've got a problem." She laid her notes on his desk and sat down beside him. "You said I should call for help, so …

'Help!'"

"Sweet! See? Wasn't that hard, was it?" He pointed dramatically at her face. "I especially liked the tentative curl of your lower lip."

"Jeez, Seth!"

"Okay … all seriousness aside, what's up?"

She sat down beside him. "The computers snagged this burst transmission about three hours ago. The thing was trying to ride undetected on a routine satellite uplink from the UK. The source, however, I think is somewhere off the Irish coast, and while there's one US Navy ship splashing around in the area, this isn't a syntax the navy ever uses. Frankly, I don't know what the heck it is."

"Well … any guesses?"

She sighed, another sign of defeat she hated. "It's … probably a programming order of some sort. It's asking another computer to do something. Closest thing in my experience would be the multiple-repeat commands we learned to send from the Jet Propulsion Lab in California to distant spacecraft. You know, 'Hey there, V-Jer, turn your antenna towards this, fire your rockets at that, and give us a precise readback.' Orders we wanted to absolutely make sure got through without error."

"But what's the urgency, Jen? What's worrying you?"

"Dude, what's it *programming*? *That's* what's bothering me."

"Okay," he said, stroking his bony chin.

"I mean, is this a targeting order for a remotely piloted vehicle, like a Global Hawk or a Predator? Is it a test? A … a programming order for a spacecraft that the owner of the satellite doesn't want seen?"

"You've run all the usual …"

"Oh, yeah," she said, unconsciously running a hand through her mane of perpetually curly chestnut hair. "I jammed it through the main supercomputers, and they can't match it."

Seth leaned forward, studying her. "You've got a hunch though, don't you?"

"No … not a hunch, really. Just a worry."

"Go ahead."

"Well, just that … if something sophisticated and in motion is being programmed, we need to know what it is and where it's headed or pointed. I mean, taking into account everyone in the world who wants to harm us and the fact that the only countries on the planet who remain our friends are Monaco and McMurdo Sound in Antarctica …"

"McMurdo is not a country, Jen."

"My point exactly. Anyway, it makes me real nervous to have what feels like a targeting sequence being sent to an unseen, unknown receiver."

"Was there a latitude or longitude in the message?"

"Maybe. There are numbers."

He nodded. "Okay, then pull our esteemed friends at the North American Air Defense Command into this, and if they act puzzled, light up Defense Intelligence."

"Whoa, Seth! I'm worried, not professionally suicidal. You want DIA pulled in on nothing more than a wild suspicion of mine?"

"We at least need to know if this is one of ours, right?"

"You think it could be a US military thing? Like a black project?"

"They don't tell us, Jen. That's why they call them black projects."

"Would they tell us if we asked real nice?" she countered, tilting her head.

"Not directly, but something would be said. Or someone very authoritative with dark glasses and a black suit would be sent over to make us calm down. And, by the by, just because the navy hasn't used a particular code pattern doesn't mean they couldn't be doing so for the first time."

"You are kidding about that, right?"

"About what? The navy?"

"The strange guys with dark glasses and black suits?"

He looked at her for a few seconds and smiled. "Maybe."

"That scares me, Seth, and I think you know it. I'm not in covert ops."

"None of us is. That's why men in black scare us."

"Okay, stop it. Seriously? Please. I don't want to know about that stuff."

"Remember, Jen," he chuckled, "just because you're paranoid doesn't mean they're *not* out to get you!"

Jenny shook her head in mock disgust and rolled her eyes. "Why do you like torturing women, Seth?"

"I don't! At least, not women in general. Mostly I just like torturing you," he grinned.

"As I always suspected."

"Seriously, Jen, they'll let us know if it's out of our bailiwick. Don't worry."

She sat in thought for a few moments. "I checked on airborne traffic, including drones passing through the area that might have birthed the transmission."

"And?"

"Nothing out there but regularly scheduled commercial flights, and none of them could use a transmission like this."

Seth was sitting quietly, waiting.

"Am I … missing something?" Jenny asked.

"Now *that*, my resident perfectionist genius, is the real question. And if we figure it out, we'll probably discover it's just some idiot in Iowa programming his toy helicopter."

"But, if we get this wrong …"

Seth sighed openly, a weary look crossing his angular features as his thoughts focused inward for a second. "Well

… if we get it wrong and something really skanky happens … like another 9/11 … nobody will ever love us again. Ever. Not even our mothers."

"Jeez, Seth."

"Welcome to life on the edge, Miss Reynolds."

She got to her feet and paused at the door, looking back.

"And for the record, y'all? I don't have an accent."

CHAPTER TWO

Ben Gurion International Airport, Tel Aviv, Israel (4:15 p.m. local / 1515 Zulu)

First Officer Dan Horneman checked his watch as he arrived at Gate B5 at Tel Aviv's airport. It was the last place he expected to be this afternoon. He had picked up an extra reserve trip from New York to Tel Aviv because it offered a four-day layover, and even if he'd stayed in the mid-level hotel Pangia rented for its crews, that would have been a great deal. Four days to relax and enjoy Tel Aviv … now shot to hell, along with the extra money! Dan had indulged himself and rented a shamelessly expensive suite at the King David Hotel and quietly cancelled the company room. He had barely settled into the luxurious digs when crew scheduling found him by phone to assign an unwanted return trip, and suddenly Dan was back in uniform, dragging his brain bag to the gate as a last-minute replacement copilot, and trying to adjust to the idea of another all night flight.

A female voice somewhere behind him failed to register at first, but its familiarity persisted at the margins of his memory until he turned to see the smiling face of Janice Johnson, her shoulder-length black hair pulled into a small pony tail riding behind her Pangia uniform hat.

"Hey there, fellow misfit," she said, giving voice to their shared outlier reputation: she for simply flying while female, he for having, as she teased him, more money than God.

Dan smiled in return as unbidden memories of their brief dating history flashed like a slightly dated movie trailer through his mind—a recent anthology that included a hedonistic week in Maui which had been as glorious for the companionship and intellectual ferment as it had been for the rather unbridled sex.

"Janice! Did you just fly this bird in?"

"Yep. And I hear you've been drafted to fly her back with our resident self-appointed diety. Captain Skygod."

"Captain who?"

"Breem. Bill Breem. God's gift to aviation. A legend in his own mind."

"Oh! I thought I was flying with Jerry Tollefson."

"Tollefson is *your* captain. You guys are the relief crew, but el supremo Breem is the primary captain."

"He's that bad?"

"To start with … spoiler alert … he and Jerry Tollefson hate each other. I mean, frothing at the mouth homicidal hate!"

"The old North Star Airlines versus Pangia Airways rivalry again?"

"No, no, Danny. Worse. Breem was a longtime captain with Stratos Air. He lost his 747 captaincy when Stratos Air was bought by Pangia, before Pangia bought us at North Star. Breem's been madder than hell about everything ever since."

"Is Breem still a training captain?"

"Oh, God, no! Not for years," Janice replied. "But he still looks down his nose at anyone who wasn't hired by the original Stratos Air, and he complains about North Star captains constantly. Breem's pushing sixty-three now, and we're all counting the days till he's gone."

"Sounds like a wonderful evening."

"Good luck, dude," she said with a smile as she leaned in and brushed his cheek with a kiss. "Miss you!"

"Why *did* we stop dating, by the way?" Dan asked, smiling in return"Because we could never get together on the same continent," she said, waving as she pivoted with her bags and headed for the exit.

Dan stood for a few moments in thought, amazed at the ridiculousness of the constant internecine warfare among angry pilots from the different airlines that had been cobbled together to form Pangia.

It was less of a war within the flight attendant ranks, but there were bruised feelings, lost seniority, and simmering upsets there as well—such as the famous thirty-year war between Pangia's two most senior flight attendants stemming from a stolen boyfriend in the late seventies. Now at ages seventy-six and seventy-eight respectively, the two were the oldest flight attendants still flying, but neither would retire before the other.

A Pangia captain was approaching the gate with a fistful of papers, his eyes on the paperwork as he passed by. Mid-thirties, Dan judged, and with a squarish, friendly face framed by sandy hair that he remembered all too well. Jerry Tollefson hadn't noticed him yet, but before Dan could snag his attention, another captain in full four-stripe regalia strode into Tollefson's face without offering his hand.

"So you're my relief crew tonight."

"If you're flying Flight 10, Bill, that would be correct," Tollefson replied, his voice cautious and all but icy.

"I thought you were still on your initial operating experience trip. What'd you do, son, scare off the check pilot?" Breem chuckled.

"Actually, I think what did the trick was finding out you were coming along," Jerry replied, his eyes boring into Breem, who wasn't about to flinch.

"Well, they warned me a boy captain from North Slope was playing relief crew."

"North STAR, Bill," Tollefson corrected, rolling his eyes. "Our airline was quite profitable and had a name."

"Oh, sorry. It's hard to remember the name of the different little operations we've bought over the years. No disrespect intended."

"Right, like calling me 'boy captain?'"

Bill Breem responded with a snort. "Well, how old are you, Jerry?"

"Thirty-five."

"I rest my case. You've done damn well getting to four stripes in a major international airline by age thirty-five. I've just been around a lot longer and so, sometimes, I'll admit, it seems like I'm surrounded by boy wonders. I apologize if the term offended you."

"It did, but I accept your apology."

"Good. See you aboard."

CHAPTER THREE

Gate B5, Ben Gurion airport, Tel Aviv, Israel (4:40 p.m. local / 1540 Zulu)

Two black sedans with heavily tinted windows slid to a stop in a scene so familiar that few of the ramp workers took anything but passing notice. Two men with dark glasses, dead serious expressions, and equally serious automatic weaponry emerged from the lead car and in a fluid and practiced routine, scanned the surrounding tarmac for threats. Satisfied, the two moved to the second vehicle and opened the rear door, ushering a short, bald, older man and a stunning younger woman to the jetway stairs. In less than two minutes, the lead driver was back behind the wheel, escorting the second car from the airport and disappearing into the busy streets of Tel Aviv, their presence on the ramp nothing more than a whispered myth.

The rapid entrance of Moishe Lavi and the woman to the forward-most seats in the unoccupied first class cabin of Pangia Flight 10 had been witnessed by no one but the flight attendants. Not even the pilots had been briefed that a former prime minister of Israel was joining them, and the lead flight attendant had been warned to collect all her crew's cell phones until after takeoff, assuring that no one who noticed could report Lavi's presence.

Still grieving the loss of the trappings of great power, Moishe Lavi settled uncomfortably into the elaborate sleeper seat, motioning immediately for his companion to lean close and take a new round of notes in the non-stop soliloquy of action items and ideas he'd been firing at her since arising at 5:00 a.m. Instead of complying, Ashira Dyan settled into her own seat and smiled, shaking her head slightly as she mouthed a warning in Hebrew to wait. Lavi started to protest but thought better of it and smiled back with a nod, his mind replaying the delicious memory of her naked form gliding across the hotel room a few hours earlier after she'd pulled away from his embrace.

Ah, sweet Ashira! he thought. Only thirty-four years old with a perfect body and shoulder-length black hair. She was like so many accomplished Israeli women who could melt you with their femininity, or effortlessly break your neck with their military training.

Especially Ashira, whose prowess as a power-hungry she-wolf entranced him even more. She was a decorated major in the Israeli Defense Force, well trained in intelligence, and a perfect secretary when she needed to be. He was well aware that the only reason she was playing the role of his mistress was the eternal seduction of great political power.

Of course, now that he'd been thrown out of office, how long would *that* last?

He thought of the long flight and what lay ahead. He could probably depend on her loyalty for a few more months before she jumped ship—before she realized he was never going to regain power. He understood that power was the aphrodisiac. If Moishe Lavi had ever been a physical prize to any woman, those days were ancient history.

Of course, he was soon to be history himself.

Moishe fished out his iPhone and fumbled inexpertly at the screen, surprised when Ashira wagged her finger.

"No!" she said, with the understated confidence of the senior Mossad agent she'd long been. "You could be tracked. We don't want any chance of being located until we're long gone. Even then, it would be hazardous to everyone aboard."

He met her eyes and nodded. She didn't understand, of course, despite her training. His enemies were many, and while the worst of the lot were well outside the borders of

Israel, they were equally determined to kill him. Especially the Iranian mullahs. Which was, he thought, why killing them first was the only viable option.

But for the moment, tactically, she was right, and that reality irritated him.

"Very well," he replied, indulging in the slight vanity of puffing his tone up to make it sound like the idea was all his own. "I think it's best to call in flight."

He swiveled his squat, aging body toward the adjacent window of the Airbus dismissively, letting his thoughts return for the thousandth time to the stand he'd made in the Knesset—the no-compromise throw down that had destroyed what remained of the coalition that had made him prime minister. He was right, of course, that they would eventually be forced to launch on Tehran. But it would be too late. It would be a doomsday nuclear exchange, and two nations would essentially cease to exist.

If Israel waited.

Moishe snorted to himself, barely aware of the presence of the two pilots as they moved past him up the aisle toward the cockpit. As much as he loved this land, he was suddenly very anxious to leave it.

CHAPTER FOUR

Mojave Aircraft Storage, Mojave Airport, California (8:10 a.m. PST / 1610 Zulu)

The manager of Mojave Air Storage looked up from his battered old desk trying his damndest to figure out how his most uncommunicative employee could have acquired a sense of humor in twenty-four hours. But the perennially taciturn man just stood there in his dirty coveralls as if he'd walked out of a Grant Wood painting without his pitchfork, expressionless except for the slight look of alarm in his eyes, his voice as humorless as a funeral director.

"Not there, huh," the manager repeated, mocking the same Eeyore-class monotone his employee had used.

"No-pah," the man replied, stretching the single word into two syllables.

The wind was whining around the cracks in the old desert line office, coating everything with the fine grit the rows of airliners outside were sealed against.

"Look," the manager began, "I appreciate that you probably stayed up all night figuring out this little joke, but … see … it really isn't funny to suggest we might have misplaced a $200 million airplane."

"Not a joke, sir. I can't find that serial number. That company in Colorado we thought was probably a front for the military? It was their airplane. One of the A330s we got out there. They need it by next Thursday. I thought you had seen the order."

"How many A330s do we have out there?" the manager asked, a cold knot of apprehension beginning to make its presence known in the pit of his stomach.

"Nine. There were nine. Now we have eight, and that

serial number … the one belonging to the Colorado group … isn't one of them."

"Okay," the manager replied, "get the team and inventory the A330s, one by one, by serial numbers and placement, and come back and we'll get this figured out."

"Pad 79, where the Colorado A330 should have been, is empty. I think we sent the wrong one away," the man said, leaving the shaken manager to reflect on the possibility that *he* might not have a job a week from now. The phone on his desk was mocking him, challenging him to call the hotheaded owner of Mojave Aircraft Storage who lived several miles away, but that was the last thing he intended to do until they were certain Mojave Aircraft Storage had actually delivered the wrong airplane to the wrong client.

CHAPTER FIVE

Cockpit, Pangia World Airways Flight 10 (1610 Zulu)

With Captain Bill Breem and his first officer seizing the designation of primary pilots, Jerry Tollefson and Dan Horneman had been relegated to the status of relief crew and left to watch the takeoff from the cockpit jump seats. As planned, ten minutes into the flight, Jerry and Dan headed back for their programmed sleep period in the cramped underdeck crew rest facility.

"Programmed" always seemed so oxymoronic, Dan thought as he settled in. Some pilots could drop off on cue, but he had never been one of them. In addition to dozens of random thoughts keeping him awake, there was the "gee-whiz" factor of being a crewmember on such a sophisticated machine, and it hadn't worn off yet. The amazed little boy in him was usually too excited to drift off to sleep and instead demanded—*demanded*—permission to stay up just to watch himself lounging in such a technologically advanced cocoon.

This time, however, sleep came uncharacteristically fast. It was startling when the alarm function on his cell phone corked off after almost four hours, the watch showing him it was 1951 Zulu and alerting him that it was time to get back to the cockpit.

Dan rolled out of the crew bunk and made his way up the narrow stairs to the main deck and into one of the restrooms, closing the door for a moment of solitude and looking at the deep circles under his eyes in the mirror. He loved this job, despite feeling like an alien in Pangia's pilot culture, but there was no evading the reality that he was approaching a meltdown of cumulative fatigue. The impromptu vacation days in Tel Aviv he'd looked forward to were supposed to address that fatigue, but now they were gone.

The circles aren't too bad! he thought, admiring his full head of dark hair which always seemed to fall into place with little or no effort. His face had never been described as thin, but his facial features were angular, almost chiseled, like an emotionless sculpture, according to Laura, the one lover he missed the most. Long before his tryst with Janice Johnson, Laura had given up trying to understand the world-girdling schedule she considered ridiculously unnecessary and had tossed that backhanded compliment at him the morning they'd parted for good. Strange that he would remember that so clearly among all the other things she'd said that morning—especially the hurtful words, like saying he would never be happy until he decided he deserved the things he'd worked so hard to acquire.

The rebound girlfriend he'd found after Laura had also backed away, equally unsure he was ever going to be comfortable in his own skin.

Gotta start dating again, he promised himself. He felt no compelling need to find a mate or make babies, but … it just wasn't much of a life without sex and female companionship, and every pretty woman he saw just reminded him of what he'd lost when Laura finally gave up.

"You're filthy rich, and I'm eager to sign a pre-nup, and there's no reason not to retire right now!" she'd all but screamed. "Why the hell are you doing this? Buy your own damned jet! What are you trying to prove?"

The vivid memories faded again, and he sighed and straightened his tie, checking the crisp, professionalism of his image before leaving the restroom in time to tag along behind Jerry Tollefson as they made their way forward.

With the cockpit door closed and sealed, Dan watched Tollefson stoically endure the overly officious handoff briefing from Captain Bill Breem before sliding into the left-hand captain's seat. Breem's briefing was the usual litany: their current position, altitude, airspeed, headwind, weather, and fuel remaining, along with their estimated time of arrival in New York, but it was delivered in the fashion of a master about to turn over the wheel to a rank amateur. Breem and his copilot were scheduled to return to the cockpit in five hours and take the arrival and landing at Kennedy.

"So," Breem finished, "your job, Tollefson, is to wake the A-Team in five hours, and don't break anything in the meantime."

Dan could see Jerry's jaw muscles gyrating, absorbing the irritation of such a demeaning order, but he held his tongue for nearly thirty seconds until Breem had closed the cockpit door behind him.

"*Alrighty*, then!" Jerry said, rolling his eyes in an expression of utter contempt.

"Is he always like that?" Dan asked, as much to commiserate as to confirm.

"Oh, yeah! Pompous asshole with delusions of adequacy."

"An original Stratos Air alumnus?"

Jerry Tollefson nodded and then stopped.

"Yes. They're not all like that, but this one is a really angry dinosaur. Angry and mean."

"I've heard of him, of course, but never met the man before tonight."

"You didn't miss anything."

Jerry busied himself for a few moments with building his nest in the left-hand captain's seat, arranging his crew bag and the company-supplied iPad as Dan Horneman had just done on the right side. Satisfied all was in its place, Jerry sat back, taking in the broader nighttime view from the cockpit of Flight 10.

The lights of Zagreb, Croatia, some eighty miles to the east were visible to their right as the Airbus cruised along at

37,000 feet, and neither pilot spoke for several minutes.

Jerry snorted, shaking his head, one more thought incapable of suppression. “The thing I can’t stand about Breem is his air of superiority and his constantly demonstrated disgust for the rest of us.”

Dan let the words parade by, trying hard not to focus on the concept of hypocrisy as related to Jerry Tollefson. He tried to see Breem through Tollefson’s eyes without seeing Jerry in the same light, but the effort was failing. He wondered if Tollefson, too, had suddenly realized the ludicrous nature of his hypocritical slam.

No, Dan concluded, *he’d never see it.*

The autopilot was doing the flying, but now that their perceived common antagonist had left the cockpit, Dan could feel tension rising between himself and the captain, evaporating what moments before had been a fleeting brotherhood between the two of them based on a classic “we’re okay, but he’s not okay” bond.

Without Breem, Dan was now the outsider, and there was, indeed, an elephant in the cockpit—a big one—and it was going to be a miserable flight if someone didn’t throw a spotlight on the beast.

“So, Jerry …” Dan began, intending to slip gently into the subject of their near-disaster in Anchorage years before, but Jerry Tollefson was already locked and loaded.

“So, *Dan* …” Jerry echoed, sarcastically, “Had enough fun playing airline pilot?”

Dan glanced over at the left seat and tried hard not to overthink his response. He’d expected something snarky, and clearly he wasn’t going to be disappointed.

“Well, I’m still here.”

“Yeah, so I noticed. With all your millions, I thought you’d have bought your own jet by now and just hired one of us poor schmucks to fly it.”

"It may be difficult to understand, Jerry, but I enjoy this challenge of being an airline pilot."

"Really?"

"Yes."

"Enjoying the process?"

"Yes. Definitely."

"Well, that makes one of us at least."

"Look, Jerry …"

"So … when we last tried to crash together up in Alaska, you didn't have a lot of flight time. Had much since?"

"I had just checked out, if you recall."

"Oh, I certainly do recall," Tollefson replied with a snort. "It was almost the last thing I ever recalled. It's interesting, talking about the merger of North Star and Pangia, since it was Pangia that hired you. At North Star, we had this irritating little tendency to hire competent pilots rather than raw trainees. Pangia, apparently, doesn't differentiate."

An uncomfortable silence filled the space between them for almost a minute.

"Okay … Jerry, look, I know we got off on the wrong foot three years ago …"

"Ya *think*?" Jerry snorted, turning to face the copilot. "But I wouldn't exactly call it getting off on the wrong foot, Danny. I'd call it perhaps the worst crew introduction in airline history." He paused studying Dan's stoic expression for a few seconds, reconsidering the force of his pent up anger. "Look, Dan, you're obviously a nice guy, but your flying sucks, and the memory of that botched approach still scares the hell out of me. But … as I say, I guess you've had a lot more experience since then."

"More than three years."

"Good!" Jerry kept his eyes on the right-seater as he reached out with his left hand and pointed to one of the instruments on the forward panel. "For example, you do now know about this little thing here called an airspeed indicator?"

"You really can't let this go, can you?" Dan asked.

"Well, I admit I get a mite testy when people try to kill me with a complete lack of aeronautical skill, okay? Or were you going to tell me it was all systemic and not really your fault? Use crew resource management as an excuse for no individual accountability?"

Dan cleared his throat, internally holding onto the throttle of his own anger.

If you were my employee, I'd fire your ass on the spot! Dan thought.

"Jerry, I don't do excuses, okay? But the fact is, if you'll recall, you gave me a visual, manual approach in high winds that day, and then, because you got distracted by a cabin smoke problem, I was totally solo, and I wasn't—"

Tollefson whirled on him, his voice raised. "You damn near killed a planeload of innocent passengers and me, Dan, and the real cause is apparently because you decided to come over and slum a bit, pretend to be an airline pilot, but one who didn't understand the basic fact that we need at least some wind over the wings. I've never had to take the airplane away from a copilot or a captain before, or since!"

"So that's the bottom line, right?"

"What?" Jerry replied, the word spoken with the report of a bullet propelled by contempt.

"Not that I'm a bad pilot, or even a good pilot who made a bad mistake, but that I've got too much money and therefore can't be part of the club."

"*What?* If you don't know how to fly safely … if this is some dilettante exercise, playing airline pilot … you shouldn't be here. That's all I meant."

Dan was shaking his head angrily, energetically, letting the dampers fall away from his usual reluctance to engage an unnecessary fight.

"Okay, bullshit, Jerry! That's just frigging bullshit! You just tipped your hand, Buddy. The real truth is, I'm a permanent outsider here because I have too much money and I was a success in another field. And ... *and* ... because I failed your testosterone check. Right? But that overblown Alaskan bush pilot cowboy shit is just as toxic as it is intoxicating. Hail the Arctic Eagles! If you're not swaggering enough and macho enough to impress us, you can't join the club, because you don't have the right stuff! And if you have too much money, you're automatically excluded."

"None of us cares a whit about your money, Horneman, and this has nothing to do with bush flying. We're professional pilots, and what we do care about is precision and safety and competence!"

"Jerry, you were exuding that cowboyish bush pilot attitude from every pore the day we almost bought it with my mistake. Remember turning off the autopilot and the autothrottles and even the damned ILS? What ever happened to the company rule about using all available nav aids?"

"You were relying too much on the automation!"

"Of course I was. You're right. Know why? Because that's how I was trained! But you don't need automation because you guys never make mistakes, do you? As long as you survive, that is. I'm surprised you don't rank each other by how many enthralled women throw their panties at you when you walk down the street!"

"What the hell are you nattering about, Horneman?"

"The profession and responsibility of flying versus the swaggering 'Hi girls, I fly jets!' version of daring airmen bringing it in on a wing and a prayer. That's what I'm talking about. You're locked in the Jurassic Age of piloting, Jerry. *YES* I fucked up. Yes! But you apparently can't forgive that, because in your world, being imperfect is not the right stuff. Well here's the truth: Real men and real pilots make mistakes."

"I've made lots of mistakes!" Jerry snarled. "I've never claimed to be perfect!"

"Yeah, but, holding everyone else … particularly me … to a standard of being perfect is the same thing. But again, it's all so easy because I'm not one of you."

Jerry snorted, shaking his head, the gesture as dismissive and disgusted as he could make it.

"Well, I can see this is going to be one hell of a fun evening!"

"I didn't start it, but I'm not going to sit here like a whipped puppy and take your unjustified contempt."

"And what if I hadn't pulled it out and we'd crashed, Dan? Would you accept the contempt then? If you'd survived and others died wholesale because of your screw up?"

"No one would have greater contempt for me than me, and for that matter, what makes you think I did escape unscathed? I had my own destroyed self-esteem to deal with, as well as all the added scrutiny from the chief pilot and the training department."

"Poor you!"

"Jerry, what kills me is that you won't even admit your own complicity in going head down on the interphone while you should have been monitoring the approach and your obviously untested first officer. What do you think the NTSB would have said about that if we hadn't made it?"

"You couldn't find the damned throttles! That's the bottom line for me. Competent pilots don't lose sight of the airspeed!"

"I'm sorry. I thought the autothrottles were engaged. As I say, I made a huge, honking mistake."

"Yeah … and about that …" Jerry Tollefson had swiveled partially around in the captain's seat, glaring at his right-seater with blood in his eye, daring the underling to talk back again as he played the challenged alpha wolf. "Whoever taught you to just sit there and watch the airspeed deteriorate without touching the throttles? What kind of moron doesn't teach watching the throttle movement or listening to the engines?"

"You wouldn't believe what I was and what I wasn't taught, Jerry," Dan said, as quietly as possible. "You asked me after you'd saved us where the hell I learned to fly, but I never had a chance to answer you."

"You made the same ridiculous mistake as those systems operators at Asiana made in 2013 in San Francisco! Maintaining one's airspeed is the prime directive."

"Which I was never taught."

"Excuse me?"

"Where did *you* learn to fly, Jerry?"

"The United States Navy," Jerry snapped. "So where were you trained?"

"I learned in one of the toughest flight training environments you can imagine," Dan said, earning a contemptuous sideways glance from the captain.

"Oh, *really*?"

"Yeah … it might as well have been a correspondence course! It was a civilian ab initio program provided by a little airline in New England desperate for pilots … an airline that didn't care if I had never even flown in a small plane and didn't think it was important. The same kind of deficient ab initio course the big airlines are now trying to use. This little carrier was looking for trained monkeys to fill the legal square and didn't even realize it themselves."

Jerry Tollefson had leaned forward to jab at the buttons of what in a Boeing would be a flight management computer, but he stopped suddenly and straightened up in his seat, fixing Dan with a questioning gaze. "What do you mean?

You telling me you didn't even have your private pilot's license when you got your first airline job? That kind of 'ab initio?'"

"Private ticket? Hell, Jerry, they hired me out of my office in Seattle. I'd never even flown a small plane. I was disillusioned about my Internet business and from having too much success too fast, and I'd always, always wanted to fly. So I decided to sell my company and go the route of any other average individual without much money. I thought that was the honorable thing to do, something that would be respected as paying my dues, you know? I had no idea how contemptuous people would be about that decision."

"What do you mean, contemptuous?"

Dan shook his head, smiling ruefully, trying hard not to say something even more sarcastic.

"It was a huge relief to sell my company and stop spending every day worrying when the whole thing might collapse. I watched my father and my family lose everything to a recession and never recover. I was very lucky to make enough and get out in time."

"When I flew with you," Jerry said, "… everyone was talking about our billionaire boy pilot. We figured you were slumming with the working stiffs."

"I hated that. I *still* hate that impression! I'd had 2,000 hours of flying airborne computers by the time I applied here, and as I said, I had no idea I was deficient. I was trained to fly primarily by autopilot and dial in altitudes and headings and airspeeds and told to keep my hands off the controls if the autoflight system could do it better. Precisely the same malady that caused the Asiana crash in San Francisco in 2013."

"A systems operator."

"Yes. Exactly. I was trained to be a dumb systems operator, not a pilot. When I hit the line, I had less than 300 hours. It was before the FAA changed the rule to require 1,500."

"Less than *300*?"

If I'd had any idea how little I knew about stick and rudder flying, I could have bought 400 or 500 hours of quality flight instruction. But what I didn't get a chance to practice were those basic skills. I had no idea that was a deficit."

"And then *we* hire you," Tollefson said flatly.

"Yeah. Sorry about that!"

"What'd you do, pull strings?"

Dan shook his head with a rueful laugh. "Jesus, you, too? I guess everyone thinks that. No, I didn't pull strings. Wish I had. Someone might have told me to back off. Instead, after driving regional jets around for almost two years and seldom ever touching the yoke, I dropped an application in the box at the very moment you guys were desperate for new first officers, and after a whirlwind ground school and a few sessions in the simulator, you got the lucky number. I mean, Pangia World Airways *knew* my limited aeronautical background a heck of a lot better than I did."

"Did they also know you were uber rich?"

"I wasn't *uber* rich, not that it has any bearing on the situation. I'm not *uber* rich. But I had no intention of telling them or anyone else I was well off. It was simply immaterial."

"So what was your net worth? Bill Gates country?"

"Hell no. I had a paltry sum compared to what I could have received if I'd kept the company several more years and taken it public before selling."

Dan Horneman met Jerry Tollefson's gaze for a few seconds, knowing what the response was going to be if he spoke in dollars. It was impossible for anyone with an average professional income to bridge the philosophical gap that separated their respective bank accounts. It was far more than numbers, it was a gulf measured in unfathomable terms of struggle and misunderstanding, and ultimately, it was always a case of 'You have what I don't, and I resent it!'"

"*How* paltry?" Jerry prompted. "Speak to me in numbers."

"About $500 million."

CHAPTER SIX

First class cabin, Pangia 10 (2000 Zulu)

Josh Begich was impressed with his own stealth. The smoking hot babe seated next to him in Seat 3A still wasn't aware he'd been indulging in a delicious, clandestine view of her substantial cleavage.

Thank God for peripheral vision! he thought.

Josh riffled another series of keystrokes across the keyboard of his laptop computer to keep her attention diverted, smiling to himself when a map expanded impressively to fill the seventeen-inch screen and then zoomed in on what appeared to be a phosphorescent aircraft against a black void, presumably as seen from space.

"Is that *us*?" the girl asked, her eyes riveted on the image as wisps of clouds appeared to pass the depiction. She shifted in her first class seat and leaned in further toward him for a better view—*his* better view. Exactly what he'd planned.

"Yes, that's us," he answered. "It's the infrared picture I'm pulling off one of our US spy satellites. I hacked into their datastream months ago and … as long as I don't stay connected too long … they never know why their camera suddenly shifts to something else."

"That … is … amazing," she said, a giveaway tone of delectable awe in her voice. "I mean, it's night, and we're still visible!"

"Yep. That's what you can do if you know these machines … and you have a Wi-Fi connection by satellite." Josh glanced at the "satellite" image running in the three-minute loop he'd constructed. It was streaming from nothing more distant than his own hard drive, and in about thirty seconds it would start again with a slight jump, perhaps giving away his deception. But the girl was apparently buying it.

What is she, fifteen like me, or sixteen? But technologically dumb as a stump.

Josh pointed to the screen again. "This jet we're on is full of computers. The whole world is now, and I can break into just about any of them."

She sat back, the slight look of awe changing to a look of skepticism. "Really?"

"Yeah. Really!" Josh replied, feeling suddenly challenged.

"So, launch a missile from North Dakota for me," she said. "You owe me for five minutes of eye-fucking my boobs!"

"Eye *what?*"

"It's okay. I'm cool with it. Now, make good on your boasts. Show me something other than a pre-cooked loop."

"Pre-cooked …"

"You're busted, dude. I saw it repeat."

"You know computers?"

She smiled a disturbing message of hidden sophistication and nodded, her eyes melting his as she sat enjoying his squirming response.

"You might say that."

"How?"

"Hey, you're the stud trying to wow the dumb blonde in the next seat, it's my turn to be mysterious. So throw down, boy. Show me something real."

Nonchalance was his thing—Joe Cool on ice—and he tried to regain that air of bravado as he shrugged his insubstantial shoulders and worked on looking slightly bored.

"Okay. I've got some pretty good moves."

"Sweet. Show me."

"It'll take a few minutes to break into the processor I'm

gonna commandeer."

"Go for it, Rambo. We've got hours," she replied with a smile. "But I'll warn you … I don't impress easy."

"What did you say your name was?" he blurted, well aware she hadn't offered it and angry with himself for yet another display of awkwardness in the presence of a pretty girl.

"Sara," she replied, eyes meeting his again for a moment before he looked away in clandestine embarrassment and prepared to do battle with a vulnerable server unseen in the distance, a knight errant out to win the damsel.

CHAPTER SEVEN

NSA, Ft. Meade, Maryland (3:15 p.m. EST / 2015 Zulu)

"Seth! It's not a primary signal; it's an echo!"

Jenny had noted the unusual fact that Seth's office door was closed at the same moment she thrust it open. It was immediately obvious that she'd interrupted a closed meeting.

Seth Zieglar's back had been to the door, but he turned now, motioning to an unfamiliar man standing near Seth's desk.

"And right on cue comes Ms. Reynolds, the analyst I was describing to you. Jenny, meet Will Bronson of Defense Intelligence."

"DIA?" she asked, off balance.

"Yes," Bronson said, coming forward to shake her hand. "We're equally curious about this SIGINT … signals intelligence … you've found."

"I know what SIGINT is," she said a bit too defensively.

"Jenny has a tendency to enter like *Seinfeld's* Kramer, Will, but other than that, she's really quite competent," Seth winked at her in a way she detested.

"I'm sorry to burst in," she managed. "I was just, well, excited."

"Sit!" Seth commanded, pulling up a third office chair for her. "Everyone, sit."

Will Bronson waited for her to settle into a chair before doing the same. "So this is not primary flash traffic you found?" he asked.

She shook her head, watching Seth out of the corner of her eye. Bronson was easy on the eyes. Heavy dark hair, clean shaven, almost squarish face, and clearly mid-thirties in an impeccable dark blue business suit and what she judged to be a Jerry Garcia tie. She could date a guy like this, she thought—provided one ever asked her out. He had a genuine smile, too, but any Defense Intelligence operative so well turned out was too smooth to be overtly trusted, and she made a mental note to think before blurting.

"I thought it was coming up from somewhere west of the Irish coast, now I think I'm merely reading echoes of a downlinked satellite transmission. It's still piggybacking on a legitimate signal, and whoever's sending it is trying to hide it. But it may well be hemispheric in scope, or wider."

"Then you're looking for it in other areas of the globe I take it?" Bronson asked.

"Yes. It could be coming down from satellites all over the place, or just a couple. I'm not sure yet."

"Show me everything you've got, if you will."

Seth was nodding approval, and after all, she had called in DIA on Seth's order. But as she began laying out the various papers and waveform tracings, she couldn't shake the feeling that his question was more "tell me what you've discovered that you shouldn't know" than an innocent search for new information.

After a fifteen-minute briefing, she couldn't help herself.

"So, is this us? Did I catch something *we're* doing … something I should totally forget? Do you have some little flashy thing that erases our short-term memories?"

Bronson chuckled as he glanced at Seth Zieglar, then returned a disturbingly intense gaze toward her. "I'm wearing a *blue* suit, Jenny … not black. And in a word, 'no.' We at DIA are equally puzzled and concerned. It's not coming from our side, and I agree, it's a programming order of some sort. That's why I'd like to work with you, and my team at Boling Air Force Base to coordinate with us, depending on my interpretation. You okay with a team effort?"

"Sure."

"Good. Because there are things going on out there … things that are classified with no need for you to know … that demand we quickly solve mysteries like this. Immediately if not sooner."

She was watching his eyes intently, but his gaze was steady, open.

Smooth operator, she thought. *Probably has a girl in every port ... or office.* Jenny pulled herself back to the moment and cleared her throat. "Wow. So this *could* be a threat?"

"It could. And as a bit of a backdoor measure of the seriousness, if you have anywhere you were planning to go or do this afternoon or evening, I'd like you to cancel."

"And what if I have an important date?" she asked, smiling.

"Break it. You're dating me tonight, so to speak."

She felt a little ripple of surprise flitter up her spine before he continued with a broad smile. "Me and three others back at my office."

CHAPTER EIGHT

Cockpit, Pangia 10 (2110 Zulu)

The tension in the cockpit was thick enough to slice. Not that the past four hours had been anything but correct and collegial, but Captain Jerry Tollefson had no doubt that Dan Horneman was eager to continue arguing about the Anchorage incident, the arrogance of the Arctic Eagles, and how discriminated against he felt for being shamelessly rich.

Screw him! Jerry thought. *He could have just apologized and left it at that, but no, he had to attack me for letting him be a lousy pilot! Bullshit!*

But there didn't seem to be any point to reigniting the argument. Horneman, he had concluded, was a weak pilot slumming in a world that neither needed nor wanted misfits. And somehow, he was trying to evade the reality that a competent, properly trained pilot simply doesn't have the luxury of making fundamental mistakes.

Rehabilitating a pilot's reputation once he's shown himself to be dangerously slow at the controls is impossible, Jerry thought. The rumor mill, after all, communicated weakness faster than light. He resented Horneman's use of the phrase "right stuff" and mud-slinging North Star's Anchorage-based pilots. Horneman didn't have it, and he never would.

He's right about one thing, Jerry thought. *None of us can be comfortable flying with a man who already has the money and success we all want. If you're insanely rich, why do this? Why play airline pilot?* It was hard to even imagine what it would be like to have $500 million or what would he do with it if he had such wealth?

Jerry brought his eyes back to the windscreen where a

streaming cocktail of darkness and high-altitude cirrus clouds made the view indistinguishable from that of a simulator. There were stars somewhat visible overhead through the clouds, but he did little more than glance at them. Astronomy had never interested him, although a spectacularly starry night was always exhilarating.

They were entering a patch of turbulence, just light chop at first, but for some reason the slight bouncing was promising to get worse. He glanced down at the glowing computer screens that formed the front panels of the Airbus, checking the radar, which showed nothing of significance as the turbulence increased slightly to just below the moderate level. Jerry caught himself wondering almost casually why, at the exact same moment, the entire forward panel and all the cockpit lights went pitch black.

"What the hell?"

Dan Horneman's voice echoed his own thoughts. Jerry sat back suddenly as if struck. The entire instrument panel, consisting of four cutting-edge sophisticated video screens and including the Electronic Centralized Aircraft Monitor, or ECAM, were blank. Normally they conveyed all the information pilots needed to fly.

"What happened?' Jerry asked. "What did you do, Dan?"

"What did *I* do? Nothing! We've just lost all our displays … ECAM … everything!"

The turbulence had grown to the level of "moderate," and from habit, Jerry reached up and turned on the seat belt sign.

"Where's a flashlight?" Jerry asked, his voice betraying confusion.

"Hold it … I have mine …" Dan said, pulling a small penlight from his shirt pocket and shining it around the forward panel.

Is there a procedure for this? I can't recall one? Dan

thought. *How the hell can we lose everything?*

"Let me … get the checklist …" Dan said, scrambling to play the small beam of light to the right in search of the Quick Reference Handbook.

"I've got a big flashlight here somewhere in my bag …" Jerry said.

"Was there anything on the radar?"

"No! It was clear."

"Never thought we'd ever need a flashlight in a Scarebus!"

"Dan, do we have a reset button for the generators?"

"I'm … I'm pulling the checklist … hold it. I don't think so … as such …"

"What the hell is going on here? Are we turning?"

"What?"

"It felt like …" Jerry began, straining to look out and up. "I guess not. Engines are still running."

"I've got the Quick Reference Handbook," Dan announced. "Lemme get into it."

"I think we've lost all the generators, Dan."

"Yeah, but … where's the battery and the RAT, the ram air turbine? It should have dropped into the airstream by now and provided emergency power."

"Okay, run the checklist."

"Which one?"

"Loss of all electrics."

"I don't think we have one like that … let me look … jeez!"

"Wait … Dan, I can see light under the cockpit door."

"Sorry?"

"I just looked back … the cabin's still lit up."

"Okay, then it's not the generators."

"This damn plane can't lose all the displays," Jerry said, "It's supposed to be impossible! We've got zero instruments except for the standby attitude."

"Okay, here's the loss of electrics checklist in the QRH." Dan began reading the items, holding the small flashlight in his teeth, searching the overhead panel for a reset button as Jerry found his flashlight and frantically tried to make sense of what was happening.

And just as suddenly, everything came back on line, all the computer screens snapping back to their previous illumination levels and the cockpit lights back on.

"Thank God, Dan! What did you do?"

"Again, nothing!" Dan mumbled, the small penlight still in his mouth.

"Well, you must have done something. Check the heading!"

"Steady on course, two seven zero degrees. Speed's the same."

Jerry could see Dan shaking his head as he stared alternately at the ceiling panel and back to the QRH. He pulled the penlight out of his mouth and turned to the captain. "I'm telling you, Jerry, I didn't do a bloody thing! I was still searching for something TO do!"

"Then, what the hell happened?"

"I guess it cured itself, but we'd better start troubleshooting. Something knocked everything off line. It could happen again."

Jerry had leaned forward, his eyes racing around the flight display.

"We're still on course, on altitude … on airspeed. Everything. I don't think it even knocked off the autoflight system."

"Autothrottles still good?" Dan asked, verifying the indications were still correct.

"Yes."

"I've never seen anything like that. Have you?" Dan asked.

"No."

"Did I miss anything in training?"

"No … I mean, individual screen failures, but they're all independent."

Both men sat stock still as if any movement might once again plunge the cockpit into darkness, both of them studying the panels and trying out various theories, the silence building before Jerry spoke again.

"There are no error messages on the ECAM, Dan. You notice that?"

"Yes."

He punched at the center display. "Nothing. We didn't imagine it, right?"

"No, it was real. We were dark for maybe a minute. It felt like a freaking eternity!"

"Jesus! I'm wide awake now."

"Me, too. Should we, maybe, advise maintenance?"

"Yeah," Jerry responded. "You want to type in the story?"

"Yes. Got it." Dan began punching in an abbreviated narrative of what had just happened to transmit to Pangia's command center in Chicago.

"As soon as you're done with that, Dan, ask Shanwick for higher. I'm tired of this cirrus," Jerry said.

"Will do."

Dan typed in both messages and triggered the send function as Jerry scanned every panel for a clue to what had happened. The captain could see the copilot leaning forward again, scrutinizing something on the screen controlling the radio systems and the Aircraft Communications Addressing and Reporting System, known as ACARS.

"What?" Jerry asked.

"It's not going through," Dan replied. "I've got no indication of a transmission."

"Maybe it's just not reporting properly. You think?"

"I don't know what to think, Jerry. Hold on, let me try getting Shanwick with a CPDLC message," he said, referring to the Controller-Pilot Data Link Communication system. His fingers moved over the appropriate virtual buttons on the computer screen to send a message directly by satellite to Shanwick, then tried the HF channel, but the call went unanswered, as did the next attempt to reach the company over the satellite phone.

Jerry watched him work with increasing concern as the copilot went through the entire array of available communication devices controlled through the touch screens, until Dan looked up and met his gaze.

"Nothing, Jerry. We've got nothing!"

"You tried VHF?"

"Yes, 123.5. No one's answering, and there have to be aircraft all around us."

"Okay, there's got to be a way to reset these radios."

"There is a procedure to reset the satellite phone, but it stands to reason, Jerry. Whatever blacked us out up here probably tripped a whole bunch of breakers in the E and E compartment."

Jerry handed over the checklist. "You know how to go down there?"

"I've only been in the compartment once, but … yeah, I know how."

"We're supposed to get company approval first."

"Okay, so once we reset the radios, I'll ask them for the okay," Dan chuckled.

"Good plan."

Dan was lifting himself out of the seat but Jerry reached out to stop him. "How much time before we hit the coast, Dan?"

"Three hours, twenty minutes to Newfoundland," Dan replied. "And we've got five hours to JFK with six hours thirty minutes fuel remaining."

"Okay."

"At least the computers are with us again. I just don't understand what the hell happened back there."

"Tell me about it," the captain replied, his eyes on some distant point beyond the nose. "This is a frickin' electric jet. I don't know how it's even possible!"

CHAPTER NINE

Shanwick Air Traffic Control Facility, Shannon, Ireland (9:15 p.m. local / 2115 Zulu)

"Pangia One Zero, Shannon on HF. Are you experiencing any difficulty, sir?"

Arthur O' Brien had triggered the selective call code for the flight he'd been watching on their new extended radar, speaking on high frequency radio. There was no guarantee the crew of Pangia 10 would hear him, but they hadn't responded to his satellite computer message and this was getting serious.

Arthur leaned in slightly as he studied the computer-generated displays of the air traffic under his control, most of them entering, leaving, or navigating the Nat Tracks–the North Atlantic Track System. He was dead tired, but his focus had snapped to the glowing symbol representing a Pangia Airways jumbo jet after it had made a completely unexpected U-turn at 38,000 feet.

He could feel his fatigue evaporating.

"Pangia One Zero, how do you hear Shannon Centre?" he repeated, his finger moving imperceptibly against the transmit switch.

Even in the subdued atmosphere of the radar room, the uptick in his voice had caught the attention of his shift supervisor, and Sean Smythe was beside him, glancing with rising concern at O'Brien's display. The Tel Aviv-to-New York flight was boring eastbound, the huge Airbus A330 now challenging a sky full of westbound jetliners approaching their North Atlantic Track System entry points, including two 747s closing on their position at the same altitude.

"Bloody hell!" O'Brien muttered, his voice low and

steady, his mind on full alert.

"He's not talking to me, and he hasn't responded to the CPDLC message, and I only caught this when he crawled back on to my scope." O'Brien said to Smythe without looking up. He mashed the transmit button again, hard enough this time to feel his finger protest. "Pangia One Zero, Shannon, how do you hear us? We see you've made an unauthorized course reversal."

O'Brien finally glanced up at his chief, and Smythe read the grave expression on the controller's face. He had worked with Arthur O'Brien for a decade and had never seen him rattled, and while this was no exception, the rising tide of tension was washing over him as well.

"Better clear the way," Smythe said, voicing O'Brien's thoughts.

"Got it," Arthur answered, his finger already triggering the transmitter as his mind shifted to the high-speed task of keeping a sky full of jetliners from colliding with the rogue Airbus. All of those westbound flights were closing in on their entry points to the North Atlantic Track System, after which they would be out of direct radio contact, passing position reports primarily through satellite-based computer messages. But for now he had to rearrange those jets approaching the coast, and it would all be done with numbers: compass headings, fired by voice into the headsets of a dozen airline pilots, shattering what had been a quiet, routine passage over western Ireland.

Turning a British Air 747 to a heading that wouldn't conflict with the Pangia Airbus was his first urgent task. Using the traditional radio call sign of all British Air flights the order rolled easily off his tongue.

"Speedbird Two Three, turn immediately to vector heading three-zero-zero, acknowledge."

The obviously puzzled voice of a pilot with an

exceptionally cultured accent replied from the British Air cockpit. "Vector heading three-zero-zero, Speedbird Two Three, Roger."

Very well ... the Air France flight next, then Virgin Atlantic, then American.

The British Air pilot interrupted before Arthur could trigger the next command.

"Shannon, Speedbird Two Three. Have we lost our Nat Track clearance then?"

"For the moment, yes, Speedbird. Remain this frequency and standby." The pace of his words was accelerating, the same motormouth tendency he had always complained about in other controllers who tried to stuff too many words down the finite "tube" of a push-to-talk radio in any given period of time. But there was no time to hesitate. Three oncoming flights had to be turned away quickly and in the form of a messy starburst maneuver there would be no time to explain.

"Air France Two Eighteen, Shannon. Turn right immediately, vector heading three-zero-five. Break, Virgin Four Four Six, immediate right turn, vector heading three-one-zero. Break, American Twelve, immediate right turn, vector heading three-two-zero."

A cascade of acknowledgments flowed through his headset from each flight, each voice registering tension as the collective group of airmen perceived the alarm and urgency in their controller's inflections. O'Brien saw the respective blips beginning to change course just as the voice of the British Air pilot cut through his consciousness again with a chilling message.

"Shannon, Speedbird Two Three. We're responding to a resolution alert."

Dammit! Arthur thought to himself. The TCAS—the onboard traffic collision avoidance system—in the British Air 747 had electronically detected the oncoming Pangia

Airbus A330 and was now commanding the pilots to make an emergency climb or descent to avoid a collision.

But which was it? Up or down? The TCAS had essentially yanked control of the 747 out of his hands, and he was prohibited by regulations from trying to interfere.

The image of a second rogue jumbo jet now climbing or diving through a traffic jam of airplanes stacked at 1,000-foot intervals above and below gripped him like a blast of arctic air. It was a game of instant contingency planning, with deadly stakes.

Arthur forced a breath and waited for the next sweep of the radar to make its way through the computers and onto the datablock on his screen, each sweep a new brush stroke in an ever changing work of electronic art. The numbers changed suddenly, showing the British Air jumbo in an emergency climb.

He could deal with that.

Arthur snapped out two more commands, ordering heading changes for the eastbound jetliners whose altitude the British Air flight was about to invade as he struggled to climb above the oncoming Pangia A330. The routine radar "picture" had suddenly become a deadly video game of changing vectors, and he watched the British Air 747's blip close on another 747 just above him as the second jet began to turn out of the way. British Air was leveling nearly 2,000 feet above his original altitude, safely clear. He knew they couldn't collide with anyone now, but Arthur's stomach had already condensed to the size of a pea watching the small computer-generated blocks of data representing each airborne aircraft merge together, then crawl apart intact with agonizing slowness.

He looked at the Pangia datablock again, wondering what else was wrong. Something had snagged his attention, and all too slowly the recognition dawned: While British

Air had responded to the resolution alert, Pangia had not. Why? The TCAS system in both airplanes were supposed to be communicating at light speed with each other, mutually agreeing that one flight would climb while the other would descend to avoid a potential collision. British Air had gone up. Pangia had remained at flight Level 380!

O'Brien looked up and locked eyes briefly with Sean, an unspoken sentence wordlessly communicated in the fleeting glance: *What the hell is Pangia doing?*

CHAPTER TEN

Mojave Aircraft Storage, Mojave, California (2:45 p.m. PST / 2145 Zulu)

The owner of Mojave Aircraft Storage slammed the receiver down as hard as he could manage, trying his best to fracture the rest of the ancient telephone desk set, speaking through gritted teeth in seething anger.

"Okay, team. Guess what? They've already launched and are on the way here from Colorado with an ETA of fifteen minutes. I called them two hours ago, and they're almost here … our clients with the missing airplane who are going to want some answers we don't have, and I seriously doubt … THAT THEY'RE HAPPY!" The yelled words bounced off the walls of the line office, but this time the general manager was a bit beyond cringing, having already endured an hour of Ron Barrett's fury and verbal abuse. After almost six hours of meticulously examining the identification plates of every Airbus A330 on the windswept desert airfield, the conclusion had been inescapable: They had, indeed, dispatched the wrong airplane a week before to Pangia World Airways, one of their best customers—an identical aircraft owned by a Colorado company no one knew anything about. The company had responded by launching their senior executives on a business jet, and Barrett was all but terrified at the upcoming confrontation.

Mojave Aircraft's attorney, Jaime Lopez, had dropped everything and raced in from nearby Lancaster to join Barrett in pacing holes in the floor, waiting for word that the missing A330 wasn't missing after all.

But it was.

Barrett was snarling again at the three people in the

office. "You idiots know that it's probably the goddamned CIA we're screwing with, right?"

"We're not sure they're government, Ron," Lopez replied, but Barrett whirled on him, his eyes tiny little pinpoints of red, his overgrown eyebrows flaring almost comically.

"Who the hell *else* would have a $200 million airplane registered to an unknown company none of us can find anything about? Not even a secretary of state listing in Colorado. Strike you as strange?"

Barrett continued pacing before speaking again, this time at a slightly lower volume. "Whoever they are, we've screwed it up and they're almost here, and I'm going to have to call Pangia Airways now and tell them they're using someone else's airplane illegally."

"Not illegally, Ron," Jaime Lopez reminded him. "They just … are going to need to return it … at our expense. We released it, true, but Pangia's pilots flew it out, so it was more of a mutual mistake. Have we pulled a copy of whatever communiqué came from Pangia Airways asking us to deliver one of their airplanes?"

The manager lifted a folder off the desk. "I checked the serial number of the jet we mistakenly sent away," he began, "but we got an email ordering us to pull that very aircraft!"

Ron Barrett was on his feet, moving to the desk to verify the conclusion.

"What?"

"I think we're in the clear!" the manager added.

"Let me see that, please," Lopez asked, moving in behind Ron Barrett, who was holding the single sheet of paper triumphantly.

"The bastards created their own problem!" Ron Barrett was saying. "How are *we* to know that's the wrong serial number?"

Jaime Lopez closed the folder and placed it back on

the desk. "We have a duty to double-check, Ron, and unfortunately, that emailed order did not come from the true owner of the jet. We are decidedly *not* off the hook."

"But Pangia misled us!"

"Did anyone authenticate this message?" Lopez asked. "Did we independently call Pangia's maintenance base and verify? Did anyone validate the email address on this order?"

Silence met the question, and the lawyer shook his head. "Guys, the sender is, indeed, listed as Pangia World Airways and the email seems to be from them, but did any of you notice that the company name is misspelled?"

"What?" Ron whirled and moved to the lawyer's side to look at the paper.

"After the 'at' symbol, it says 'Pangiawordlair dot com.' Why would a major airline be unaware that its email server's name is misspelled? This isn't just a repeated email address, this is the address from which the message was *sent*! And I just looked … each of the previous orders from Pangia comes from 'Pangiaworldair dot com.' In the message we received, there is one more addressee listed, 'XL@pangiawordlair dot com.' The 'l' and the 'd' have been juxtaposed."

"What are you saying?" Ron asked.

"I'm saying," Jaime Lopez said, metering his words, "… that on the face of it, it looks like we dutifully responded to a request that was specifically designed to look like a valid order to deliver to Pangia's possession a $200 million aircraft that does not belong to Pangia. I'm saying that the email address of whoever sent the order may be bogus. And I'm saying that the fact that we received, and innocently acted on, that order does not change the reality that we handed over someone else's property without their permission."

The cascade of sound from a decelerating jet outside marked the arrival of the team from Colorado Springs, and Ron Barrett looked up, swallowing hard, his mind on the millions of dollars he'd spent to buy this storage operation, and how quickly it could all disappear.

CHAPTER ELEVEN

Shanwick Air Traffic Control Facility, Shannon, Ireland (9:45 p.m. local / 2145 Zulu)

Devon Knightly, the evening lead supervisor of Shanwick Control, had been waiting for the connection with Pangia's command center in Chicago. At last someone identified as Pangia's operations chief came on the line, the voice puzzled and brimming with questions.

"Devon, is our crew squawking a radio-out or hijack code?"

"Neither. They're still on the normal assigned code. There was no warning or radio contact of any sort before their 180-degree course reversal. My lads had a bit of a struggle clearing everyone out of his way. We were hoping you folks might be able to reach him by Sat phone or ACARS," he said. ACARS had become a near-universal airline link between airborne cockpits and dispatchers.

"Understood …" the man replied from Chicago. "I'm told we're trying, but no response yet. But I've got a more urgent question for you. If you project his new course out, is it steady? And if so, where does it appear to lead?"

"We did that, sir, and yes, it appears steady, and if you project it out over hours, it would take them right back across the Med and to their point of origin, Tel Aviv. It's almost as if his flight computer decided to return to the first fix."

Devon let his mind fast forward to an image of the big Airbus approaching the Middle East, and the mere thought of an unauthorized airspace breech anywhere in the area throttled up his already racing sense of urgency.

"That's what we've been thinking," the airline operations chief was saying, "… along with the worry that they could have changed the transponder code to let us know if they'd lost radio contact. It's more like they could be fighting a major problem and looking for an emergency landing point."

"It's possible, I suppose," Devon replied, trying to push the Middle Eastern images out of his mind to concentrate on the conversation, but it was as if a panther had silently padded in the door to stand there with deadly potential, impossible to ignore.

Devon Knightly pushed himself back to the moment. "All we see here in Shanwick is your crew flying the reverse course at the same altitude. Of course, he's got London, Paris, Frankfurt, Dublin, and Amsterdam all available for emergency landing fields … and yet the fact that he appears to be headed back to the Middle East raises the possibility of a hijack."

"Can we keep an open line with you, Devon?"

"Most assuredly. I'll have someone standing by for you. Oh, one other matter. Your aircraft's course reversal triggered a resolution alert on a British Air seven-four, and the Speedbird started climbing. So the TCAS boxes were agreeing that British Air would be told to climb whilst your aircraft would be directed to descend."

"Yes?"

"Well, you see, your chaps remained at the same altitude, as if they didn't get the same alert."

"Oh! Okay, got it," the Pangia chief replied.

"I should go, seeing as how I've a growing list of air defense and air traffic control facilities to alert. The British, for one, are going to be quite annoyed. Please let me know the instant you contact your crew by whatever means."

"Will do."

CHAPTER TWELVE

Aboard Pangia 10 (2200 Zulu)

In the cockpit of Pangia 10, Jerry Tollefson replaced the crew interphone and shook his head in the negative. "The passenger satellite phone system is dead, too. No one's getting through back there."

"Are we going to ask if anyone has a portable satellite phone?" Dan asked.

"You're kidding, right?" Jerry snapped. "No one carries those anymore."

"What's wrong with trying?" Dan asked.

"It's a waste of time."

"Jerry, it's a simple PA announcement. There are two satellite networks for private sat phones, and if someone has one ..."

"Okay, okay! Then tell Carol to ask, if it makes you feel better."

Dan hesitated for a few moments as he suppressed the response that was sitting like bile on the tip of his tongue. He nodded instead, before switching to interphone to ask the flight attendants to make the announcement.

A few bumps roiled the cockpit as a patch of chop accelerated to light turbulence, the same way it had as they'd flown westbound over the Irish western shore a while back, the Irish Cliffs of Moher unseen seven miles below.

Jerry reached up automatically and switched on the seat belt light as Dan looked at the radar depiction, which was showing nothing of interest.

"Clear ahead."

"Yeah, that was the forecast, except for the UK and Ireland."

"Which we're way beyond now." The moving map

display continued to show their westbound course as steady, with the horizontal situation indicator and its compass rose pointing to the same heading of 290 degrees.

"Okay," Jerry began, "Let's review this. We're in a super sophisticated electric jet at 38,000 feet going at 80 percent of the speed of sound, on course, on time, in the soup with no radio communication of any sort."

"That's about right."

He gestured to the array of computer-generated information on the front panel, the ECAM, or Electronic Centralized Aircraft Monitor. "No warnings on the ECAM, no clue as to why, but all backups are down and the damned ACARS won't even work. What do we make of that? Does anything ring a bell? Am I missing something?" Jerry asked.

"If you're missing something," Dan answered, "… so am I. We're still flying, and everyone on both sides of the Atlantic knows our flight plan, and we have enough fuel, but this is creeping me out."

"Me, too."'

"What would you think about my going below to have a look at the electronics bay," Dan asked.

"Yeah, we were going to do that. See if we have any breakers out or … or other obvious problems."

"Got it. I'll need you to motor your seat as far forward as you can stand."

"Roger."

Jerry was already pulling on his quick don oxygen mask as Dan lifted himself out of the copilot's seat and stood momentarily behind the center console, rubbing his neck.

Stay conscious, Cappy, Dan thought, aware how much of a balm the sarcasm would be if he could just say it out loud, as if Tollefson didn't remember the rule that when one pilot was out of the seat above 30,000, the other put on his oxygen mask.

But the words remained unspoken as Dan moved quickly to the cramped space behind the captain's seat and raised the floor hatch, squeezing through to the ladder, disappearing below and reappearing less than four minutes later.

"Anything?" Jerry asked, replacing his oxygen mask in the side compartment and moving his seat back.

"Nothing unusual. It is a bit nonstandard down there in the way it's laid out, but otherwise normal."

"But everything with a light is blinking, huh?" Jerry asked.

"Well, nothing I saw needed resetting. No smoking black boxes, nothing."

"So … how could we have lost everything? Tell me that."

Dan took a deep breath, forcing himself to think clearly as he slipped back into the right seat. "I don't have a clue, Jerry."

"Well, you said you know this bird better than I do, so …"

"I didn't say that to challenge you, Jerry. I've just studied this bird's systems very thoroughly since she's an electronics nightmare. But the bottom line is, there's nothing obvious down there."

"Which leaves us with what?"

"As I said, I don't know, but I'd recommend we prepare to land in New York without benefit of the radios."

"Rather obvious conclusion, since they aren't working," Jerry sniffed, aware he was pushing Horneman, and equally aware the copilot was purposefully taking the digs without pushing back. "Okay, Dan, here's a procedural question for you. Since we've got a big problem, do you think we're honor bound to wake up the asshole?"

"Breem?"

"Who else?"

"Jerry, this probably isn't the book answer, but don't we

have enough trouble as it is?"

Jerry Tollefson nodded aggressively, the hint of a smile on his face as he glanced over. "Probably the first thing we've agreed on all evening."

CHAPTER THIRTEEN

Mojave Aircraft Storage, Mojave, California (2:00 p.m. PST / 2200 Zulu)

As the owner of Mojave Aircraft Storage, Ron Barrett was already profoundly frightened by the possible liability of turning over a $200 million jet to the wrong people, but the fact that the principles of the mysterious Colorado Springs leasing company had responded to the news by immediately flying their private jet to Mojave made him even more nervous.

Within minutes of arrival, Ron and Jaime Lopez were climbing aboard the Gulfstream and taking the proffered seats across from the CEO of Air Lease Solutions, a distinguished looking man in his fifties identified as Paul Wriggle. Wriggle's two corporate assistants, Sharon Wallace and Don Danniher, were also introduced but stood quietly aside.

Paul Wriggle seemed the perfect physical specimen of a buttoned down, serenely confident corporate leader, Ron thought—all the attributes he wished he had. Trim, athletic, chiseled features, and sharply dressed in a monogramed shirt complete with cuff links, Wriggle was obviously a man in complete control, and if not wealthy, then at least well off.

Wriggle outlined the basic facts surrounding their missing, misdelivered Airbus A330 and the need to solve the problem as quickly and amicably as possible. "We recognize this was an honest mistake, gentlemen. It's fixing it quickly that's important. What we need to know right now is where our airplane is at this moment, when we can get her back, and what are the model characteristics of the one you should have sent to Pangia Airways?"

"Sorry … why do you need to know about Pangia's?" Ron Barrett asked, regretting the challenge immediately. "I mean … certainly we'll give you everything we've got in terms of info, but … I guess I'm not following the logic."

Wriggle leaned forward. "Well, if the two aircraft are essentially identical in equipment, configuration, engine type, and flight hours, we might as well just call up Pangia and propose an even swap."

"Just like that?"

"Simple solution, don't you think? You know any reason to suspect the A330 that's sitting out there right now is any different? You already said it was three serial numbers different from ours?"

"No reason" Ron replied, feeling the proximity of potential deliverance.

"So, a quick solution would be to have our pilots take Pangia's bird back to Colorado Springs with us today, and we'll just take care of the rest."

Ron Barrett knew he must have a confused look on his face, but two new concepts had flashed by and he was having trouble keeping up.

"You … have two more pilots aboard here somewhere?"

"No … my guys up front are A330 qualified."

"But … how do you …"

"Get this aircraft back?" He gestured to Don Danniher. "Don and I are Gulfstream IV type rated. We'll fly this ship back. Is Pangia's A330 ready to fly, by the way?"

"Ron looked at Jaime who was nodding. "We went ahead and de-pickled her just in case. We just need a fuel order."

"Excellent."

"But, excuse me, Mr. Wriggle," Jaime Lopez continued. "We're legally responsible for Pangia's aircraft and they'd have to release her formally and with the appropriate paperwork before we could, ah …"

"Let us fly away? Understood. So happens Pangia's CEO is a good friend of mine, and I have no doubt we can work a deal in a matter of minutes to accept the aircraft pending resolution of the problem."

"We would need signed paperwork, sir," Jaime continued.

"We can do that electronically," Wriggle shifted around to catch his assistant's eye. "Can't we, Sharon?"

"Yes, sir."

Something about the crispness of the reply caught Ron Barrett's attention. In fact, he thought, this entire team had an almost military sharpness about them, and their professional deference to their boss was startlingly sharp, like electricity crackling through the air.

Wriggle had pulled out an old model flip phone and was tossing it to his assistant, who caught it deftly.

"Sharon? Find Rick Hastings's number on my list there and get him on the line post haste. Tell him what we need." Wriggle turned back to Ron. "As you probably know, Rick Hastings is Pangia's CEO."

"Right," Ron replied, having had virtually no idea who filled that role.

The woman named Sharon moved toward the back of the Gulfstream's cabin as she worked with the keypad on his phone.

"Mr. Wriggle, may I ask …" Ron began. "Are you guys CIA?"

The partial explosion of a belly laugh from their host caught even Wriggle's staff off guard, although they briefly laughed as well.

"Nothing … whoa …" Paul Wriggle said, wiping his eyes, "… nothing so dramatic, Ron. Oh that's funny!"

"Sorry, I …"

"No, no, no, that's fine! It's just a hoot for me to ever think of myself as involved in the intelligence community.

No, you see, you correctly discerned that we're not your average aviation lease company, but since I'm sure you've discovered that we just have one A330, which would be unusual, it would be logical to ask what the heck we're up to. So I'll tell you, in the strictest confidence. In a nutshell, we're working on a special government project to provide and maintain a clandestine alternate to Air Force One."

"Really?"

"Really. Which is why I have to impress on you the extreme need to treat anything and everything you know or think you know regarding our missing A330 as the equivalent of a top military secret."

"We … can certainly keep quiet," Ron managed.

"No, it's more profoundly important than that. We have to make sure that we thoroughly understand each other on this, Ron. You've created some heavyweight liability for yourselves, so aside from just appealing to your patriotism, which I don't question, we've also more or less got you by the short hairs legally. As long as you agree to keep this as an unbreakable top secret, we will agree not to sue you into penury and destroy your business. Sound like the makings of a deal?"

Ron was nodding as he watched Jaime doing the same thing. He returned his focus to Wriggle. "I … yes, that's a deal."

"Good. I've got some paperwork to give it teeth, but I didn't anticipate a problem getting you to understand. Break the promise of absolute silence for any reason, we come after you with all guns blazing, and, as you realize, you have no defense."

"Mr. Wriggle, why is your airplane so special, or different, that this kind of secrecy is needed?" Ron asked. "Has it already been modified?"

"It was going to be extensively modified, but we were

just in the design stages, which is why we just needed a place to park it for now. Frankly, it was too conspicuous around the Colorado Springs airport where we were keeping it, so we chose your facility because it could blend in with the other A330s … which it, of course, did all too well. No, it's a garden variety A330."

"So … I guess I shouldn't ask this but … you're a private company working for the air force unit that flies the president?"

Sharon had moved slightly closer, still standing, as if anticipating something, but Ron's attention was on Wriggle's hand as he pulled a small leather case from a back pocket and opened it to reveal a gold badge.

"What's that?" Ron asked.

"This company is a private corporation, Ron. I, however, am also a component of the United States Secret Service, and this company is working under a Secret Service contract. We protect the president, and we go to great lengths to make sure that the bad guys can't get close to him. Sometimes we even waste immense amounts of fuel flying Air Force One around empty while the president flies in a nondescript plane. So, you can see why we'd be working on an alternate flying White House that, among other things, couldn't possibly be used by the president because it's a French-built jet. One that never sees Andrews Air Force Base. One that's not painted like Air Force One."

Sharon Wallace had moved to Paul Wriggle's side and leaned over to whisper something to him. The CEO nodded and turned back to Ron Barrett.

"Okay, Pangia wants to just fly the airplane back to us and get theirs. It's in Tulsa at their maintenance base and hasn't been placed into service yet, so no problem. They're sending the approval right now to release their bird to us. You're printing it, Sharon?"

"Yes, sir."

"So that should be it."

The remainder of the transaction had taken less than twenty minutes, and despite Jaime Lopez's reluctance to sign the multiple-page agreement without a thorough vetting and some legal research, Ron Barrett was determined to get ink on paper and one additional A330 in the air. It seemed an agonizing eternity watching the pilots preflight the Airbus while Wriggle and associates departed in the Gulfstream, but at last the big Airbus lifted into the desert sky to Ron Barrett's audible relief, and Jaime Lopez's consternation.

Jaime had taken Ron by the arm as they waited. "It's not just us, you understand. This agreement muzzles everyone in our employ. We can't even tell our people why they have to stay silent, just 'Shut the hell up!'"

"Yeah, Jaime, I get that."

"Yes, but what you probably *don't* get, and why I was trying to at least read through everything, as your *lawyer*, and consider all the implications, is that if one of our guys speaks out of school in a bar or whispers something in a whorehouse at midnight, even if he's only guessing and BS'ing, if that crosses their line and they find out, we're done, man! Investment gone. Game over."

"I don't understand what you're getting at, Jaime."

Jaime Lopez released the contents of his lungs in a long and weary sigh. Ron Barrett was an energetic guy but thick as a rock sometimes, and his almost total lack of understanding of legal obligations was a constant trial.

Jaime studied his shoes and mentally calmed the growing need to explode before trying one more time to get across the staggering scope of what had just been promised.

"Okay … what I'm *getting at,* Ron, is that when it comes to anything that happened with their aircraft or even rumors thereof, you just promised to nursemaid, monitor, shadow, and control every single solitary employee, full-time or part-time, and their families and friends and kids and concubines, twenty-four hours a day, seven days a week, essentially forever!"

Aboard Gulfstream N266SD

Holding a relatively fresh cup of coffee in hand from the unattended galley, Air Force Lieutenant General Paul Wriggle eased himself back into the left seat of the business jet and glanced at Lieutenant Colonel Don Danniher in the right seat. There was no trace of a smile on either man's face.

"That was quite an act we just put on, Don. Do you think they bought it?"

"You mean, that we're on a mission for the Secret Service?"

"Yep. Will they comply and stay quiet? Did I tell them too much?"

"The Barrett guy's an emotional moron, General. He's terrified, and his lawyer … who's a bright guy … will do his best to keep him and their entire operation quiet. Probably about now he's explaining to Barrett the promise he just signed. And I think you had to tell them what you told them."

"That's good. Of course, we're not using their storage services again in this life."

"Amen," Danniher replied. The two men sat in silence for a few seconds before Don Danniher glanced over at his boss, a thin smile on his face.

"Sir, may I speak frankly?"

"Certainly."

"If I called Central Casting in Hollywood and ordered an actor to play a Secret Service agent, I would be upset if they sent you. Sir."

"So, what are you saying, Don? That I'm a bad actor?"

"No sir, but you are far too authoritative to be a Secret Service agent. You look like and sound like and are, in fact, an air force general officer, sir. Not a weasel with a badge. Where'd you get that thing, anyway?"

"Directly from the president."

"Really? The current one?"

"Can't tell you, Don. But it is a real badge and a real commission directly from POTUS," referring to the acronym for the president of the United States. "Only problem is, even the Secret Service doesn't know about this little commission. And, by the way, our Secret Service guys are not weasels."

"Yes, sir."

"Okay, Don … we've got some serious thinking to do," Wriggle continued.

"I'm the one who agreed to park our bird with Mojave to get it away from prying eyes around Colorado Springs, but we're going to face this need again very quickly. We're not going to have the budget to resume testing for at least six months. So where can we fly it and store it in the meantime, so no one's aware of it?"

"There are still hangars available at Groom Lake in Nevada, General, but we rejected that choice because of the intense satellite scrutiny. If the Russians and NSA aren't watching every move there, a hundred civilian UFO hunters are."

"Yeah, that's all we need," Wriggle snorted. "Big headlines: US government flying space aliens on strange Airbus A330 … with the following tail number!"

The two men fell silent for a few minutes before Paul Wriggle shook his head again.

"Okay … let's keep thinking," Wriggle continued. "Provided we can make the swap with Pangia today, we'll need a hiding place inside three days."

"How high did Sharon have to go in Pangia's management, General?"

"Not high at all, since she never called."

Don Danniher looked startled.

"Really? When did you and Sharon arrange that?"

"Minutes before. I taught her a code phrase that, if she hears it, means to invert whatever I just said."

"What is it?"

"You have no need to know, now do you, Colonel," Paul answered, smiling at the copilot.

"I guess not."

"I wasn't kidding when I said I know Rick Hastings, their CEO. He's a fellow retired air force general, but I haven't called him yet. Sharon found a civilian at one of the FBO's in Tulsa who agreed to go over to the other side to check Pangia's ramp and make sure our airplane hasn't been painted yet … as well as check the fuel load. "

The cockpit door opened, and Major Sharon Wallace slid into the space between the two pilot seats without a word. Paul Wriggle looked at her and frowned.

"What's the matter, Sharon? Did you get through?"

"Yes, sir. A line supervisor at one of the fixed base operators at Tulsa International. The fellow called me back and said he saw our airplane, November Three-Three-Romeo Mike, on hardstand eighteen in front of that giant hangar in Tulsa."

"The old World War II aircraft factory?"

"Yes. He also said that hardstand twenty is open, so we can probably just slide our A330 into that spot, and they'll send a fuel truck out to give us enough for the flight back to the Springs."

"Excellent."

"One other thing." She handed him a piece of paper.

"I just found this on the BBC wire. One of Pangia's

international flights is in trouble. Sketchy details, an unexplained course reversal on a Tel Aviv to JFK flight, the crew is radio silent, and it may be a hijacking into the Mideast. I'm sure Pangia is dealing with a kicked over ant hill about now."

"Please explain the deeply worried look, Sharon," he pressed.

"Because, sir, the plane involved is an Airbus A330, and this is going to put an internal spotlight on their A330 fleet, which means we should make the swap as soon as humanly possible."

CHAPTER FOURTEEN

Cockpit, Pangia 10 (2220 Zulu)

"Jeez, Dan, we're idiots!" Jerry Tollefson said as he lunged for a small panel on the center console.

"What?" Dan Horneman jerked his head to the left to read Tollefson's expression, alarmed at the tone.

"What do we do with the transponder when the radios are out?"

"I don't … oh, Christ! You're right. The radio failure code"

"Hell yes! We should have been squawking 7600 on the transponder."

"Probably no one out here to see the code anyway, Jerry. Don't chew on yourself. I didn't think about it either."

"Yeah, but air traffic control's radar goes out a lot further than they admit." He dialed in 7600 and sat back, looking anything but relieved. "I'm assuming this thing is still transmitting. If so, when we're approaching Newfoundland they'll figure it out. Dammit! I can't believe we forgot that!"

"This cirrus layer is clearing," Dan remarked, peering out of the forward windscreen at the starfield beginning to come into view. "I kind of expected it would be with us all the way."

"Doesn't solve our radio problem, but it may help air traffic control keep everyone comfortably clear. I mean, we'll follow the assigned routing exactly, but they need to know we can't hear them or respond."

Dan chuckled. "Somehow I think they've probably got that one figured out. We're at least one position report behind."

The two of them fell silent for a minute until Jerry

gestured outside.

"This really unsettles me, Dan. I know we can easily call Kennedy Approach or New York Center by cell phone as soon as we get over Canada, but what if there's a war going on down there and they're not talking to us because they can't."

"A *war*?"

"Well … we're out of touch with the world, okay?"

"I doubt the planet's coming to grief, Jerry. We're the ones with the radio problem and a strange power failure."

"You think it's all us?"

"Yes," Dan replied. "There's zero static on our VHF radios, which means *our* radios are dead, not theirs. Ditto with the satcom … no lock, no sign the unit's working. We're not even sure the transponder is working. I mean, I see the little reply light flashing …"

"That means the radar beams are hitting us, Dan. And boy, look at that." Jerry said, pointing to the transponder readout. "We're … what, 700 miles west of Ireland and that thing is blinking like a hundred beams are hitting us per minute."

"Could mean it's malfunctioning, too."

"You try the high frequency radios? I mean, it may be World War II technology, but …"

"I tried, Jerry. No static, no nothing."

"I pulled out my cell phone a minute ago, and, believe it or not, for a second I got a signal."

Dan laughed ruefully. "The captain left his phone on, huh? So *that's* the problem! Your cell phone's fried the equipment!"

"Yeah, right," Jerry replied, smiling in spite of himself.

The starfield overhead was in full bloom now, the constellations coming clear as Dan let his mind drift away from the radio problem and admire the beauty of the celestial show they'd been denied for the past few hours. He found himself searching for Polaris, the North Star, to the right, but couldn't be sure which one it was. Sometimes this time of year he could see the Aurora Borealis, the so-called Northern Lights, as they danced like moving curtains of colored light over the North Polar Region.

Strange, he thought. *Polaris has to be there of course, but I can't find it and I can't even see the big dipper. I must be really tired or something.*

Dan tore his gaze away from the window and reached down to dial up the lights on his side of the cockpit as he noticed a distant glow far away to the right. He peered out the right side window for a better look at what had to be light filtering through the bottom of an overcast beneath them. But that made no sense, given their position practically over the middle of the North Atlantic. The Azores were way to the south, to their left, and out of sight, even with a clear sky.

Must be the lights of a fishing fleet, he thought, recalling the intense floods of commercial fishing vessels working off the Washington coast as a kid. Or maybe those were a collection of deep sea drilling rigs, though he remembered those as being hundreds of miles to the north. Whatever they were, it was an interesting phenomenon.

Dan returned to the task of boosting the cockpit lights as Jerry started paging through diagrams of the electrical system on his iPad, searching for an answer. Dan watched for a few seconds before forcing his attention to the various panels and displays, trying to sense if anything was amiss that they hadn't seen. And for some reason, at the end of his scan and almost as a personal joke, he decided to consult the all but forgotten little mechanical compass at the top of the center windscreen, the so-called "whiskey" compass which owed its name to open cockpit days when cheap bourbon was often used to float the internal compass rose when the normal alcohol solution leaked out.

Dan pulled out a pocket flashlight and pointed the tiny beam on the compass rose, mechanically reading the numbers.

Zero nine five degrees ... zero nine six, something like that. He turned off the light and automatically flipped the number around in his mind, knowing their planned heading was 278 degrees magnetic. Pilots had an easy mental shortcut—a crutch—for quickly adding or subtracting 180 degrees, the same way pilots flip the compass heading of one runway number around to read the reciprocal. Start with zero-nine-five degrees, add 200, subtract 20, and in this case, voila! 275 degrees. *That would be about right*, he thought.

Dan replaced the flashlight in his pocket, overriding the sudden suspicion that he was missing something.

CHAPTER FIFTEEN

CIA, Langley, Virginia (5:30 p.m. EST / 2230 Zulu)

"Sir, you are *not* going to believe this!"

As Jason Duke knew well, the use of such a breathless phrase was not the most judicious or professionally sophisticated way of approaching a veteran CIA leader—especially if delivered while leaning into his office doorway in early evening. But with all the mind-numbing routine intelligence traffic he'd handled over the past few months as the man's overeducated gopher, breaking the news of this unfolding situation was almost a breath of fresh air.

Walter Randolph—a rumpled-looking, 40-year veteran spook and now deputy director of Central Intelligence—motioned the younger intelligence officer in with an unmistakable gesture to close the door behind him. Randolph took the reading glasses off his craggy face and sat back in his chair, focusing on the younger man while nibbling on the earpiece of his glasses.

He looks ridiculously like Lyndon Johnson when he does that, Jason thought.

"What, exactly, am I not going to believe, Jason? You sound like an overly exuberant intern."

"The Pangia flight, sir. We pulled the passenger list. Moishe Lavi is aboard."

Randolph carefully closed a classified folder he'd been studying and leaned forward to place it on his blotter before responding. He looked up, studying Jason Duke's face, his hands folded in front of him.

"You are correct, Jason. I don't believe you."

"I confirmed the inbound information with Homeland Security. It's an Israeli passport, non-diplomatic, but it's the number we have in our database."

"What the hell would Lavi be doing aboard an American flag carrier? He only flies El Al."

"Don't know."

"Who's with him?"

"A secretary, apparently, from the Israeli Defense Force, by the name of Ashira Dyan. Her passport checks as well."

"We know Ashira. She's his official IDF mistress. Any idea why Lavi is inbound?"

"Well, why he *was* inbound, we think, may have something to do with the UN, but we've found no appointments or arrangements for him yet. Not even a car company to pick him up at Kennedy, which is a bit odd."

"You *think*?" Walter Randolph rolled his eyes. "Newly defeated warhawk prime minister of Israel who's used to an entourage of dozens buys a commoner's ticket to the US, and, what, a cousin is going to meet him in a beat up Ford?"

"We're checking all the car companies."

"I don't doubt that, I'm just … holy crap! And this airplane is headed right back to Tel Aviv?" Randolph was on his feet and pacing.

"The airline says their airplane is electronically reporting that it's still westbound toward New York, and all the reported GPS coordinates are fiction as well. They're saying it's not possible for someone to mess with that automated datastream in flight, so they're clueless as to what's happening. But European air traffic control confirms that if the aircraft remains on the same eastbound course, it will pass over Tel Aviv hours from now. The aircraft came from Hong Kong before Tel Aviv, so if there's no one in control up there and the computers steer for Hong Kong after passing Tel Aviv, they'll pass just south of Tehran."

"Wonderful excuse for the Iranians to overreact. Do the Brits know Lavi is aboard?" Randolph asked.

"Not yet, I think. But I need you to sign off on informing MI-6 formally."

"Do it. They're on our side … usually."

"Okay."

"Where's the director?"

"Home, sir."

Randolph took a deep breath. "Very well, I'll wake him."

"It's that serious, you think? They're still hours from the Mediterranean."

Walter Randolph fixed Jason with a questioning gaze which quickly morphed to amusement. "A little reality test, Jason, if you please. The man who wanted to commit Israel to a preemptive nuclear strike on Tehran in the last few months is thrown out of office when his government collapses and even his supporters react to the exposure of his plan with utter horror. The head of the IDF revolts, and the president of the United States has to publicly flail and repudiate our ironclad ally for even momentarily thinking such thoughts. Iran remains on what for us would be DEFCON 2," referring to the nation's defense readiness condition, "a hair-trigger from launching one of the nukes we know the mullahs have to wipe Israel off the map, which is their stated goal. Then Moishe Lavi leaves office ranting and raving that he will not give up until *they* are neutralized. Now this same wild-eyed man ends up on a rogue jetliner with an American flag on the tail … and did I mention that the mullahs don't trust us? So the damned French-built A330 is headed back toward the Middle East with no radio contact and apparently a clueless crew, and even though the plane is still over the English Channel, and, as you say, hours away from the Med, it's headed straight for Tel Aviv, which, coincidentally, is a very short distance from Tehran, geopolitically speaking. So, who do *you* think we should notify? Walter Cronkite?"

"He's … dead, sir."

"Which is a damn shame, but you get the point."

"Yes, sir. I do see your point. Ah, points."

"I'm not beating you up, son … you brought me into it immediately … but this is potentially a very big problem. A White House Situation Room level problem. And guaranteed, Defense Intelligence is all over this as we speak. We can't let them get ahead of us."

"I've got a team coming together, sir."

"Good. Give me a conference room number, and I'll be there inside thirty minutes. You've got anything you need on this, okay? But for God's sake, and mine … and, for that matter, the director's … *please* let me know instantaneously or sooner if they turn that bird around or land it somewhere safe."

"Got it."

Walter Randolph waved his arm in mock dismissal. "Go forth and sin no more, my son!"

"Excuse me?"

The deputy director was chuckling and looking down as he replaced his glasses and adjusted them on the bridge of his nose. "Just something a past director used to say to me in my intelligence infancy. Ignore my nostalgia. I've been here far too long."

Randolph sighed and settled back down in his desk chair, feeling both the years and his lack of regular attendance in the gym. The weight was creeping back onto his otherwise considerable frame, and he was becoming vertically challenged. Officially, the agency still thought he was six feet two, but at age sixty-nine, he was compressing vertically and expanding laterally.

He picked up the receiver and pressed the buttons that bypassed everything else to connect him with the director's secure phone at his home in Arlington. Chuckling to himself, he waited for the familiar voice to answer with the same expectant "Yes?" one uses when each ring of the instrument is a potential announcement of Armageddon or an unhappy POTUS.

"Jim? Walter here. You are *not* going to believe this!"

CHAPTER SIXTEEN

Aboard Pangia 10 (2230 Zulu)

Carol Crandall still liked being called "Head Mama" whenever she served as chief of the cabin crew, although at the age of thirty-two she was hardly a grizzled veteran. She thought of her lead position now as one of her more junior flight attendants, Kate Guthrie, pushed through the first class divider curtains to see her. Carol motioned Kate into the forward galley as she moved back into the cabin to refill the wine glass of an elegantly coiffed lady who had been buried in a book since takeoff from Tel Aviv.

Still not drunk, Carol thought. She was one of their million-mile frequent fliers who had already downed the better part of a bottle of Chablis, the aura of very expensive perfume surrounding her.

Uncharacteristically, the lady glanced up and nodded thank you—first time she'd responded for hours. Carol suppressed a chuckle and joined Kate in the galley, pulling the curtains as she motioned back toward the cabin.

"She's up to page 200. She keeps re-reading certain parts."

"I'm not following you," Kate said, looking puzzled.

"The *Vogue* model in 4A. She's got a custom cover on her book and thinks I can't see."

"Okay."

"It's the latest mommy porn book everyone's reading. Wild sex by page eighty-six. *Really* wild!"

"How do you know … never mind." Kate was smiling, but thinly, as she waved it away, and Carol could see something was really tugging at her.

"What's up, sweetie?"

"A worried passenger back there, who now has *me* worried. Maybe I shouldn't be, but ..."

"Tell me."

"This guy tells me he's an amateur astronomer ... he owns a small telescope and belongs to some amateur organizations ... and he's telling me this because he's in a window seat and he swears the stars are all wrong."

Carol arched an eyebrow. "Excuse me?"

"No, listen ... I don't think he's a kook. He's on the left side and says he should be looking at something very different than the Big Dipper and the North Star, which is what he's seeing, on the left. That would make sense, right? The North Star should be on our right?"

"I suppose. What's the point, Kate? Passengers get mixed up all the time?"

"It's on our left."

"What's on our left?"

"The North Star."

Carol frowned. A call chime rang, and she needed to check it out.

"See, if we're flying west toward New York like we're supposed to be, the North Star would be on our right. So would the Big Dipper. I leaned down to see what he was talking about, and the man is right. The Dipper is on our left, the North Star is on our left, and the only planets visible are on our right. Mars, for instance."

"He could be wrong. *You* could be wrong."

"I'm not an idiot, Carol. I'm a Wisconsin farm girl ... I know the night sky, too."

"What's the bottom line here? The world is upside down?"

"Seriously?" Kate said, cocking her head before taking a deep breath, unsure whether that response was going to get her in trouble.

"I'm not trying to make fun of you, Kate. But what are you trying to say? Spit it out, girl."

"We're flying the wrong way."

"We're over the Atlantic, almost midway I would think."

"Maybe … but we're headed back to Europe then, because we're flying east. The guy even pulled out a little compass, and it said the same thing."

Carol smiled. "You know how much this jet costs, with all those sophisticated instruments up front, not to mention two pilots who probably know how to read a compass?"

"Carol, please listen! I don't care how sophisticated the airplane is, the stars are saying it all: We're flying the wrong way. Has something happened they're not telling us about?"

That hit a trigger.

Carol stood in thought for a few seconds, wondering if the pilots had made the serious error of keeping their lead flight attendant out of the loop on something important. She'd had it happen before, and it was an infuriating insult, not to mention a breach of the way the pilots were trained to treat the cabin crew as part of their team.

"Wait a second," Carol said, her expression hardening as she scooped up the interphone and punched the buttons for the cockpit.

"Yes?"

"Is this the captain?"

"Nope. It's the copilot. Carol? That you? Dan here."

"Dan, is there anything you gentlemen want to tell me that you haven't?"

Silence on the other end for a few seconds before a hesitant answer.

"Ah … what did you have in mind, Carol?"

"I need to come up."

Carol turned to Kate and gestured for her to follow as the cockpit door interlocks were turned off and the door opened from within. The two women quickly moved inside and secured the door behind them.

"That is technically a breach of protocol, having two of you ..." Jerry Tollefson began, stopping when he glanced at the flint-hard expression on Carol's face and the ashen look on Kate's.

"Okay, what's wrong up here? Are we returning to Europe or the UK?"

"Returning? No! We've got a radio problem, but everything else is normal."

"You mean, the passenger satellite system?"

"Yes," Jerry began, glancing at the copilot. "That ... and ... several more radios. Basically, we had a real strange loss of all our panel and instruments and computer screens for several minutes a while ago, but everything came back on ... except the radios. We've lost all normal communication with air traffic control and the company, but they know where we are, and we're squawking a radio failure code, and ..."

"Why are you asking, Carol?" Dan interjected, earning an irritated glance from Jerry.

The lead flight attendant had leaned forward and was reading the compass rose on the horizontal situation indicator. She nodded and glanced at Kate, who she'd forgotten to introduce.

"You should tell me about things like that. I'm supposed to be an integral part of your crew."

"I apologize, Carol," Jerry said. "We were still actively trying to work on the problem. I was going to tell you folks as soon as possible."

Carol gestured to her companion. "This is Kate, who's been working steerage. She's got an astronomer back there who claims that we're flying east."

"*Excuse* me?" Dan said, the words propelled by something between a snort and a chuckle.

Carol shot him an icy stare as Kate answered.

"Ah … he's not an astronomer … I mean, an amateur one, maybe, but …" She repeated the exchange in full, and Jerry Tollefson turned around completely in his seat facing forward to squint out the window. "Dan, turn the overhead lights down."

"Got it."

Jerry straightened up suddenly and looked forward at the forward panel, then at Dan's panel, then back at the two women—puzzlement showing in his face.

"You're right about the Big Dipper, and … I'm not sure about Polaris … and yes, they should be on Dan's side, but …"

His attention was diverted by Dan who had suddenly scrambled to follow suit and leaned forward and was now squinting at the whiskey compass, a small pocket flashlight beam now illuminating the instrument.

"Holy shit!" Dan muttered.

"What?" Jerry demanded.

"Good God! I saw this a half hour ago and misread it. I can't believe it, but I fucking misread it! It's reading one-zero-three, for God's sake, with our HSI's steady on the opposite course. I must have flipped it by a 180 degrees to 280 something, but it's … it's east, basically."

The alarm on Jerry Tollefson's face was palpable. "What do you mean, you reversed it?"

"I flipped it 180 degrees."

"How the hell could you do *that*?"

"I don't *know*, Jerry," Dan shot back, trying unsuccessfully to keep the sarcasm out of his voice. "I guess I just *assumed* we were flying west!"

"Well … what the hell heading *are* we flying?"

"Apparently 103 degrees, Jerry!"

The two pilots glared at each other for a heartbeat,

distrust and disbelief chiseled into their expressions..

"So, we *are* flying east?" Kate asked, breaking the silence.

"God, I hope not!" Jerry said through clenched teeth as he turned to yank his company iPad out of his flight bag. He flipped the cover open and toggled it on, selecting a map program and watched in frustration as a small target in the middle crawled across a blank screen with no map references.

"Dammit! I forgot it has to have an Internet signal for the map."

"Wait, Jerry … I have a little thing on my … personal droid … that gives a good magnetic compass heading …" Dan lunged for his flight bag, fumbling loudly for the small smartphone he kept stored during international trips. "Give me a minute … the damned thing has to spin up!"

An interphone call chime rang, and both pilots ignored it at first.

"It's coming online … hold on … if I remember right, the app is purely magnetic with no external connections needed—"

The call chime rang again, and this time the captain looked up at the overhead panel, irritated to be interrupted.

"Would you like me to get that, Captain?" Carol asked softly, well aware both men were highly agitated. She could feel Kate's wide-eyed fright without glancing at her.

"What? Yeah. Here." Tollefson punched the intercom button on the center console as he yanked off his headset and all but tossed it at Carol.

"What are you finding?" he asked Dan.

"Just a second … takes the stupid thing a friggin' eternity to reboot …" He punched a series of commands onto the touchscreen, waiting for what looked like a miniature attitude indicator to appear, which finally swam into view.

"There! Now, let me get this close to the window … the magnetic heading rose is right there at the top, and it's saying … SHIT!"

"What?"

An almost feral glance from the copilot confirmed it before the words.

"It's saying east, Jerry! About one-zero-zero degrees. Jesus God, we've been flying into opposite traffic without contact!"

"You're serious? How long, man? And where the hell are we?"

"Captain?" Carol interjected, her voice soft and urgent, her hand still holding the headset against her ear.

"I don't know, Jerry. I remember feeling like we were in a turn during the blackout, but when the instruments came back up …"

"How the hell could they be lying to us?" Jerry asked, staring again at his forward panel. "This jet's worth a fortune … I should be able to trust the readings!"

"Captain …" Carol tried again, but Jerry was fighting complete disbelief, staring again at the forward panel as if the answer was about to pop into view.

"Dan, check to see if anything's offline, and ladies, stand back while he gets out of the …"

"*Captain*!" Carol, said, this time forcefully enough to get his attention.

"What?"

She held the interphone out. "You're going to want to hear this. Now!"

Jerry donned his headset once again while locked on Carol's eyes. "This is the captain. What's wrong?"

Carol could see the man's shoulders slump ever so slightly as a look of hopelessness passed across his face like a veil.

"You're sure? Can you tell what type?"

"What?" Dan demanded as Jerry swung around to his left and pressed his face against the glass.

"What's going on, Jerry?" Dan demanded as Jerry looked back at him.

"We have company. Probably fighters. One off our left wing. Check your side."

The copilot complied, filling in the rest of the nightmare. "Oh, crap, I have one here, too."

"Who do you suppose they are?" Jerry asked.

"I don't know … just like you said, where the hell *are* we*?*"

"God, I wish I knew!"

"We can't talk to them. Wait, let's turn up the cockpit lights as far as we can. Don't want them to think we're not in control."

"Do it!"

Dan turned to the two flight attendants. "I need you guys to get back to the cabin! Extra people up here will look like hijackers!"

Once again, Jerry shot the copilot an exactly-when-did-I-lose-control glance as Carol nodded and ushered Kate out of the door.

Jerry had been sitting in a near catatonic state for several very long seconds, and Dan was choosing the words he'd need to break him out of it, when the captain came back to life on his own, rifling through a small handbook.

"What are you doing?" Dan asked.

"Looking for the universal signals for obeying whatever they want us to do!"

"Okay. I know those procedures by heart," Dan said. "You do realize we're in deep shit here, right?"

"Our instruments are lying to us!" Jerry replied, a plaintive whine in his voice.

"Let's just take care of the problem," Dan shot back. "We haven't screwed up anything yet," he said, almost choking on the words. "How's our fuel?"

"I've already checked. We have at least five hours. Dan? Can you think of any reason a passenger would have a portable VHF radio back there?"

"A what?" The copilot thought through the question for what seemed like an eternity before shaking his head. "No. We could ask, but … we'll panic people."

"I think we're already there," Jerry answered.

"Are there emergency radios in the life rafts?" Dan asked.

"Not any more. Too expensive and not needed. Someone always knows where we are."

"Right. Like we knew where Malaysia 370 was."

"Dan, turn the lights up all the way."

"Got it."

"He's shining a flashlight at us … the guy on the left. I think it's an F-15. Maybe US markings."

"Our guys, then?"

"Maybe!"

"Then we're probably still over the UK somewhere." Dan added.

"He's shining his flashlight on his helmet and tapping it."

"That means he's asking for radio contact, Jerry. Shine your light on the left side of your face, wave your left hand back and forth by your ear, and shake your head no!"

The flashlight teetered on the brink of falling as the captain regained his grip and nervously followed the instructions, both tapping and waving around his ear.

"You getting a response?" Dan asked.

"Yes! He got it, I think. He's holding the flashlight on himself again and nodding and pointing ahead."

"Okay, Jerry, he's going to do the follow-me night intercept maneuver. He'll get out ahead and a little below, flash his lights, light his afterburner and turn to our right and we follow."

"Got it."

"He'll guide us down to a suitable field. He's probably talking to Chicago for us."

"You think they know by now?" Jerry asked.

"Who?"

"Chicago. Our company?"

"Jerry, I think half the world knows by now. There! He's moving."

Jerry's left hand went to the sidestick controller.

"Don't punch off the autopilot yet … not until he's crossed from left to right in front of us. I'll blink our position lights twice, and then you follow him."

"Okay. Shit, shit, shit!" Jerry muttered. "I have no idea how much trouble we're in, but this can't be good!"

"Relax, Jerry. We didn't do anything wrong."

Once again the sharp glance to the right, the hard expression betraying irritation, and for some reason Dan couldn't resist a postscript: "We'll sort it out on the ground, Jerry."

The position lights of the F-15 blinked off and on several times to the left and slightly below their altitude before the big fighter began crossing ahead of them, its twin afterburners lighting in two startlingly bright twin streams of flame which looked like they might even lap the nose of the A330. The F-15 pilot completed the crossover and kept moving off to the right at a slight angle as the afterburners went out.

"Okay, Jerry. Punch it off and follow him."

"Of course! That's what I'm doing!"

"Jerry, he means now."

Jerry's left hand was deflecting the sidestick controller, but the aircraft was not turning.

"I know that!"

"But …"

"I'm … trying."

Dan glanced to his left, puzzled. "What do you mean, 'trying'?"

"It's not following my commands,"

"What? Damned computers!" Dan reached for the switches controlling the autoflight system, finding them off. He turned them back on and then off.

"That should do it. Are we free?"

"No."

"No? But autoflight and autothrottles are completely disconnected!"

"I'm telling you, I'm shoving the stick to the right and she's still straight and level."

"How's that possible?"

"Dan, how is *any* of this shit possible! We should have direct law."

Dan had eased back onto the right seat. The F-15 had moved a bit further to the right and then turned back to steady his heading while he waited for the jumbo jet to respond. Somewhere behind them, the F-15's wingman was waiting, undoubtedly with armed ordinance.

"Jerry?"

"This is NOT happening! All the computers are off, and I still can't get a response from the sidestick. Try yours."

Dan grabbed the right-side control stick, commanding a steep right bank as Jerry let go.

Again the utter lack of change was akin to a physical impact.

He tried again, moving the stick carefully through left, right, up, and down commands, but the aircraft remained rock steady, refusing to follow the commands.

"Jerry, what's going on here? How can we not have direct control?"

"I don't know, man! Do you remember anything in the book about a situation like this?"

"No!"

"Nor do I. But she won't let go. There's no electricity going to any part of the flight computers."

A deep sense of foreboding had been percolating away in Dan's stomach for the past two minutes, and now he felt just outright nauseous. He looked at his right hand, which was deflecting the right sidestick controller ordering what should have been a precipitous turn to the right in an aircraft devoid of any power to the autoflight computers that might oppose him.

And yet the flight path had not changed.

"Nothing, Jerry! It's like we're along for the ride," he said quietly.

The captain was sitting there, Dan noticed, in utter disbelief, the F-15 now maneuvering back to his original position to their left, his wingman somewhere behind.

"Any ideas, Dan?"

"Everything's on an interlock with the autoflight system. Mess with anything, it'll disconnect. Right?"

"I always thought so," Jerry replied, the strain audibly affecting his voice.

"Okay … let's try this." Dan Horneman positioned his left hand on the throttles and clicked the disconnect button for the autothrottles, yanking the levers back to the idle position. The complete lack of response from the aircraft felt like a physical blow.

"Jeez … nothing!"

"Try the speedbrakes," Jerry prompted.

"Whoa! Not at this speed!"

"Just a little … to see if it works!" Jerry snapped, pulling the lever slightly out of the detent himself, but feeling no response. He pulled harder, but there was no change in the aerodynamics of the aircraft. "Maybe drop the landing gear?"

"If we try and it works, Jerry, at this speed it'll blow the gear doors off."

"Right. Then we won't."

"Dan, you said you know the systems … there's got to be something we're controlling that doesn't depend on electrons."

Even in the midst of the growing crisis, Jerry's acknowledgement that his copilot's knowledge might have some value was a startling concession.

"I'm all ears, man, if you can think of anything," Jerry continued.

"Well …"

"How about the nosewheel steering? That's hydraulic."

Dan was chuckling the laugh of a condemned man, "Yeah, that'll work at 33,000 feet!"

Jerry looked slightly embarrassed, "Yeah. Got it."

"Sorry, man. It's just that I never really thought of it before, you know?"

"Thought of what?"

"That there's nothing on this flight deck that's physically connected to anything usable in flight! This bird is nothing but a freaking video game!"

"There's … *nothing*?"

"Okay, the rudder is connected by cable to the hydraulics, and the pitch trim is also partially manual as long as we have hydraulic pressure, and the alternate gear extension system uses a cable, but that's it. Everything else involves electrons. Flight controls, throttles, speed brakes, landing gear, trim system … everything's electric. We might as well be sitting in a capsule on the ground controlling this machine by satellite telemetry, like the drones—or unmanned aircraft systems—that the air force uses."

"But, Dan, no one in their right mind would design a

system that could lock out its pilots if there's no counterpart on the ground, right?"

"Well, sure as hell no one else is flying this beast. And all the flight instruments have been lying to us. They're *still* lying to us! Look at that moving map! It's saying we're over the Atlantic heading west, and instead we're barreling southeast toward Paris!"

The interphone call chime rang, and Dan punched it up on his panel to find Carol on the other end with a simple but disturbing question.

"What?" Jerry asked.

"Carol wants to know if she should wake up Breem and company?"

"Shit."

"Is that your final answer?" Dan chuckled.

"No, dammit! That's all I need is his royal ass up here firing off orders."

"Jerry …"

"I know, I know. All available resources, and we've got a bona fide disaster going on."

"I wasn't going to say that. I was going to point out the company regulation regarding relief crews and emergencies."

"Tell me."

"Whoever is in charge when an emergency occurs remains in charge. The only exception is if a check captain decides to remove a relief captain for cause."

"And Breem's no longer a check captain."

"Right. It's your ship."

"Tell her to wait fifteen minutes, then wake them. Maybe the bastard will have some ideas. Who's his copilot?"

"Wilson. I forget his first name."

"Okay. Do it."

Dan passed the order to Carol and rang off.

"We've got to get control of this thing," Jerry said,

suddenly pulling himself up in the seat and taking a deep breath. "Okay, look … let's go back over everything and see if there's something we've missed that could regain control. What if we reversed everything you tried a few minutes ago? I mean, there's got to be a logical explanation for this, if we can keep from panicking."

"Panicking?" Dan asked with a rueful chuckle he couldn't stifle.

"Yeah."

"Too late, brother. I'm already there."

CHAPTER SEVENTEEN

CIA, Langley, Virginia (5:45 p.m. EST / 2245 Zulu)

At the top of the intelligence food chain, patience is seldom a virtue, Walter Randolph thought, as he punched in his aide's secure phone number.

"You promised updates, Jason."

"I was just getting ready to call, sir. I've been on the line with our air force command post at Lakenheath in the UK. Their two F-15s had to break off. The Pangia flight wouldn't, or couldn't, follow them back to London."

"Explain, please."

"The lead pilot said the pilot of the A330 was gesturing and acting like he was going to follow their orders, but the aircraft never altered course. He said there were others in the cockpit when he first flew alongside, but they beat a hasty exit. Logically, if the pilot won't follow the F-15s, even though he's signaling that he intends to, that might indicate that he *can't* follow."

"In other words, intimidation. Did the rest of the aircraft look normal? Did the fighter report on that?

"Yes, sir. There are lights throughout the cabin, and faces visible in most of the cabin windows."

"Where are they?"

"Southeast bound over the English Channel headed for France. The French are already scrambling fighters to intercept."

CHAPTER EIGHTEEN

Cockpit, Pangia 10 (2245 Zulu)

"Jerry, I've got a GPS lock."

"On your iPad?"

"Yes. My personal one."

"I thought you needed an Internet signal?"

"I remembered an aviation program I downloaded that has a stored map … wait … okay, we're about …"

"What? What are you showing?"

"Jeez! This can't be right!"

Dan peered at the small screen again, blinking and refocusing to make sure he was interpreting the map correctly.

"Where the hell are we?" Jerry insisted.

"Jerry, hold on."

"*Where*, dammit?"

"Not over the Atlantic, that's for sure! According to this thing, we're over France and aiming straight for Paris from maybe a hundred miles northwest."

"No shit?" Jerry's voice had almost a whining tone.

"Looks like we just passed over the channel south of London."

"France? Seriously?"

"That's what it says, man, but I'm a little short on believing computers about now."

There was silence from the captain for a few seconds before Jerry sighed heavily and replied, almost under his breath. "I hope it *is* Paris ahead."

Dan looked up, puzzled. "Why?"

"Paris would be a perfect place for an emergency landing … provided we could get control of this beast."

Jerry turned to his left, looking outside where one of the

F-15s had been up until minutes before.

"He's gone."

"I figured. The one on the right is gone, too. If we're really over France now, they'll send up a couple of Mirages."

"Dan, they wouldn't shoot us down, would they?"

"You're the ex-military guy, Jerry. You tell *me*!"

"I just flew Tomcats off a carrier. I never got involved in diplomatic stuff, and that was decades ago anyway."

"Okay, look, I do happen to know this. The French are diffident friends at times, but, no, they won't shoot us."

"I hope you're right."

"But we can't fly this heading forever without running into some people who might."

"Meaning?"

"I don't know, man. I … haven't projected this heading, but it probably takes us over the Middle East and some places we don't want to be."

Jerry was shaking his head in apparent disgust, and somehow Dan knew what was coming.

"I can't believe you saw the compass showing the wrong heading and you didn't … recognize it!"

Okay, so let's play "shift the blame!" Dan thought. *A good pilot with the right stuff and a modest bank account would never make that mistake, right Jere?*

An appropriate retort had formed in his mind, but he forced it back. They were in the middle of a real emergency, and an internecine dual wasn't going to help regain control.

"Okay, okay …" Jerry was continuing, "the main thing is, we've got to get communication back! The factory where they hatched this airplane isn't that far. Toulouse. Maybe someone down there knows how to regain control."

Dan's head snapped up from the iPad as he released his seatbelt and motored the copilot's seat back on the rails, then sideways. He swiveled around to face the captain, fixing

Jerry with a steady stare and an index finger held high.

"Okay, listen. We've got to regain control of this ship, and we have to realize those F-15 pilots are going to report that we refused their orders, and the only reason we would do that is … is …"

"If we were being forced to, or we're deviating on our own."

"Chicago won't believe we've gone nuts. *I* wouldn't if I were them."

"So … we're hijacked in their view? What does that do to us?"

Dan sighed deeply, looking at the floor for a second before meeting Jerry's rather feral gaze again. "I don't know, but … they'll keep everyone out of our way, I guess." His eyes suddenly shot down to the transponder control head. "We *are* squawking radio failure, right? The 7600 code, not the 7500 hijack code?"

"Right."

"Good."

"But someone could be forcing us to do that. That's what they'll conclude. I remember reading about the Soviets shooting down a Korean Air 747 back in the eighties."

Dan was waving away the thought. "That risk is a long ways off. Right now, Captain, we need to prioritize."

Dan noticed that his use of Jerry's title seemed to have an impact. Almost imperceptibly, the left-seater sat up a bit, looking around as if suddenly realizing he was the one in charge.

"I was going to say the same thing," Jerry began, a slightly defensive tone overlaying the barely-contained panic both of them were feeling.

"I recommend," Dan said, watching the captain for any sign he was pushing too far, "… that our first move should be to find a radio or a cell phone or something we can use to talk to the guys who built this jet and get some help on how to get its goddamned attention!"

Jerry Tollefson nodded. "Yeah, agreed." He started to punch the PA button on his interphone panel, but Dan stopped him.

"Wait! Let's stay coordinated. What do you want to ask them?"

"What *you* said. A usable cell phone or a radio of some sort."

"That means we've got to fess up to what's happening."

Jerry nodded. "Yeah, I get that."

Dan hesitated, wondering if Jerry could pull it together enough to not panic the passengers and gauging whether an offer from the copilot to do the deed would be resented.

Whatever, he concluded. "Want me to do it, Jerry?"

The captain started nodding in obvious relief. "Go ahead. No, wait! I'm the captain … I should."

"Go for it, then. Hurry."

Jerry punched the appropriate button and adjusted his headset microphone, activating the PA. He sat in silence for a few seconds, collecting his thoughts and trying to imagine the best way to break the news that everyone aboard was being flown by an electronic ghost.

"Ladies and gentlemen, this is your captain ... Captain Tollefson. I need you to listen very carefully. As some of you had already noticed, we have reversed course and are, at this moment, about a hundred miles northwest of Paris, France. We have experienced a very unusual failure in our autoflight system, and although we are in no present danger with plenty of fuel, many of you also noticed that we were intercepted by US Air Force jet fighters a while ago. The reason is that we have lost all of our radios ... not just the satellite system for Internet and phone calls. And, we have

been unable to get the system back, so we can't talk to air traffic control, even though they know who and where we are. I now need to enlist your help. If there is anyone aboard who has a radio capable of transmitting and receiving aircraft frequencies, please ring your flight attendant call chime immediately. For those of you with cell phones that work in Europe, I ask you to take them out now and turn them on, and if you have a steady signal and can reach anyone below, we need to borrow that phone in the cockpit immediately. For anyone with a handheld satellite phone, we also need to know if you have a lock-on signal. Anyone who can assist, please immediately ring your call chime."

Call chimes could be heard through the cockpit door, and Dan triggered a call to Carol.

"I'm opening the door. Just give us anything you collect from the passengers."

"What in heaven's name is going on, Dan?"

"We can't disconnect the autopilot, and we need to talk to someone on the ground about why."

"Can't … *what?"*

"That's why we turned around and didn't know it."

"Can't you …"

"Carol! Please! Just go get us phones that work. We'll explain later."

"You need to explain more now," she replied. "To everyone! You should see the looks back here, and I don't want panic.

Jerry had punched off the PA to call the cabin, and his finger now poised over the PA button once again as he shot a questioning look at Dan.

"What?" Dan asked.

"Was I too vague?"

Why don't we just tell them we're in a giant pilotless

airplane! Dan thought to himself. But Jerry was asking for guidance. This wasn't the time for flippant answers.

"I think," Dan began, "… that if I were back there as a passenger, I'd rather know the entire unvarnished truth. They will undoubtedly find out later."

"Yeah, got it," was the reply. Another deep sigh and Jerry punched the button again.

"Okay folks, let me describe to you precisely what we're dealing with up here. It's our policy not to dance around or obscure anything. In a nutshell, our autoflight system will not disconnect, and we have not yet been able to find a way to regain manual control. Further, the airplane reversed course on its own while falsely displaying normal indications that we were westbound and over the Atlantic headed for New York. Normally we would just pull circuit breakers and disconnect the system, but it is resisting our efforts to do so. Now, machines and computers are not sentient, so there is a simple explanation for this, and we will find it. But that's the reason we need to establish an alternate way of speaking with folks on the ground, so we can solve this problem more quickly. Both of us up here promise to keep you fully informed at all times."

Dan was nodding as Jerry punched off the PA. "Well, done, Jerry. Tough job well done."

A genuine flash of appreciation crossed the captain's face like the momentary flare of a candle on a dark night, and at the same moment the cockpit door burst open. Captain Bill Breem, his face almost purple with apparent anger, stood in the doorway, his voice loud enough to be heard in first class.

"WHAT THE FUCK IS GOING ON UP HERE?"

Jerry half turned in his seat and smiled as disingenuously as possible.

"And a good evening to you, too, Bill!"

First class cabin, Pangia 10 (2255 Zulu)

The passenger call light had brought Carol routinely to the side of a fashionably unshaven male in his forties who looked up and motioned her closer.

"Ma'am, could I talk to you, perhaps in the galley?"

"You have a cell phone or radio, sir?"

"Well … yes, but it doesn't work. I …"

"Right now I need to deal with an airplane full of call lights," she said, strain showing clearly on her face.

"Yes, but … I need to … to *report* something the pilots may need to know."

"Report what?"

He glanced at the seat row ahead, noting the teenage boy who had partially closed the lid of his laptop, but the glow of an aircraft instrument panel could still be seen on the screen.

"Ah … in private, when you can … please," his cultured British accent easy on her ears.

She nodded, not unkindly. "Follow me, please."

The man scrambled out of the aisle seat, unnoticed by the woman in the adjacent window seat still too absorbed in her book to notice, and followed Carol forward to the galley where she had him step inside the curtains.

"Okay, tell me."

"The pilot said he's having trouble with the autoflight system. I … believe I may possess a clue as to why."

"Go ahead."

"I believe the young chap sitting ahead of me in 3B is fooling around with the controls of this airplane."

"Excuse me? How?"

"He's a computer hacker, and he's trying to impress the

girl next to him. He's been manipulating programs for the past hour. I know computers. He's up to no good."

The look on Carol's face told it all: She didn't believe a word of it. Worse, she didn't think it possible.

"I'll tell the captain, sir. Please go back to your seat now, and thank you."

"You're quite welcome, but you do understand I'm dead serious?"

"I understand." He felt her hand on his arm, propelling him gently but with unmistakable firmness back into the aisle and to his seat.

But she didn't go straight to the cockpit, he noticed. Instead, she went aft and returned with a bag of collected cell phones first, disappearing then into the cockpit. Surely now she would inform the captain, he thought.

He studied the scene one row ahead, the shoulder-length blonde mane of the girl in 3A falling to the left of her seat against the window, sound asleep, the kid leering at her now without subterfuge, his eyes all over her as she slept. He sat with his partially closed laptop showing that same cockpit view. Whatever he'd prepared on that screen to impress her, he obviously wasn't going to change anything until she awoke.

CHAPTER NINETEEN

CIA, Langley, Virginia (6:00 p.m. EST / 2300 Zulu)

CIA Deputy Director Walter Randolph surveyed the packed conference room and said a simple "good evening" as he sat at the head of the table. Thirteen earnest faces now turned to him, their papers, tablet computers, and note pads at the ready.

"Very well, folks. As my able assistant Mr. Duke has, I'm sure, briefed you, we have a winged problem that may just be boomeranging back to Tel Aviv. At least we *hope* whoever is controlling Pangia Flight 10 intends it to go no further than Tel Aviv. We know Mr. Lavi is aboard with his handler, and in the case of Miss Ashira, the word "handler" is a bit of a double entendre. I do not know where our uniformed DIA rivals at the Pentagon may be on this. Further, at the director's insistence, I am to meet him at the White House Situation Room in thirty minutes. So, speak to me, starting with the flight dynamics."

Randolph planted his elbows on the polished table and supported his aging face, letting his eyes bracket whoever was speaking. Full attention mode, he called it, but in fact he was listening on a secondary level as well for something that didn't quite mesh, some fact that seemed incongruous. Sometimes fifteen minutes later a tiny snag would surface from his subconscious gray matter, and often, too often, it was a missing piece of the puzzle.

The facts came hot and heavy: The aircraft was on the same heading as if it were bore sighted on Tel Aviv; the French fighter pilots were reporting Pangia pilot attempts to communicate visually but no luck with handwritten signs in the windows; Pangia World Airways was clueless about a potential cause and they suspected a hijack; and the Airbus was streaking toward an already upset Switzerland whose leaders perceived there might be a military issue with this rogue flight, of which they, being a neutral nation, would want no part.

Walter raised a hand to stop the briefing suddenly. "Whoa. Several statements back ... Charmaine, was it you reporting on the passengers and cargo?"

"Yes, sir."

"And you said in addition to the normal baggage there was what? Cargo?"

She nodded. "One cargo storage igloo. We don't have the manifest."

"Can't we get it? After all, we're the CIA."

"We're working on it, sir."

"Good. Random bags are one thing, but a cargo container containing unknown cargo and coming out of Israel with Moishe Lavi on board has me a bit more than concerned. Do we suspect something explosive?"

Several heads were shaking no. "No, sir. At least given the neutron backscatter equipment always used at Ben Gurion, nothing nuclear."

"But we all understand, do we not ..." Randolph continued, visually polling the faces around the table, "... that if the Iranians get interested, they won't buy that assurance for a moment? And, we have no assurance that a Lavi sympathizer isn't running the neutron backscatter detector array at Ben Gurion."

The sound of the conference room door opening a bit too aggressively caused everyone to look toward the intruder. A woman Walter Randolph didn't recognize but sporting the requisite CIA badge moved immediately in his direction, her face a mask of seriousness as she handed him a folded note written on the stationery of the director. Walter studied the note and nodded at her. "In five minutes," he said quietly, pocketing the note as he forced his protesting body to its feet.

"Well, as expected, the head of Israeli intelligence is requesting an urgent conference with our director, and I have the honor of delivering an emergency briefing so our esteemed leader isn't blindsided. He already knows the basics, but this will be a high-wire act. Send me a runner with anything new you may get in the next ten minutes, and I want everyone coordinating on a multi-pronged assessment of every possible outcome you can envision. Including ones involving nuclear detonations."

The deputy director moved quickly out of the room, acutely aware of the deathly silence behind him.

CHAPTER TWENTY

Cockpit, Pangia 10 (2300 Zulu)

There was no place Dan knew of for a truly private conversation between crew members except for the crew rest facility, but that was over 150 feet aft. There was also no avoiding the reality that someone had to get Bill Breem under control, and that someone was him.

Asking Breem's first officer, Tom Wilson, to temporarily replace Dan in the copilot's seat had been the first step, and Breem hadn't even noticed. Dan stood and faced the angry captain, all but physically pulling him away from the running verbal gun battle with Jerry Tollefson, who was not about to surrender control.

"Captain Breem, may I have a word with you in private?" Dan asked, his voice deep, calm, and as steady as he could manage.

"Not now!"

"Yes, sir. Now. Right now. Please follow me out of the cockpit."

"Who the hell are you …" Breem started.

"Legally, sir, I am the second in command of this aircraft, and I'm asking you as a fellow professional to follow me outside to the galley for a private conversation, and this request is on the record."

"On the record?" Breem snorted. "What are you now, a fucking lawyer?"

Dan pointed at the ceiling. "No, Captain, but you and I are being recorded by the cockpit voice recorder, there's a tiny microphone right over our heads, and that will not be the case in the forward galley. What I have to discuss with you is probably best left off the record."

Breem hesitated, uncertainty fighting anger as he glanced upward and gave in with a nod.

"This better be good, son."

"Jerry? Tom's got the right seat. I'll be back in a few minutes."

Jerry Tollefson had been on the verge of exploding, but he nodded now without a word, and Dan stepped out of the cockpit and waited for Breem to follow. They moved silently into the forward galley, where Dan asked Carol to step out for a few minutes.

"So what do you want?" Breem asked, his voice reasonably low but his eyes betraying alarm.

"Captain, I have to tell you that I recently attended a training course in Chicago where this very issue of emergency command was discussed. One of the company lawyers came in along with our union counsel, and they confirmed … and I am confirming to you … that the company rule Captain Tollefson was citing to you a minute ago absolutely governs."

"I'm the senior captain!"

"Yes, sir, you are the senior captain in terms of experience and rank and even seniority number, but you were not the pilot in command, the flight captain, when this emergency began, and therefore the man who was in that position, Captain Tollefson, is the captain of this ship for the duration of the emergency."

"Screw that. I'm relieving him."

"Sir, you cannot legally do that unless you are a check captain relieving him for cause, and you are not a check captain, and there is no cause. Therefore, any attempt to pull him out of that seat is legally somewhere between an attempted hijacking and a felonious mutiny, a federal crime in any event, and I, Captain, will be a witness against you, if you attempt it. At the very least you would end up losing your position, and maybe your job, and, possibly, your freedom."

A lifetime of practice in the art of derision and arrogance had taught Bill Breem how to back down without appearing to give in, and he used his skills now by smiling a snarly smile and glancing away momentarily, as if confronted by fools.

"I am well aware that if Tollefson wants to hold onto command he legally can, and if we survive this, I'm also aware that his refusal to let go will end his career, and you, sonny, can be a witness any way you want."

"As long as you understand that he is in command. We need your help, not more struggles over who's in charge."

"Kid, I was a fucking international captain when you were still wetting the bed! I don't need a lecture from the likes of you."

"I certainly hope not, sir, but as of a few moments ago you definitely did.""Yeah, whatever."

"Captain, look. I've addressed you with courtesy and used your rank each time, and I would appreciate some corresponding recognition that my name is First Officer Dan Horneman, not 'sonny.'"

Seemingly for the first time, Breem actually looked at Dan, sensing that the wisest course might be to shift gears.

"All right, point taken. Dan, is it?"

"Yes."

"I'm sorry to be so tough on you, Dan, but this is really aggravating to be rousted out of a deep sleep long after a problem develops on my … on this flight … and then hear about it on a frickin' PA while I'm walking to the cockpit. Very embarrassing."

"Understood. But we need your help working this out."

"Okay, then tell me in as much detail as possible what's going on."

CHAPTER TWENTY-ONE

Cockpit, Pangia 10 (2310 Zulu)

Bill Breem had been on his own down in the electronics bay for the past five minutes trying to figure out what was happening, while Dan had climbed out to look for a more detailed electrical diagram. But when he returned to the cockpit, a brief exchange with Jerry was all it took to convince Dan that Captain Tollefson was losing it, and the implications were seriously worrying his copilot.

Tom Wilson had also left the cockpit for a few minutes, and Dan seized the opportunity to sit back down in the right seat, looking at Jerry.

"What's going on?" Dan probed.

Jerry was all but hyperventilating as he held up and shook the latest cell phone he'd tested.

"Nothing, Dan! Not a goddamned thing! We might as well tape notes to rocks and drop them!"

"Jerry … take a deep breath," Dan said, startled at the beet red color of the captain's face, and worried that Breem would pop up from the E and E compartment below like an opportunistic meerkat and renew the "who's in charge" debate.

The captain looked back as if his copilot was yet a new distraction he couldn't comprehend.

"*Excuse* me? Who the hell do you think you're talking to?"

"You need to know who's your ally, and that's me. I'm talking to the captain of this ship. I just chewed on Breem to make sure you stay the captain of this ship! And I'm doing what any good first officer would do, offer my best professional advice."

Jerry's eyes had flared as he leaned forward over the center console, his index finger in motion as if pointing a gun at the copilot, his voice almost in a hiss.

"Listen, Danny, when I need someone to wet nurse my attitude, I'll …"

"You'll do what?" Dan interrupted with equal force. "You'll license me to speak if it pleases your highness? Giving you tough advice is what teamwork is all about, Jerry—as you well know. You taught crew resource management, remember?"

"I don't need to be insulted."

"I'm not insulting you, Jerry. Jesus, is everyone here so thin skinned? I'm merely suggesting that the situation is momentarily overwhelming you the same as it is me, and we *both* need to take a deep breath."

Jerry snorted as he shot an acid look at the copilot.

"Why?"

"Because you're worrying me, okay?"

"How? How am I worrying you? Aren't *you* worried? Jesus, man, we can't get control of this jet and …"

"JERRY! Listen to me! You wrap yourself around the axle like this and you could have a stroke or heart attack, and I can't solve this dilemma alone. Okay? Mark it off to enlightened self-interest. Calm down, Captain, sir! We need calm, cool leadership! Steel nerves, like when you were flying Tomcats in the navy. That's a challenge I can't even imagine."

"What? Calming down?"

"No, hitting a pitching postage stamp of a flight deck on a ship at 150 knots in a massive fighter and living to tell about it!"

"Oh."

At last a sigh, Dan noted, as the captain slowly nodded and said, "Yeah … okay. You're right. Sorry."

"May I make another suggestion about the situation?"

"Yes, you may! I don't have a clue where we go from here."

"Okay, we've only tried a few of the phones. Let's get the cockpit door back open and get Carol and Tom and maybe one other of her crew up here to start working their way through the rest of this bag of phones until someone maybe makes contact with someone on the ground. Meanwhile, if you'll strap in, I'll go back down to the electronics bay and see if Breem has any new ideas, and if we can figure something out."

"Why should I strap in, Dan?" Jerry snapped suddenly, as if a wave of resentment had suddenly washed over him. "We have absolutely no control over anything up here," he added, ringing the call button for the flight attendants.

"What if the bird suddenly reverts to manual law and pitches over violently and you're caught unprepared sitting sideways while I'm off the flight deck?"

Jerry looked up and stared at his first officer for a few seconds as if seeing him anew, the flash of anger diminished as he nodded.

"Okay, Dan. All right. I get that." He turned back toward the front panel and fumbled with his seatbelt before motoring the captain's chair forward on its rails. The call chime sounded, and Dan lifted the handset to approve Carol's reentry, punching the overhead release button simultaneously.

"How can that help, having you go back downstairs, except to keep an eye on Breem?" Jerry asked, as Carol came through the door.

"Remember when we lost the radios and thought we were still flying west, and I went below and reported back that this was a nonstandard configuration?"

"Yes."

"Jerry, there's a whole part of the compartment down there filled with a cabinet of some sort I've never seen before on a 330. I didn't try to open it, but since something has electronically locked us out of our own controls, maybe it's something to do with that cabinet. I need to look at it again."

"Right."

"Gentlemen, what can I do?" Carol asked, her voice filled with tension, as she eyed the bag of phones and the fact that neither pilot was yet using one.

Dan quickly explained the assignment and she turned to recruit one of the other flight attendants waiting just outside. She reached for the door to close it, and Dan caught her hand.

"Leave it open, Carol," Dan said. "We can't even control the aircraft. I'm not particularly worried about anyone else trying. You agree, Jerry?"

The captain nodded, his thoughts elsewhere, as he tried once more to click off the autoflight system, to no avail.

"Okay, I'm going down to the electronics bay. Jerry? I need you to motor your seat as far forward as you can stand again. When you move your seat back, you all but seal off the hatch."

"Got it."

"Wait…" Carol responded. "Before you go, I need to at least tell you about this one report from a first class passenger."

Half out of the right seat, Dan stopped. "Go ahead."

"I'm sure it's useless information, but there's a young teenage boy, an unaccompanied minor, in the seat ahead of this fellow, and he's got some sort of computer program running that our passenger thinks could mean that he's somehow … I'm embarrassed to even repeat this silliness … but that somehow he's hacked into the cockpit systems and is causing all this."

Suddenly Jerry Tollefson was completely engaged. He

stopped motoring the seat forward and half turned to his right to ask Carol to repeat the details.

"The kid's got a computer program on?" Jerry asked. "A UM? No parents aboard?"

"That's right."

"NOW?"

"Yes. Right now."

"Jesus!" Seat belt straps were flying as Jerry moved the seat back and scrambled out, brushing past Carol to reach the cockpit door, fire in his eyes as Dan caught his sleeve.

"What?"

"Jerry, that can't be the answer."

"Yeah? Then tell me what *is*? Closest thing to an explanation I've heard so far."

"At least wait till I strap in," Dan managed, but the captain was already through the cockpit door with Carol on his heels.

First class cabin, Pangia 10

To the passenger who'd reported his suspicions, all concerns that he wasn't going to be taken seriously evaporated as the captain himself fairly burst into the cabin. The four-striper moved straight to the boy in Seat 3B and leaned over, grasping the edges of the seat, shaking it slightly.

"Look at me!" the captain demanded. "Are you electronically messing with this aircraft?"

The girl in the window seat had suddenly snapped awake.

"What?" the kid managed.

"Let me see that computer!"

"That's my …"

"GIVE ME THE COMPUTER! NOW!"

The laptop was rotated on the boy's lap, and the captain's

eyes narrowed as he took in the instrument panel of an Airbus A330.

"Listen to me kid, or you'll spend the next twenty years rotting in a French prison. You're going to undo whatever you've done! You hear me? You reverse that immediately and return full control to my cockpit."

"But I …"

"NOW, DAMMIT!"

Several first class passengers were getting to their feet, unsure what was happening, as Carol closed in at the captain's side, a hand on his arm to calm him down. But it wasn't working, and the commander of Flight 10 leaned over again, his big hand closing on the lapel of the boy's shirt, his breath in the boy's face.

"You little bastard! I swear I'll beat you senseless right here if you don't do what I'm telling you to do! RELEASE MY COCKPIT!"

"Captain …" Carol, began.

"YOU HEAR ME?"

"*Captain!*" she tried again.

`"WHAT?" Jerry Tollefson asked in a growl, glancing over his shoulder at Carol.

"He's trying to answer you!" she said. "Let him speak."

Jerry released Josh Begich with a violent lurch and straightened up to his full height, glaring at the terrified boy.

"I … didn't do anything!" Josh stammered, his eyes huge, his right hand at his own throat as if to check if it were still intact. "Honest, sir, I …"

The girl in 3A was gesturing wildly to the laptop, her eyes huge as well.

"He had a loop going … he was trying to fool me earlier, but it was just a recorded loop!"

Begich was in total confusion, nodding at first, then shaking his head. Three male passengers had stood and were approaching cautiously, unsure who needed to be brought under control, but Carol was motioning them back.

Jerry reached down and twirled the laptop once more so he could see the screen.

"What's your name, kid?"

"Ah … Josh … Josh Begich …"

"Where are your parents?"

"My dad's meeting me in New York."

"So we're at flight level three-eight-zero, and so is this display. Our instruments show a heading of two-four zero, and so does the panel on this screen. You're reading our panel, aren't you?"

"Captain, he was just trying to fool me …" the girl said again. "He was … just being a dork."

"I heard you!" Jerry snapped at her, his eyes boring into Josh's. "What am I looking at on this screen?"

"I … it's a mockup … it's a cockpit like yours, sir, but … but I'm not connected to anything. I just had it running the heading and everything … where I thought we were."

"And if I turn this computer off and rip the battery out?"

"Nothing will happen to the plane! Honest! I was just … just …"

"Our cockpit is offline! Is that a coincidence, too?"

"I heard your announcement, sir, but it isn't me."

Jerry grabbed the laptop and handed it to Carol. "Take it to Dan. See what he thinks." He turned back to Begich, pressing a finger to his chest. "If I find out you're lying, kid …"

"I'm not! I'm not lying … I wouldn't … really! I swear!"

Jerry swiveled around, reading the distress in his lead flight attendant's eyes. He followed her gaze to the three male passengers who'd been standing at the ready. All three were watching him now with deep alarm, saying nothing, as if unsure whether it was safe to even sit down with a madman captain screaming and threatening kids. He shook his head and waved them off. "Sorry to alarm you guys. We thought ..."

One of the men was approaching. Short, rotund, and balding, he nevertheless had an air of authority about him and Jerry shook his head at first when the man's voice reached him, low and accented.

"Captain, may I speak with you in the galley there."

It was, Jerry realized, more of an order than a request, and for some reason the embarrassment of attacking a snot-nosed teenager cancelled his desire to pull rank and duck back in the cockpit. Instead, he followed the man in, finding a perfunctory outstretched hand, which he took reluctantly.

"I am Moishe Lavi," he began, watching for a reaction that didn't come. "I know a few things about command and leadership, Captain, and I know we've got a very big problem, but may I make a humble suggestion?"

"What, that I cool it? Yeah, you can, because I know you're right, Mr. ... Lavi was it?"

"Yes."

"I apologize."

"Tell me what you think is happening to this plane, Captain?"

Just for a second Jerry thought he saw a means of polite escape, but pilot platitudes such as "We're working on the problem" or "We have it under control" sounded one light year beyond ridiculous, and so he remained where he stood, knowing somewhere in the back of his mind that somewhere he'd heard the name "Lavi," and not being able to make the connection was bothering him, too.

"Actually, sir, I don't have any good ideas to explain what's happening to us. Neither the copilot nor I have ever even heard of anything like this before. I ... we just left Israel, as you know, and I have to wonder if some enemy of

Israel did this … but, I don't even know how to define "this."

"An enemy of Israel?" Lavi looked off balance for the briefest of moments. "You mean the Iranians? Why would you suspect them?"

"I don't, at least not an active suspicion, and not just Iran. I mean, we have no explanation for what's happening, so I suppose that's a place to start."

"I see. And you can't regain control?"

What? Jerry thought. *Am I not speaking clearly?* He stifled the urge to make a sarcastic comment, still suspicious that he should know this guy.

"No," Jerry answered, restraining himself carefully and describing the untouchable video game the cockpit had become.

"And if nothing changes, what are we to do then, Captain?"

That's the question I don't want to hear, Jerry thought to himself. *What if! What if we can't solve it before we run out of fuel? What if even then, even when all the electrics are offline, we can't even dead stick it to an engine-out landing?*

Moishe Lavi saw the expression on Jerry Tollefson's face even before Jerry realized it himself.

"Excuse me, please, Mr. Lavi," Jerry said, trying to mask the sudden tension in his voice. "Please go back to your seat. I have to go back up front."

Jerry turned without a word and propelled himself into the cockpit, pulling the door partially closed behind him. Bill Breem had surfaced from the electronics bay and was perched on the jumpseat and Jerry registered the fact that Dan had the kid's computer on his lap, an amused expression on his face.

"What, Dan?"

Dan shook his head. "Carol told me what went on. This is just a clever recording. I changed a bunch of parameters and nothing changed up here."

The sigh from the captain's mouth as he slid back into the command chair was almost heartrending, Dan thought.

"I thought …"

"I know. Unfortunately, it's not that easy."

"One other idea, Dan."

"Go ahead."

"If the engines stopped, and the RAT wasn't deployed, and the battery was disconnected, there's no way whatever or whoever is holding us hostage could *not* let go, right?"

There was desperation in Jerry's voice, but what was pulling at Dan was completely frivolous—the fact that the last line of defense for electrical and hydraulic failure had a derisive acronym: RAT, the Ram Air Turbine.

"Dan?"

"Jerry, the only way that would happen, if nothing else we try works, is when we run out of fuel and the engines stop. Even then, a total disconnect would only occur if we slow down so far the engines can't provide windmilling voltage. Then, provided we could keep the RAT from popping out and giving us electricity, which, by the way, we can't, because it's automatic, and provided I could find and disconnect the only battery bank downstairs, then the remaining problem is, we'd have no basic flight controls and we'd be descending, with all instruments blank, unable to influence anything. I don't really think that's a good solution."

"I wholeheartedly agree, that's not a solution," Breem added, his voice no longer carrying a sarcastic tone.

"I'm not an idiot," Jerry said. "I know that. But in that moment of complete disconnect, we could then deploy the RAT, power up the controls, and maybe get her back."

"For how long?" Dan asked. "To glide down somewhere? We'd be out of gas, and we can't artificially turn off the fuel since nothing up here works."

"We haven't tried to use the engine cutoffs."

"Jerry, I don't think we want to just *try* that. You want to gamble, knowing that if it works and the engines stop, we still can't get them back and fly the airplane manually …" he let the thought trail off into the oblivion it deserved.

"What else have we got?" Jerry asked.

"Methodical analysis. We're off the emergency checklists on this. Yes, we have no formal guidance, but this stuff isn't metaphysics. Therefore, we have a lot of deduction and methodical analysis to go through, step by step. Let me get back downstairs and see what I can find … if anything. Captain Breem, did you have any insights down there?"

Bill Breem shook his head and looking a bit pale. *A bit different when you're facing the monster yourself, isn't it, Captain Bligh,* Dan thought, making sure those thoughts weren't being transmitted in his expression.

"I've only been in that compartment a few times, gents," Breem said. "But you're right; I've never seen a cabinet like that or even heard of it."

"Well, we know the flight controls worked on this ship out of Tel Aviv, and no one's been in here with a welding torch, so presumably any huge switch array that's been thrown down there can be unthrown, so to speak."

"And if it can't?" Jerry asked.

"Too early for apocalyptic thinking, my friend. Do you want the worst case? Ultimately?"

"Yeah, Dan. Give me the worst case."

"Worst case is we all die. But the inconvenient truth is, we're all going to die someday anyway, so all we can do is delay that inevitability as best we can, and when you work back from that premise, there is hope."

First class cabin, Pangia 10

Forty feet aft of the cockpit Moishe Lavi had regained his seat and settled in, his eyes focused somewhere far away, as Ashira could clearly see. She knew this look, this sudden air of detachment, always the face he showed when something very strategically challenging was roiling his fertile brain. She had learned how to bide her time in learning what it might be, and even then—even in the throes of sexual delight when his guard was down and his cock was up and in total control—he would sometimes mislead her with an ease Prince Machiavelli would have admired.

She watched now in silence, her own stomach contracted at the news of the pilots' loss of control and now Moishe's studied response. She waited patiently for his return to the mundane cabin of the aircraft, trying to guess his mind.

As Moishe Lavi returned to his seat, Carol quietly pulled open the cockpit door and stood just inside, her eyes wide as she waited for at least one of the pilots to turn toward her.

"We have a signal!" she said, causing both pilots to turn toward her.

"Sorry?" Dan managed.

"On one of the cell phones we gathered. We have a signal, and we have an operator!" She held out the handset, and Jerry grabbed it with the zeal of a starving dog lunging for a scrap.

CHAPTER TWENTY-TWO

First class cabin, Pangia 10 (2330 Zulu)

Ashira had been ready to offer at least one of their top-of-the-line satellite phones to the crew, but Moishe had vetoed the idea, directing her instead to hide the transceiver. There were many things Moishe did that irritated her, but his order had mostly twanged her suspicions.

Ashira was watching him closely, but Lavi was paying no attention, as he sat hunched over a laptop computer that seemed to have his undivided attention. Finally he looked up, locking eyes with her as he snapped the lid closed.

"So, we are returning."

Ashira's eyebrows had arched slightly. "To Tel Aviv?"

"Yes … and no. We may fly over our homes and then head for Tehran."

"WHAT?" she managed.

Moishe Lavi looked almost smug, and while he sometimes reacted to stress this way, it made no sense.

"How do you know this?" Ashira asked, her mind whirling through all the ways any in-the-clear communication could be intercepted and used against them.

"I have Internet … I have email … I have sources, Ashira, and I remain in charge of me. You should know that."

Cockpit, Pangia 10 (2340 Zulu)

Feeling as if another lifeline had been snatched away from his fingertips, Jerry stopped the constant re-dial attempts and placed the borrowed cell phone in his lap, forcing himself to sit in thought for a second.

"Did they hear you?" Dan was asking. "Did they

understand we're locked out of the system?"

"I think they did … but they said it was coming through badly … like every other word. You heard my end."

"What were you responding to when you said, 'We couldn't be if we tried'?"

Jerry turned toward his copilot with a crooked smile. "They asked if we were hijacked."

Dan shook his head in amazement. "If we can't believe all this, I wouldn't expect them to. That was operations in Chicago?"

"Yeah … and one of our vice presidents, no less … if I heard him right."

"Okay, Jerry, I'm going down to the electronics bay again. Please motor your seat full forward."

The captain gave a perfunctory nod as his first officer lifted the floor hatch and once again carefully squeezed behind the captain's seat. He descended the diminutive ladder into the crowded corridor of electronic racks and blinking lights carrying his airline-issued iPad which was already keyed to the limited electrical schematics pilots were allowed to view. Bill Breem had begged off going down again, describing his wiring knowledge as too rudimentary to be helpful, an uncharacteristic admission stated with a degree of embarrassment.

Even knowing electrical and electronic circuits as well as he did, Dan had never seen the real engineering schematics for the Airbus A330 either. But there was an innate logic to the way even Airbus organized the hundreds of miles of wires that formed the electronic keel beam of the plane. Most of the complex cable harnesses, as they were called, were buried behind baffles and conduits or beneath the floor panels he was standing on, and as he snapped on the interior lights and looked carefully in all directions, nothing seemed out of place.

Where the hell do I begin? Dan wondered. *How would you disconnect an entire cockpit, yet continue to feed it bullshit flight information for the displays?*

The presence of the unfamiliar cabinet toward the rear of the compartment had been his target before descending the ladder, but there was always an ethereal hope that he'd missed something big and obvious on the first excursion beneath the cockpit. But nothing looked even remotely like a single switch that could reconnect everything, restoring their ability to actually fly the airplane.

Dan moved carefully aft, shining his flashlight around on the various exposed electronic racks, trying to take nothing for granted. But even the electronics boxes with blinking diagnostic lights appeared to be normal.

He reached the unknown cabinet and whistled to himself. The size of it was larger than he'd remembered. Almost eight feet in length, about five feet high, and spanning perhaps three feet laterally, the side made out of what looked suspiciously like a weight-wasting stainless steel. But despite his best effort, he couldn't locate even a hint of a hatch or service door.

At the forward end, he could see a cascade of cables entering the cabinet, but without pulling up the floor panels it was unclear where they were coming from. The sheer size of the cable harness, however, looked formidable—as if every circuit in the airplane was routed through the big box.

Gotta get inside this thing! No warnings, no labels, no nothing. This makes no sense! You don't put a major component in an airplane and weld the whole thing shut. There's got to be a hatch on here somewhere.

He moved carefully towards the aft end of the cabinet, examining every square inch he could reach by running his fingers along the smooth, unpainted metallic surface.

Okay, logically, if there are no openable panels, then the entire side has to come off or swing open.

He ran his fingers over the top of the right side from aft to forward, realizing at last that there was a ridge where the sheet metal was bent from the vertical to horizontal, overlapping the edge by perhaps two inches, the overlap unseen on the top. He examined the entire front-to-back breadth of the seam, feeling for a latch or screws or some sort of fastener.

On the third pass, he found what felt like a round depression, just the size for an index finger to push in on some type of button.

The space between the top of the cabinet and the roof of the electronics bay was only two inches, not enough to see over, but he could feel the button give a little when he pushed it, and spreading his legs to get a steady stance while holding the edge of the metal rack to his right, Dan shoved his index finger down with as much force as he dared.

He felt the lock begin to move as an earsplitting "*CRACK*" coursed through him. Just as quickly, the memory of the noise faded as he sank to the floor of the electronic bay.

How much time had passed he couldn't tell, but regaining consciousness felt like swimming up from the bottom of a giant bowl of soup. It wasn't immediately clear to Dan whether he was coming in or out of a dream, anesthesia, or a nightmare. He opened his eyes to a sideways, floor level view of a strange compartment that ever so slowly began to look familiar again. He lay there afraid to move for a moment, wondering if he still had arms and legs and whether they would respond if he tried to move.

There was sound all around him now, and he recognized it as a slipstream, which would mean he was in flight somewhere. He struggled to put the pieces of the puzzle together, and the thunderclap realization of where he was and what had happened caused him to sit bolt upright, ignoring the dizzying pain in his head.

There was a burning sensation on his right index finger, and something wet, warm, and sticky was on the back of his head and when he probed it, his hand came back covered in blood. The steel-faced cabinet was still in front of him, looking all the more impregnable and intimidating. Obviously it was booby-trapped, and he'd walked right into it.

There was a voice in the distance … a female voice, Dan judged … and he knew he should look to the right and see if there was a woman attached to it. Or maybe he was still dreaming. It would be so much better to just close his eyes and rest a few minutes.

Or a few hours.

But the voice was insistent, irritatingly calling his name, and he struggled to look to the right, spotting a disembodied Carol, only her head visible as she stuck it below floor level looking for him.

He tried to reply, but his voice sounded too weak for even him to hear.

"DAN! WHAT HAPPENED? DAN, ARE YOU OKAY?"

Carol pulled her head up and out of sight, but it was replaced instantly by the rest of her descending the ladder and coming to him, some sort of towel in her hand.

"Good Lord, what happened?" she asked, as Dan struggled to answer that question himself. There had been a button and he had punched the button, and … and …

"That … thing … shocked me."

"Shocked you?"

He started to nod, but she was holding the cloth to the back of his head.

"Ow!"

"You're hurt! Stay still!"

"Voltage … I think it's got a protection … ah … circuit … shock thing …" Dan could hear his voice trail off as if it belonged to someone else, but slowly his conscious thoughts were coalescing. He had been electrically zapped by something when he tried to open the cabinet. That meant that whoever had put it here did not want it opened, at least not in flight. He could feel his heart racing and wondered in passing if it could have killed him.

"That cabinet … holds the key," Dan said, but she didn't hear.

"Can you walk, Dan? I need to get you upstairs to attend to this cut."

"I've … I've gotta get into that thing."

"Not until I get this bleeding stopped."

With Carol guiding him, he reached the ladder and propelled himself up to the cockpit with her behind, aware that Jerry was watching him emerge with an incredulous expression.

The process of bandaging the gash on the back of his head took several minutes while Dan explained what he could remember to Jerry, who was looking quite feral.

"You say it's booby-trapped?" Jerry asked.

"Yeah. In a phrase. I wasn't expecting that."

"Can we … can we maybe use gloves and get past it?"

"Dunno. Could be it has other security safeguards as well, but that's got to be the key. There are huge wire bundles running into it from the front side under the floor. I've never seen anything like that in an A330, although … to tell you the truth … I've only been down in two other hellholes. But those two had nothing like that, just an open bay of electronic racks where that thing is situated."

"I've never been down there at all," Jerry said.

"Any luck getting through on any of those other phones?" Dan asked.

"No. They're still trying."

"I was hoping to find a way to restore the radios, but it's hopeless to trace wires. Millions of them. Wait, Jerry … did anything change up here when that thing zapped me?"

The captain shook his head no.

"I was hoping it had. That might mean it's just a short. But … I think this thing intends to defend itself. God knows how many volts of electricity it hit me with, but I don't think its intent was to kill."

Jerry's eyebrows were up as high as they could go, the alarm in his voice visceral.

"What are you talking about, Dan?" Bill Breem interjected. "You make the damned thing sound sentient."

"It may be. God, that stunned me! But it's the key. You don't build a defense system for routine electronics on a plane. Has to be something someone doesn't want us screwing with, and since we're not in control, the box that IS in control doesn't want us taking over. So, that fits."

"What fits?" Jerry asked. "I'm not following you."

"I'm not either," Bill Breem added, a genuinely engaged look on his face.

Dan took a deep breath as Carol nodded her okay to turn forward in the copilot's seat. "I mean, we've been relieved of control thanks to something electronic, and it's more than likely that whatever that is, is in that cabinet, and the cabinet is protecting itself because it doesn't want us taking control back."

"Who is 'IT'?" Jerry asked. "I mean, I know you're referring to the cabinet, but who's controlling the cabinet?"

"Ah … yeah. That's the friggin' question, right?" Dan said. "If we knew that, we might know how to fight it off."

Jerry cursed and turned left toward the side stick

controller, grabbing it and mashing the priority button before deflecting the stick full to the left.

Nothing happened, and he flopped the stick back and forth violently as if trying to break it away from its base.

"Goddamnit!"

"I know. Nothing," Dan said.

"Who the hell would install such a thing in a commercial jet? Has Pangia gone mad?"

"Why would you think our airline would have …" Bill Breem began, letting his voice trail off as the ridiculousness of the question hit him. It was here, therefore someone in their airline had to know, and had to have decided not to tell the pilots.

"Okay, guys," Jerry continued. "If that thing IS in control, we've got to defeat it. Can we cut the cables?"

Dan was shaking his head vigorously. "No. Too risky. But … what the hell *is* it? Is it some sort of surrogate control center? Is it supposed to protect us and instead it's gone nuts?"

"I don't have a clue, but I want it gone."

"Yeah, Jerry … me, too, but if we go cutting cables to something we don't understand that seems to be in control and defending itself, we could crash. If we cut the wrong cable, remove that thing's ability to fly and don't restore ours, we're done."

"We've got to do something!" Breem said.

"So what do *you* think we should do?" Jerry asked through gritted teeth, looking squarely at Dan but expecting Breem to respond as well.

Dan could feel the cobwebs dropping away at last. The burning sensation in his finger and mild headache were trivialities he could ignore.

"Okay, it's a straightforward problem in essence. It's electrical. Find me some thick gloves, insulate my shoes, put on the thickest coat I can find, and I'll go get that goddamn cabinet open. That's step one."

"And step two?"

The single laugh that escaped unbidden turned into a guttural giggle, as Dan shook his head. "Jerry, even if I wrote thriller fiction for a living, I wouldn't have a clue where this story goes next!"

CHAPTER TWENTY-THREE

Aboard Gulfstream N266SD (2350 Zulu)

General Paul Wriggle looked out at the lights of Telluride, Colorado, passing below and to the right of their Gulfstream. He'd been there many times and loved the place, even with its rarified altitude. He wished he could just spend his time flying airplanes and looking at incredible sights like this, the sodium vapor lights reflecting off the ski slopes, as night skiing progressed in the crystal clear air. Not that he didn't appreciate the professional opportunities for accomplishing things and meeting the challenges that his rank and assignment provided. He enjoyed being a general officer, even more so than he'd imagined he would when he was a lowly second lieutenant just entering undergraduate pilot training out in Enid, Oklahoma. But flying was such a joy, especially when he could park the plane at destination after a completed mission, like an actor leaving a bravura stage performance that never needed a follow-up meeting.

Not quite as good as sex, he thought to himself with an involuntary smile, *but maybe the next best thing!*

He considered throwing off the seatbelts and going back to the cabin to check on Sharon's progress, then thought better of it. They would be ready to start descending into the Springs in about twenty minutes, and he'd already had the pre-arrival bladder break.

He was lucky to have Major Wallace on his team, he thought. An absolute Radar O'Reilly when it came to anticipating what was needed, and incredibly adept at finding logistics solutions for almost any challenge. She could accomplish more in twenty minutes than most staff members could in a day.

He changed his mind again and decided a pre-descent leg stretch was a good idea after all.

"Don? You've got the con. I'm going back for about ten minutes."

"May I point out, sir, that 'you've got the con' is navy-speak, not air force?"

"You may," he smiled.

Sharon Wallace was hunched over the satellite phone when Wriggle walked into the cabin, and she looked up briefly with a "please wait" gesture. He settled into the swivel chair next to her as she finished the conversation and turned to him immediately.

"Sir, we have a problem. A bunch of them. I was just coming to tell you."

He sat forward, on alert. "What's the matter, Sharon?"

"First, the FBO I called in to fuel our aircraft in Tulsa called to reconfirm which airplane we were talking about. I repeated our tail number and serial number and the spot. He rang off, then called back ten minutes later to say the airplane isn't there, despite what the other guy told me."

"Isn't *there?* Did he check all the ..."

"Yes, sir. All the white tail A330s. And he checked their hangars. He said the aircraft on spot eighteen is definitely not our Three-Three-Zero-Romeo-Mike. The serial number is three numbers off from ours. He got out and checked the identity plates in the nose wheel well, to the extent that Pangia's ramp patrol got suspicious and chased him off. Obviously the first guy I engaged was sloppy as hell."

"Shit! Where the hell is our ship?"

"I'm afraid I already know, General."

"Well, *tell* me, Sharon!"

"The call I was on when you came back was the FAA command post in the DC area. I had a bad feeling. I hate to tell you, sir, but the registration number of Pangia's hijacked

A330 is 330RM. In other words, ours."

As a matter of style, Paul Wriggle had never appreciated the use of dramatic pauses, but he couldn't help himself. He sat staring at Sharon for several very long seconds as he tried to process what she'd just said.

"You've got to be kidding!"

"I wish I were. No wonder they couldn't find her in Tulsa. Pangia wasted no time putting her on the line."

"As a *white tail*?"

"Must be, sir. No way could they have painted her in a week."

"And the damn flight is *hijacked?"*

"It gets worse, General. I picked up a late news dispatch about the Pangia flight before those calls came in. It's *not* a hijack. The flight crew is reporting that something has electronically locked out all the controls on the aircraft, and the crew can't fly it, descend, change course, or anything."

Wriggle snapped forward in his chair, eyes wide.

"Oh, my God!"

"No one knows why, sir. Or at least, *they* don't why … or so the news media are saying."

"Jesus Christ, Sharon!" General Wriggle managed, his eyes flaring wide.

"Those were the words," she added. "The pilots can't disconnect the autoflight system. And it's our airplane.'"

"How the hell could this happen?" the general managed, his eyes casting around the carpet as if searching for an answer or reprieve that just had to be rolling around the floor.

"Our guys are an hour behind us in the other A330 headed for Tulsa," Sharon continued, "and undoubtedly, every level of our government will be involved shortly."

Wriggle was waving her to be quiet as he stood and started pacing.

"And we're constrained by law and regulation from

saying too much to anyone," the general added, half under his breath.

"Sir, should we stop our team from landing Pangia's airplane in Tulsa for now?"

Wriggle was breathing hard and struggling to stay composed. He looked up at her as if only half understanding. "What?"

"Our guys hauling Pangia's A330 behind us, sir. We told them to proceed to Tulsa."

"Ah … no. Have Don get hold of them. Have them land in the Springs and just wait for instructions."

"Yes, sir."

"Quick. Go ask Don to confirm whether we have enough fuel to make Washington, DC. I think we do, but …"

"Will do," she said. Sharon disappeared forward into the cockpit returning less than a minute later.

"Don says it would be tight but we can make it. Two hours and twenty minutes from now. We have a kick-ass tail wind."

"Where is that Pangia flight? How much fuel and time do they have left?"

"I … have no idea, sir. We can probably calculate it. They were a Tel Aviv to New York flight with normal reserves, if we knew the departure time …"

"No. There's no time. We'll land at the Springs and work this from our secure lines."

She started to turn for the cockpit again, but he stopped her.

"Wait … Sharon, do we still have classified capability on this satellite phone?"

"Yes, sir."

"Okay, tell Don to head direct to Andrews. I'll work on things from here. I need our staff assembled at the Springs and waiting for instructions."

“What are we going to do, sir?” she asked.

“I don’t know. I really don’t know! I’m thinking. We had no contingency plans for anything like this. That airplane was never supposed to be out of our control, dammit! And nothing like this is even supposed to be possible.”

Silence filled the space between them for a very uncomfortable few seconds before Sharon Wallace filled it.

“We have to help them, sir,” she said.

The general’s eyes locked on to hers with a pleading look she knew he could never articulate.

“Sharon, goddammit, don’t you think I know that?”

CHAPTER TWENTY-FOUR

NSA, Ft. Meade, Maryland (7:10 p.m. EST / 0010 Zulu)

"Jenny? What happened? Where'd he go?" Seth Zeiglar was leaning in the door of the small conference room, which now held nothing but her.

She looked up from what was apparently deep thought and shook her head as she shrugged her shoulders.

"Frankly, I'm not sure. Ten minutes ago we were fixing to go back over everything we knew … or thought we knew … about the signals, and Will Bronson gets a text, immediately makes some lame excuse, and he's on his feet thanking me for nothing and then evaporating."

Seth came in, closed the door behind him, and sat down, looking concerned. "So, what did you find together?"

Jenny sighed and tossed the papers she'd been holding on the table. "We validated my theory that the signal sequence is an echo that has been apparently piggybacking on several dozen communication satellites around the globe. That, in itself, is a pretty good trick, requiring some very creative programming, and I told him that, in my opinion, this isn't something you can set up in a matter of days. Chances are, the transponders involved have been quietly prepped for many months … maybe years."

"Prepped in what way?"

"Quietly reprogrammed from the ground to carry this mystery signal on their normal datastreams from an existing transponder whenever it receives a carefully coded order. But Seth, what I haven't discovered is, where is the mother burst coming from? I was working to pinpoint it when the signals stopped. I'll have to go into the historic data now."

"Geographically, you mean?"

"Yeah. Where's the uplink coming from? That might give us a clue as to who's behind it. "

"Wait, Jenny, you said the signals *stopped*?"

"Yes!" she scooted her chair toward him in excitement, an index finger in the air. "There was what appeared to be an answering burst, then an acknowledgement, then nothing. We ran a series of signal comparisons and found that the programming message changed after the answering burst."

"Something responded?"

"Yes, just about three hours ago. Some station somewhere accepted the programming order, or at least that's what we assume happened. So, just like I said before, the question eating at me is: What entity or machine has been told to do or not to do something? See, if this wasn't nefarious, why the hell would someone go to this extreme to keep the process coded and secret?"

"Was there any sudden breakthrough idea you came up with or some suggestion made that might have triggered our DIA man's departure?"

"No. Just the message he received. I didn't get to read it. And suddenly he's evacuating. At least it felt like an evacuation."

Seth Zieglar shook his head. "Well … my guess is something much more dramatic just came up. And I'll bet … if we did a little digging on the current classified alert channels …"

She was already brightening. "Yeah! Got it. I'll dive in."

"Tomorrow, Jen. Tomorrow you dive in. You should go home now. You do have one of those, right?"

"One of what?" she said, puzzled.

"A home. I seem to recall a long suffering cat in your life."

"Oh, that would be Duke. But he's okay alone. He only dies of malnutrition if I'm gone more than a week."

"Lucky cat."

"Lemme work late on this, Seth."

"You can if you want, but … is this going to help us?"

"Don't know. Can't tell. Want to keep digging."

"It gets spooky around here late at night."

"I know, but I'm not alone."

Seth pulled himself to his feet and waved. "Okay. Have a great evening! I'll be home if you uncover the plans for the attack on Pearl Harbor."

"What? I don't think I understand."

"Just … a joke. Don't stay so late tonight that you don't make it in tomorrow on time, okay?"

"Got it," she said.

Ten minutes later, a fresh coffee in hand, Jenny settled back into her work station and keyed up one of the secure intelligence channels just as the phone rang with Seth on the other end, his voice, she thought, a touch too cheerful.

"Okay, Jenny, mystery solved. Our Mr. Bronson just called my cell phone and essentially said it turns out to be a classified DOD thing, and don't worry, he'll explain later, and thanks so much for the help. He said he was greatly impressed by you."

"You're on your cell phone, right?" she asked, well aware that somewhere in their own NSA building their words were flowing into an immense datastream recording bank and being examined for trigger words or phrases. The public might have been exempted now from phone monitoring but definitely not NSA personnel.

"That would be a correct assumption. In any event, unless you just want to stay and play video games, go home. Nothing to see here."

"You're sure?" she probed, evaluating the nuances of his reply and the time he took to speak it.

"We … have no reason … of which I am currently aware

… to not take our compatriots at their word. So … unless it's making up for what you didn't get done today on normal tasks, go home."

"Uh, huh. Okay. G'night Seth."

"Likewise."

She disconnected the line and stared at the phone's screen for the better part of a minute. *What the hell was that?* She'd worked for Seth long enough to know his vocal patterns, and that was a very stressed version of her boss. Stressed and unnatural.

Jenny shivered involuntarily, wondering what kind of interdepartmental intrigue would cause a chain reaction like she was apparently witnessing: DIA doing strange things and perhaps causing Seth to make calls to her with information she inherently couldn't trust.

I'd make a terrible spy, she concluded. *I'd see duplicity everywhere. Hell, I DO see duplicity everywhere.*

The memory of a close encounter with a psychologist two years before swam unbidden into her consciousness. She'd thought she'd found a clandestine ring of spies within the confines of her own department, and the suspicion had grown to unbearable proportions before Seth and his boss had in essence done an intervention to calm her down. Paranoid tendencies, the doctor had cautioned her, could be fanned by such thinking. Seth should *not* have used that word with her, ever … although she wasn't sure the diagnosis had ever been shared with him. It embarrassed her terribly, especially when the Snowden case erupted and for a few hours she thought he was a validation of her suspicions—until it turned out he was from an entirely different department and a contractor to boot.

Jenny looked back at the computer screen and re-focused. The secure channel was still blinking and the flag indicating a breaking bulletin had popped up, an initial alert regarding a commercial flight that had suddenly reversed course off the west coast of Ireland and might be a hijacking. She glanced at it passively as she mentally replayed Seth's call.

A sudden wave off from the Defense Intelligence Agency had been phoned not through channels, but to Seth's cell phone. And Bronson not calling her meant what? An insult? A determination to prevent her from knowing anything more? Had she suggested something that worried them? And if the programmer and the programmed were both DOD entities, why the hell hadn't the Defense Intelligence team known that themselves when they walked in? Surely Bronson didn't need a team of people wasting an afternoon just to ferret out the little that she knew. He could have had that information for the asking.

Or, she smiled to herself, for dinner and a little intimate persuasion. *Two glasses of wine and a few kisses, and I'd sing like a canary!*

She forced herself back to the serious mode.

No, it felt like a turf thing, and she was used to tug of wars between intelligence agencies that were supposed to be fighting for the same team. Such had been going on from time immemorial.

I shouldn't have teased Seth, she thought, recalling his attempted joke about Pearl Harbor. She knew that story very well, and how all the American intelligence agencies at the time had been withholding information and fighting each other so ridiculously that firmly predicting an impending attack on Hawaii had been all but impossible.

So, is this the DIA pushing us away? she wondered. *Probably not.*

But, there was something about Bronson's hasty departure, and now his rather disingenuous wave-off, that raised a flag. A big one.

Jenny sipped her coffee and let her thoughts bounce

around for a few seconds before realizing something about that hijack story on her screen was lobbying for her attention. She re-read the details, noting the time that the airliner had reversed course without clearance was around 2100 Greenwich Mean Time, or "Zulu" as it was now called.

A little more than three hours ago.

Jenny sat bolt upright in her chair. "Three hours …"

She leaned over suddenly, pulling the folder of papers they'd been working with all afternoon toward her, rifling through the notes to find a particular line.

The one, singular answering burst from something out there that had accepted their mystery signal had come at 2052 Zulu.

Now when, exactly, did that airliner's turn begin? How do I find out?"

She re-read the screen before recalling the existence of the FAA's Air Traffic System Command post. A quick search through a very restricted database turned up the duty officer's number and she punched it in before realizing that a call from the National Security Agency, even on the best of days, could rattle cages and raise shields. And there was never a question about being on an NSA line alone—she had a monitor out there in the form of an active human or a passive datastream.

Monitors be damned, she decided as the line was picked up.

"Vint Hill, duty officer."

"Yes, hello. Jenny Reynolds here, at the Pentagon. A quick question, if I may."

"Go ahead."

"That Pangia flight we're all watching, do you know precisely when it reversed course in Zulu time? I need to verify the *start* of the unauthorized turn."

"May I ask why?"

"Yes, ma'am, you may ask … but I can't tell you."

She could tell the woman on the other end was weighing suspicion against the relatively innocuous nature of the request.

"All right. I think I understand that."

"If it helps, I didn't call on our secure lines because this isn't a classified question. I'm going for speed."

"Right. Hold on." Jenny could hear papers being shuffled in the background before the answer came through. She issued a heartfelt thank you and hung up before any additional questions could be asked, comparing the two numbers and feeling a small shudder ripple up her back.

Jesus God! Two minutes apart! First the answering burst, then two minutes later the turn. How many 'Holy Shits!' are there in the word 'coincidence'?

She sat back down, tracking the various components of the puzzle. A strange programming order repeats for at least half a day over clandestine satellite channels, apparently waiting for an answering burst. The United States Defense Intelligence Agency, with a straight face, tells her they know nothing about the transmissions or their purpose, and a team forms around the one NSA employee who discovered the mystery. Then, suddenly, there IS an answering burst, and the primary transmissions stop—and a civilian US flagged airliner, with passengers aboard, reverses course as if hijacked and heads back to the Middle East.

And the DIA team leaves as soon as they hear.

She could feel her face heating up in anger at being used and tossed aside by DIA's Will Bronson, who undoubtedly had known all along whatever was happening was the military's doing.

But, wait a minute, she cautioned herself, *he came over BEFORE the aircraft reversed course. Bronson was already here when the answering burst came through. Why stage such a charade if they really did know what was happening, who was sending the transmissions, and what was going to happen?* Jenny sat back and tried to unleash her subconscious to work on the problem.

That doesn't make sense!

But her conscious mind couldn't let it go.

No. There was no need for a charade. We called them. All he had to do was tell me to sit down and shut up, and I would have. He and his team were involved because there was something we stumbled on that they didn't know about. But what?

Wait ... how many people were on his team? I never spoke to anyone back at Boling. But he did. So, maybe at least one or two.

She pulled a legal pad over and started listing the items:

* They didn't know who was sending the signal.

True. That's why they needed my help in locating the source, which we never discovered.

* They weren't sure what the programming signal was trying to accomplish.

Hmm. Maybe. They might have recognized it as a dangerous transmission doing exactly what I was afraid it was doing: programming some possibly airborne or orbiting machine.

Her logic was getting tangled, she realized. Beyond the high probability that Bronson and his team came over because there was something they did not know, it was too murky to be sure of anything.

But, as soon as they got word that ...

She stopped herself again. The connection she was

making between the errant airliner and Bronson's text message was a leap. No, it was worse. It was her tendency to connect dots that didn't yet exist. She hadn't even read the text he'd received. Maybe it had nothing whatsoever to do with the airliner. Maybe it was a laundry list, or his mother asking him to bring a quart of milk to dinner.

But what if it did connect? The thought was rising like a silent tide. *Maybe Will Bronson didn't know what was going to happen, but obviously he and his people knew enough to get concerned when someone at NSA discovered a sky full of strange signals.*

Dammit, none of it was anything but speculation! She desperately wanted hard conclusions.

Jenny let out a long sigh, unconsciously shaking her head as she reached for the water bottle always by her computer and took a long drink.

Okay. Strict logic, girl. No intrigue. No leaps. No return to my paranoiac youth. Point one: This can't involve some sort of secret planned military test or exercise or Bronson would never have come over here to begin with, let alone involve his minions back at Boling. They would have already known what those signals were. Point two: If they suddenly connected the dots between the answering radio burst and the airliner hijacking, and that prompted his hasty evacuation, that doesn't prove the DOD is involved. Maybe it just means that they needed to get back and handle the intelligence questions that will inevitably follow the offshore hijack of an American aircraft.

But there was a point three, and she couldn't avoid thinking about it: *What if whatever's happening somehow involves some clandestine operation by our military that has to be hidden at all costs? The fact that we know about it means the operation is leaking, and may be spinning out of control.*

Jenny sat in silence for a minute reviewing the chain of thoughts. She drummed her fingers on the edge of the mouse pad, then flicked her hair back and picked up a pencil to chew on the eraser—a comforting habit since grade school that her father had hated. It angered her that Will Bronson hadn't called her personally, and she blushed slightly at the thought that her pique might be more primal than professional.

But, dammit, no matter how cute the man was, could he and his team and the DOD in general really be covering something up? Was that why they called Seth, to get him to quiet her down?

This is stupid! she concluded, not entirely buying her own resolve. *This is a hijacking, not something involving radioed orders to a drone. Nothing but coincidence.*

Jenny realized she was looking longingly at the phone, desperately wanting to call Seth for adult supervision. His security status wasn't high enough to justify a classified line at home, and there was no way she was going to be reckless enough to talk about this on an open line, so …

Suddenly she was fumbling through a personal address book in search of his home address, calculating just how long it was going to take to drive there, and just as quickly deciding that such a move was the sort of frightened, impulsive act that could seriously undermine his confidence in her. He'd said goodnight. Leave it alone.

Yet, there were secrets beyond that computer screen begging to be unraveled.

With a strange combination of excitement, apprehension, and resolve, she turned back to the keyboard.

CHAPTER TWENTY-FIVE

The White House (7:20 p.m. EST / 0020 Zulu)

No matter how many times he entered the Situation Room, Walter Randolph felt the weight of history bearing down on him. A long procession of American presidents had grappled with unfolding crises in here, he thought, some more successfully than others. How many photos had he seen over the years of grim-faced men and women gathered around this table?

How many times had he been one of them?

Walter took a seat at the far end and opened his laptop, confirming the secure channel before signing in. At the same moment, James Bergen, the director of Central Intelligence, rounded the corner looking almost presidential himself, his custom-tailored suit devoid of even the hint of a wrinkle as he flashed his practiced smile the media so loved—a smile characterizing the country's chief spook as an affable grandfather.

"Walter! Sorry to keep you waiting. The president should be here shortly. He's already been briefed that Moishe Lavi is a part of this equation." Bergen shook Walter's hand firmly, settling his five-foot-ten frame into the leather chair and waiting for the presidential aide to depart before turning to his chief deputy.

"So, what have we got that I didn't hear from you on the way over?"

Randolph leaned toward him, keeping his voice low.

"Two things. We know Mossad would never let Lavi out of their sight, but somehow Lavi managed to ditch his tail in Tel Aviv and was off the ground before the team shadowing him knew he was even headed to the airport. They're stunned,

I'm told, and knowing our Israeli friends, some heads will roll, but that means only Lavi loyalists are aboard that jet to keep an eye on him. In other words, no adult oversight."

"Not good, and not necessarily consistent with a trip to the US. What else?"

"I have a very worrisome tip from ... let's just say a reliable asset in a sister agency, not that we would ever spy on each other."

"Perish the thought. I can't let us do that. Go on."

"James, DIA's deep into this already. Turns out they dispatched someone to go to NSA headquarters this morning, and we think they're working on the same problem."

"They're that far ahead of us?"

"Yes. My information is the DIA was talking to NSA when the aircraft changed course, which is very strange."

"Maybe dumb luck?"

"Maybe, maybe not. Something more's afoot here. The Pentagon is involved to a greater degree, I think, than would be reasonable if all they were doing was worrying about Lavi and the Israeli Air Force."

"So, what do you suspect?"

The noises accompanying the entrance of several people ended the quiet exchange as the national security advisor came in just behind the assistant secretary of state, both men following an air force colonel and a navy admiral. There were greetings all around before the assembled, all-male team took their seats and unburdened notebooks just as the president, wearing a tuxedo, swept in ahead of two Secret Service agents. He rolled his eyes as he gestured over his shoulder.

"Gentlemen, as of this moment I'm supposed to be stroking egos at an East Wing shindig featuring the mind-bending combination of Yo-Yo Ma and Carlos Santana. The first lady is already irritated at this diversion, and that could translate to a cold and lonely night. And I don't like cold and lonely nights. So, quickly … what's going on with this hijacked airliner? James? CIA first."

Bergen restrained himself from a sideways glance at the two military officers in the room, both of whom would have already been briefed by their Defense Intelligence counterparts.

"Mr. President, this is not a hijacking as far as anyone can tell. The flight was Pangia's Tel Aviv to New York run, and it was halfway there when it turned around and headed back toward the Mideast. The crew didn't even know it at first. The airline reports their pilots can't physically control the airplane or kill the autopilot, and the most immediate problem is that Moishe Lavi is aboard."

"Can't control it? Do we know why?"

"No, but it has us concerned. We understand Mossad is also deeply concerned, and if Iran hasn't picked up on this by now, it will be only a matter of time before they do."

The assistant secretary of state had a finger in the air as he nodded agreement. "The Israelis want to keep a hot line to our conclusions and information."

"Agreed, but only if the channels are airtight," the president said. "How would Tehran know any of this, James?"

"The communication between the crew and their Chicago headquarters was on open channel cell phone, a phone collected from a passenger. God only knows who picked it up, but the story has already broken worldwide as a suspected hijack, which it isn't."

"Why can't the pilots control the airplane?" The president asked again, looking from face to face. "Is there something I don't know? I didn't think it was possible to remotely hijack an airliner like that. In fact, that's exactly why …" the president stopped himself and waved away the rest of whatever he was going to say.

"It isn't possible, as far as we know …" James Bergen began again, acutely aware that the air force colonel and navy admiral were saying nothing and everyone was wondering what statement the chief executive had choked off. "But that's what the crew has reported."

"You think the airplane has been turned into some sort of remotely controlled instrument … controlled from the ground, for instance?" The president asked.

The CIA director glanced back at his deputy, and Walter picked up the answer.

"We have no reason to believe, at present, that this Airbus A330 is capable of that sort of remote control, sir. The A330 is a complicated, electronic airliner, but the pilots can always override the autoflight system."

"And yet they haven't … or they claim they haven't, right?"

"Correct. But we've run backgrounds on all the crewmembers, and there's no indication of any potential compromised loyalty. The captain is an ex-US Navy fighter pilot."

"Are there any weapons aboard?" the president asked.

"Mossad says no … they routinely scanned the bird on taxi out with a neutron scanner. But … there is a cargo igloo—a pod—aboard, and Pangia Airways seems to be having trouble finding the manifest."

"I'm a pilot, remember? I know the Airbus A330, and it doesn't have bomb dropping ability. A cargo pod would be useless as an external weapon."

"Yes, sir, but there's always a worry that something explosive could have been sneaked aboard in that cargo pod, something that could explode the aircraft."

"Evidence?"

"Not yet."

"Okay, what are we scared of, gentlemen, other than losing a plane full of passengers … not to make light of that, even though, to tell the truth, losing Moishe Lavi would probably be a godsend for world peace."

"Sir, in the broader picture, we've got to consider the possibility that somehow this aircraft is being pressed into a mission that could involve Lavi's repeatedly stated intentions to either launch a first strike on Tehran or provoke an attack that would force an Israeli nuclear response."

The president of the United States looked incredulously at his CIA team and then searched the eyes of the rest of the men in the room.

"Seriously?"

"Yes, sir."

"You're telling me the pilots are loyal, and there's no way to control this airplane from the ground, and there's no nuclear material on board, but you're expecting it to head for Tehran and by looking like a threat, trigger a strike on Israel which would trigger a nuclear response and a Mideast Armageddon? Are we serving hard liquor in here?"

Much to Walt's relief, the air force colonel came alive. "Mr. President, if that aircraft heads for Tehran with Moishe Lavi aboard they could be flying a Cessna 172 and the Iranians would use it as an excuse to go ballistic. Perhaps literally."

A long sigh marked the end of the president's attention.

"Okay, I get that. Get me more facts, guys. I assume you have no recommendations for me at present and we do have some time?"

"Yes sir, we have a couple of hours, and no, sir, we have no immediate recommendations," James Bergen responded. "Not CIA, at least."

"Nor the Joint Chiefs, sir," the admiral chimed in. "At least, not yet."

The president stood and grinned as he looked at the two uniformed officers. "You fellows also representing DIA in this visit?"

"Not really, sir. We're reporting for the Joint Chiefs."

"But … you and DIA and CIA are playing nice, right?" The president swept his eyes back and forth between CIA's James Bergen and DIA's General Richard Penick. "No one's playing games with the information or strategically timing the release of anything to me, right?"

"No, sir," they said practically in unison.

"Okay. Because to make a lighthearted reference to a very serious subject, I get really cranky when that happens. Don't forget we're on the same team. Summon me back down here when you've something to recommend, the first lady's wrath notwithstanding. Meanwhile, I'll be in the east wing looking appropriately enthralled." The president turned, then turned back with a finger in the air. "Wait…that's not fair. I dearly love and respect both Carlos Santana and Yo-Yo Ma. Just … *together?"*

CHAPTER TWENTY-SIX

Cockpit, Pangia 10 (0020 Zulu)

"Goddammit, *you* talk to them!" Jerry tossed the commandeered satellite phone toward his copilot in deep disgust, and Dan had to lunge to the left to catch it in mid-air. "As far as *they're* concerned, if the book doesn't say it's there, it isn't!"

The passenger who'd finally volunteered the satellite phone had held out on them at first, apparently afraid of running up a big bill. But the "can't fly the airplane" part of Jerry's PA had changed his mind, and at last they'd scored a steady signal. Dan cleared his throat and raised the phone to his ear, taking care to keep the extendable antenna in the forward window as he identified himself and waited for a reply.

"Dan, this is the maintenance director. The captain was telling us there's a metal cabinet in the electronics bay, and obviously, if it's there, it's there, but we're completely puzzled back here because according to our information on this bird, there are no cabinets or large enclosures in that compartment. Are there any decals or placards on the side of it?"

"No. I looked carefully," Dan replied, describing the cabinet. "The thing shocked the hell out of me and knocked me out briefly when I tried to open the side of it. I'm pretty sure that's a security defense system. Plus, I can tell you it's firmly attached and engineered into that part of the electronics bay ... not just something sitting there loose." He described the cables running in and out and his growing suspicion that every electronic control in the cockpit had been shunted to whatever was in the box.

"So ... in your opinion, that box is not something that could have been added on a quick turnaround or in an hour or so?"

"Hell, no!" Dan said. "The sheer volume of the cables running into the front of this thing along the floor and the solid construction of it means it would have taken major downtime to get it installed, and there would had to have been all sorts of disassembly and reassembly in a maintenance hangar somewhere. I mean, we're talking weeks, probably! Has she been on the ground somewhere for that long out of our control?"

"We're checking, Dan. We've got our ship routing department as well as the A330 team on another line from Toulouse, and they're just as mystified as we are. They say there's never been anything like the cabinet you're describing engineered into one of their birds, not just the ones they've built for us."

"I'm pretty sure that cabinet holds the key, so to speak."

"We ... have no idea ... but I suppose you could be right."

"So here's my plan, unless you guys can come up with something else, I'm going to get on thick gloves and a coat and insulate my feet and go back down to see if I can get the side of that box open. If so, maybe there's a switch inside, or some clue as to whether it's causing this freaking nightmare … which it has to be."

Dan could hear the genuine angst on the other end as

what had to be a sophisticated speakerphone picked up the group's reaction.

"We can't think of anything else to recommend. Just be careful."

"I will. We don't have a lot of time. We're over Croatia now, and I estimate Tel Aviv in three hours. To be brutally frank, if we don't regain control, we'll flame out in approximately four hours."

Dan punched the disconnect button on the satellite phone and sat in silence for a few seconds before looking over at Jerry and across at Bill Breem and Tom Wilson, his copilot.

"You heard?"

"Yeah," Bill Breem replied. "Enough, at least. But how the hell can I believe that this company somehow doesn't know about a bus-sized box in the basement of this plane?"

"Bit smaller than a bus …" Jerry said, with a sharpness he immediately regretted.

"You know what I mean," Breem added.

"Yes, I do."

Someone was standing in the open cockpit door, and Jerry glanced around to find Carol pointing back over her shoulder.

"Someone wants a word with you. Is it all right to bring him up?"

"Who, Carol?" Jerry asked.

"I believe you spoke with him before, Captain. Moishe Lavi."

The sigh was more apparent than audible as Jerry's shoulders slumped slightly even as he nodded approval, but the copilot's head had jerked around, and Jerry was instantly puzzled to see Dan's eyes flare in surprise. There was no time to ask questions, however, as Carol stepped aside and the stocky passenger moved into the same space, nodding at both pilots.

"Prime Minister Lavi! I had no idea you were aboard," Dan managed, extending his hand, which Lavi took gratefully.

The confusion on Jerry Tollefson's face was now turning to alarm, and Dan nodded at Lavi as he shook his hand and offered a simultaneous introduction.

"Jerry, I'd like you to meet the prime minister—"

"*Former* … prime minister," Lavi interrupted.

"Yes … the former prime minister of Israel, Mr. Moishe Lavi."

Jerry swiveled part way around and extended his hand as well, shaking his head in embarrassment.

"Sir, I apologize. I knew your name sounded familiar earlier, but … I just didn't put it together."

"No apology necessary. You had a crisis in progress, Captain."

"Yeah, well … we still do, unfortunately"

"So I see. And that's the reason for my intrusion. Is there any change in our situation?"

Lavi's eyes were on the captain, but Carol, standing at a distance in the cockpit door, was tracking the sudden change of expression on Dan Horneman's face as his startled and pleased recognition of Moishe Lavi connected to the fact of the former prime minister's reputation and his presence on this flight, the rising implications boiling over in all geopolitical directions before coming back to Dan's consciousness and registering on his face as abject alarm.

There could be no realistic possibility, Dan thought to himself, that Lavi's presence and their current plight were connected somehow, but then it was a nightmarish thought he had yet to explore, let alone reject. Dan listened to the two of them talking, but the only voice he could seem to hear was his own mind fairly screaming that, regardless of how they ended up in this predicament, there was a huge new reality: If they ended up in the airspace of an Arab country with Lavi aboard, they would become perhaps the world's juiciest target. There would be no need to dance around some explanation of a gunner thinking he had an intruding military airplane in his sights. Hamas, Syria, Iran, Egypt … hell, even Iraq and Saudi Arabia would probably trip over each other for a chance to launch a missile to kill Moishe Lavi, in or out of office!

"Ah … sir …" Dan interrupted. "We may have a very big problem."

Lavi looked over at Dan, as did Jerry, who had been explaining what they'd tried so far.

"Yes?" Lavi replied. "You have a bigger problem than complete loss of control?"

"Yes, sir," Dan replied. "We're headed back for Tel Aviv, but we have no idea where this airplane is going to turn or fly after that, if we can't regain control. It could go straight ahead. It could release us. Or it could try to fly back to the previous point of origin, which is Hong Kong."

"I like Hong Kong," Lavi smiled.

"So do I, sir, but that's not the point. We don't have enough fuel to last more than ninety minutes after Tel Aviv … perhaps less … and a course direct to Hong Kong is a course directly over Iran, and just south of Tehran."

"I understand," Moishe Lavi replied, meeting Dan's steady gaze with a pleasant smile and an expression as neutral as the sphinx, leading Dan to wonder if his words had registered.

"My point, sir …"

Lavi had his hand up. "I understand. If Iranian airspace is invaded by an American airliner originating in Israel, even in an emergency, what will they do?"

"Yes, sir, but … what if they know that *you* are aboard?"

"They undoubtedly already do. They are insane and genocidal idiots, but they have fairly good intelligence sources."

"Would they shoot us down to get you, sir?"

"The Iranians would shoot us regardless of my presence or absence. They look for any excuse. But I have a suggestion for you. If you have not regained control by the time we arrive overhead Tel Aviv, it would be wise to let me come back up here and use your radio to speak in the blind to Tehran's air traffic authorities when we get close enough to the border, and through them, to the mullahs who will undoubtedly be listening."

Dan couldn't restrain the look of near horror on his face.

"Why, sir? Even if we get the radios working … and they aren't now … that's the very *last* thing I would think we should be doing! That would confirm that you're here and a great target …"

"Trust me, son. I know the Iranian leaders better than they know themselves, and I know how to interfere with their thinking. The only chance we have if this ship flies into Iranian airspace is my presence on the radio."

"You're going to *reason* with the people you want to exterminate?" Dan asked, quite unaware of the implications of his question until the words had escaped his lips.

The expression on Moishe Lavi's face hardened. "Please let it be noted that I never, in my entire political career, ever advocated using on any nation the same genocidal aspirations that Israel and the Jewish people have commonly and historically faced. My quest was to neutralize Iran's ability to explode nuclear weapons over my country."

"I'm sorry, sir. That was an unfortunate choice of words," Dan said.

"Yes, it was. Apology accepted. And you are correct

about the futility of reasoning with the institutionally insane. It is not possible. But manipulating them by reference to their own interests is the height of diplomacy, and I know this methodology, even in relation to the Iranian mullahs who, despite their constant pious nonsense about the delights of leaving this world to cavort with their ridiculous vision of seventy virgins in their hellish, misogynist version of heaven, are truly not suicidal."

Dan shook his head in apparent sadness. "Lord, I wish we had time for a leisurely discussion around a hotel pool somewhere. What I wouldn't give to have just a small fragment of your knowledge of the world."

"But we have 'promises to keep and miles to go' before such pleasures," Lavi responded, "to borrow liberally from your poet Robert Frost."

"Indeed," Jerry said.

"Please keep me informed," Lavi added, before turning back toward the cabin.

"Jesus Christ!" Tom Wilson said almost under his breath, unaware of the religious irony of his words.

Jerry glanced back toward the cockpit door to confirm they were now alone as Jerry shook his head.

"Well, *that* was embarrassing … not recognizing a VIP," Jerry said.

"What was disturbing to me, Jerry," Dan began, "… is that he's either got ice water in his veins, or he's actually okay with this. Maybe … maybe it provides another diplomatic challenge, I don't know, but …"

"If we do end up aiming for Tehran, should we take him up on his offer and have him communicate with the Iranians?" Breem asked.

Dan shook his head aggressively. "Absolutely not! Guys, if we let Moishe Lavi speak for us," Dan replied, "… we sign our death warrants."

CHAPTER TWENTY-SEVEN

NSA, Ft. Meade, Maryland (7:30 p.m. EST / 0030 Zulu)

"Gotcha!"

The latitude and longitude figures Jenny Reynolds had finally distilled from working through a hunch were in bold now on the screen, but she pulled out a notepad and wrote them down just in case the fruit of her labors should suddenly disappear. Jenny glanced at the piece of paper and folded it, stuffing it in her purse as she glanced at the time. Eight minutes since Seth had called and ordered her to go home, this time without even a hint of humor or friendliness.

"Why, Seth?" she'd asked, "I don't understand. You told me it was okay to stay and work."

"And now I'm telling you it isn't. Get your stuff and go home. Leave the building. Now. You understand that's not a request; it's an order."

"Do you have to sound so mean?"

"I'm not being mean. There are things we just can't discuss on the phone. I'm not mad at you, there's just a … change in plans. Trust me, Jenny. Go home. Call no one. I'm going to call security in a while to make sure you're out, okay?"

"Okay."

She'd punched the phone off in a mix of anger and hurt and apprehension, and turned back to the computer determined to finish her search.

It had turned out to be far easier than she'd expected, tracing the so-called "mother burst," and now she found herself torn between wanting to superimpose the lat/long coordinates on a map or run for the door. The coordinates might just be able to shed light on the mystery of who and why strange programming signals had been sent in the blind and apparently accepted by an airborne airliner.

The blinking symbol signifying a news bulletin appeared on the left side of her screen and she clicked on it as she stood and gathered her iPad and purse. Several new paragraphs about the hijacking came into view, and she skimmed them, sitting back down in her chair to focus on the verbiage. The fact that Pangia Flight 10 was headed in the wrong direction was old news, but the information that the pilots couldn't disconnect the autoflight system was something entirely new. *How on earth ... oh my God, that's what the answering burst was all about. It disconnected them!*

A noise in a far corner of the cavernous room made her jump slightly, and she hurried to collapse and save the lat/long page information to a secure drive before standing up to look around. There were always a few other analysts working away into the evening in their various corners of "cube-ville," but she could see no one, and even her last foray to the coffee machine had turned up no fellow late-nighters. That, in itself, was a bit unnerving.

The noise reached her again, this time like metal on metal at a distance, and an old feeling of impending terror that she had worked so hard to keep at bay began to settle around her shoulders like a dark cloak. Lifelong experience with anxiety attacks had taught her the symptoms all too well: tightening stomach, sudden sweat, a creepy feeling of coldness and impending attack, hands shaking, and a cascade of thoughts accelerating into a blind panic which would only intensify if she did nothing but sit still and try to reason with herself.

Jenny leaped to her feet and headed for the door, forcing a look over her shoulder to verify that no one was behind her. There were, of course, only imaginary footsteps following in her mind, spurring her to run. But even though she knew there was nothing really closing on her from behind, her imagination propelled her as she shoved through the double doors and slammed into the chest of a very large uniformed guard.

"Oh!" Jenny staggered back, eyes wide, breathing hard, as the guard caught her elbow to steady her.

"Sorry, ma'am. I didn't see you coming out of there. You okay?"

"Ah … yes. Yes, I'm … you just startled me. I didn't mean to …"

"It's cool! I'm still standing. Were you leaving for the night?"

"What?" She looked closer at the man, his large dark face beaming a sympathetic smile as he released her elbow. He towered over her, maybe six feet four, a wall of uniform.

"I just asked if you were leaving for the night?"

"Oh! Yes, I was. I am." Jenny shook her head and took a deep breath, her hand up in a stop gesture. "I'm sorry to sound flaky, it's just … I don't work nights much and this place gets spooky."

The requisite exit search and clearance procedures at the NSA's entrance hall behind her, another guard waived her out of the parking lot and she checked the address she'd preloaded on her iPhone before merging into traffic southbound, then just as quickly pulled to the shoulder and braked to a halt.

The need to know where those "mother burst" coordinates were on the face of the planet was suddenly irresistible, and she pulled out her iPad and triggered a map program, entering the lat/long coordinates before pushing the button.

The center of the satellite map picture suddenly coalesced on a series of buildings set in a sea of parking lots. The image looked vaguely familiar, and she zoomed the picture, noting the expected satellite antenna farm on the roof before zooming back out and looking at the adjacent map in increasing disbelief.

No, that's not possible! I hit the wrong button.

She re-checked the coordinates on her slip of paper against what she'd entered. They matched perfectly. There was a highway running adjacent to the building complex with the number "295" showing on the map adjacent to the target, and she looked up and out of her windshield now into real life to see the very same number on a highway sign no more than twenty feet away.

Her eyes went back to the screen, the recognition now inescapable: If the mother transmission had come from those coordinates, they had come directly from the heart of the National Security Agency complex at Fort Meade.

Her building.

Right under her nose.

Oh dear God! No wonder Seth wanted me out of there! We ARE involved!

The steady stream of traffic whizzing by mere feet from the side of her little Prius came into focus, and she clicked off the iPad now and eased herself back into traffic, mind whirling, hands shaking.

Somewhere half a world away from her, there was an out of control airliner plowing through the night with what had to be frightened people aboard, and the radioed order that apparently triggered the whole impending disaster had come from her building!

She thought of the exit process minutes before as she left the building and the guard's careful examination of her purse for flash drives or any other storage medium. Thanks to that traitor Snowden such a search was now routine. The presence of a simple scribbled note in her purse shouldn't have alerted him, but with her fears rising exponentially, she wondered now whether taking even that information out of the building was a violation. Would there be a security team even now coming after her? Surely, she wasn't supposed to know that the originating programming signal she'd discovered so many hours ago—the same one that had apparently caused an airliner to change course—came from their own building. How could she erase what she knew? It would be like un-ringing a bell.

Oh God, what do I do now? Who do I tell? I have to tell someone.

The electronic warble of her smart phone caused her to almost lose control of the car, and she struggled to stay on the road while fumbling for the instrument. There was a strange phone number on the screen. She knew not to answer it, but the longing for deliverance won out, and her finger found the green button.

"Jenny Reynolds?" a male voice asked. It was somehow familiar, but she was far too scared to coalesce the memory.

"Yes."

"This is Will Bronson. You remember? From this afternoon?"

"Yes."

"Where are you, Jenny?"

"I'm …"

"Are you still at work?"

"No. In my car." *And scared to death*, she wanted to add.

"Good. Were you going home?"

Why would he want to know that? she wondered, trying desperately to stay ahead of the conversation but losing the battle to sheer panic.

"Jenny?"

"Uh … yes … no … I was, I was going to go drop in on my boss, at his home. He's over by …"

"Don't."

"What?"

"Jenny, I would like you to change course and meet me.

Tell me approximately where you are, and I'll arrange a place to meet."

"Why?"

"Because ..." he hesitated. "Because I want to take you out tonight, and I won't take no for an answer."

As much as she wanted that to be true, she knew it was a dodge for anyone eavesdropping, and she had barely a split-second to decide whether to trust him.

A split-second was all she needed.

"Okay. You won't have to take no. I'd ... like to see you, too. I'm just a mile south of my building on the Parkway, heading south."

"Take Greenbelt Road exit west. You know the Beltway Plaza Mall?'

"Yes."

"Pull up in front of JCPenney and turn on your four-way flashers. You're in a red Prius, right?"

"Yes, but how did you ..."

"I'll find you. Don't call anyone."

"Will?"

"Yes?"

"How ... how do I know I can trust you?"

"You don't. I'll need to prove it. Dinner and a movie, to start with?"

"Okay. Wait, to *start* with ...?"

"See you in ten."

CHAPTER TWENTY-EIGHT

Aboard Pangia 10 (0030 Zulu)

Dan Horneman took a deep breath as he finished buttoning up the heavy coat he'd borrowed. He was standing beside the offending metal cabinet in the electronics bay beneath the cockpit of Flight 10. The thing was still booby-trapped with electrical power, but as long as he was careful, his plan might work.

He turned toward the forward hatch leading back to the cockpit and nodded to Carol, who was watching carefully, deep concern etching her almost flawless face.

There was no way to reach over the top of the thing without all but bear hugging the metallic side. Provided the voltage within wasn't too great, all the layers he was wearing should prevent electrical arcing, he thought. The previous shock was enough for one lifetime, but he had been skin to metal with the thing while grounding himself with his other hand to close a circuit that could have killed him.

Not this time.

Slowly feeling his way along through thick leather gloves, Dan followed his memory until his index finger settled into the hole. It took a bit of twisting and pushing to force his glove-clad finger in deep enough to touch the top of the metal plunger, but at last he could feel it, and after checking to make sure his face wasn't touching skin to metal, he shoved the plunger down hard, feeling nothing yield. He shoved harder, his finger protesting in pain, knowing that before he'd been hit by a bolt of electricity before reaching the release point.

If there *was* a release point.

Dan withdrew his finger and pulled his hand and arm away, thinking through what he'd felt. There was a plunger, but unless it was a dummy set up just to suck in and shock an intruder, there had to be a release mechanism inside.

Once more he took his flashlight and poked around every part of the cabinet he could reach or see, wondering if he could have missed another hole or hatch or panel somewhere. But he found nothing.

Okay, I'm just not pushing it down far enough.

He needed a small wooden stick, but finding wooden sticks in a jet at 38,000 feet was ridiculously unlikely.

Dan stepped away from contact with the cabinet and pulled off his glove, fishing in his uniform pocket for the clippers. Small, metallic, and just slim enough, it might work, he thought. Once again he donned the glove and maneuvered himself into position, carefully inserting the body of the nail clipper into the hole and feeling it align with the sides, the cutting head settling squarely on the plunger. Slowly, gingerly, he moved the tip of his index finger to the more narrow back end of the clipper and pushed steadily, feeling the plunger descend, keeping the small tool aligned with his index finger until it was in almost to the limit.

The "click" of the internal locking cam releasing was felt more than heard, but suddenly the top of the cabinet rotated toward him.

He grabbed each end and lifted the entire side off its lower channel moving it far enough aft to expose more than half of the electronic nightmare within.

There in the middle was a large warning placard in red block letters:

WARNING! THE CONTENTS OF THIS VAULT ARE PROTECTED BY HIGH VOLTAGE ELECTRICAL CURRENT THREE TIMES THE MINIMUM SUFFICIENT TO KILL A HUMAN. DO NOT, UNDER ANY CIRCUMSTANCES, TOUCH OR OTHERWISE

ATTEMPT TO MANIPULATE OR INTERACT WITH ANYTHING INSIDE WITHOUT FOLLOWING DEACTIVATION PROCEDURES.

There was an ordinary keypad to the right of the sign, with keys large enough to be pushed by a gloved hand, but there was no indication of the code.

What in hell IS this thing? Dan thought, already knowing the most important part of the answer: It was obviously what had disconnected their entire cockpit and locked them out of the basic ability to fly the jet. Whatever it was supposed to accomplish strategically, tactically it was controlling the show, and that had to end.

Dan ran his eyes carefully up and down the racks of electronics, finding no switches large or small and only a few blinking LED lights. No other placards or identification plates adorned any of the equipment, and all of it was packed in so tightly that there seemed no way to reach around behind any of the boxes.

Jesus, where do I start?

He could hear Carol's voice calling to him, and he turned toward the hatch, flashing her a thumbs-up. She nodded and smiled and withdrew her head undoubtedly to report to Jerry that he was in, but in to what? The more Dan examined the contents of the cabinet, the more his stomach knotted. Whoever had installed the infernal thing had no intention of bluffing. Even if he could work with the thick gloves, there were no wing nuts on any of the boxes that might free them up and allow them to be pulled out, and if the system was wired to resist interference, it might even fry the electronic engine controls and flight computers, leaving them with a dead and falling airframe.

He allowed himself a few seconds of horror, imagining what kind of death that would be, helplessly watching your plane and passengers fall to destruction while you flailed at dead, useless controls, unable to do anything. His mind flashed back to the gut-wrenching story of the Germanwings crash, and his own unbearable rage thinking about the terrorized captain of that flight, locked out of his own cockpit and pounding helplessly on the door as his suicidal copilot descended into the Alps.

To a lesser extent, Dan was fighting that same kind of rage and frustration, and he forced himself to slow his breathing and concentrate. He had a bit more than three hours, and he had to believe that anything that could be engineered into place could probably be reverse engineered. If only it wasn't booby-trapped.

He slid down to the floor alongside the thing, watching it for a minute, letting his subconscious have a crack at his feelings, which were running amok.

The wave of hopelessness washed over him again, but for some reason he felt himself swim through it, rejecting its nihilistic conclusions. After all, an hour ago they weren't even aware there *was* an offending cabinet full of control-stealing electronics. Now he was staring it in the teeth.

Wait a minute!

The new thought came unbidden, but the recognition was powerful and it caused a sharp intake of breath and a surge of hope at the same time. Dan sat up a bit straighter and followed the logic trail.

People don't put warnings on invulnerable things! If it was impervious to disconnection, there would be no placard.

He could see the wires going in and could trace at least some of them to racks outside the cabinet that he could reach and wouldn't shock him. If he could find the right wires, the right controls, and figure out which of the boxes inside the cabinet were connected to which ones on the outside, he had a chance.

No. No, it's more than that! he thought, eyes widening. *There is a key here, and something that they were afraid would be discovered. Something that CAN be discovered. It's a freaking Easter egg hunt.*

In other words, it wasn't "if," it was "how."

CHAPTER TWENTY-NINE

Beltway Plaza Mall, Greenbelt, Maryland (8:00 p.m. EST / 0100 Zulu)

"I've got you in sight, Jen. Take the first parking place and lock it up."

She had to admit, Will Bronson's voice was reassuring, not that she had the slightest idea what was happening, or whether she was falling into a trap like some silly little girl with daddy issues doomed by her own search for paternal protection. She had promised herself that she would never, ever be that girl.

"Okay." She punched off the phone, slid the car into an empty space, and got out, locking it with her remote and then standing there feeling very off balance. She could see no cars with drivers looking for her. Where was he?

Will Bronson's deep voice reached her ears from inches behind.

"This way, Jenny."

She yelped and whirled around, wide-eyed.

"Oh my God!"

"What?"

"Don't EVER sneak up on me like that!"

"Sorry," he said, taking her arm and moving them toward an entrance to the mall.

"There are about twenty-one different movies playing tonight," he said somewhat breezily, "… but I thought we'd eat first. What would you like?"

"Seriously?"

His head was on a swivel, looking in all directions as they crossed the lane to the entrance, and she was certain he wasn't just scanning for traffic.

He held the door open, smiling as she moved inside.

"I thought we'd duck into one of the restaurants in here," he continued, "… or if all you want is McDonald's, we can do that as well."

Jenny took his arm and stopped him, turning him around to face her.

"Really? This is a flash date?"

A virtual anthology of reactions played subtly across his face, the dominant one a shadow of sadness as he shook his head no and replied yes.

"Of course it is. I have friends who own this mall, so there's a private entrance into my favorite place. Come on." She followed him at an accelerated pace down the half-empty corridor, keeping pace in her high heels to an unlabeled side door which he held for her, slipping in behind as it closed.

Before them was a loading dock and a black SUV waiting with engine running and no one else in sight. Will opened the right side door and Jenny climbed inside, and just as quickly they were moving out of the loading dock into the night.

"Okay … I owe you some explanations."

She turned to face him, eyes wide. "Ya *think*? Your favorite *restaurant?* This is the strangest pickup I've ever had!"

"Jenny … please. Another place, another time, I'd give anything to just take you out. Right now we have a mutual problem."

Dammit! she thought, tears welling up for about a half dozen reasons as she struggled to hold them back. "Okay … Will … if that's your real name …"

"It is. Will Bronson. And I am with DIA, just as I told you."

"So, what haven't you told me?"

"The signal we were chasing together all afternoon?"

"Yes?"

"It came from NSA's building."

She was nodding, and it was his turn to look puzzled. "I know."

"You do?"

"I figured it out just before you called. I traced the coordinates but didn't put them on a map until I was in the car. I saw that report, too, that the airliner's pilots can't control the direction of the aircraft. But … how did *you* know?"

"Later. Jenny, there's more, and this is shaping up to be a very big problem. The White House is alerted, my people at DOD are on high alert, and to find that the initiating signal came from our own NSA is what sent me out the door."

She stared in his eyes closely, uncomfortably for a few seconds. She'd always been told that trying to read the soul of a trained agent by looking in his eyes was a fool's errand, but she had to try.

"You're not sure who to trust either?"

He was nodding. "DIA is a bit of a schizoid agency. Our overlords wear uniforms with high rank, we're controlled by the civilian side, and I've seen us sent on useless errands before to keep us busy while the brass does whatever the brass wants to do."

"In other words, this could be a clandestine military operation not even you guys know about, and an illegal one at that?"

"I don't know, but I'm worried, and you and your boss are targets if so."

"Whoa. You mean … we're in *physical* danger? From our own *government*?"

"I doubt … *physical* … but clearly professional danger."

"And, you're the one who's going to keep me safe, right?" she shot him a slightly incredulous look.

"I'm damn well sure going to try."

"Why?"

Seeing such a confident man suddenly flustered, even for a second, was startling. He recovered as quickly.

"Two reasons. I like your insight, and this is a puzzle one does not solve alone. Second, if you're a damsel in distress, it's my nature."

"Thank you, Lancelot." It was only half sarcastic, and clearly he took it right.

"M'Lady."

"So, shall we share everything we know?"

"Yes. That's the first reason I wanted to snag you out of the ether."

"Okay. I'm etherless. You first."

"The code you were chasing is a registered military code."

"What? What do you mean, registered? It didn't come up on any database."

"It wouldn't. There is a top secret-crypto level list of codes and algorithms used by deep secret units and projects, but we register them in case something like this happens."

"Something like what?"

"In case a very bright and beautiful NSA analyst finds one and calls DIA in. You remember asking if this was us?"

"Yes."

"Well, that's how we answer the question before we go ballistic, or trigger anything ballistic or aerodynamic. That list lets us know we have met the enemy, and we is they, to quote Pogo."

"Who's Pogo?"

"Long story. A cartoon possum philosopher from years back. Point is, the list tells us whatever we found comes from our side."

"So it's—and thanks for the bright and beautiful compliment—it's …"

"You're welcome, and you are!" he smiled.

"I'm what?"

"Foxy … beautiful … alluring … bright and beautiful."

"Mr. Bronson, are you flirting with me?"

"Yes."

She hesitated, suppressing the smile she wanted to flash. "Okay."

"It is?"

"Hey, flattery works. So the code is ours? It's military? Why didn't you tell me sooner?"

"I didn't run that check until I got back to Boling."

"Is that why you left so suddenly?"

"No. It was finding Lavi aboard that flight that triggered the recall."

"Who?"

"That's right … you probably don't know." He explained the presence of the former Israeli prime minister and the implications. "As soon as news broke of Lavi's presence, my boss wanted me back to deal with the implications. He had no idea that what we were working on together at NSA might be related. I checked the secure database when I got back, and bingo. But, Jen, that's why I'm worried. It's on the registry, but even my boss couldn't crack through the security level to find out *which* project or agency registered it. That level of security is about as high as it gets."

"You mean, the White House?"

"Well, probably one or two steps lower. Four star general or secretary of defense levels. I asked my boss to get permission, and he refused. It spooked him. He told me to forget about it and go do something else. That's when I left."

"But, Will, jeez. This is saying that the United States has frozen the controls of a commercial airliner and I assume put everyone in peril."

"They may have, but it gets worse, Jen."

"Try me."

He outlined the significance of an uninventoried cargo pod and the fact that fifteen minutes before he'd called, evidence emerged that Tehran had become aware of most of the story.

"Moishe Lavi's still got too many confederates in Israel. We can't be sure there's not just enough nuclear material in that cargo pod to spur the Iranians to act."

She sat back, studying his face again. "Wait … Lavi may be behind an attempt to frighten the Iranians, but you're saying the signal that froze the aircraft's controls came from us."

"Yes."

"Could someone on our side be setting up a war, then? In conjunction with Moishe Lavi?"

He snorted and looked forward, shaking his head before looking back. "If this is a purposeful act, and why wouldn't it be with the intensity of the signal distribution you ferreted out, what would someone be trying to accomplish? Killing Lavi? They could do that with a sniper at Kennedy on arrival. Hell, half of Mossad wants him dead, the other half was nominating him as the Messiah. No, there has to be a point to it."

"Will, first of all, how could mere radio signals lock up a civilian jetliner? Could someone have hacked into the computers?"

"We don't know. *I* don't know. The jet came out of Tel Aviv … maybe someone installed some strange equipment on the ground there or monkeyed with the computers or computer memory. Just … proceed from that assumption, that whatever has locked up their controls was triggered by those radio bursts and was purposeful."

"You think someone in the military is sitting in a little cubicle somewhere programming that flight? Like a drone?"

"Maybe. Although they haven't changed heading or

climbed or descended yet, so I'm not sure there's active control going on. But *someone* did this."

"Would it benefit anyone on our side to start a nuclear war with Iran?"

"It might. It would be a surrogate war, Jen. The Israelis would fight it for us, and they wouldn't let Iran clear leather, so to speak. The very second the mullahs light off a missile, they'll be toast."

"The glow-in-the-dark kind?" she asked quietly.

"Yep. Then all hell breaks loose, the Islamic world goes completely barking mad, Russia and China get involved in diplomatic opportunism, and it's always possible the mullahs still get a death shot off at Israel. Have you been there, by the way?"

She nodded.

"It's tiny. It wouldn't take many split atoms to reprise the Holocaust."

"Dear God. What can we do? Can we go pick up Seth and keep him safe and get his ideas?"

Will shook his head. "I'm not sure your man Seth isn't part of this, whatever 'this' is."

The answer seemed otherworldly, forcing a frightening image of Seth as something other than her trusted boss and confederate.

"Then … who do we tell, Will?"

"Until we know for sure what we're dealing with, no one's going to be spring-loaded to believe either or both of us. Even the CIA, who is nipping at DIA's heels right now trying to find out what we know, hasn't figured it out. Or at least that's where I think they are. But, see, if this is something our military or any segment of it is doing, it's a very deep, very dark secret, and we've already unraveled enough of it to be a very large threat."

"And we can't tell anyone? Not even the president?"

"Tell him what? That's the problem. All we know for sure is where the transmission came from."

'But, *that* at least is a fact!"

"Yes, as is the fact that the code was registered. But what if some faction at the White House is also involved?"

She searched his face for a few seconds, feeling very helpless.

"You're scaring me, Will. Seriously."

"I'm not far behind. If I get us on a secure computer net, can you help find some answers?"

"Aha! I can see your thinking now. Jenny's a cryptologist so she can naturally hack into any information."

"I can hope, can't I? What I was wondering was whether you might be able to decrypt the instructional code that the Pangia flight apparently uploaded."

"I'd need a key of some sort. I tried every way from Sunday."

"I may have one."

"Where? How?"

"Just … trust me. If I can get you a key to the code, or any part of it …"

"Then maybe I can. But why?"

"Well …"

"Oh! Jeez! You want me to countermand whatever orders that transmission contained!"

"Precisely. I don't know if it would work, but …"

She sighed deeply. "Yeah. Got it. But Will, I think you're expecting too much of me. You're not sitting next to Garcia from *Criminal Minds*!"

"I love her!"

She's not real, Will. No one can dance over keys and pull up information that easily."

"I know."

"But … if we can find a way into any net, and if you can

provide a key, I can sure as hell try."

"That's what I was hoping you'd say, and that's also where we're heading."

"Where is 'where'?"

"A safe house with a net portal."

She turned a bit more toward him, looking puzzled.

"You really do use safe houses?"

"Yes."

"Which … would mean you're into covert ops."

"Yes."

"Which means I'm dancing with a real live James Bond."

That sad look crossed his face again. "I wish."

"What? That you were Bond?"

"No. That we were dancing."

CHAPTER THIRTY

The "Kirya" IDF military complex, Tel Aviv, Israel (2:00 a.m. local / 0100 Zulu)

With a heavy sigh, the interim prime minister of Israel settled his overweight frame into a chair at the head of a large conference table in the military command complex known fondly as "the hole." Having the title "prime minister" inserted before his name was still a shock to Gershorn Zamir's own sensibilities, but he was slowly warming to it. The greater problem of what to do about the previous PM and his terrifying determination to start a nuclear war had propelled Gershorn from his home across town to a meeting he really didn't want, but couldn't avoid. And the news that Lavi was aboard the American airliner hurtling back toward Israel and essentially out of control was alarming everyone.

"Ladies and gentlemen, please proceed," he said in Hebrew, keeping the informal arc of ministerial conduct intact, as far as he could imitate it.

Lieutenant General Yossi Alon, chief of the general staff, ran through everything they knew, outlining the various responses they were preparing based on what Pangia Flight 10 might or might not do when, and if, it appeared overhead Tel Aviv in less than three hours.

And suddenly it was quiet with all eyes on him.

Gershorn Zamir leaned forward, nodding at the general. "Thank you, Yossi. Very well, I have a few questions. If the crew cannot regain control and they overfly us and turn towards Iran, as you've warned is possible, what then? Let's say they head straight for Tehran, the mullahs are watching, and regardless of what Washington tries to tell them, they get ready to launch their one or two nuclear warheads. You said the Airbus hasn't enough fuel to make it all the way to Tehran, so they would flame out and crash barely over the border, and no longer be a threat to Tehran. But would the bastards use this situation as an excuse to launch on us?"

"It all depends on whose finger is on the button," the military intelligence chief said. He added a quick analysis of the command and control who's who of Iran's central command, and what it would take to license a nuclear launch. "While we have three levels of civilian authority needed to launch, Moishe Lavi's ideas to the contrary notwithstanding, Iran's C2 capabilities … C2 means command and control—"

"I know the term, general," Zamir interjected gruffly. "I was Israeli Air Force, after all."

"Yes, sir. Sorry."

"But back to the fuel status. Can't we assemble enough help, including the US and Russia and whoever to persuade Tehran not to start a war unless the aircraft doesn't turn around or fall out of the sky? They can't possibly be so stupid as to think an Airbus is a bomber, right?"

"We're setting up all the diplomatic help we can get right now, sir."

"Very well. Also, does anyone here really believe Moishe is somehow in control of this airliner? I mean, seriously, do we really think he's using it to actually bomb Iran, or get them to pull the trigger? Is it possible that he's merely a passenger?"

The intelligence chief raised his finger. "We have virtually nothing to support the idea that Lavi is in control, or that he's anything other than a passenger, as you say. He ditched surveillance on the way to the airport, but that's the only thing even slightly suspicious. Well, except for a cargo pod in the belly of that jet that Pangia can't seem to find a manifest to cover. But that's nothing."

"Very well."

"I need to describe Iran's current nuclear command posture. What worries us is that their C2 abilities are a confused mess, with no real centralized authority. No one has any doubt that they possess the means to hurl the few warheads they have at us, despite all the sham nuclear inspections … which, if I may say so, had about as much value as Neville Chamberlin's pre-World War II nonsense about trusting Hitler."

"Yes, yes, we all agree on that. Ben Netanyahu was right. Go on."

"Within an hour or two of right now, I would not at all be surprised if the decision on the table in front of the various members of Iran's so-called leadership will be whether to pre-delegate a ready-to-launch posture. That would mean assembling the missiles and granting launch authority to some lower commander out in the desert. And that is probably our worse-case nightmare scenario, because at the slightest suggestion, however ridiculous, that this out-of-control Airbus might truly be attempting to sneak into Iran to bomb their nuclear capabilities, some idiot sub-commander will probably hit the button. Obviously, we all know … although the rest of planet seems ignorant of it … that Iran's military commanders are not trained primarily as professional soldiers, but as religious zealots valued for their ideological conformity and zeal."

Zamir sighed, drumming his fingers on the table. On one level he respected Moishe Lavi's internal crusade to act against such an implacable foe, but on another, Lavi's myopia was terrifying. And now the man himself was riding a potential instrument of everyone's destruction.

"Sir?" Someone was asking, and Gershorn Zamir realized he'd been drifting.

"My apologies. I was deep in thought."

"Do you need me to repeat?" the intelligence officer was

asking.

"No. No, but I need to repeat the key question you have grappled with on a daily basis, and this has nothing to do with covering my or anyone else's posterior. If the bastards launch, can we shoot it down in time? Will the iron dome work against a nuke?"

Listening to a room of high-powered and high-ranking military officers all take a deep breath at once was unnerving, almost as much as the subsequent cautionary glances among the group. But General Alon nodded and took point.

"The 'it' versus 'them' is the key to the problem. We believe that we have an 80 percent to 90 percent chance of blowing up anything they launch in boost phase, without a nuclear detonation, and long before it gets close enough to us to use the Iron Dome defense system, which is proven. The problem is that the mullahs know those percentages, and they are very likely to launch a barrage of missiles, only one of which will carry the killer warhead. So, which one do we shoot? Our percentages go down significantly the more missiles they launch. We have proton scanners to spot fissile material, this is true. But they also know how to use lead shielding to foil our view, and they're not beyond launching a barrage of missiles with just enough nuclear material to trigger our detectors, but no bomb. So, the bottom line is this: If they launch more than five missiles, our chances of guaranteeing that Israel will not be hit by a nuclear detonation reduces to 50 percent. These are not acceptable odds."

"Which," Zamir added, "… is precisely why the Knesset cashiered our old friend Lavi, because even if he had been correct about hitting Iran's nuclear program now, we can have no guarantee that a single nuclear warhead couldn't make it through our Iron Dome." Zamir let his words sink in for a few beats before continuing. "So, if this American flagged airliner turns the wrong way and heads down the throats of the mullahs, do *we* shoot it down?"

"If we must," came the answer, short, to the point, and chilling from General Alon.

"And how do we decide if we must?" the PM asked, suddenly shaking his head, "For God's sake, is that *my* decision? A plane full of innocent lives in international distress, and Israel kills them all on the outside chance that the genocidal regime in Tehran will overreact?"

Utter silence filled the conference room and Zamir felt guilty about essentially attacking his team, but, dammit, they had to understand the gravity of such a decision and the way the rest of the world would view it. "We're gambling Israel's future with Israel's respect in the world community, assuming we have some left. I need a better option."

"You asked for worst case," Yossi reminded him quietly.

"I did?"

"Essentially."

"Very well, give me the best case response based on the worst case situation with the airplane. I'm going back home. If the problem is not resolved by the flight crew in two hours, wake me up again and I'll come back here and we can make the appropriate decisions. I'll assemble the necessary people to satisfy the authority requirements to approve our response, up to and including a nuclear launch, if, God forbid, we are forced into it. And, gentlemen?"

"Yes, sir?"

"Pray. Pray hard."

CHAPTER THIRTY-ONE

Aboard Pangia 10 (0120 Zulu)

Bill Breem and Tom Wilson had gone back into the main cabin on a mission to interview passengers who had responded to Jerry's request for anyone with aviation electronics experience, and Carol was back in first class. For the first time in hours Dan and Jerry were once again alone in the cockpit.

"Dan … I owe you an apology."

"For what?" Dan asked, truly puzzled.

"For judging you. Everything you said earlier."

"Well … accepted, of course, Jerry."

"I'm beginning to think the wrong person's sitting in the left seat."

Jerry was staring straight ahead, his voice almost too low to be heard, and Dan Horneman wasn't sure for a second that he'd understood the captain correctly. He leaned over the center console toward Jerry as he sat sideways in the copilot's seat.

"Surely you're not contemplating turning control over to …"

Jerry turned toward him, a truly lost look in his eyes.

"Of course not. But … I mean, I'm sitting up here helpless as a freaking baby, and you're the only one who seems to have a clue what to do. Sorry … I'm just very, very frustrated. "

"Me, too."

"And … something I was trained to never be."

There was silence before Dan interjected.

"What's that?"

"I'm scared shitless, man! There. I said it."

"It's completely normal to be scared."

Jerry looked over at him suddenly "So why aren't *you*, Dan?"

The question was entirely without rancor, and Dan could see the man searching for anything to hold onto that would justify the four stripes on his shoulders.

"For the record, Jerry, I am just as terrified as you. I just may be a better actor."

"You may be. You're Mr. Cool."

"Look, Jerry, we all need the anchor you provide. This is a team effort, and this team needs a leader, which is you. Quit thinking you've got to be John Wayne tough."

"Yeah," Jerry breathed, the shadow of a smile marking his changing attitude. "I should have been asking that. What would Duke Wayne do?"

"Probably get all the passengers in a circle! Look, Jere, let's talk about the plan. We don't have a lot of time. You heard what's down there … I think I should test my theory as fast as I can."

"You mean about rewiring?"

"Not … rewiring, but … finding the point at which any of the boxes down there have been routed to the big cabinet, cutting that connection and re-mating whatever wires with the appropriate input on each box."

Jerry was shaking his head. "I don't think I followed you about that. I wanted to run it past our maintenance people in Chicago, but the damned battery died on that sat phone, and Carol says they haven't found a replacement or the charger. Apparently the charger is in the passenger's bag."

"I know. We're silent again."

"Yes. But Dan, back to the wiring thing. Please explain it to me."

"Okay, let's say I find your DVR at home isn't sending a video signal to your television because the video signal has been routed through a big amplifier that's malfunctioning. If I disconnect the video lead between the DVR and the malfunctioning amplifier, and instead connect it directly to an input slot on your TV, where it belongs, suddenly you get to see whatever you're playing on your DVR. Get it?"

"You think it's that simple, Dan? Down there, I mean?"

"In principle, not in fact. I'll have to trace and understand and cut wires and splice them to have any hope of making this work, but, essentially, that's what's going on down there … all the outputs from all our normal electronic instruments, including autoflight and autothrottles, are being shunted off into that cabinet, and then the electronics in that cabinet are replacing the signals with their own versions and sending them off to the controls, while sending us false displays. I don't care about the displays, I want our controls back."

"And if you're wrong?"

"That's why I want to attack the radios first. Just one VHF. If I can find how to repower one VHF radio, or maybe even the satcom, it'll validate the method. If that works, I want to try the autothrottles. There is a risk, of course, that they could just wind the engines down to idle if I cut anything, but if I'm right, I might be able to restore our control."

"That's a hell of a risk, Dan."

"And if we do nothing and wait until we run out of fuel …"

"I understand that."

"So, what do you think, Captain, sir? Should I at least try the radios?"

Jerry pursed his lips and nodded, his eyes forward, deep in thought, anger propelling a derisive snort. "Who the hell put that damned thing down there, Dan? Is our airline lying to us? Is this now a standard specter shadowing us on every flight?"

"Can't be. I've never seen an installation like that before."

"But it's apparently there to take over. When? If we're incapacitated or … or hijacked? But in the hours since it apparently turned us around and switched off the cockpit, the damn thing hasn't varied our heading or speed or altitude one iota. So is it *flying* the airplane or did it just freeze the controls?"

Dan exhaled sharply. "Damn, I didn't think about that."

"You mean, that it hasn't varied anything since the turn around?"

"That it might be malfunctioning. Good God!"

"Does that change anything in your thinking?"

"Maybe. Maybe not. But I need to get moving, if I'm going to try."

Jerry nodded again, this time emphatically. "Nothing else is helping us, and Chicago doesn't have a clue. Yes, Dan. Let's go for it."

Carol had quietly re-entered the cockpit and was waiting, standing just behind the center console, as Dan turned to her.

"I need a quick scavenger hunt. I need anything close to black electrical tape or any tape that's sticky and insulating. I need the sharpest steak knives you can find in your galley, if any. And I need wires … but I'll probably just have to make do with what I find down below."

"Do you need anyone down there with you?" she asked. "I could …"

Dan was shaking his head no as Jerry raised a finger.

"Wait … Dan. This airplane is crammed full of computers and that snot-nosed kid I wanted to kill may be more expert than we know. Carol? Bring that kid up here, will you?"

"Certainly," she replied, disappearing back into the cabin as Dan smiled to himself. Captain Tollefson was once again in the game.

CHAPTER THIRTY-TWO

Aboard Gulfstream N266SD (0120 Zulu)

Major Sharon Wallace was studying Paul Wriggle from across the Gulfstream's cabin. They were rocketing on the heels of a tailwind toward the nation's capital for what would quite likely be the end of their program. Discovering that their misplaced Airbus was over southern Europe with a locked out crew had impacted her commander hard, and she could only guess at his blood pressure, but it couldn't be good. The words didn't need to be spoken. They all knew.

Sharon unconsciously twisted her hair through her fingers, a nervous habit that normally the rest of her compatriots loved to tease her about.

The general was hunched over the satellite phone waiting for the team to assemble below in the Springs, Lieutenant Colonel Don Danniher was flying the Gulfstream alone, and the other two pilots they'd begun the day with would be on final approach now for Colorado Springs in Pangia's A330.

Wriggle was a good man, she thought. A good leader who did not deserve this kind of stress, and for the moment—with a single satellite phone in the cabin—all she could do was sit and watch him deal with the nightmare and wait for his orders.

Across the cabin, Paul Wriggle forced himself to focus as he sat with the secure satellite phone pressed against his ear, listening to the voices of his executive team back on the ground at Peterson Air Force Base in Colorado Springs.

He could visualize the cramped suite of nondescript offices they had purposefully selected in a back building on the base, as well as the underground chamber they'd built surreptitiously below one of the basements—a wonderfully clever design for security all around. Teaming with electronics and secure fiber optic connections back east, the 24/7 security had been expensive but well worth it. Even the Peterson base commander had no idea of what was happening in building 4-104.

"We're all here, sir. Finally."

"Okay," Wriggle began. "This is an emergency meeting of Air Lease Solutions," he said, using the code words to expunge all use of military references. He knew very well the prime security directive against talking "around" classified information, but in this case there was no choice, and even though the line was approved for classified information, it made him very nervous.

"We all understand down here, Paul," Colonel Dana Baumgartner, his second in command said. The use of the general's first name was a reciprocal code.

"Has everyone there received and read my message on what's happening?"

"Everyone," Baumgartner replied.

"All right," Wriggle began, "Obviously, this is not a drill. The entire program is imperiled, as are the people out there who've been inadvertently involved. First, have you checked whether we somehow uplinked a transmission of orders?"

"We have checked," Colonel Baumgartner replied, "… and the answer is absolutely not. There were none. Our last test run was three weeks ago. It was a good, routine test by all parameters, but, of course, there were no operational receivers in the … air … to receive. The test sequence was the same one we've run for two years. No change. But nothing has been triggered in the last, well, three weeks. And as you know, we only trigger the test to keep everything open while we complete the network."

Paul Wriggle was rubbing his forehead.

"That's our machine out there," the general said. "That wasn't supposed to be the case, but it is, and from the sound of it, sometime this morning she either listened to something we sent, or misinterpreted something someone else sent, and she took action as a direct result. I suppose it's also possible that she unilaterally decided to turn herself on. Unfortunately, the best fit is an unfortunately timed test transmission."

"We're … well, Paul, we're absolutely sure nothing was voluntarily transmitted."

"Voluntarily? Why the hesitation, Dana?"

"Because we're just now checking the last twenty-four-hour history of all our servers, and I just got word that one bank of computers may have been off line for a few minutes yesterday evening, and we don't know why."

"Off line? Why would that cause an unwanted transmission?"

"It shouldn't, but we all want 100 percent certainty, so we have to know why anything dropped off line, and what it did when it came back on."

"Does anyone else but us have, maybe, a copy of the standard test sequence? Or could someone have cracked into a copy of the overall form of code we use? Could this be sabotage, in other words?"

There was a burst of conversation in the background before another team member answered, the voice recognizable as their chief scientist, a brilliant civilian named George Choder.

"No one is supposed to have a copy of anything, and certainly initiating an … order, for want of a better word … would take the entire string, and we haven't even finished writing that yet. Plus, no one knew our … machine … was anywhere other than California. But despite all that, I wouldn't rule out sabotage. This could *not* happen accidentally."

"Suppose our machine heard just a test transmission.

Could it obey and lock up based on that?"

More conversation in the background, now even more intense, as many seconds passed.

"We … don't think so, but we don't know, Paul. But we want to emphasize that there was no purposeful test transmission this week! We weren't ready for live tests, so … I don't know the state of our machine's programming."

"You mean, the other end, our, ah, operational machine, *could* have been receptive? It *could* have reacted to whatever it heard?"

"We don't understand the question," Dana Baumgartner said.

Wriggle sighed out of frustration at the elliptical conversation. It would be far easier to just say "airplane," but anyone overhearing would then have zero doubt what they were discussing. "What I'm saying is," Wriggle continued, "… can you guarantee me that if our machine was operational, and if it heard the test sequence whether recorded or live, that it absolutely could *not* trigger it's lockout function? Is that what you're saying?"

"No, we're not saying that at all, Paul. We're saying we *can't* guarantee that, because no one was ready for the machine to fly … to operate, I mean. We hadn't checked that part of the programming. It wasn't ready."

"Then we've got a huge problem," Paul Wriggle said. "Regardless of how she got out of our hands, that machine is our responsibility, and we've got to get her to release control. I mean now. Who's our programming expert for the receiving end of the equation?"

"Well, sir, that spotlights another worry," the colonel replied. "That would be one of our people who has been on vacation, but she didn't come back as scheduled two days ago, and we've been frantically trying to locate her for the past hour."

"Give me the initials."

"Golf Hotel, sir. She was supposed to be up in Rocky Mountain National Park, but we can't find her, and the phone and her iPad are both turned off …"

"I apologize for sounding suspicious, folks," the general continued, knowing the potential effect of his voicing a loyalty doubt, "… but we're in very dangerous territory here. Does Golf Hotel have the ability to trigger an uplink signal remotely, by herself?"

"She shouldn't. But … again … none of this was an anticipated possibility."

Choder's voice interceded. "Ah, sir, I would bet my career that Golf Hotel would never do anything like that, but to be honest, she has the control of the receiver's programming and I'm afraid we've more or less left that to her until now. She probably knows better than anyone … well, hell, she *does* know better than anyone, what state the programming is aboard our, ah, machine."

Paul Wriggle pulled up a mental image of the woman they were discussing. Gail Hunt … in her forties, single, very quiet, hired out of Boeing Military in Seattle with a long-standing top secret clearance. He resisted the tendency to wonder if her being momentarily AWOL from a vacation could portend something more sinister, but it had to be considered.

And she wasn't a particularly happy employee.

"Paul? You still there?"

"Yes. Absolutely."

"I … have to tell you we'd had some concern about Golf Hotel in recent weeks, and … and there was a certain amount of animosity over a personnel decision. That's why her not coming back on time is a worry, and I was just handed a note that the place she … wait a second."

He could hear the questions in the background if not the

answers: "Is this right? Where?"

There was a fatigued sigh on the line, and the colonel came back on. "Okay…she was supposed to be at the McGregor Lodge in Estes Park, and they say she never checked in."

Paul Wriggle shook his head as he drummed his fingers on the adjacent table and pressed the phone even tighter to his ear. "Let me ask this again, to make sure. Do we have the programming prowess among the rest of you to know what our machine was programmed to do at this stage if turned on?"

"In a word, sir, no. That was going to be a team effort that she was to lead. That's why she wanted the aircraft out of the desert, if you'll recall."

"Wait … *she* wanted it out?" Wriggle asked.

"Yes. I thought you knew. The request started with her last week. She wanted the ship back here so we could get the onboard programming complete."

"I didn't realize that. But she had no idea it had left Mojave last week, correct?"

"We don't think so. She was already on vacation, and someone there would have had to tell her, and from what we've learned, the Mojave people didn't even realize they'd screwed up and pulled our airplane out until today."

"That's correct. Okay, listen up, folks … if our machine thought we wanted her to … to … trigger a locked situation, could she just as easily be persuaded to unlock? Think carefully, because those people are in trouble, and we've got to act now if we can."

"Paul, shouldn't we inform … I don't know, the air staff, the White House. Someone?" Dana Baumgartner asked.

"And say what, Dana? We're not even supposed to exist. And even if we could report it that easily, what is anyone else going to do that we can't do ourselves?"

There was embarrassed silence on the other end.

"So, again, I need an answer. Can we countermand whatever order our machine thinks it's been given?"

It was Choder who spoke up. "In theory, yes, if we had the final programming done. But we're searching right now for some notes or anything to tell us where GH left the onboard processor. If it was fairly rudimentary, then it should obey the "all clear" code … if we could transmit it. If it was more complex, a simple unlock order may not work."

"But," Wriggle asked, "… if all it did was respond to the enabling code, can't it be turned off?"

"We didn't send that enabling code!"

"Someone did! Is there any danger in *trying* whatever generic code we have?"

"No. But, Paul, that's not the point. Point is, our global network is not complete. We're just over 60 percent coverage. We could go blasting an unlock message all over the planet, and that bird might not hear it."

"Do we know where the holes are in our coverage?"

Another chilling delay filled the void.

"Yes, sir. We know most of the holes."

"Is the Mediterranean covered, or is it a hole?"

"It's pretty much an incomplete hole, sir. We've got much of northern Europe and the UK, but … but the Med is spotty."

"Can the thing be turned off from inside?"

"Yes. There's a code you can enter from any of the flight management computers."

"But … you're going to tell me we don't have a clue what that code is, correct?"

"Yes, sir. I suppose we are. We really need to find Golf Hotel. But the thing is, the flight management computers will look like they're dead because the displays turn off. One wouldn't normally think you could enter anything."

There wasn't much cord between the receiver and the

base of the satellite phone, but Paul Wriggle stood now, pulling as tight as he could to allow at least some pacing. He had to keep them moving forward, and, for that matter, he was far too agitated to sit for another second. There couldn't be much time left for their airplane, and the people aboard.

"Okay, get the release sequence, open the network, and blast it continuously as far and wide as you can. How soon can you get that going?"

"We figure an hour or less."

"Text me the moment you start the transmissions, and the moment, if any, that you get a response. Keep looking for Golf Hotel … ask the rangers in Rocky Mountain, call any friends we have at FBI for help, check state police and morgues, and meanwhile someone please make sure she hasn't left some weird message on her desk or her email. Also … someone call Ron Barrett, the owner at Mojave Storage and find out who the employee was who made the mistake. Let's make sure it's not someone who knows our lady, okay?

"Yes, sir."

"Do your best and do it as fast as you can, please! I'll be touching down at Andrews in two hours, and if we haven't got this nightmare resolved by then, I'll be enroute to our boss. Where things go for us from there is anyone's guess."

CHAPTER THIRTY-THREE

Aboard Pangia 10 (0135 Zulu)

Dan was working on assembling a toolkit full of scavenged items from his and Jerry's flight bags and the forward galley when Carol brought Josh Begich to the cockpit door.

"May we come in, gentlemen?"

Dan nodded, reaching out to shake the young boy's hand. "Absolutely. What's your name, and how old are you?"

"Josh, sir, and I'm almost fifteen," the boy replied, his eyes wide and watching warily, lest the captain recognize him and resume his attack. Jerry, however, was studying the forward panel.

"Are you good at wiring things, splicing, insulating, tracing?" Dan probed.

"No, sir. Well, I know basic circuits and stuff. But I'm good at programming."

"Okay. Stay up here."

At that moment Bill Breem and Tom Wilson appeared with a male passenger in tow they identified as Frank Erlichman, a man in his fifties with a perpetually startled look on his weathered face.

"Frank, is it?"

He nodded. "Yes."

"And your background, sir? American?"

"Yes. Well, born in Germany but now from Duluth. I'm an electrical engineer. I know wires and circuits, and was an avionics repairman five years back," Erlichman explained, with a slight accent.

"Okay," Dan said, "Let me explain what's going on and how you two can help.

Dan briefed them on what he was planning, ignoring the

wide-eyed look of fear on the young boy's face.

"There's only room for two of us down there. Mr. Erlichman? You come down first. Josh, please stay here, sit in this right-hand seat when I get out of it, and let the captain run you through whatever wiring diagrams we can pull up on our iPads. They'll be pretty rudimentary, but they might help you figure out the philosophy of the wiring as it should exist, and there may be a diagram of where all the black boxes are in relation to what they do. Look at the autothrottle and then the autoflight system in general. I'm stabbing in the dark, fellows, but the only reason I think we have a chance is just this: Whatever that damned cabinet down there is for, I don't think the designers ever expected anyone to mount a serious and sustained effort to retake control. I'm just guessing, of course, but I don't think they had security uppermost in mind, or I would have never been able to open the side of it."

Once the captain's seat was forward again, Dan descended the cramped access ladder, guiding Frank Erlichman down after him, and giving a quick orientation tour of the cabinet and the racks of electronics.

"Dan?" Frank asked, "May one ask, how much time do we have? I am aware that we can't fly forever."

"We have about three hours before we're out of fuel."

"What then happens?"

Dan shook his head. "In all honesty? I don't know. It could mean we regain control when the engines die and the power goes off for a few seconds before the battery kicks in, then we can glide somewhere to a landing. It could mean we sit here helpless and crash."

"Thank you for being straight with me."

"Okay, let's get to work. Don't touch anything on or in that cabinet, just in case it's still electrified or booby-trapped."

"I understand."

"I'm going to look for the VHF radios and start with that. You look for anything that looks like autothrottles or autoflight. Do you speak French, too, by any chance?"

"Yes."

"Good. I forgot to ask. I don't know if any of the placards are in French or English, but either way, we're okay."

The maze of wires going into tightly packed and insulated wiring bundles and harnesses was nothing short of mind boggling, and Dan kept himself focused on reading the little metal placards on the bottom end of each electronic box, increasingly pessimistic that anything would be plainly labeled. Most of the boxes were American made, with each placard full of serial numbers and date of manufacture and convoluted model numbers, but on the third rack and fifth row, he finally caught the letters "VHF" for one of the aviation-band radios.

Got it!

On the rack itself, the "VHF #1" position was emblazoned, and he loosened the circular nuts holding the radio cabinet in place and gingerly pulled it out of its cradle.

Nothing in the wire harness going into the rear of the cradle showed any signs of change or tampering. It was as if the harness was a standard factory construct, and the plug itself provided no help—only small numbers associated with each pin position could be seen when he disconnected the plug and examined it.

Dan felt his heart sink as he stared at it. What arrogance to think he could figure this out without a schematic. But as Frank moved to his side, the passenger reached out to point to the disconnected rack plug and nodded.

"You recognize something?" Dan asked.

"There is a standard pattern. Power supply, input, output, antenna leads … all of it pretty straightforward."

"Really? Anything look nonstandard here?"

"You said the radios went off? All of them?"

"Yes."

"And there were no lights then on the control heads, no indication of power?"

"Nothing at all."

"Very well. You see, if I were going to build a box to seize control remotely, I wouldn't need to use the radios. I would just see to it that they were turned off."

"What are you saying, Frank?"

"We should try to find power to plug in … here and here … to these pins … and you might just reactivate the transceiver. The antenna seems to be in place."

"I wish we had a circuit tester or ammeter."

"So do I. But these instruments are all powered by the same voltage. Any positive and negative lead should work."

They searched the adjacent rack before finding a small box several feet away with blinking lights on the front. Dan unscrewed and removed the box, disconnected the cannon plug on the back of the rack and waited for the aircraft to react.

Nothing.

"Okay, which are the power leads?"

Frank took over, cutting the two appropriate wires and pulling them through far enough to reach the back of the VHF radio. He stripped a section of insulation from each of the cut wires to the radio and spliced the power leads in, and immediately two small LEDs on the front lit up.

"Wait here," Dan said, scrambling to stick his head above cockpit floor level.

Jerry was already waiting for him. "The number one radio just lit up, Dan! What did you do?"

"Too long to explain. That's just step one. Call out if anything changes up here."

"Can I use the radio?"

"Hey man, knock yourself out. We should be adjacent to Italian airspace by now. Maybe Rome control could hear us."

"Hey … wait a second … it's not transmitting."

Dan pulled himself out of the hatch to stand beside Jerry's chair.

"What do you mean?"

"The audio control panel here … it's still dark, and even though I know I had the switch selected to the number one radio before all this crap began, when I hit the transmit button, nothing happens."

Dan reached down and worked with the panel, then looked at his panel on the right side.

"You're right. We've only turned the thing on. Can you change frequencies?"

"Yes. That's just manual, or at least it works."

"Can we hear anything?"

"Let me find the right ATC frequencies for where we are, and I'll let you know, but it isn't going to help us much unless we can talk."

Carol was standing beside him, and Dan turned to her.

"Any luck on radio batteries for that satellite phone we were using?"

"No. That was apparently the only one on board."

Josh Begich looked up, listening to the exchange.

"You know, that telephone can't be too exotic in terms of what kind of charging power it needs. Perhaps we could find a charger aboard and modify it? I would bet a lot of people have chargers in their carryon bags."

"I'll make the announcement and see what we can find," Carol said, turning to Dan. "And I'll send Jeanie up to relay for you."

"Okay, stand by on searching the bags. There's not much room down there. Jerry? I'm going back down and keep at it."

"Go for it, Dan. Hey … take a minute to get something to drink or hit the head if you need it."

"I'm good, but you need a break?"

"Yeah, next time you come up, I need to get out of this seat for a minute."

Josh was looking over at the two of them. "I thought you couldn't control anything?"

"We can't," Jerry replied, knowing where this was going.

"But, that means that if you need to get up, nothing will change while you're out of the cockpit, right?"

"Ever hear of Murphy's Law, kid?" Jerry asked.

"Uh, no. Is that an electronics law?"

"No, it's life. Anything that can go wrong, will go wrong. If I unstrap and leave the cockpit with Dan downstairs, guaranteed that's the exact moment we'll get control back and go into a dive or something."

Josh looked even more confused.

"Really?"

"Yep."

"Okay, but then we'd have control back, right?"

Jerry looked up at Dan who was suppressing a laugh, then back at Josh Begich.

"I'll have to explain this to you later, kid. It's like the facts of life."

Dan returned to the underdeck area with renewed hope, but the look on Frank Erlichman's face was funereal.

"What's wrong, Frank?"

"I traced the autothrottle circuit. I doubt we can touch it."

"Show me. What do you mean?"

Frank led him forward to a separate electronics rack, pointing to a large electronic box and the nomenclature on the identiplate.

"I think this is what you were looking for. But please

look at the wiring harness. I traced the basic wires and they go to the cabinet, and then another autothrottle related box, then back to the cabinet, and as far as I can tell, there is no way to be sure you can regain control by cutting anything."

"It would be a gamble, in other words?"

"A big one."

Dan looked at his watch, the gesture well understood by Frank who had an ashen look about him.

"Okay … let's think about this. The engine power is frozen at the same level as when this happened," Dan began, counting off points on his fingers. "That means they're not *controlling* it, most probably, they've just disconnected our ability to set it. Regardless of the back and forth wiring, the big question is: Which one of these boxes, if turned off instead of on, would restore our ability to move the throttles?"

"You're playing, I think, with fire," Frank said. "These are computer controlled and not as simple as the radio."

"Well … you may have a point. We turned the radio on but still can't transmit on it because we didn't turn on the audio selector panel."

"We can probably find that circuit."

"No … let's … could we try a few things for the throttles and be ready to reverse if it doesn't go right?"

"There are no switches. You mean, pull the racks out from their plugs?"

"How about stripping a section of wire, cutting it in the middle, and if all hell breaks loose, just re-twisting the ends together."

"We can't do that with gloves, and there is substantial voltage."

"I have to try."

Once again Dan stuck his head above floor level to brief Jerry and the others on what he was about to do and position Carol to relay any information from Jerry if there was a change.

With five minutes of work stripping wires, they were ready, and Dan used a glove to insulate his hand while running the exposed wire into a pair of uninsulated nail clippers.

"Okay. Here goes."

The sound of the click as the clippers snapped through the 18-gauge wire was almost inaudible, but Dan could feel the tiny impact in his gloved fingers. At first, it seemed as if there were no further reaction, until he realized he was leaning forward slightly against the *deceleration* of the airplane.

The power is coming off! he thought to himself, just as a voice yelled down from the flight deck, relaying Jerry's words.

"PUT IT BACK! PUT IT BACK! THE ENGINES ARE COMING TO IDLE!"

"OKAY!" Dan yelled back over his shoulder as he prepared to re-mate the cut wires, positioning them so he could make firm contact and then twist them back together. He could feel the big aircraft continuing to slow. He was too far ahead of the wing mounted engines to actually hear them, but the decreasing sound of the slipstream told the tale. The thought crossed his mind with lightning speed that if the engines didn't rebound when he touched the wires, they were truly at the end of the line, and the thought made him almost desperate to touch the wires together again, just as something else was warning him to wait.

What the hell am I missing? Dan thought. The pressure to act was accelerating to unfathomable levels as he forced his mind to divulge whatever it was thinking in the periphery of the subconscious.

Oh, jeez! Yes!

Dan turned to yell at the face he saw watching him from

the hatch.

"PUSH THE THROTTLES UP! SEE IF THEY RESPOND!"

"What?"

"TELL THE CAPTAIN TO PUSH THE THROTTLES UP!"

Carol nodded and disappeared, and the seconds slowed down to an agonizing pace as time dilated and Dan lost track of reality. The two ends of the wire were still in his respective hands, and the big jet was getting progressively slower. Without more power they would slow and stall, and unless the autoflight system was truly engaged, they would fall out of the sky.

Dan tried to force himself to touch the wires and finish it, but another part of his brain was screaming to wait a few extra moments in case deliverance was at hand. When a surge of thrust reached his consciousness, Dan was unsure whether he was imagining it or feeling it.

Carol's voice from above broke the suspense:

"IT WORKS! HE SAYS IT WORKS! WE HAVE MANUAL THROTTLES!"

Dan looked at Frank, realizing neither of them had been breathing. He gasped for breath then and smiled at the shaken passenger.

"Thank God!"

"Indeed."

"Let's get these wires taped and very far apart."

"I can do that for you!" Frank said, a very large grin on his face. The jet was reaccelerating, the slipstream sounds rising back to where they'd been.

"I'm going up for a minute. Standby to reconnect those wires if something goes wrong."

Dan all but levitated out of the hatch to find an ebullient captain fine-tuning throttles he could actually control.

"Jesus Christ, Dan! Well done! God, I'm not going to buy you a beer when we get on the ground, I'm buying you a friggin' brewery!"

"Full manual control of the engines?"

"Yes! Goddamit, yes! And I can hear air traffic control on the radio. Bosnia, I think. One-twenty-one-five," he said, citing the emergency frequency. "I can't talk to them, but I can hear the buggers. I don't know how fast we're going, but I'm gonna slow us down a bit by feel to conserve fuel while you work the rest of your magic!"

"We're just starting the process, Jerry."

"I know, but hell, you can try to kill me in Anchorage anytime, Bro!"

Dan smiled, a cascade of emotions coursing through his head, all of which he forcibly suppressed.

"You have no side stick control, though?"

"No. And all the displays are fiction. But I'm pretty sure I can feel this baby well enough to slow her down without stalling."

"Pretty sure?"

"All I've got. But we can control something for the first time in hours! How'd you do it?"

"The truth?"

"Yes. Of course."

"I guessed, Jerry."

"Okay."

"And the next guess might not be as lucky."

CHAPTER THIRTY-FOUR

Silver Springs, Maryland (8:45 p.m. EST / 0145 Zulu)

Jenny Reynolds sighed. Her laptop was fighting back, and she was getting seriously pissed.

She sat back for a second, rubbing her eyes before casting them around the surprisingly spacious apartment. She'd only imagined what a clandestine "safe house" would be like, but never had she actually been in one.

Jenny glanced at her watch, reading nearly 9:00 p.m. The Pangia flight would be over Tel Aviv in less than two hours now, and Will had apparently pried enough information out of his unsuspecting confederates at the Pentagon to confirm that nothing aboard had changed: The pilots were still unable to control the jet, and the rising level of alarm from Washington to Tehran was becoming deeply worrisome. Worse, Will had had the temerity to lay the singular hope of deliverance on her shoulders.

"I'm just guessing, Will. Let's get real here. Even if I can figure out how to reverse whatever that original order was, that might not be enough to solve it. They could be taking telemetry orders from some live control room now and impervious to anything I send. Besides, this server is blocking me at every turn, and even if I write the right code, I don't know how the hell we're going to get it broadcast on the right channels in time."

"Just do your best."

"I *am*, but at precisely what point are we going to let someone else but us know what we suspect?"

"One more hour. Nothing bad's going to happen to them for another hour. After that, it could be very bad."

She'd stood then, moving to him as he stood by the door

and taking him by the arm, locking eyes.

"I need a commitment, Will! Got it? If I can't make it work by one more hour from now, we need to call a rainmaker. So who would that be?"

His eyes broke the lock and looked away, toward the window, then toward the door.

"No!" she snapped. "Stop that! Look at me, dammit!"

Will Bronson turned his gaze back to her, looking startled. "Okay, okay. Calm down."

"Do you even *have* a plan?"

"Sort of."

"*Sort of*? What do you … what do you mean sort of, for Chrissake?"

"Look, Jen, I'm not sure who we're battling here."

She cocked her head slightly as if seeing him for the first time. "Really?"

She sat studying him, realizing he was perspiring ever so slightly and looking far more uncertain that she'd recognized before.

"You know what I think?" she asked suddenly. "I think there's a deeper subtext here, dude. I think what you're trying hard *not* to say is that you're not sure whether you're protecting your bosses at the Pentagon and trying to undo what they've done in time, or whether we're fighting some renegade group in the government, or maybe even some crazy individual? Am I right?"

He tried to pull away from her, but she tightened her grip. His voice was rising, betraying angry frustration.

"Okay, I *don't* know. That's the point. That's why I came to find you tonight because I *am* worried who's behind this and if it *is* our side and we're messing with that flight for some legitimate reason, and I go and breach security to tell the world …"

"Goodbye career," she finished the sentence for him.

"Yeah, and maybe worse. You, too."

"All right, now I need YOU to focus. You just used the phrase 'for some legitimate reason.' Is there any legitimate, reasonable, conceivable justification for putting those people in peril, if this is something our side did?"

Will looked down in thought for a small eternity before sighing and nodding, then changing the gesture to an emphatic head shake. "No."

"Then I need that commitment. One hour more. If I can't be sure we've freed them … and it's only a bizarre Hail Mary pass we're talking about … if I'm not sure, who you gonna call?"

He turned toward her slightly, fully engaging, which was a good sign, she figured.

"Jenny, there is no one I can be sure of in a situation like this. No one. Not even my team, who are hunkered down waiting for me to tell them something good. Do you understand what I'm saying to you? In the entirety of the government of the United States of America, since the enabling signal came from our own National Security Agency, I can think of no one completely safe who could take action in time. Hell, it may already be too late to take any action in time, but you've got to try."

She leaped to her feet again. "Oh, really? Tell me again why *I've* got to solve this? My government seems to have gone crazy and is trying to kill a planeload of people and maybe start a nuclear confrontation and I'm responsible *how*?

"Sit, please," he commanded suddenly, the earlier composure returning if not the air of confidence. Something hard in his voice led her to choke off an objection and comply.

Will Bronson picked up another lightweight chair and plopped it down in front of her backwards. He sat on it, leaning his chin on the back, staring at her.

"What?"

No response, and she was getting steamed.

"WHAT, damn you?"

"You really want me to tell you why … how you're responsible?"

"Is there an echo in here? Yes! That's what I asked."

"You wrote the code."

She stared at him in disbelieving silence.

"I … *what?"*

"I wasn't going to tell you, but you wrote the code they used to start this mess."

"Like hell I did! I've been trying to decipher … what are you saying?

"The registration of codes I told you about? I wasn't lying when I told you I was denied access to who registered it. But there is a track to whoever created a unique code or variant. Do you recognize the digital signature Three-Three-Six-Nine-Alpha?"

Jenny looked at him speechless for a few seconds, her mind running back to previous assignments over the years, some of which had required a personal code, which in her case had always been 3369A.

"That's … my digital signature, but I swear to you I've never seen that transmitted code before. And I wouldn't have anything to do with …"

"You signed it."

"No, someone *used* my coded signature! I've spent the whole day trying to figure out the logic in that codec. If I'd written it …" She stopped, her face suddenly looking pasty.

"What?"

"Oh crap!"

"*What* Jenny?"

"I didn't think about …"

"Please, tell me."

Her hand was in front of her mouth, her eyes drifting away for a few seconds before she looked back at him.

"Jesus God, Will! That's the key! Someone scrambled a very old code of mine, and I've been irritated all day because it had some familiar overtones but I couldn't tell why. I didn't write this version, but they used one of my encoding sequences and then scrambled the hell out of it." She turned a shade whiter as she met Will's gaze, understanding.

"This means NSA is involved!"

"Maybe. Could be. Highly possible,"

"But if I know the core philosophy of the code, maybe I CAN decipher it!"

She started to turn back to the computer and stopped herself, a dark cloud crossing her face as the final tumblers fell into place. She hadn't been just the helpful girl from NSA. She had been the target all along.

"I see now. NSA. You thought I was the bad guy, didn't you?" she said softly, watching him as he stood and put the chair aside.

"Jen …"

"No, level with me. This whole thing was because of my digital signature and the signal coming from NSA, right? So what were you going to do to me if I didn't produce the code? Seduce me? Torture me? Kill me?"

"*What*?"

"This is one of your safe houses and I'm sure you could kill someone in here quite handily and some … some team would come flying in to dispose of the body and the evidence."

"Jenny, calm down. That's not what I or the DIA do. That's Hollywood."

"Oh really? The DIA doesn't do covert ops? You're *known* for covert ops!"

"That's not me."

"How were you planning to make me talk, huh?" Her eyes were narrowing as she warmed to her anger. Here she'd thought he respected her and enjoyed working with her and—

"JENNY!"

"What?"

"What would *you* have thought in my shoes?"

"I ..."

"We have a major emergency and little time. Thank God we were wrong about you. I get it. Now let's work like hell, okay?"

She looked at him carefully, the steam dissipating, and nodded.

"Okay."

"We're essentially alone on this. Just like I said."

"Okay."

"And, I would never kill you or torture you!"

"You left one out," she said, turning back to the laptop.

"Did I?" he said, feigning ignorance.

"Get me coffee, Will Bronson. You can seduce me later."

CHAPTER THIRTY-FIVE

The White House (8:50 p.m. EST / 0150 Zulu)

CIA Deputy Director Walter Randolph had made the round-trip from the White House to Langley and back reluctantly, but meeting with his team was vital and there was simply no way of assuring an unmonitored electronic conversation in or around the Situation Room. He looked up from his briefing papers now as his driver was waived through the West Wing gate, spotting the director of Central Intelligence who was waiting. James Bergen climbed into the rear seat as Walter leaned forward to engage the driver.

"Ralph? Just drive around for about fifteen minutes, okay? Then back here."

The guards waved the car back through the gates as Bergen sighed and rubbed his eyes. "I hate days like this and just hanging around waiting for POTUS."

"I know. Feels a bit subservient."

"We serve at the pleasure of the president, Walter, my boy. At least I do. Okay, what have we got?"

"A growing international confrontation that could either dissipate like the morning fog or end up in a nuclear exchange. How's that for extremes?"

"Details, Walt."

"We have confirmation now that Tehran is fully aware of Moishe Lavi's presence on the Pangia flight, because they have formally notified all adjacent air traffic authorities that any flight with Lavi aboard is prohibited from entry into Iranian airspace. They've assembled what passes for their air force general staff, and they've even sent a direct nastygram to Pangia headquarters to make sure Pangia knows their jet with Lavi aboard will be, as they put it, 'refused admission to Iranian airspace,' meaning they reserve the right to shoot them down."

"Okay. We expected all that. What else?"

"Well, we've also discovered an interesting little tidbit that is probably quite seismic: The Airbus that Pangia is flying doesn't belong to them, and the airline apparently didn't know it."

"Excuse me?"

Randolph explained Pangia's shock at being informed they were flying the wrong Airbus A330 and how they had pulled it out of the desert and hurried it into service.

"The storage company in Mojave, California, made the mistake, Jim. We sent two of our people up there in the past hour. The employee responsible for sending the wrong airplane to the airline is a Carl Kanowsky, and Mr. Kanowsky has suddenly disappeared, and it turns out the name is probably an alias. Our team suspects that all the information the man gave the employer to get hired about six months ago when those white tails arrived will turn out to be false. And, the jet Pangia Airways *thought* they were flying, the one which should still be there in Mojave?"

"Yes?"

"It's gone, and the owner of the storage company is feigning surprise."

"What are we thinking, Walt?"

"First, we're thinking that delivering the wrong aircraft to Pangia Airways was not an accident, and that the substitute aircraft that was sent to Pangia's facility in Tulsa had been purposefully prepared specifically for this flight with something electronic installed that would seize control of the airplane when triggered. This may well be a carefully laid plan."

"Laid by whom?"

Walter Randolph laughed and cocked his head. "Well,

Jim, who's aboard?"

"Really? You think the old bastard engineered *this*?"

"He's dying, Jim. Sorry … that sounds like a line from *Star Trek*, but, seriously, you remember our little inside bombshell that Lavi's hiding the fact that he's been diagnosed with pancreatic cancer?"

"I've never bought that, Walt. I think it's a planted feint. We know he's had heart trouble, but cancer?"

"The cancer stuff may be false. But remember we got that word one month before he pulled his wildly unexpected goal line stand in the Knesset, which, if he isn't dying, makes little sense. Lavi has always known how to live to fight another day. That throw down was a complete reversal of character."

"Walt, he acts as hale and hearty as he was at age twenty. Certainly his bedroom athletics haven't diminished."

"True, but let's just suppose for the sake of argument that he *is* dying. Look at the motivation. If you were the great Moishe Lavi, how would you like to go out? As a footnote in history, the failed leader who never removed the Iranian threat you had likened to Hitler, or as the self-appointed deliverer of your people?"

"The Messiah complex."

"Yes."

The CIA director sat for a few seconds in thought. "I'll admit it's not impossible. But what would he have gained by planting the cancer story?"

"A cover for uncharacteristic behavior," Walter Randolph continued, "… which could also mean a cover for the solution he'd devised against the mullahs."

"Shaky, Walt."

"But possible."

"So, who would have engineered this global effort for him, whether he's dying or just intent on suicide?"

"A loyal faction of Mossad … perhaps even a faction of the IDF. We can only speculate at this point, but too much is lining up here which smells like a very clever clandestine operation. And remember, his drive for a first strike at Tehran was already blocked before he was thrown out of office because of their extensive civilian safeguards. This may be his only way."

"Provoke Tehran, you mean?"

"Yes," Walter replied. "And personally at that. The way he appears to be doing it may border on the brilliant, but that depends on what other planned tumblers fall into place. In other words, if he has confederates in the Israeli Defense Force and the Israeli Air Force ready to feed inaccurate tactical and strategic information to the leaders at critical moments in order to make them believe they have no choice, Lavi might just be able to bypass all the normal safeguards."

"You mean, feed them disinformation on which Iranian missile sites are fueling, what radars have snapped on, satellite communications, and autonomous launch authority? Having his clandestine confederates feed the Israeli command staff bogus updates in a crisis?"

"Precisely, Jim. All that, and more. Everything necessary to make it appear that the only responsible course of action for Israel is to launch a nuclear first strike against the mullahs. In the so-called fog of pre-war, with the dice loaded, Mr. Lavi and his commandeered jetliner may be flying one in for the homeland."

"Good God."

"Walt, how about DIA dancing with NSA before the plane turned? What's up with that?"

"We're working on squeezing some explanations out of NSA. We're also chasing down a picture of the missing Mojave employee for a face recognition scan. Bet you anything he's Israeli."

"But, Walt, why was DIA on this to begin with? Is there any chance …"

"That we're directly involved with helping Mr. Lavi?" Walter sighed, long and ragged. "I hope to hell we're not involved."

"Walt … wait a minute. There's a loose end bothering me here. Where's the airplane that Pangia thought they were flying? You said it was missing from that California facility?"

"We're tracing flight plans. No luck yet. Apparently when it left California, it was using a bogus call sign."

"See, I keep thinking, if this was a purposeful mix-up, who would want to fly off with that other plane? I'm not following that."

"Frankly, Jim, neither are we."

CHAPTER THIRTY-SIX

Silver Springs, Maryland (9:45 p.m. EST / 0245 Zulu)

"I think I've got it!" Jenny Reynolds jabbed a fist in the air as she turned to Will Bronson.

"Really?"

"Yes! I figured out the enabling order, and I've reversed it … in theory. Now the small remaining problem is how to get it transmitted to that aircraft on a frequency it's monitoring."

Will rushed to her side looking somewhat bewildered at the complex strings of letters and numbers on her laptop screen. "Didn't you get a read on the frequency when you picked up the transmission?"

"Yes, but remember it was a piggybacked signal, kind of like a harmonic. But that's not the problem. I can transmit it in the clear, but I have to have something to transmit it over, and I don't have the authority to just tap into any satellite transponder I want to commandeer."

The electronic warble of Will Bronson's cell phone caused Jenny to look up as he pulled it out and studied the screen, a frown darkening his features as he turned away from her.

"What?" she asked.

"Keep working, please," he said, getting to his feet and moving toward the far end of the room, his voice low and tone urgent with words she couldn't hear and was trying to ignore. Normally she could hear the other side of a cell phone conversation, but he was holding the phone so tightly to his ear she could hear nothing.

Suddenly he was back, standing uneasily beside her, a distracted expression on his face.

"Okay, what's wrong?" she asked.

He shook his head and tried to laugh, but the effort was disingenuous.

"We need to hurry."

"No kidding. What was that call? Why are you looking haunted all of a sudden?"

Again he glanced toward the door before turning back to her. "Jenny, my agency thinks I've gone rogue."

"What?"

"Or some rogue faction at DIA thinks I'm a threat. "

"Meaning?"

"Meaning we've got to get that code you figured out transmitted and get out of here."

"I thought this was your safe house?"

"It's DIA's safe house, and I'm DIA, and … apparently … some of us are of the opinion that you and I are up to no good, or hell, who knows, maybe they think I've kidnapped you!"

"Can't we just explain it to … them? You want me to talk to someone … a proof of life kind of thing?"

He was shaking his head vigorously.

"If there was time, Jen, yes, but remember we don't know who sent the first messages, and they came from your building. Get finished, and let's get out of here."

"Is someone on the way?"

He leaned in close to her, eye to eye. "Jenny, just work as fast as you can. We need to go, or we might not have the chance to solve this. Just save your work and don't try to transmit it yet."

She nodded slowly, momentarily lost in his eyes again. "Okay. But why? If I have a chance to transmit it, why not try?"

"There's a good reason!"

"Which I need to know."

"It has to do with monitoring. I don't want anyone

cancelling out whatever you send. We could have only one chance."

"And time is running out, right?"

"One shot, Jen! You want to gamble?"

She snapped back to the computer, re-focusing on where she'd been when his phone rang. Both of them stared at the screen in silence for a few moments.

"I know a transponder you could use clandestinely, but we can't trigger it out of this place," he added.

Jenny sighed and bit her lip, racing her mind's eye around a planet full of communications satellites and trying to recall a classified vulnerability she'd read about within the last few weeks. It was a geosynchronous communications satellite over the eastern Atlantic, which would cover the Mediterranean and some of the Middle East, but what was the vulnerability?

"Jenny?"

"Shh-h. I'm thinking."

"About what?" Will got to his feet and stood aside quietly, watching her as she tapped a pencil on the desk and then started nibbling the eraser like a crazed chipmunk, occasionally shaking her head as if in deep dialogue with an unseen colleague. He was wholly unprepared for her to turn suddenly and yelp.

"What?"

"I think I've got it. I *hope* I've got it!"

"Okay. Can I ask what?"

She was already back at the keyboard typing frantically, bringing up a series of pages of some technical site and landing finally on a blinking cursor. She typed in a series of keystrokes and waited as some distant server considered her request.

The screen filled suddenly with a blue background and a series of open fields.

"Yes, yes, yes! I did remember. They were testing this one transponder and someone left the portal open with a very mundane sign-in code."

"Meaning?"

"Meaning I've got one shot at uploading the reversal string and firing it toward the Med. If we're lucky, it will repeat three or four times before self-cancelling. But, hopefully, that will be enough."

"And the frequency is the same?"

"I'm not certain, Will, but I think this covers the same spectrum."

"Will NSA intercept it?"

"Yes, but not immediately."

"Then for God's sake, don't do it! Not from here."

"Will … why?"

"Save your work. Here's a flash drive. Save it, and let's get the hell out of here."

"What aren't you telling me, Will Bronson?"

"That we may have every cop in the Beltway looking for us! Please, let's go!"

She worked quickly to transfer the computer code to the flash drive, her head spinning with the pressures of time and Will's sudden panic over transmitting. But the opportunity was there and the transponder was waiting, her finger poised over the execute key he hadn't seen her pull up. She glanced over as he moved to the window to check outside, and tapped the key, immediately collapsing the transmit page. Maybe it would be tracked and maybe it wouldn't be, but she'd taken her best shot. He was wrong to want to wait, she was sure of that, yet something wasn't quite making sense about his concerns.

Just as suddenly, he was back at her side, nodding as she ordered the computer into hibernate mode and snapped it shut, handing him the flash drive.

"Okay. Done."

"What do you mean, done?" he asked, searching her eyes.

"I mean it's on the flash drive and saved, I'm ready to get back to that transponder when you think it's safe, and I'm ready to get out of here. Okay?"

"Okay."

"Although I'm worried we may have blown the one chance to stop this," Jenny said, wondering why she was lying about it. What was she doing, testing him?

Will was already turning toward the door, his hand on her shoulder.

"Worry not. I've got it under control."

CHAPTER THIRTY-SEVEN

Aboard Pangia 10 (0245 Zulu)

Still flush with hope, even an hour after restoring the throttles to manual control, Dan Horneman prepared to descend the ladder to the electronics bay once again, pausing behind the captain's seat to put a hand on Jerry Tollefson's shoulder.

"Hang in there, Captain!"

Bill Breem had spent the last hour standing behind the copilot's seat, watching and working with Josh Begich, trying to figure out wiring diagrams they'd called up on Dan's company iPad.

Jerry turned as far around as he could, nodding at his first officer. "Yeah, you, too, Dan. Be damned careful down there."

"I will."

Dan looked back at the copilot's seat where Josh Begich was punching his way through electrical diagrams. Carol was back in the cockpit, waiting to kneel as best she could in the cramped space behind the captain's seat to be the relay for Dan. He could see the strain on her face as she struggled to smile at him.

Frank Erlichman was anxiously waiting for Dan at the bottom of the ladder.

"Any progress, Frank?"

The man nodded, his words precise and spoken in a slow meter in pace with the seriousness of the situation. "I have been tracing wires as fast as I could, and I believe I know where the main controls have been spliced; although whoever wired this modification did such a professional job you would never know it wasn't a part of the original wiring harness."

"Show me, please," Dan replied, following the man to the right side rack. "We don't have much time."

"Ja, I think," Frank continued, "… if we cut here and here … ready to reconnect as before … and then splice these wires with these … we might be able to reroute control of the autoflight system. But … it is a big gamble."

"How much?"

"Pardon?"

"How much is guesswork and how much is certain, Frank?"

The man looked the copilot in the eye without a trace of humor and laughed ruefully. "It is all guesswork. I am not certain of anything."

"Okay. Is there a safer approach?"

"Yes. I think so. Those racks in what you call the cabinet?"

"Yes?"

"It is full of relays. Why would it be full of relays if the purpose wasn't to shunt power and control?"

Dan looked at the long rows of small, square metal cubes and a semi-ancient memory popped into his head, a memory of trying to explain what a relay was to his mother, who thought it somehow would explain what her son was doing to make money in the software business.

"Think of it this way, Mom," he'd said. "All the lights in town have gone off in a storm. Now the storm is gone, and I want to turn all the lights on again. But that's a huge amount of electricity, and I want to just flick a little switch. So, instead of routing a river of power through tiny wires that would burn up, I use a relay. I flick a switch, a little power goes through a little wire and powers an electromagnet, the electromagnet causes a metal rod to move a much bigger switch from "off" to "on," and I never have to get close to that much bigger and more dangerous amount of electricity."

It had been a noble attempt, but when she explained to friends that Dan controlled the city's light system, he gave up.

Frank, he realized, was talking, and he'd let himself drift.

"In other words," Frank repeated, "… I think that is how it is done. My thinking is that the relays are not normally powered on, so that when they're not powered, all is normal. When something causes them to come on and do their job of switching, that's when everything changes. The flight controls, for instance. The relay is energized, one of them cuts the power going to and from your flight controls … your sidestick controls on the flight deck … removing your manual input to the autoflight computers. Instead, it sends false information to the same autoflight computers, enabling them to be commanded perhaps by radio from outside, or by some internal program. In any event, as long as those relays are active, you can't interfere."

"Like someone just unplugged our cockpit controls and plugged in an alternate set of controls."

"Exactly."

"And we're just along for the ride. Okay, I'm with you."

"Well …" Frank continued, "… my theory is that if we interrupt the power that's letting those relays disconnect your cockpit, they'll shift to the off position and let go of the various controls."

"Great!"

Frank Erlichman was shaking his head energetically. "But wait, please. I have to warn you that if we're wrong … if we shut down the wrong one … even turning it back on might not cause it to latch again. Without a wiring diagram—"

"I understand, Frank. But we have to try. So we just selectively and physically pull the relays out of their respective sockets and see what happens?"

"No, no, no! If we pull a relay, it will depower that relay, yes, but it will also break whatever circuits are flowing through it when the relay is not powered on."

"Oh, Lord, of course. When the thing is off, the normal power to, for instance, the sidestick controllers, flow through that very relay."

"Yes. We need to depower each relay without pulling it out of the socket."

"So how do we do that? We can't get to the back of this cabinet where all those wires come in."

"I'm sorry ... I don't see a way without finding the power leads and cutting them."

Dan leaned against the starboard electrical rack for few seconds, letting his mind race over the options. He was missing something, and it was pissing him off.

All available resources ...

The phrase echoed through his conscious mind like a rebuke, and he raised an index finger in a wait gesture.

"Stay here. Don't pull anything. I'll be right back."

Scrambling up and down the small ladder through the narrow hatchway to the cockpit was getting easier, or he was becoming less aware of the bruises. Carol saw him climbing out and was just regaining her feet when he emerged, taking her by the shoulders to move her aside gently on the way to the right side of the cockpit.

"Josh ...?"

The boy's head snapped around toward him as he flashed a wait gesture to Jerry who was looking puzzled. Bill Breem was looking at him as well, but saying nothing.

"Okay. Help me figure this out, if you can. Both of you." Dan described the cube-shaped electrical relays and the inability to reach the power leads behind them. Breem began asking questions, and he and Dan were firing ideas back and forth too intently to notice Josh Begich trying to snag their attention. Frustrated, the boy reached up and grabbed Dan's left forearm.

"You guys are missing it."

"Missing what?" Breem asked, not unkindly.

"If a relay is powered on one side and the other side is holding open the circuit you want to close, pulling that relay out of its socket for a few seconds or even minutes will do no harm. You can pull the relay, pop the cover off, cut the power leads, then put it back in and the little switch inside will no longer be powered, the little plunger rod inside will be spring-loaded back, and the circuit it was designed to interrupt will no longer be interrupted, it will be restored."

Dan looked at Bill Breem who was nodding.

"He is absolutely right."

Dan turned back to Josh. "Okay, but what if we get the wrong one and want to repower it? If we've cut the power leads inside …"

"Well, the relays I'm used to working with have little prongs on the back going into the socket. Just bend the power prongs aside, and if you need to repower it, bend them back and plug it back in."

"Josh, you just earned your keep! Thank you. That's what I was missing."

Dan whirled around to return to the electronics bay as Jerry caught his arm.

"I've slowed us down considerably, Dan, and I think we've got at least two hours before we're over Tel Aviv now. At least it looks like we're still bore sighted."

"Got it. Pray hard, buddy. I'm going to start pulling things."

Within five minutes Dan had put on the insulating coat and gloves he'd used before and with Frank briefed and standing beside him with a pair of needle nosed pliers, he reached in gingerly and grasped the first cube, pulling it smoothly from its socket.

A sudden uncoordinated bank to the left almost propelled Dan's face into the metal frame of the open cabinet, but he managed to pull his head back just enough to avoid the inevitable bolt of electricity that would have accompanied the slightest touch. Frank had braced himself against a non-electrified rack, but his eyes were wide now as Dan looked at the relay cube in his hand and tried to decide what to do. He could hear Carol's voice from the hatch relaying Jerry's cry of alarm that they were in a steep bank, and he could feel the big aircraft in a severe sideslip, the rudder commanding a right turn as the wings tilted to the left, the frightening sound of the slipstream hitting the side of the A330 in a way it was not designed to be flown.

Still thrown to the left, Dan turned to reinsert the cube as they hit some sort of turbulence just enough to knock the relay from his hand. He heard it clatter and skitter to the bottom of the cabinet and knew there was too little time to chase it down. He could hear Jerry's voice clearly through the hatch yelling to restore whatever he'd changed.

The relays all appeared to be identical, and he made a split second decision and grabbed for one off to the right side of the row of cubes, pulling it out and shoving it in place of the first one he'd removed.

And suddenly the severe sideslip stopped, the Airbus returning to coordinated flight, whether in a bank still or not, he couldn't tell.

"What's happening?" he yelled at Carol, whose terrified face could be seen through the hatch.

"Jerry says we're still turning left, but we're not slipping," she shouted.

Dan got to his knees and shone the small flashlight at the bottom of the cabinet, being careful not to touch his face to the frame. He spotted the loose relay and gave chase, sticking his arm perilously into a maze of equipment and finally closing his hand around the precious little cube, then scrambling to his feet to plug it back in place of the substitute he'd removed.

"He says the turn is continuing," Carol yelled. Dan pushed past Frank, motioning for him to stay in place, and climbed the ladder far enough to hear Jerry directly.

"What's happening, Jerry?"

"Man, don't do whatever that was again, please! I thought we were going to go inverted!"

"Are we wings level now?'

"No. We've turned around almost 270 degrees and are still turning left. Wait … from the horizon it looks like the bank is lessening and the whiskey compass says we're coming back to the original course."

"We just did a 360?" Dan asked.

"Apparently. Did you put everything back?"

"Yes. For the moment."

"I don't know, Dan. I don't want to experience that ride again."

"I need to keep experimenting, Jerry."

"Well, whatever just happened, this thing has been commanded to return to the original course."

Dan scrambled out of the hatch and stood at Jerry's side to eliminate the need for yelling back and forth.

"You think that's what's happening? Someone's actively controlling us?" Dan asked.

"It's possible. It was weird. The slip stopped, the wings leveled, and then it started turning again to get back to course. Are there any antenna leads down there that might be feeding it commands from a satellite? Can we disconnect them if there are?"

"I hadn't looked, but there might be."

Once more, Dan descended the ladder back to the electronics bay, where Frank Erlichman was waiting with a pleading look betraying any attempt to project calm.

"Jerry raised the issue of whether someone's fighting us move for move," Dan explained.

"Similar to what would be used to fly a remotely piloted vehicle. I think they call them a drone?"

Dan nodded, as he crouched by the ladder and let his eyes run over the mysterious cabinet.

"Yes. Like a remotely piloted vehicle, an RPV, or these days we call it a UAS, unmanned aircraft system. If that was so, maybe we could disconnect the telemetry antenna and block any further orders from coming in."

"But what if the relays did not unlatch?"

"Yeah, I know. We disconnect the active control from the ground, but we still can't regain cockpit control."

"For there to be active control or just a signal which turned this thing on, there would need to be a satellite connection, and I found a lead in the big cabinet labeled satcom." Frank pointed aft and Dan followed, as he moved to the open cabinet, looking for the thick wire he had seen.

"I see it. And … there appears to be a cannon plug. Okay, help me with this logic. If this cabinet activated and took away our control in flight, it either did so by some freak accident … in other words turned itself on … or it received a radio signal. If I was going to go to all the trouble and expense of engineering this thing in the airplane to seize control from the flight crew, I wouldn't depend on VHF radios or anything with limited range. I'd use a satellite link, separate from the passenger system or our cockpit satcom with the company."

Frank was nodding. "And you think if the antenna lead here is disconnected, it might let go of us, whether we're being actively controlled or not?"

"I don't think we're fighting a live person, Frank. Jerry up there nailed it a while ago, I think, when he said we haven't changed heading once since this all started. How could that be active control?"

"That is logical," Frank replied, watching Dan think it over, his eyes glued to the satcom antenna lead.

"Frank, I think we have to disconnect the satellite antenna, at least for a while. If we *are* under active control, and we *don't* disconnect, and we keep turning off different systems, like we've already done with the throttles, whoever's at the remote controls will try to compensate somehow. But if we deprive it of the basic satellite connection ..." Dan's voice trailed off.

Frank Erlichman nodded solemnly. "I see two possibilities. If we disconnect the antenna lead and nothing happens, I would think that proves we were probably not under someone's active control. That doesn't mean the satcom couldn't have been the means of someone on the ground programming us previously. Second, if we disconnect the satcom and this cabinet unlatches and returns control, it proves we *were* under active control and now we're free."

"I think I followed all that, but the bottom line is, we've got to try to disconnect. Could you hand me those gloves?"

The cannon plug connector for the satcom antenna was easy to reach, and Dan looked up to find Carol once again in position, leaning down through the hatch as he held onto the lead.

"Tell Jerry I'm ready to disconnect this antenna, but if we're under someone's active control, like a remotely piloted vehicle, this could be a big risk."

She disappeared for a few moments then reappeared, nodding essentially upside down as she stuck her head down far enough to be heard.

"Dan, he says we need to take the risk. Be ready to reconnect it if something bad happens, but go ahead and disconnect now."

"Okay." He glanced at his watch, which was showing exactly 0252 Zulu.

Building 4-104, Peterson Air Force Base, Colorado Springs (0252 Zulu)

Colonel Dana Baumgartner yanked the phone to his ear on the first ring. The discovery of what appeared to be both the lock and unlock codes in Gail Hunt's classified office safe had precipitated a mad scramble to upload the unlock sequence and open the fiber optic channel to NSA's computers, a process that required a maddeningly lengthy series of steps that had taken the better part of an hour. No way, Dana thought, could anyone have accidentally triggered that satellite array. Sabotage was the only answer.

"The unlock code is just about to go up, sir, on your order."

"Do it! Now! Are you sure it's the right sequence?"

There was a telling hesitation. "No, sir, we're not. It's our best guess, based on Gail's notes."

"Had she changed the numbers before?"

"Yes. Often. For security."

"Blast the disconnect code out there, and let's hope it's the right one."

"Yes sir. Transmission in sixty seconds, and we think we now have the Med covered."

Aboard Pangia Flight 10 (0254 Zulu)

Dan held the two halves of the connector and hesitated, wondering whether there was any other aspect he hadn't considered.

A fleeting memory of an impromptu lecture he had once given to his employees in the early days of his company came out of nowhere, an admonition for them to listen to intuition, but he couldn't tell whether it was intuition or the shock of the aircraft's earlier reaction to the pulled relay that was staying his hand.

Is there any reason I can think of why we'd want to maintain this connection? Somewhere there seemed to be an answer to that question, but he couldn't get his mind around it, whatever it was. Something was definitely tugging at him, yet the logic was inescapable: If someone was controlling them from below, this would solve the problem!

Dan took a deep breath and pulled the two halves apart, totally isolating the satcom receiver.

CHAPTER THIRTY-EIGHT

Andrews Air Force Base, Maryland (10:20 p.m. EST / 0320 Zulu)

Essentially, Lieutenant Colonel Don Danniher realized, he was flying the instrument approach solo.

A cold drizzle made the landing at Andrews a bit more challenging than he had expected, and the presence of a totally preoccupied general in the left seat hadn't made it any easier. Not that he minded, necessarily. He was well aware of the high stakes and the dilemma that had his boss wholly distracted and tied in knots.

The staff car Sharon Wallace had ordered for the general had pulled up moments after they'd braked to a halt on the transient ramp, but the destination General Wriggle was going to give the driver was one of the bits of information Don assumed neither he nor Sharon Wallace had any immediate need to know.

Paul Wriggle threw off his shoulder straps and seatbelt and disappeared wordlessly into the jet's main cabin to change into his air force uniform. Sharon had already descended the Gulfstream's stairs to tell the driver the general would be a few minutes in coming. She returned to the jet then, standing in the entry space behind the cockpit as Don emerged.

"How are you doing?" he asked, knowing well the question had more depth than the words alone would indicate.

She responded with a strained smile, glancing at the closed entry door to the cabin. "I'd feel a lot better if I knew Pangia was talking to their pilots with code in hand, so to speak."

Don Danniher nodded. "I agree."

"Can you talk to him?"

"He knows, Sharon."

"Of course he does, but … time is critical here. This feels like brinksmanship."

"You know what our legal constraints are on revealing any aspect of this program."

"Yes. I signed the same papers. Don, talk to him. Please!"

Danniher nodded and opened the cabin door, closing it behind him and slipping into a seat across from where the general was adjusting his tie.

"Don …"

"Sir?"

Paul Wriggle turned to look at his copilot, then pursed his lips and shook his head, deciding not to voice whatever he had been thinking, then changed his mind again and turned back.

"Check my math. That jet … *our* jet … has an hour and a half to go before reaching Tel Aviv."

Danniher checked his watch and nodded. "That's correct, as of the last position we had."

"How long have we been blasting the disconnect code?"

"The first transmission was at 0252 Zulu, about thirty minutes ago, with no answering transmission. We did trigger transmitters covering the Mediterranean, though."

"And we have the code now they can punch in manually, right?"

"Well … same caveat as before … it's what they found in Gail Hunt's notes. If there isn't a subsequent change, then that's it. Sharon put it on your iPad and in your briefcase, with full instructions."

"And we don't know whether anyone has direct radio or satellite contact with them? Right? Some way we could verbally pass the code and how to enter it?"

"No sir." Don shifted forward in the swivel chair. "And, sir, I know we discussed the fact that if we call Pangia directly to find out, they're not only going to want to know who's asking, but we may tip off every intelligence service listening to such a call, but …"

"That's right. That's why we're here in DC."

"Sir?"

"Don't ask," Wriggle said, pulling on his tunic and turning. "While I'm gone, fuel us up and get on the secure line back to Dana and the team, and call me the instant they get a confirming response from the jet … if they do."

"Yes, sir. But in regard to Pangia?"

"I've got their CEO's personal cell number, Don."

"Yes, sir, but about the possibility of direct contact with the aircraft, I think …"

"No calls to their Command Center yet, okay? But if you discover through any safe channel that the pilots are talking to someone on the ground … a line we can get to, even a VHF radio to one of the air traffic control facilities … let me know immediately and get all the information necessary to pass up to them."

He could see the troubled look on Danniher's face.

"What, Don?"

"Begging the general's pardon, sir, but may I speak very frankly?"

"You always have that authority. Go ahead."

"Sir, I know the stakes for us are critical, but I don't think we have the moral right to wait another minute if there's any way to get hold of that crew. We don't know whether our broadcasts will work or not, and …"

"I understand that, Don."

"But, General, every minute that passes that that crew has no control is another rise in international tension, and maybe even brinkmanship. I seriously urge you to make the call to Pangia right now. Sir."

Paul Wriggle sighed heavily and studied his shoes for

a few moments before meeting his executive officer's eyes again.

"Don, I don't have time to explain my full reasoning for delaying."

"My job is to point out …"

"Yes!" Paul replied, pointing his finger in an affirming gesture. "Yes, it is. And it is also your job to trust that your commander knows what he's doing."

I wish I could trust your decision not to warn the aircraft, Don thought to himself, forcing a nod.

Wriggle studied his eyes for a second. "Answered without enthusiasm, I see, but the orders stand. Understood?"

"Yes, sir."

Paul Wriggle slipped into the back seat of the nondescript town car and passed his destination to the master sergeant at the wheel of the staff car after asking his name and security clearance.

"Should I put the star flag on the front, General?"

"No, but thanks for asking. We want to keep this low key."

"Yes, sir."

He pulled out his cell phone and entered the required password before paging down to the phone number he was looking for. The line was answered on the second ring, and he gave his name and rank and an identifying digital "signature" code, waiting impatiently for the individual on the other end to acknowledge.

"We have you and the applicable protocols logged in, sir. How may I assist?"

"I will be at the west entrance in fifteen minutes. I need immediate access to my reporting authority. Highest priority code."

"You're certain, sir? Highest code? This is a busy evening."

"Yes. I'm sorry, but absolutely yes. On my authority and accountability."

"Yes, sir. Understood. An escort will be waiting."

He punched in a fast dial number then and waited until Colonel Baumgartner had come on the line back in Colorado Springs.

"What have you got, Dana?"

"A mixed bag, Paul. We haven't located Gail Hunt yet, but we got into her credit card account and found her last charge was for gasoline in Lyons, Colorado, which is a gateway to Estes Park."

"Nothing beyond that?"

"Nothing. Also, we've been blasting the unlock sequence on every network link we have, but we're getting no answering response, and just a minute before you called, I got the word that our conduit has shut down."

"Translate that, please."

"We … transmit the signal to an intermediate location that I think you know, and they boost it on an uplink, and from there it networks out. That primary server has been turned off, or at least is suddenly refusing our signal."

"Any ideas why?"

"Yes, sir. A few. None of them good. And at least one involves a project compromise."

"Okay. Keep trying. Dana, were any of us thinking that Gail had something to do with the aircraft switch?"

"I'd hate to think that, but she's the key, and without her, we don't even have a clue whether the codes we've been blasting are correct. Where the hell *is* she, you know? Disappearing the very day our airplane is pulled out of the desert doesn't sit well with me."

"On the outside chance that … well, she's involved, try

sending a picture of her to Ron Barrett, the owner of Mojave Aircraft … no, on second thought, don't."

"You mentioned Mojave … and that's becoming strange. We had a call from Ron Barrett for you, and he was about a millimeter from hysterical. He said two federal officers from the Transportation Security Administration had shown up there this afternoon to grill him and his lawyer, and the agents reportedly told Barrett that his employee … the one who made the mistake with our machine … was using an alias and now can't be found."

"*TSA*? What the hell would they …"

"Obviously not TSA."

"Oh. Of course. The Company?"

"CIA, yes."

"More likely DIA."

"No, Paul, it makes sense. One of our friendlies in the Beltway tipped me off an hour ago that Langley was kicking over trash cans looking for explanations, and supposedly the Situation Room has been lit up for this."

"A bit excessive, don't you think? Any direct bead on us?"

"Negative. Not so far."

Wriggle sighed, rubbing his forehead.

"I'm on the ground in the Beltway now. Where is our jet? I figured an hour and a half out of Tel Aviv."

"We concur, but it's slowed down."

"What? What do mean, 'slowed down'?"

"By over sixty knots, and before you ask, that's not explainable by winds at that altitude."

"Do you think the crew has retaken control?"

"Their heading is still the same, but the speed could indicate something. We're just not sure what. If they change course, however, depending on where they head, it could mean we're dealing with something entirely different."

"Tell me, Dana."

"Someone could be using our machine and our equipment as a shield for what they're really up to. You … *do* know former Prime Minister Moishe Lavi is aboard, right?"

"*What?* No!"'"

Dana Baumgartner filled in the details, and Paul Wriggle felt his head swimming.

"Oh, my dear God! No wonder the Company and the Situation Room is involved!"

"Does that … have a particular meaning to you, Paul? That Lavi is aboard?"

"At the very least it means the diplomatic explosiveness of this is far beyond anything I imagined. Good lord! Okay, Dana, I'd better ring off for the moment."

"I'll call the minute we get anything new."

"Yes. Please."

He punched the disconnect and sighed, hesitating in deep thought for what seemed like a very long time, before making the decision and pulling out a folded note from his shirt pocket. Don was right, he thought. Further hesitation was unsupportable. He carefully punched in the telephone number on the note and triggered the call, wondering how in hell he was going to verbally navigate the razor edge he would need to walk. He glanced at his watch, calculating the time zone change to Chicago, and almost missed the answering voice on the other end.

"Hello?"

"General Rick Hastings, please," he said.

"This is Rick Hastings. Who is this?"

"Paul Wriggle, Rick. One of your classmates from undergraduate pilot training."

"Hey, Paul! Kinda late for a telephone reunion, don't cha think? But it's good to hear from you. What's up? I assume you're not calling to chat about the Cubbies?"

Paul chucked. "I would *never* chat about the … God, you never give up on the Cubs, do you?"

"Of course not! That's what sets Cubs fans apart. Eternal mindless optimism. So what's on your mind, Paul?"

"Short and sweet, okay?"

"Of course."

"First, I'm still on active duty. I'm a two star now, heading a program I can't discuss. I know we haven't talked since you retired as a three star, and I apologize for never formally congratulating you on becoming CEO of Pangia. But that's the subject: Pangia. You have an airplane in trouble, I may have the solution, but flag rank officer to flag rank officer, I need your immediate assistance and an almost complete absence of questions about how I know what I know."

Paul could hear Hastings changing hands and almost dropping the receiver.

"Holy moly, Paul! That's quite a preamble."

"I know it."

"Well, I clearly have the fiduciary loyalty to this company to consider now."

"We're flag rank, Rick. That never changes. Remember the prime directive about joining the star club? Although I shouldn't have to mention it."

"No, you shouldn't, Paul. A bit rude, I'd say, but I'll hear you out."

"Can I get some assurance?"

"Assurance? I'll do the right thing for our service, and our country, Paul. You don't have to ask for that."

"Very well."

"What is it, man?"

"Do you have any communication with your flight crew?"

"No. We did, sporadically, via a handheld satellite phone, but we think they ran out of battery. We know they'll call back if they can."

"So there's no current means to relay something to them? Not even ACARS?"

"Not that I know of. Why?"

"I've got a code sequence, Rick. If we can get one of the pilots to punch it into what would probably appear to be a dead flight management computer, they'll probably get back complete control."

There was a chilling silence on the other end.

"Paul, are you telling me our service is screwing around with that airplane?"

"No! Absolutely not!" Paul Wriggle said, suppressing the small, burning kernel of doubt in his gut that he had a bead on everything that was happening. "What's happened is a complete electronic accident."

"You know something about this substituted airplane, don't you? I just found out a half hour ago."

"The aircraft swap was a total accident, Rick. Yes, that's my bird, and she has some special equipment I can't admit exists."

"Well, buddy, the whole fucking world is liable to hear about it now!"

"Maybe, maybe not. But I think I have the code that, if punched in, returns the damned thing to normal. If we can get it to the pilots without broadcasting a hint of an explanation …"

"Jesus, I don't believe I'm hearing this! You know how many passengers are aboard that flight?"

"Yes, and one in particular, whose presence makes getting this solved supercritical. No questions, Rick. We can sort it out later. Can you get to the pilots?"

Another long silence and a deep sigh as Paul noticed the Washington Monument passing off to the left.

"I'll throw that question back to our operations center.

As far as I know, we've lost all satellite contact, ACARS telemetry, and sat phone, as I told you. I don't know what else we can do? But what's the bloody number?"

It was Paul Wriggle's turn to sigh. The cell phone was in the open, a non-secure channel, but it was too late to kvetch about that now. They could always change the code in future versions.

"You use the MDCU, the Multifunction Display Control Unit keypad. Select 1 Right, and twelve boxes will open. Type into scratch pad the twelve-digit number sequence I'm going to give you, then line select 1 Right, putting the numbers into boxes. Then select 1 Right again to activate. He read the twelve-digit sequence and forced a read back, stopping himself from mentioning the fact that they'd been blasting the code all over the planet with no response.

"This will do it? Just this?"

"Yes. But, Rick, a very large warning. It has to be entered with absolute precision. After three wrong entries, it permanently locks out the computers."

"Okay. I'm on it. You realize the questions are going to come like a fire hose, and I can't stop all of them?"

"Yes. Please do your best. I'll call back in a little while. I promise you a full explanation. Just … no time now."

He punched off the phone, aware that the destination was just ahead, and he fumbled around in his back pocket for the appropriate ID, preoccupied with the question of whether he had just committed a federal felony.

CHAPTER THIRTY-NINE

Situation Room, The White House (10:20 p.m. EST / 0320 Zulu)

The significance of the terse little conference in the corridor was not lost on the director of the Defense Intelligence Agency. Major General Richard Penick knew CIA Director James Bergen and his deputy, Walter Randolph, only too well, and trusted neither. Sharing a routine Senate grilling with Bergen every now and then as marginally-trusted intelligence community leaders was part of the job. But the multiyear ferocity of the food fight over which agency should control the nation's human spies, cryptically referred to as HUMINT, was making blood enemies out of formerly respectful rivals, until it had become almost an intelligence civil war.

It was especially interesting, Penick thought, that Walter Randolph and James Bergen were so engrossed in their private little exchanges, they hadn't even noticed him brushing past with a small wave.

General Penick moved into the Situation Room and nodded to the civilian aide who'd accompanied him, primarily to watch for incoming messages, but there was no question that she was also there for appearances: The director of DIA, and a three star general at that, should never be seen without at least one aide. If that wasn't written as a rule someplace, Penick thought, it damn well should be.

The woman shook her head ever so slightly to indicate there was nothing new to report, and that irritated him all the more. To have a major potential intelligence challenge with Israel and Iran occur simultaneously with one of his agents appearing to go silent was upsetting. Whatever was happening, it also involved the NSA, and it was a sure bet his CIA counterparts knew something and were waiting with barely concealed glee to blindside him.

Penick took his seat, trying hard to maintain a smile but hating this aspect of the job. In the military, blindsiding a major general was a career-ending move. In the civilian intelligence community, it was known as sport.

The president had become fond of walking briskly ahead of his aides, advisors, and body man and breezing into meetings with little or no warning, which he did now, loosening the bow tie on his tux as he rounded the corner. There had been too many occupants of the Oval Office, Walter thought to himself, who had no military experience and had been too tentative and wildly out of step with reality, but the current chief executive was not one of them, and it was deeply comforting to know the man understood the parameters—and the limits—of both military force and intelligence.

"Okay, folks. What's the status of the Pangia flight?"

One of the national security advisor's deputies ran through the basics: Aircraft still not under crew control but a strange 360-degree turn, as well as a significant slowing.

"Okay. James? Walter? What about Moishe Lavi? Is he just along for the ride? Or is this something more nefarious?"

Walter Randolph wanted badly to get to his feet and command the room, but it would be seen as inappropriate and an upstaging of the president, so he remained in place and substituted a few silent moments of referring to his papers before looking up and locking eyes with POTUS, then beginning to speak.

"First, a few new discoveries. The Airbus A330 that's causing the problems does not belong to Pangia." Walter quickly outlined the switched aircraft and the airline's utter shock at the news, the missing, bogus employee in Mojave, and the allegation that former Prime Minister Lavi may be dying of pancreatic cancer. "Mr. President, with all this, we increasingly suspect the possibility of a covert op being run on behalf of, or even directly by, Mr. Lavi, and one originating at least in part within our borders."

"Good lord! How probable is that?"

"Well, sir, the facts are lining up a bit, and the motive is very clear, if Lavi is involved. First, the missing Mojave employee. We believe he is actually a well-known ex-pat operative who at one time or another has worked for a half dozen agencies, including the CIA. His real name is William Piper. His aliases are too many to mention, which is something for a man in his late forties. He looks like a GQ model, and we figure he has a very good plastic surgeon somewhere keeping him young. We think we've picked up his tracks in Tulsa where the airplane was prepared for commercial service the following week, and we also have reason to suspect he has a confederate, some sort of mole, in Pangia Airways. The owner of this mysterious, identical airplane that was pawned off on Pangia as theirs … an airplane which has to have been fitted clandestinely with some sort of electronics a regular Airbus would never have … is a secretive company in Colorado Springs, which is obviously a front for someone—and not CIA, I hasten to assure you. This outfit bought the subject A330 new off the line in Toulouse and had it sitting in storage long enough to modify it for precisely this mission."

"A front organization in the Springs?" the President asked, looking startled.

"They're incorporated as Air Lease Solutions, but we can't find any evidence of a single lease they've done as yet, and they only own one other airplane, a Boeing 737, also new. Of course there hasn't been enough time to track down any of their principals, but we're working on it as fast as possible. Considering the fact that Piper once also worked for Mossad some fifteen years ago, and the fact that he was last supposed to be retired from being a spook and living in Haifa with his Israeli girlfriend, this fits most of the fingerprint requirements for a carefully planned operation: They acquire and extensively modify the electronics on the aircraft and wait for the right moment to substitute it for one of Pangia's identical airplanes, knowing that the A330 would most likely end up on the long distance, round-the-world run … especially if a confederate was doing the ship routing in Chicago. Once the aircraft is on the way, Mr. Lavi buys a ticket … which he did, in fact, buy at the last minute … and once they're airborne, either take control of the aircraft through an installed package of electronics triggered by an external, probably satellite-fed signal, or internally. It's not impossible that Mr. Lavi himself is controlling the aircraft from his first class seat. Maybe with a special laptop the aircraft is programmed to obey. Mix in an unknown number of sympathizers and coconspirators in the IDF and the Israeli Air Force ready to overstate the case and push everyone into hair-trigger tension, make sure Iran is informed very early in the process of who's aboard and what might be happening, perhaps call in a sleeper agent in Tehran to whip up paranoid hysteria at a critical moment among the top military leaders, and you have the makings of a manufactured disaster."

The president's hand was out in a stop gesture. "Whoa! All this just to provoke a response from Tehran? The mullahs could just order the plane shot down!"

"Very true, and if Flight 10 gets close to the border, Iran will undoubtedly launch their fighters to do exactly that, and it's likely they will be flying toward an airliner escorted by Israeli fighters with hair-trigger rules of engagement. Also, as we all know, there are factions in Tehran who were so outraged by Lavi's quest for a first strike, they want the same thing launched by their side and, of course, we must never forget that power in Tehran rests in the hands of people openly dedicated to wiping Israel off the map and evaporating all the inhabitants. Any way you cut it, you have at the very least a potentially escalating confrontation. This jet is a spark flying toward a pool of gasoline."

"But we don't know if Lavi is a passenger or a progenitor?"

"Yes sir. And, we don't know what aces Lavi may have hidden up his operational sleeve, if this is all his doing."

"What is Israel saying?"

"Precisely what you would expect, Mr. President. They are on alert; their command and control apparatus is on line in The Hole in Tel Aviv. We also know that the new prime minister was there a few hours ago and is fully engaged with the civilian decision-makers who would have to be in agreement for any nuclear usage, and even though we are not supposed to know this about our allies' preparedness, they have pilots waiting now in their cockpits, with the fighters fully armed. We assume the missile crews are on hair-trigger alert as well."

"I see," the president said, leaning on both arms, his hands planted on the table. "Anything else? Not that that's not enough."

"Yes, sir." Walter glanced at the DIA chief with a carefully forced, neutral expression. "There is one thing we haven't had an opportunity to share with General Penick, since we picked it up just before you got here, but we have grave concerns that part of this clandestine operation, whoever is running it, may have involved our own NSA in some way, and we think DIA may have had someone looking into this already."

James Bergen watched a homicidal look flicker across General Penick's face before the DIA chief caught himself and nodded evenly.

"Yes, sir, we had one of our men deployed to NSA this morning because we detected some strange satellite signals and wondered if they were military and we wanted their assistance."

"So, what did he find?"

"We … don't know yet, sir, because it appears he's … suddenly dropped off the radar. We don't know if he's refusing to come in, or why he's gone silent, or who he was talking to at NSA, if he even got there."

"You've misplaced one of your agents?"

"Misplaced is a bit harsh, Mr. President. We're quite concerned about him."

One of the presidential aides quietly appeared at the president's side and at his nod spoke a few words in his ear too low to be heard.

The president nodded in response and returned his gaze first to General Penick, and then to James Bergen. "James, what do you suspect? Forget this parochial shit and spit it out."

"Very well. First, since we know the aircraft was operating normally until halfway into its flight and then suddenly turned around without the pilots' knowledge, and in addition the aircraft or something in the aircraft's systems locked the crew out of being able to control their plane, the highest likelihood is that the triggering event was a radioed order of some sort, which could have been transmitted via satellite, a ground station, or even from the cabin of the aircraft. So, if there *was* such a signal, since DIA was already looking into strange signals *found* by someone at NSA, then my immediate concern would be knowing precisely what NSA discovered, and, quite frankly, getting assurance that NSA hadn't somehow been involved directly or otherwise in transmitting anything. I have to add that this was news to us that DIA and NSA were looking into strange signals."

"My God, you're suspecting a covert operation involving the NSA supporting Moishe Lavi?" the president fell silent, looking, Walter thought, suddenly a bit chalky. Just as quickly he recovered and stood up. "So what are your recommendations, gentlemen?"

"We think," James Bergen began, "… that Israel may need some steady words of caution and calm from you, Mr. President, if the scenario doesn't change."

"How would it change?"

"The crew may regain control. It appears they have partially done so with the speed and at one point they did a complete circle."

"But they're still headed for Tehran."

"No sir. Tel Aviv. But there are two basic scenarios, both with a bad flight plan. One, Lavi isn't in control, this *is* an accident somehow, but when the airplane arrives over Tel Aviv, instead of disconnecting, it will mindlessly turn to go back to its point of origin before Tel Aviv, which was Hong Kong, which means straight over Iran and just south of Tehran. Second, this *is* a Lavi operation, in which case, the aircraft will also inevitably turn and head for Tehran."

"There's not a lot of airspace between Tel Aviv and Tehran that a 500-mile-per-hour jet can't cover rapidly," the president mused. "About 600 miles, I figure. How long before they're over Israel?"

"One hour, sir."

"And we still can't talk to them?"

"No."

The president was nodding. "I know Moishe reasonably well. He's a egomaniacal bastard, but it would be consistent with his personality, whether he's dying or committing suicide, to do it with a full professorial explanation. If that's what's really happening, I promise you he's got a satellite phone ready to connect when he's ready to speak. I'll be back down in forty-five minutes, or sooner if you need me. James? You and General Penick here pull out all the stops to find out what that phone number is and be ready to connect me to him if it's humanly possible to do so. And … keep me posted on your missing man, General. That's worrisome."

"Yes, sir."

The group got to their feet as the president left, and General Penick leaned close to his civilian aide's ear as he leaned down to pick up his briefcase.

"You were talking to our operations team a minute ago?"

"Yes, sir."

"Get them back on the line and tell them to lock down this city until they find that goddamned agent, Bronson."

CHAPTER FORTY

Aboard Pangia 10 (0320 Zulu)

"Nothing new happening up here!" Carol yelled, and Dan nodded as he sat on the floor of the electronics bay, glancing at the passenger who had been invaluable in helping solve an impossible riddle.

Frank nodded, too, his smile quite thin, the tension starkly transmitted by the tightness of his facial muscles. Small talk was difficult in the constrained space with the noise levels of cooling fans and slipstream, and Dan averted his gaze back to the strange cabinet, determined to give it a few more minutes before deciding precisely where they were in the process. The satcom antenna leads were dangling loose where he'd left them nearly a half hour before. No further orders could be received from anywhere as long as those two halves were disconnected, if there had indeed been any external control to begin with.

But that same nagging feeling that he hadn't thought this through enough was rising again, the same feeling he had when playing chess and a gleeful move to place his opponent in check was about to turn out to be premature—the opponent poised to take advantage of the one move he'd failed to consider.

Why am I assuming there is a person on the other side of this nightmare? Dan thought, wondering if the personification of a nemesis wasn't obscuring some larger truth. *Why would anyone or any entity do this to us?*

Carol's head had disappeared from the hatch, and Dan found it suddenly unsettling to not see her there. He had all but ignored the beauty of her auburn hair cascading down through the hatch, so great was his forced discipline to concentrate on the nightmare at hand. *Nothing wrong with concentrating! We're in trouble. No time for thinking sex-related thoughts*, although she was a very attractive woman. But here he was facing an uncertain future, his mind suddenly grasping for relief—something good to think about—and Carol's femininity triggered a moment of regret that he'd paid far too little attention to his love life in the past few years.

My alleged love life, he thought, triggering a random pain that echoed back to his teens and threatened to open doors of longing he'd long since tried to nail shut. He forcibly switched off those thoughts and turned his mind back to the life-threatening dilemma at hand.

There's always a reason for anything that takes time and money, and whoever built this thing obviously has a huge investment in it working. But to do what? Kill us?

Dan looked at the cabinet again. Obviously designed to switch off the cockpit and hand the control to … someone? What if, he mused, it was a two-stage deal? First, remove control from the cockpit, then stage two, switch the active control to someone on the ground through satellite interface? What if only stage one had occurred, and that had been an accident?

And what if someone below was trying to "fix" that mistake right now and reverse stage one?

The two disconnected ends of the satellite communications antenna were suddenly mocking him, and Dan called Frank out of his brief reverie as he pointed to them.

"Follow my logic. We disconnected and nothing has changed for a half hour. That proves we weren't under active control, so it should be okay to reconnect, *especially* if someone below accidentally triggered this thing and might try to use a satcom signal to reverse their mistake."

"So … reconnect?" Frank asked.

"Yes. Why not?"

"How much time do we have?"

"Before what?"

"Before running out of gas."

"Maybe two hours. Maybe a bit more."

"Then we should do it quickly," Frank said.

"Agreed," Dan replied, adjusted the gloves, and grabbed the two ends, screwing them back into uniformity.

When the job was complete, Dan sat back, aware Frank was looking at him.

"What?"

"That was precisely my question, Captain. What do we do now?" Frank asked.

"We start experimenting again and yanking relays, as fast as we can."

CHAPTER FORTY-ONE

Silver Springs, Maryland (9:25 p.m. EST / 0325 Zulu)

"So where do we run to, Mr. Bond?" Jenny asked, only slightly amused with her reference.

Will Bronson had been all but hunched over the steering wheel, guiding them into the night traffic southbound toward the heart of DC and obviously deep in thought. He looked over now almost in lack of recognition, a smile returning uneasily to his face as his eyes focused on her.

"Sorry. I was concentrating on where to go."

"Any Starbucks will do," Jenny said, not in jest.

"Too public, and a public server will be child's play to trace."

"Who cares, Will. We're running out of time. If I had a portable hot spot … wait, I *do!"*

"Jenny, we're being watched!"

"Okay, and I'm willing to trade my damned job for a planeload of passengers. Aren't you?"

"That's not the point."

"What *is* the point, Will? I think I have the code figured out, but we need to be broadcasting it everywhere. I have only one transponder I know that might be usable. Who else can we turn to?" Jenny fumbled in her purse, pulled out her smartphone, and worked the screen to trigger its internal hotspot.

He was shaking his head and breathing a bit too hard, and Jenny heard the indecision in his voice.

"I think I know where to go for a secure channel, but … you're right about the lack of time."

"Then hush up for a moment and let me work this," she replied, head down, making a tiny mental note that "hush up" might be too Southern a way to shush a spy. Then again, he was acting less and less like a serenely confident operative.

She pulled her laptop out of its case and fired it up, connecting to the cell phone's Wi-Fi channel, then retracing her previous steps to the entry portal of the satellite array she had previously tried. She entered the appropriate string of keystrokes and tried to suppress the urge to scream "Dammit!" when the entry denial included confirmation that her previous attempt had never made it through their firewalls.

"This isn't working, Will," she said in disgust, tucking back an errant cascade of hair behind her ear.

"Okay, then we'll have to find that secure entry point."

"No. No, you don't understand," she said, turning to him. "I only had one satellite channel, and it won't let me in. We don't just need a place to get into the Internet, we need a transponder or about a dozen of them. I think I'd better call Seth at home, and in the clear."

"No!"

"Why not? No way he's the bad guy. I know you can't guarantee that, but I can."

"You can't call him in the clear, Jenny. And I promise you he doesn't have the horsepower to intervene and find a transponder for us."

"Yeah? Well, Sherlock, find me someone who does, or I see no choice but to try."

"I'm working on it," he replied, negotiating Dupont Circle and steering them down Massachusetts Avenue.

Quietly, she opened a direct to text program and typed the most innocuous message she could think of.

"Seth, I'm with Will and have unlock solution for P10, but one hour left and can't broadcast. Need advice! Jen"

Jenny hit the send button and simultaneously collapsed the program just as an oath reached her from the driver's seat.

"Oh, crap!"

"What?"

Will Bronson was staring intently into the rearview mirror.

"We've got a tail."

"What? Really?" Jenny whirled around in the seat, her eyes jumping through a series of headlights behind them, none of them close enough to finger as a tail.

"I don't see who you're talking about."

"He's back there. Came around the circle trying to stay aloof. Obviously a solo, not a team, which is good."

"You're sure?"

"I'm rather well trained in this, and high performance driving response," he shot back, eyes darting between the crowded street ahead and the rearview mirror before screeching into a sudden left turn across traffic and darting into a side street, almost losing control in the process and barely missing a parked SUV.

"JESUS, Will!"

"Sorry."

"What are you afraid of, anyway? That they'll shoot us?"

"We need a portal and a transponder, and being in any sort of custody won't achieve that in time," he replied.

"Custody? What the hell do you mean custody?" she said, hanging onto the handgrip above the passenger window as he accelerated through the back streets.

"Not now. Gotta concentrate."

Once more she turned to search behind them, seeing nothing that would qualify as a chase car, yet Will was throwing them through desperate maneuvers. Slowly, a rising tide of doubt began to trickle into the corners of her mind, where uncertainty had already created a void. The sudden departure from the safe house, no overheard voices on his phone calls, now a phantom chasing them, and a potentially precious cargo she couldn't deliver.

There was a tiny vibration in her hand and she looked down at her phone's screen to see an answer from Seth:

Company says Will is rogue and dangerous. Get away now, call me ASAP! Use any excuse.

CHAPTER FORTY-TWO

Situation Room, The White House (10:28 p.m. EST / 0328 Zulu)

"Sir, Piper may be in DC right now."

Walter Randolph switched the handset to his other ear and let Jason Duke's words coalesce.

"Talk to me, Jason."

"We know DIA is searching for their man who was at NSA this morning, the one we've wondered about. You said DIA briefed the president someone had gone rogue, and we think it's the same guy, named Will Bronson. We don't have much on him. If he's an operative, he's a new one or we haven't been watching appropriately."

"How do Bronson and Piper match up, Jason?"

"There's an NSA woman … a Jenny Reynolds … involved somehow, an analyst, purely a desk type. She and Bronson are together. Apparently Bronson was working with her earlier at NSA headquarters."

"Okay."

"But we think the real Bronson never made it to NSA. God knows where he is, but we think this Jenny Reynolds woman is with William Piper and has no idea who he is. "

"Why?"

"Sorry?"

"Why would Piper be spending time with her? Are they lovers?"

"Could be, I suppose, although our source is her boss and he doesn't think she'd ever met Bronson or Piper before. But here's the thing. If this is Piper, and he is behind whatever satellite transmission triggered an internal hijack of that aircraft, and if he's working for Lavi, the last thing he wants is someone figuring out how to send a countermanding code and turn it off. We're trying to find Bronson, looking in his apartment, car, et cetera. Highly likely we'll find a professionally disposed of body. Meanwhile DIA is going nuts and whipping everyone into a find-Bronson frenzy. We're afraid they'll shoot him if they find him."

"Purposefully?"

"No, sir. Overreaction. Even the police are involved now."

"And you think the Reynolds woman knows that code?"

"We think she has the ability to figure it out. He's probably protecting his interests. She has no idea what he does to people who are no longer of use to him."

"I've seen the file. But what if she's his confederate? What if she's the means of sending the triggering message that started all this?"

"Her boss doesn't think that's possible."

"Right … like every serial killer. The neighbors swear he was a great guy."

"In any event, we need to find them fast, before DIA kills them both and we lose any answers."

"Any track on where they are?"

"Yes and no. In DC at some apartment earlier tonight, but they left that location. DIA and we are bumping into each other trying to pick up the trail."

"Jason, what are the chances the woman really does have the key? The unlock code, so to speak."

"Her boss says she's the best, and if anyone can figure it out, she can."

Walter rubbed his eyes as his deputy waited for the inevitable thought process to end with an order or observation.

"Okay, you've been in the thick of the chase for hours. Pull back and grab some perspective. We have a phantom operative who planted himself for, what, six months in

Mojave just to dispatch the wrong aircraft? And now we think he's down to the wire trying to prevent the undoing of his dastardly deeds, right?"

"Essentially."

"Jason, could Piper have done this all alone?"

"Sir, what I can't grasp is what was engineered into that airliner that he could activate that would lock out the pilots. I don't know airplanes, but that seems impossible."

"Let's say he could, technically. For the sake of argument. Could he have pulled all this off solo?"

"Maybe. Probably. Piper is clearly one of the best. He's almost a legend, and we never expected to see him back stateside. We're thinking that with six months of uninterrupted access to the airplane his employer thought was sealed and mothballed, he could have actually installed something very complex. He's an electrical engineering graduate, you know, with a lot of practical experience."

"I missed that. From Cal Tech, too, correct?"

"Yes. And we also know he's a Lavi loyalist, because it was Moishe Lavi, while he was running Mossad a few years back, who set Piper up in luxury with all the females he wanted after he did God knows what for them. No, he's a loyalist, and if this was planned as Lavi's last play, you can bet Piper's a part of it. But we'll have to find bodies to make this scenario real. Where's the real Bronson? Where's the real Mojave employee?"

"Where will Miss Reynolds end up? And maybe more."

"Yes, sir."

"Call me the moment you've got a bead on him, and we'll share with DIA."

"Sir, we figure those pilots are just a hair more than an hour away from Tel Aviv. Just so you know."

"Understood."

The Oval Office

Flanked and trailed by the same advisors and Secret Service agents, the president negotiated the relatively short distance back to the ground floor without discussion, waiving off his secretary and the waiting chief of staff as he pushed through the door into the most famous office on the planet, closing it carefully behind him as he looked at the lone visitor and shook his head ruefully.

"Jesus Christ, Paul! So it *was* you."

"Mr. President, I'm afraid so."

"When I heard the pilots couldn't control the aircraft, I thought of you, but when I heard Colorado Springs was the aircraft's home, the coincidence was too much. But then again, one of my most trusted generals would never let anything like this occur. Right?"

"I'm very sorry, Mr. President."

The president crossed to the desk and consulted a folder before looking up again.

"What the hell happened, Paul? You wouldn't believe the briefing I received downstairs a little while ago."

"I probably would, sir."

The president motioned him to the couch as he sat heavily into an adjacent captain's chair.

"Give me the basics."

Paul Wriggle quickly summarized the series of disastrous discoveries starting with the Airbus A330 ending up as a commercial flight, the efforts to broadcast a disconnect signal, the complete mystery of how the cockpit lockout happened, and his call to Rick Hastings.

"Dammit!"

"Yes, sir."

"Hastings doesn't have to keep quiet."

"I couldn't wait."

"I can see that. That briefing I just received makes me think there's a high possibility Lavi is behind this. Of course, our spooks down there think your outfit may be a front for Lavi."

"Well, you certainly know better, Mr. President."

"Yes, I do. But a black project has to stay invisible, and we just dropped the cloak. By the way, have you ever heard of a William Piper?"

"No, sir. Why?"

"He's the guy who apparently sent the wrong airplane to Pangia … your airplane."

"He's the one working for Mojave Aircraft?"

"So I'm told. I don't know whether they're sure of this, but if it is the guy the CIA thinks it is, he's a former Mossad operative."

"Oh, dear God! I only just found out from my team on the way here that Lavi's on board. I … we have no idea how anyone could have known about our aircraft, let alone where it was. I guess it is possible that we could have run afoul of a clandestine operation. One of our key people has gone missing, a lady named Gail Hunt, and she's the one developing the lock and unlock codes."

"One of DIA's men has gone missing as well here in DC, just since this morning."

"Really?"

"Paul, what do we need to do right this moment to get those people out of danger?"

Paul Wriggle sighed and shook his head. "I honestly can't think of anything we're *not* doing, especially after my call to Hastings. Undoubtedly he'll try to get that code to his crew."

The president was up and pacing in front of the large desk.

"What if I order NSA to use everything they've got to help get a signal out?"

"That could help. We don't have much time, but if they could trigger a broadcast on a transponder that we haven't been using that covers the Med, it could work."

The President yanked up the phone and ordered the call. When finished, he turned back to Paul Wriggle.

"The Company thinks NSA itself may have been co-opted and at least someone there is working for Lavi. Any chance they could be right?"

"I … have no way of knowing. During normal tests, we send the activation signal …"

"The one that causes the aircraft to lockout the cockpit?"

"Yes. If there was an airborne aircraft with the system operational, we would send that signal to NSA by fiber optics and they broadcast it automatically worldwide. It's very hard to detect … we built the network carefully. All the pathways and protocols were set up to use without human intervention from their end. Like an open channel we could trigger at will. Someone at NSA probably caught wind of that and knowing nothing about the project, assumed a breach.

The president was nodding. "Somehow DIA was alerted to your signals and got suspicious."

"Mr. President, whatever signal activated the aircraft systems, it did *not* come from us. At least, not volitionally."

"Which brings us right back to the possibility that our Israeli friend *could* be behind this, which means Moishe Lavi has the upper hand." The president sighed deeply, his eyes studying the carpet.

"What can I do, Mr. President, considering that hara-kiri is not part of our culture?"

A brief smile flickered across the president's face. "I wasn't going to offer you a ceremonial sword, Paul. We'll piece this together and the future of the program, if any, later.

Right now we've got to restore control to that crew, or, in worst case, stop Iran from taking the bait."

"Anyone in Tehran you can reason with?"

"What are you now, auditioning a standup act?" the president said with no intent at humor. "Yes, there are a few sane people with official positions in Tehran, but not when it comes to something like this. We're talking North Korean paranoia fueled by religious myopia. And … when it comes to staying Israel's hand … forget it. When they're huddled in The Hole, they know precisely where the trip wires are, and when one is touched, that's the ball game for restraint. Think Bebe Netanyahu and his relentless pursuit of Hamas even with the world yelling at him to stand down."

"Got it."

"No, everything rides on returning control to those pilots. You built the box. Something unplanned turned on the box. How else can it be turned off?"

"Mr. President, there … might be one other avenue."

"For God's sake man, tell me!"

"But it would involve the Israeli Air Force, and telling them far more than we want them to know."

CHAPTER FORTY-THREE

The Kirya, Tel Aviv, Israel (5:45 a.m. local / 0345 Zulu)

The very fact that he'd had to return to the Hole had elevated Prime Minister Gershorn Zamir's blood pressure, but the evolving seriousness of Tehran's reaction had sobered virtually everyone in the leadership of Israel.

Gershorn nodded at Lieutenant General Yossi Alon, acknowledging the briefing just completed, the details of which were still ringing in his head: Tehran already putting its forces on alert, constant intelligence stream from the CIA, an urgent request for Mossad to confirm the whereabouts of a William Piper, who was considered to be an operative for Moishe Lavi, and, most importantly, there was the need for the prime minister to make a series of trigger-point decisions on how to intercept, handle, and perhaps terminate the flight of Pangia 10.

And now, suddenly, a call from the president of the United States.

Gershorn excused himself to an ante room to take the call, returning within a few minutes and settling into his chair once more with a cursory explanation.

"Expressions of concern, support, and deep worry that this man Piper may be the engine of Moishe Lavi's operation … if there is one," he said, looking around the room once more, locking eyes with everyone looking back at him. "Very well, I accept the general staff's recommendation. Launch our fighters; intercept and escort the oncoming flight from 200 miles out. Keep the radio channels open to this room, with any order to bring them down coming from me alone. Our pilots must understand this." He paused before speaking the appropriate code words necessary to take the defensive forces and nuclear armament to pre-launch readiness. With all elements of the civilian chain of command converging on the Hole, any launch decision could be validated and executed within seconds. The scope of the response, if anything left a launching pad in Iran, was essentially his decision, and the mere possibility had roiled his considerable stomach. It felt like Armageddon was upon them.

CHAPTER FORTY-FOUR

Aboard Pangia 10 (0345 Zulu)

Jerry had called Dan and Frank out of the electronics bay for a quick strategy conference, fully including Bill Breem, who had been extraordinarily docile. Josh Begich was still sitting in the copilot's seat looking very young and very frightened, with Tom Wilson, the relief copilot, standing behind him.

Jerry, by contrast, had shed his previous panic and was becoming appropriately analytical and in command, Dan thought. The last PA announcement Jerry had made had bordered on the masterful: calmly and professionally filling the passengers in on precisely what had happened when the aircraft did a complete 360 after scaring everyone to death with the sudden sideslip.

The captain looked at his small team and nodded to Carol to squeeze in as well.

"Okay, guys, I've slowed us about as much as I think is safe at this altitude, and that's bought us some time, but … we'll be over Tel Aviv in about an hour. We must … we absolutely must … regain control of this ship before then."

"And if we don't?" Frank Erlichman asked evenly.

"I'm not entertaining any negatives. You and Dan have worked wonders down there, but we have more to go. Any reason you shouldn't go back and start yanking everything in sight?"

Dan sighed, shaking his head. "I see no alternative."

"Nor do I," Frank added. "I'm glad to be able to help you. Help us, really."

Jerry glanced at Josh, whose eyes were turned toward the copilot's flight management computer. The screen was dark, but he was staring at it as if determined to wish it into phosphorescent life, as he randomly punched buttons.

"Josh? Are you with us?" Jerry asked. "You gave us some valuable input before."

The boy looked up and nodded without enthusiasm as his finger punched yet another button. "Yes."

"You okay, Josh?" Dan added, surprised when the boy met his gaze reluctantly, unable to hide a tear in his eye and nodding unconvincingly.

"What's the matter, Josh?"

"I don't want to die."

"Nor do we."

"I've … I've never even … you know."

"How old are you, Josh?"

"Fifteen. Well … fourteen, actually. Fifteen in two weeks."

"We'll get you back on the ground, Josh," Jerry said, feeling a chill climbing his spine for giving voice to what might well turn out to be a lie.

"And you *will* live to get laid, my friend," Dan added, trying to recall the last time he had immersed in such heavenly pleasures himself.

Carol was standing at the back of the cockpit and keeping an absolutely even expression, though Dan could almost *feel* her wanting to smile.

"Thanks," Josh replied, looking up as he punched yet another button on the multifunction display control, as unprepared as the rest of them for the Airbus to suddenly and smoothly roll into a thirty-degree right bank.

Jerry turned back forward in his chair, eyes scanning the instruments that had been lying to them for so many hours, then he looked at the whiskey compass. The attitude indicator was showing the turn, and suddenly the entire instrument display shifted around from the fictitious westbound course over the Atlantic to the same heading as the whiskey compass.

"What the hell!"

"Josh, what did you do?" Dan asked the boy, who was wide-eyed and scanning the keyboard he had essentially been playing with.

"I … I punched …"

"What did you punch? Do you remember?"

Josh nodded. The aircraft, still turning, was now more than forty-five degrees off the original heading and turning west.

"Here! I punched this key."

Dan leaned forward, eyes riveted on the key he was touching. "That's the execute button. The enter button. But do you recall what you punched before that?"

Josh was shook his head. "I was just pushing them at random because it … it felt good to control something."

"I get that. But try to recall what sequence. Were you doing numbers on the main pad or … or those squarish buttons along the edge of the screen?"

"The numbers. I remember putting in my phone number."

"Dan, we're still turning."

"Yeah, I see that."

"It might come back around to the same course again."

"Hopefully, not. Anywhere but back on that heading."

"Okay," Jerry said, turning to Josh. "Was it your entire phone number and then the execute key?"

"Yes, I … wanted to call home, you know."

"Got it," Jerry replied, feeling a deep pang of guilt for being up here while his wife and children were probably scared to death back home in Evanston. "Okay, write out that number. Dan, see if that could have been interpreted as latitude, longitude, or something, or maybe a compass heading."

"We've done a complete 180," Dan said, watching the progress. "And we're still turning."

"I think he typed in what the box thought were coordinates."

"Hell, Jerry, we didn't think the box might be on. The screen was dark …"

"Neither did I."

Josh handed over a slip of paper with eleven numbers.

"Much longer than a latitude and longitude," Dan added. "Here, punch in three digits, Josh. Punch zero-zero-five and enter."

Josh turned to the MDCU and entered the numbers, and they all held their breath, but the aircraft was still turning right, now less than ninety degrees from the original course.

"If this thing steadies out on the same course to Tel Aviv, then all we've done is delay things."

"But that's something! We just bought, what? Four minutes?"

"Yeah. Josh, punch in your entire phone number one more time and hit execute. Let's see if it does it again."

"Dan," Jerry interrupted, "Look at this! It's telling us the truth … the instruments, I mean."

"Try disconnecting autoflight," Dan said, holding his breath.

"Already did. Nothing. And the sidestick still doesn't work. But something's new."

The aircraft was leveling its wings now, and back on the previous course to Israel.

"Josh?" Jerry said. "Keep punching things and hitting execute, just … just write down what you're entering each time."

"Okay," Josh responded, turning back to the MDCU, visibly relieved to have a mission.

Dan took a loud breath. "Okay, meanwhile, Frank and I are going back down to start pulling relays, starting with anything autoflight related I can get my hands on."

First Class Cabin, Pangia Flight 10

Ashira Dyan was well aware of her conflicting loyalties: First, there was her lover and employer, Moishe Lavi, but she was with him, in part, because Mossad wanted her to be. And the broader intelligence mission of Mossad was in Israel's best interests. But precisely where did all those coincide and where did they clash?

She wished she could phone the one who had recruited her so long ago and ask the key question: Is this a coincidence, Moishe being on an electronically hijacked jet apparently headed for Tehran?

Let's not dance around this, Ashira, she could almost hear her handler say. *If the pilots are telling the truth, someone is controlling this airplane, and it has to be Moishe's doing.*

Indeed, what were the odds of an accidental presence?

And, she thought, *he's almost enjoying this!*

She knew him so well. He could be as inscrutable as a statue at times, but it was also true that he couldn't really hide deep upset from her entirely. There were always contradictory signs, as there were now. His refusal to let her volunteer their handheld satellite phone when the crew was begging for them was one, as well as his unusual reluctance to let her see what he had been writing so diligently on his laptop.

That feeling of apprehension again crept past her professional training.

So *what if he has engineered all of this, and is determined to start the war so we can finish it? If I could stop him, should I? If he's behind this, there will be many confederates on the ground, all of them working to make Israel's launch decision inescapable."*

She should confront him. But then he would merely deny

it, and she would be no closer to the truth. Same denial, same amused expression.

No, there seemed to be one choice left, and that was to somehow gain control of his laptop. If he'd used a trigger program to take over the aircraft, perhaps she could find it in time and undo it. She had most of his passwords.

The inevitable pragmatic realism that was the bedrock of her personality reasserted itself, as it always did. If he was in control on this aircraft, he would be expecting her to confront him, and the only way around his usually brilliant maneuvering would have to be complete surprise.

CHAPTER FORTY-FIVE

The White House (11:45 p.m. EST / 0345 Zulu)

Working from a tiny anteroom off the Oval Office, Paul Wriggle had a phone to each ear coordinating what the president had just approved: securing the Israeli Air Force's immediate assistance in passing the unlock code to Flight 10's computers.

"We can do that?" the president had asked. "You built that into the system?"

"Yes, but we've never tested it. It's an operational back door, a way of reaching the computers aboard our aircraft from a radio signal relayed through a fighter flying alongside, one with ultra-high frequency military range capability, which all of them have. With the proper gear, we could even fly the airliner from a second seat in such a fighter, but that was just a contingency. But what we have already built in is the ability to reach the computer and lock out the cockpit with a UHF transmission … and reverse it with the right codes."

"How fast? Does it take special equipment?"

"As Rube Goldberg as it sounds, sir, all it takes is using the keypad tones from a cell phone … just hold the cell phone's speaker against the pilot's microphone, and the all-important string of numbers can be transmitted over the UHF radio. Unlike their flight deck computer screen, you can try as many times as you need and it won't lock you out if the sequence is wrong. The downside is that we'd have to provide information that is technically illegal to discuss."

"Executive orders, Paul. Don't worry about giving the information to the Israelis. Get that arranged as fast as you can."

CHAPTER FORTY-SIX

Aboard Pangia 10 (0350 Zulu)

"Okay, guys, we've got about thirty minutes before we find out where we're going next."

Jerry Tollefson met the eyes of everyone in the crowded cockpit, including Carol and two of her flight attendants.

"I'll do another PA announcement as soon as I know whether we're turning or not, but in the meantime … if we can't regain control any other way and if we do turn in the wrong direction … I'm going to have everyone strap in and get ready for our last, best move."

"Jerry … Captain … we've got some seriously terrified people back there, including some of my crew. Please talk to them sooner rather than later."

"I will."

"And … what you called the nuclear option? Cutting the power?" Carol asked, her voice steady but her features decidedly pasty.

"Yes. If Dan can find it, cutting the main electrical power lead to that damned box."

Dan and Frank Erlichman quickly descended back into the electronics bay to start pulling as many relay cubes as possible in the hope of finding the one that would restore directional control without turning them upside down. Dan had lost count of the number of times he and Erlichman had descended the small ladder from the cockpit. But once again they were standing in front of the offending cabinet, its mere presence mocking them, the remaining minutes to Tel Aviv ticking by with increasing urgency. Carol was once again scrunched in behind the captain's seat, kneeling so that she could stick her head down through the hatch to relay any messages to Jerry, who had been out of the captain's seat no more than twice the entire duration of the cascading emergency.

Jerry looked over at the teenager he'd all but attacked so many hours ago, wanting to say something supportive. But after unsuccessfully punching numbers into the MDCU at random and taking a quick bathroom break, the kid was back nose-down in the MDCU operator's manual and nodding every few seconds as if the arcane language actually made sense.

"What do you think, Josh?" Jerry asked, unable to restrain himself.

Josh Begich looked up and smiled tentatively. "Sir, I think … I think the unit is actually working and only the screen has been turned off. I was working out how to program a different destination."

"Really? Have you tried yet?"

"No … where would you like it to take us?"

"New York!" Jerry said, realizing the futility of it with depleted fuel reserves. "Okay, then maybe Tel Aviv. Where we originated."

Tom Wilson was still positioned behind the copilot's seat, and he leaned in a bit. "Jerry, aren't we already headed there?"

"True. Okay, program in the coordinates for Cairo, just to see if it will change course."

Josh carefully entered the digits and pressed the execute button.

"Nothing," Jerry pronounced, watching the heading, his voice calm and matter-of-fact, where hours before he would have thrown something out of sheer frustration. Maybe it was weariness, Jerry thought. Maybe his more laid-back demeanor was a dangerous measure of resignation, a realization that he couldn't necessarily control everything.

Whatever it was, in some ways he seemed like a stranger to himself, someone he was watching from a distance, and even amidst the angst and the fright, that fascinated him.

"Jerry," Carol's voice reached him from directly behind. "They're pulling the first breaker now."

"Thanks. Josh, keep experimenting. Just, as I said before, write down everything you punch in before you hit execute."

"Yes, sir."

The startling sound of an air traffic controller giving an inflight instruction to an EgyptAir flight momentarily confused Jerry before he recalled that the main VHF radio had been activated an hour ago, but with no transmit function. Almost absently, he pushed the transmit button on the sidestick controller.

"And Cairo Control, Pangia 10 with you, I just wish you could hear what the hell I'm saying up here, because it would sure be nice to be able to speak to the rest of the known universe, or at least someone in it!"

Jerry relieved pressure on the button, listening absently to what seemed a response.

"Pangia 10! Cairo Control! We do hear you, sir. How are you reading this transmitter?"

Jerry looked down at the VHF control head on the center console, wondering why Dan was taking the time to tap in from below to tease him with a bad accent. Recognition slowly dawned that it wasn't Dan's voice at all.

From Bill Breem's vantage point, Jerry seemed to rise a couple of inches in his command chair, as if re-inflating, glancing around quickly to assure himself no one else was holding a microphone.

"Holy ..." He grabbed for the sidestick.

"What was that, Jerry?" Breem asked, but Jerry was already mashing the transmit button.

"Cairo, Pangia 10! If that's really you, we have you loud

and clear on 122.7."

He turned as far to the right as he could. "Carol! Tell Dan we have two-way VHF restored! And tell him to keep on pulling things!"

"Loud and clear also, Pangia 10," the Cairo controller was saying. "We are aware of your emergency. How can we assist, sir?"

"Can you patch us into a discreet frequency and set up a telephone relay to our company?"

"Standby, 10, I believe we can arrange that." The channel remained silent for a few seconds before the controller confirmed it, and Jerry passed the main number for the Operations Control Center in Chicago.

CHAPTER FORTY-SEVEN

Aboard Pangia 10 (0355 Zulu)

"Pangia 10, your company is calling, and we have them connected," Cairo Control relayed. "Please go ahead."

"Chicago, Flight 10."

"Captain Tollefson, is that you?"

"Yes. Who is this?"

"Rick Hastings, your CEO. Captain, please listen closely. There is one thing I need you to do with great care and precision."

"Yes sir. What would that be?"

"It's a series of numbers I need you to enter into your MDCU."

"We've already discovered that even though the screen is blank, it can accept some inputs. We're just not sure which ones."

"I may have an answer to that, Captain. I'll read the procedure I want you to follow and the numbers, and then I need a precise readback."

"Go ahead."

Hastings read the steps and the code and listened as Jerry read it back without error.

"Okay, good. While I have you, please punch that in and execute, and tell me the results."

"Mr. Hastings, I suppose now is not the moment to ask you what the hell is going on and why do I have this … this … code?"

"You would be correct, Captain. It is neither the time nor the forum. Just do it, please."

"Standby," was the response, followed a minute later by the report Hastings had dreaded. "We put that in precisely as instructed, sir, and virtually nothing has changed."

"You've tried your controls?"

"Yes, sir. Nothing. We're working like hell to disconnect whatever idiot thing that is in the electronics bay that has taken over, and, as you can tell, we got the radio back and the throttles, but nothing else."

"Input that again."

More seconds of line noise and vocal silence before Jerry Tollefson returned to the line, his voice terse.

"We put it in three more times, sir, and nothing is different."

"*Three* more? I only instructed one more."

"No, sir, you said to input it again. Well, we tried three times and to no avail. May I ask where this number sequence came from?"

"No, but I can tell you your airline has had nothing to do with this whole affair. We're working as hard as we can to help you."

"Well, Mr. Hastings … I'm sorry, I forgot … *General* Hastings … we're begging for anything substantive you can do. Maybe that was the wrong number sequence?"

Unseen, half a world away in a Chicago command center, Rick Hastings sighed, remembering Paul Wriggle's warning that the third bad attempt would permanently lock out an MDCU no one knew was active to begin with.

"Captain, I don't know that we've got anything else at the moment. I'll get back to you the moment we do."

"Not much time left, sir," Jerry added.

"I know it."

And just as quickly, the connection was broken.

The White House

On the president's direct order, General Paul Wriggle

had remained in the Oval Office, distant from any possibility of the team in the Situation Room wondering about his presence, and his purpose. Contemplating what had become an expanding disaster on many fronts, Wriggle found himself alone when his cell phone rang with Dana Baumgartner on the other end.

"We've found Gail Hunt, General. Tell me how much detail you want, but she skidded off the highway to Estes five days ago and has been trapped in her car in a gully since then. One of our guys started searching for her and found the skid marks, and … she's been airlifted to Denver, alive but unconscious."

"Good Lord! Thank God she's alive. What's the prognosis?"

"Good, we think."

"Don't hurt her, Dana, but push as much as you can to get that code, if she can recall it. We're down to no time left."

"She's unconscious, General."

"Do what you can."

He punched the phone off only to have it ring again, this time with Rick Hastings on the other end.

"Paul, read me that disconnect code and the entry sequence again." Clearly it was not a request, and there was no point in asking.

"Standby … I have it here," Wriggle said, opening his notebook and relaying it once more."

"It didn't work, Paul! My crew punched it in precisely as stated, and it didn't work."

"Oh, shit," was the only phrase that seemed to fit.

"Oh, shit, indeed! Now what do we do? You seem to know what the hell is going on. My guys punched it in four times, so if it was the wrong code, by your statement, we're locked out now and screwed."

"It was the only code we had. My people were pretty

sure ..."

"*Pretty* sure? Jesus Christ, man, why didn't you tell me it was uncertain?"

"I didn't know it was! The woman who wrote the code was missing. She's just been found in a car wreck near Estes Park, Colorado, barely alive after five days in a gully, and we can't question her yet."

"You want to start telling me what is going on, Paul? Or should I ask the president, if he's still with you? We have less than an hour and a half of fuel on that bird and something your ass is involved with is about to kill everyone aboard."

"Rick, I can't give you answers to that basic question yet. Not on an open line, at least. If this is your direct line, I'll call you back as quickly as I can, if there's anything more we can pass to your crew. I can tell you this ... we have Israeli fighters heading to intercept them, and one of them is prepared to relay the unlock code on a channel they can't lock out."

"But if it's the wrong damned code, Paul ..."

"I know, I know. One of my guys is at the bedside with our lady in Denver. They're trying to get her conscious long enough ... I really can't tell you the rest of it."

"We've got a fuse burning down toward an explosive, Paul."

"I know it. Believe me, I know it. I'm standing in the freaking Oval Office! Back as quick as I've got something to pass."

Paul Wriggle punched off the cell phone and sat in horrified thought for a few seconds, hoping Dana Baumgartner called again quickly. Finding Gail Hunt hovering near death in her wrecked car had answered one riddle and left others, chief among them how to deactivate a unit they never activated to begin with, and if the codes they had found in her safe were wrong, could she recall the real one? The chances of a

Moishe Lavi-led conspiracy was less than one notch below certain in his mind now, but thank God Gail hadn't been the cause of it.

Impatience won out, and he triggered the speed dial number for Colonel Baumgartner, not even bothering with hellos.

"Any news, Dana?"

"Coming around. She'll make it. Hypothermia and dehydration, but the main injuries are just fractures."

"No way to question her, I suppose?"

"Steve Reagan's there at bedside now. He's the one who found her, and he's going to try."

"The unlock code didn't work, Dana," Paul, said, filling in the details.

"Oh, lord,"

"That means the broadcast unlock code is probably crap as well."

"Agreed."

"We have just over an hour I'm told until flameout. Even at the risk of Gail's life, adrenalize her or do something to get the information. He filled in Dana on the newly launched mission to relay the unlock code through an Israeli fighter's UHF radio. "We were going to use the same code, but now that's apparently futile."

"Could the crew have gotten it wrong?"

"Highly unlikely. It was apparently passed with great care on a clear channel with confirmed readbacks. If we can't get the right code, we're done … and they're done. And, there's always the chance the thing has been monkeyed with and not even Gail has the right numbers."

"Got it."

"Hurry! Please."

"Paul, shouldn't we get our engineers together and see if they know how to physically pull the plug?"

The words felt like a ballpeen hammer to the head. "Oh, Jesus! I should have seen that! It was right in front of us, and I've been hung up on the damned codes."

"We designed it to be tamper-proof, and the cabinet is booby-trapped, but …"

"Anything is worth trying. How long will it take?"

"I have to roust them out of their homes."

"Go! I'm standing by."

Paul Wriggle punched off his cell phone and looked up, embarrassed that the president had been standing there and he was singularly unaware of it.

"What do you have, Paul?"

"Nothing good. We got through to the crew with the code, and the code's incorrect. The Israelis are preparing to intercept, also with the wrong numbers, but we did find our lady who wrote the code. She's been in a bad accident and may not be able to talk to our guys, but we're trying."

"An accident?"

Paul filled in the details in brief.

"Good God!" The president sat down on the couch opposite Paul Wriggle.

"I spoke to the acting Israeli PM. He's in a tough spot, Paul. He may have to order his fighters to shoot them down."

For a moment it didn't register.

"Shoot who down? The Iranians?"

"No, Paul. Pangia 10. Our commercial jet with God knows how many people aboard."

"Why?"

"It will be split-second decision-making, but if Flight 10 approaches the Iranian border, and if any of the Iranian missiles are erected on the launch pad, the only sure-fire way they'll have to stop an action-reaction cascade that would end in an attempted nuclear exchange would be to remove the basic trigger—the intruding airplane. The Iranians might do that themselves instead of launching on Tel Aviv, but the Israelis are not about to take a chance."

"Lord!"

"And the Iranians, according to what I just received from NSA, are fueling missiles as we speak. I just spoke with Moscow, but they won't be able to stop a paranoid response. One more thing," the president said. "If Lavi is behind this, he will have planned for damn near every contingency, including an attempted shootdown by his own forces, which is why he'd have confederates laced through the Israeli command structure to make sure it didn't happen."

"You mean, the PM could give the order, but …"

"Right. It wouldn't be carried out, because Lavi needs that airplane in Iranian airspace to force the mullahs to launch, which will license Israel to wipe out their nuclear abilities and several cities."

"And … we're powerless?"

"No, not if we get the right code or pull the right plug or those pilots figure out something before crossing the line."

Paul looked at his watch. "Less than ninety minutes from the Iranian border, if I calculated it correctly."

CHAPTER FORTY-EIGHT

Washington, DC (Midnight EST / 0400 Zulu)

The staccato bursts of red and blue strobe lights atop a police cruiser lit up the street behind them suddenly as Will barely recovered control from his latest tire-squealing turn, the accelerator still to the floor.

"Will, what the hell are you doing?"

"We can't stop."

"That's a police cruiser!"

"Maybe."

Only twice in her life had Jenny Reynolds felt the presence of a deep and sudden fear so overwhelming that it was all but paralytic, but that feeling returned now like a breaking wave as she replayed Seth's emergency text in her mind. Will Bronson, or whoever the hell the man next to her really was, continued to jerk and weave through traffic like a madman, the squad car now solidly on their tail, siren blaring. Whether they were still being tailed in turn by whomever Bronson had been trying to shake was an unknown, but Bronson was flinging the SUV around like their lives depended on shaking the cop. Policemen, she knew, loved nothing better than an adrenaline-pumping chase, but such chases seldom ended well for the quarry.

"Stop this car, Will," she commanded, her voice low and terse.

"No."

He'd seen her glance at something on her iPhone and was already suspicious. But there was no way to predict her suddenly pointing at something in the darkened residential street ahead as she screamed at ear-splitting volume: "STOP!"

His foot jammed hard on the brakes, and the SUV went into a four-wheel skid, the police cruiser slamming on its brakes right behind and almost rear-ending them.

"What? WHAT?" he demanded, eyes aflame and looking panicked. The doors of the police car had already been flung open, and two cops had emerged from each side clearing leather with their weapons.

"I'm getting out!" she said, her hand on the door latch as he suddenly jammed the accelerator to the floor again, knocking her door closed before she could get a shoulder into it, the engine roaring, but not loudly enough to mask the sound of gunfire as the rear window of the SUV exploded in glass shards.

The time it was taking for the two startled officers to turn and dive back into their car was all Will needed to dart off into a side street and begin another frantic slalom course, braking suddenly in an alley several wild turns and blocks away, peeling into a blessedly empty back driveway nestled between two high hedges before killing the lights and turning off the engine.

This time Jenny succeeded in flinging her door wide and leaping from the SUV before he had a chance to react.

Somewhere in the distance the sound of a helicopter approaching reached his ears. It would be a matter of minutes at best before the airborne Night Sun spotlight located the SUV, its shattered rear window clearly visible. The quick search necessary to illuminate two running figures would be child's play after that.

Will was breathing hard as he took a few seconds to calculate the odds of various options, but there seemed only one. He left the engine running and flung open the door, jumping out and reclosing both doors before running as hard as he could in the direction Jenny had taken.

She had the key to this whole thing. Hell, she *was* the

key, he thought. And he mustn't lose her …

Somewhere in the back of her mind Jenny realized that running for your life and taking the time to carry your high heels in order to save them were rather conflicting goals. But she had a death grip on both the pumps and her computer case as she accelerated into the fastest dash she could manage. She couldn't hear footsteps behind her with the background roar of DC traffic even at night, but she was sure Bronson would be hell for leather after her, his long legs giving him an easy advantage, and the cops and whoever else was chasing them hot on his trail.

I don't believe this! she thought, the surreal nature of everything that had accompanied the last few hours continuing to accelerate into total confusion in her mind. She had the means to save that airplane full of people—maybe— and time was running out, and people were trying to stop her. Why?

So who the hell is *he?* she wondered, pondering Seth's note just long enough to stumble and almost fall on her face on a concrete walkway. She stubbed her toe but recovered enough balance to stay on her feet and force the pain away to keep moving.

A sloping lawn on her right led up to a modest home, and she veered off, slipping a bit in her stocking feet as they hit the soft grass, scrambling around the side and down a driveway, jogging left through an unfenced backyard and then across the next street between yet another pair of houses, running mostly on the balls of her feet. She could hear the startled comment of someone who'd seen her flash past, and for a second she weighed the prospect of seeking help and entry into someone's house versus continuing to be a running target.

Running won out, but she wondered if she'd shaken Bronson or if he was still pursuing her. Maybe, she thought, he'd been confused by her zigzagging, but just to hedge the bet, she broke left at the next driveway and doubled back toward the street she'd just crossed, all but diving behind a tall hedge in someone's front lawn and trying to squelch her heavy breathing as she watched for any sign of him.

There was no one, at least no one running or in obvious pursuit. There was a helicopter overhead a few blocks away, obviously searching for them.

She thought of her cell phone. Maybe it was time for a 911 call? Or would what's-his-name be tied into that network as well?

I don't even know who I'm running from! she thought.

A sudden sound to her left caused her heart to leap, and she turned to find a thankfully calm and curious Labrador who had ambled over to see who was hiding behind his owner's hedge. Still on guard, she petted him, listening for footsteps that weren't there.

Maybe, she thought, the home she was crouching beside had a Wi-Fi she could use, but then the glow of her computer screen would be a dead giveaway.

The dog was licking her ear and whining, and she reached to the left to push him away only to have her wrist grabbed as Will Bronson whirled her around to face him and slammed her back onto the ground, straddling her.

"Scream and I swear I'll strangle you right here," he hissed, a strong hand on each wrist, penning her arms to the damp ground.

"What are you going to do, rape me? Have at it, bastard."

"Rape … *what? Seriously?"*

"What else should I conclude? You're straddling me, and you just threatened to strangle me!"

"Why did you run? We need to stay together!" he asked.

"Why did *I* run? You're the one driving like a maniac! Why? We've got cops shooting at us! Who are we running from anyway?"

His head was on a swivel, looking in all directions, then back at her, speaking tersely and low.

"Our agents. The cops. Federal police. I don't know, but I'll bet there's what they used to call an all-points bulletin out for us and not getting us caught, killed, or locked up seemed to serve the interests of saving that planeload of people. But answer me, Jenny. Please. Why are you running from *me?*"

"Because, apparently, you're not who you claim to be."

"Aha! According to whom?"

"Seth, my boss, and the CIA. So, who *are* you, really?"

"It was that message, then?"

"What?"

"You got a text in the car and got all cold and silent."

"Yes. That text. It said to get away from you. I'm beginning to see why. How the hell did you find me, by the way?"

"Your 'Find my iPhone' function. Comes in handy."

"Shit."

He sighed, a bit too loudly. "All right. You know my name, but … there's more."

"Of course there is!"

"I'm not an operative … a spy, Jenny."

"Right. And I'm not really female. Yank my panties off and you'll find out."

"*What*?"

He looked almost comically perplexed, she noted, as if she'd flung another language at him. He was shaking his head as if to rid it of whatever cobwebs had filtered her words.

"What is it with you women and sex, Jenny?"

"We *women*? *WE* women? What kind of sexist nonsense is that?"

"Just what it sounds like! Yes, you women! Jeez! Rape? Pulling off panties? We're in the middle of a freaking crisis here, and that's all you can think of?"

"Not all. But you have to admit that some of my most sensitive lady parts are in rather intimate and vulnerable proximity to you at the moment."

"Oh, yeah." He raised up on his knees, taking the pressure off her hips. "Listen to me. I *am* with DIA, but I'm just an analyst who stumbled onto what appeared to me to be a suspicious operation. I've seen several before in my department and have always felt guilty for doing nothing. This time I had to act."

"An analyst? Whoa, wait … an *analyst*?"

"You say it like it's a bad thing."

"No, I just thought …"

"I'm an analyst just like you, Jenny! I have no training as a spy."

For a few seconds she found herself forgetting the bizarre nature of their little chat, he astride her in a flower bed, and she stared at him before responding.

"Well … it's true you sure as hell don't drive like a spy, you know, someone with … with …"

"High performance driver training?"

"Yes. That. Wait … what operation are you talking about?"

"Yours. I intercepted your call for help this morning. I was supposed to notify an entire chain of people, but I didn't. Apparently someone found out, or overheard the call, I'm not sure how. But I happen to know DIA has been setting up some very secretive satellite networks, and I'm very suspicious of what they're doing because no other part of even DIA itself is supposed to know. We don't operate like the old clandestine cell system, yet that's the kind of stuff I've been picking up. When your call came in, it seemed like an example of precisely what they've been whispering about. I thought it might give me a chance to confirm my suspicions and do something about it."

"What in tarnation are you talking about?"

"The ability to remotely control airliners. Maybe crash them on cue. At least that's what I think it's about."

"Why didn't you tell me this before?"

"Because I thought you were working with *them*, okay? You wrote the code, as I said."

The code again, she thought, feeling a flash of guilt and foreboding. But who would have had access to that code, and how could she have prevented it? That was years back!

"Let me up, dammit!"

He got to his feet and pulled her up until they stood together between the hedge and the house as she brushed herself off.

"There's still an airliner …" she began.

"Sh-h-h!" he cautioned. "Keep it low!"

"There's an airliner about to be toast because of all this," she continued.

"I know."

"So, were you trying to keep me from transmitting?"

"No. Hell no! I was trying to find a way to make it work without getting arrested."

"Okay, well … *Will* … why don't we motor on over to 1600 Pennsylvania and let the big guys sort it out. No time for much else."

"Okay," he said, defeat in his voice.

"Okay? Really, just … *okay?*"

"Yeah, I'm fresh out of clever ideas."

"I have no reason to trust you, y'know. I mean, *no* fucking reason!"

"I know it."

"But I have no time to figure it out, either."

"I don't know how we can make it to the White House or anywhere else with everyone looking for us.

"We have to try."

"True."

"Maybe we could flag down a cab?"

He shook his head, his eyes cast in the direction of what had to be three helicopters now crisscrossing several blocks distant, the powerful light beams of the police helicopter cutting through the trees and the shrubs they were hiding behind.

"A cab's not possible. They'll all be alerted by now."

"We have less than forty-five minutes, and the release sequence I came up with may be garbage, but if this is as big a crisis as I think it is, they'll have to listen. If we can get there, that is."

"There's a car in the driveway," Will said, almost under his breath.

"Should we knock on the door and ask for a ride?"

"What? No!"

"Then how can we use their car?"

"We're going to borrow it."

"Borrow … wait … I thought you weren't a spy? You're telling me you know how to hotwire a modern car and steal it, with all the interlocks?"

"No, but follow me and stay low. Maybe we'll be lucky." He pulled her toward the driveway where a small, late model Toyota was parked, letting go of her hand to slip to the driver's side.

The door was locked.

He checked the darkened front windows of the home once again before carefully triggering a tiny penlight to scan the interior, looking for a way in, oblivious at first to Jenny's voice which could barely be heard against the noise of helicopters, traffic, and a distant siren.

"Will."

No response.

"Will!"

He turned to look at her, then puzzled that she was holding what looked in the dim streetlight like a credit card and pointing to the street.

"What?"

"An X car. A community rental car, is right there, right over there by the curb, and I have a membership."

"A *what?"*

He followed her gaze to the tiny two-seater and gave chase as she ran to the driver's side, sliding her membership card to open the locks.

"You know how to drive one of these?" she asked.

"Drive it? I thought you pedaled it!"

"Funny."

"The thing's embarrassing."

"It's a smart car."

"It's a pregnant roller skate, and we could hardly stand out more if this thing was painted international orange and shooting fireworks."

"Got a better idea, Mr. Bond?"

"No," he said, pulling the door open and stuffing himself inside just as a police car squealed around the corner in front of them, it's headlights a split-second from illuminating the interior of the X car as they swept the line of houses.

Jenny and Will ducked toward each other as if on cue, Jenny almost prone to her right, Will leaning left atop her, down barely enough the stay out of the headlights as the cruiser shot past. Jenny was making a conscious effort to keep her foot from touching the brake and flaring the brake lights in the cop's rearview mirror.

"Clear, you think?" she asked.

"Couple more seconds."

"If he sees us, just say we were making out."

"Jenny, this car's too small for a kiss, let alone anything more."

"Yeah, but I'm on the bottom again, and you're enjoying this!"

Will raised up slowly, scanning behind them, finding the street dark, although the beams from the searching police helicopter were less than a block away.

"Okay, let's go," he said.

She fired up the tiny engine and put the car in gear, feeling it lurch away from the curb.

"Right turn at the end of the block."

"I know the way to the White House, Will. We've got to hurry and stay on the main roads. Just … just look casual."

"Casual?"

"Yes."

"How the hell does one look casual driving a golf cart down a city street at midnight?"

"I don't know. Stop scowling … look relaxed."

"I can't relax. We've got half the town after us."

"And … that could be a problem," she said.

"What?"

"I forgot these cars report their GPS position constantly. If someone's been watching my account …"

"Wonderful. They can just monitor us and intercept us."

"There's no other choice, is there?" she asked. "We couldn't outrun a skateboard in this little thing, but at least it's moving and we have a little over a half hour."

CHAPTER FORTY-NINE

Aboard Pangia 10 (0410 Zulu)

"They said we'd get an escort, and there they are," Jerry announced as two Israeli F-15 fighters pulled into wingtip formation, their markings barely visible from the reflection of the lights in the A330's passenger windows.

"Can we talk to them?" Tom Wilson asked.

"I don't know. If they have only UHF, we can't."

But a male voice cut through the question on the discreet frequency they had set up with Cairo Control.

"Pangia 10, how do you hear?"

"Pangia 10 here. Are you our escort?"

"Affirmative, Pangia. One of us on each wing. And we are relaying a UHF signal that you may not hear in your cockpit."

"Excuse me … we don't have UHF."

"Pangia, we were told to broadcast this just in case. Stand by."

Jerry glanced at the opposite window, seeing only the reflection of a flashing red position light somewhere in the darkness. A full minute dragged by.

"Pangia 10, would you please check to see if you've regained control?"

"I don't know what you've been told, sir, but we didn't hear anything you broadcasted. But … let me try."

Jerry grasped the sidestick controller and tried to punch off the autoflight system once again, keeping a shadow of hope alive that maybe magic had been wrought somehow.

But there was no response, and he reported it to the fighter escort.

"Are you guys armed?" Jerry asked.

“We are always in alert status, sir,” the pilot replied, the elliptical response telling enough.

First Class Cabin, Pangia 10

“There’s my lovely keeper,” Moishe Lavi smiled as Ashira slid into the seat beside him. “What, may I ask, is on your mind?”

“You.”

“Really?” he asked, looking pleased.

“I think there’s something you’re not telling me because you wrongly think I’d object.”

Moishe adopted the slightly amused look he was fond of throwing at her when she approached a serious subject. It wasn’t as if he were discounting her, but at heart he was the superior, and one in his position did not adopt a serious expression of interest in a subordinate’s concerns until she’d earned it.

“And what am I to think you would object to?”

It was her turn to smile and sidestep the question. “I’ve long been prepared to give my life to Israel, and I will willingly follow you into whatever lies ahead.”

Moishe was looking at her now with great care, searching her deep brown eyes and for once thinking substantially beyond the sexual.

“Ashira, my love, do you truly think this … this electronic hijacking is *my* doing? Is that what you’re indicating?”

“Isn’t it?” she asked. “If it is, it’s a stroke of genius, and I’m sure there are others involved to make sure the first strike is the result. You were right all along, of course.”

He started to protest, then thought better of it and merely smiled. “You would follow me into death, then, to eliminate the threat?”

“Of course. I suppose that means we haven’t much time,

but I wanted to tell you."

"And you would be disappointed if I told you that I have had nothing to do with the problems on this airliner tonight?"

"I understand that you need to say that. I suppose I just wanted to see it in your eyes. I knew you wouldn't let us down, even after losing office."

He took a deep breath and prepared to say more, but the PA system clicked on:

"Ladies and gentlemen, this is Captain Tollefson again. We have restored radio contact with the ground and have a great number of people and agencies trying to help us restore control of the airplane, and we have made some progress. But as we approached Tel Aviv, some of you may have noted that we picked up a protective escort of Israeli fighters off each wing. We are in contact with them. We are not out of tricks, so to speak, but the reality is that we just passed over the airport we left so many hours ago, Ben Gurion International in Tel Aviv, and whatever electronic bandit has locked us up did not release the controls but turned us apparently back in the direction of the last major port-of-call for this flight, which was Hong Kong. Of course we do not have sufficient fuel to reach anywhere close to Hong Kong, so we have to resolve this within the hour. And one of our greatest concerns is that in approximately one hour we will have overflown Jordan and Iraq and will be approaching the Iranian border with no permission to cross. I will communicate with you when there are any changes."

Ashira was nodding and smiling lightly. She patted Moishe Lavi's hand and started to get up before adding as an afterthought:

"Oh, may I borrow your laptop for a few minutes? I want

to compose my thoughts, and I'm out of battery."

"Of course," he replied, handing over the machine. "Just close my word program. I've already saved my things."

"Thank you. As we approach the end of this, I want to hold your hand."

"You shall," he said, the seriousness of his tone flipping the last tumbler into place in Ashira's mind.

She rose to her feet, a bit unsteadily, moving to a window seat on the opposite side, and opened the laptop, pretending to type while keeping a close eye on Lavi. But as she probed deeper into the computer and its programs, the effort became more frantic and equally unproductive. There was nothing overt, and whatever he had been writing was well protected with a password she couldn't seem to break. Even the keylogging program she had clandestinely installed months ago was reporting nothing, which meant his countermeasures to thwart exactly what she'd been trying to do were very effective.

Finally sitting back and pretending to wipe a tear from her eye, she faced the fact that she had nothing left to try. He had defeated her. No evidence, no programs that could be even remotely connected with seizing control of an airliner, and not even assurance that Moishe Lavi *was* the party responsible for their plight—although she was certain that was the case.

As she prepared to turn the machine off, a tiny icon she didn't recognize appeared in the lower margin of the screen, and she double-clicked on it, triggering a routine official screen with the Israeli flag. What was clicking away in the left corner, however, caught her eye. Two digital clock readouts, one counting up, the other down, the digits changing every second.

She peered closely at the elapsed time, 06:08:23, and calculated backwards to the start of the flight, some eleven hours in the past. Where would they have been six hours ago at around 500 miles per hour?

The calculations in her head were simple, and she ran them twice more to be sure. Somewhere off the coast of Ireland, most likely, and somewhere around the time the aircraft had turned around without the pilots' knowledge.

Still, that could be coincidental.

The second digits were counting down, reading 00:53:49, and she felt a deep chill rising up her spine with the realization that it must be the time to crossing the Iranian border with Iraq. They had fifty-three minutes, and the only reason for the two clocks she could imagine was Moishe Lavi keeping track of what he'd started.

It was true, she concluded. Somehow a cabal of his followers had cocked and loaded the gun, and he'd pulled the trigger!

She loosed a final try, a series of known passwords trying to pry open the door to whatever this electronic vault was, knowing just as surely as she had to try, he would have made certain it couldn't be undone.

In her entire life—even as a baby in Russia before her parents immigrated to Israel—Ashira had a reputation for being incredibly tenacious. She never quit.

But perhaps for the first time in her adult life, she felt herself involuntarily relax in the face of certainty: There was nothing else she could do now. Life was to be measured in minutes, and the choices were no longer hers.

CHAPTER FIFTY

St. Paul's Hospital, Denver, Colorado (10:20 p.m. MST / 0420 Zulu)

The image of faces filtering through a deep fog had come and gone in the previous hours, but Gail Hunt still wasn't putting it together.

And she was *so* tired!

Suddenly, however, a face she absolutely recognized coalesced in front of her. *Steve!*

What was Steve Reagan doing here, she wondered, along with the suddenly crystalline question of where, exactly, was "here"? He was saying something, and she tried hard against a sea of weariness to listen. A question maybe?

Gail forced her eyes back open. He was still there, smiling it seemed. Good ol' Steve! She could always depend on him. She opened her mouth to acknowledge him, but there was no sound.

She tried again, understanding at least some of what he was saying, the words very distant at first. *How am I*? she echoed in her mind. *I don't know ... how AM I?*

"Fine!" she managed, the startled expression on Steve Reagan's face confirming her voice had worked.

But now he was pushing her. Something about numbers or codes in her desk safe. Triggering codes. De-triggering codes. *In my safe*? Steve should know better, she thought. Never keep … in safe.

She slipped away into a drifting sleep, but his voice tugged her back.

Gail opened her eyes again and tried hard to focus. Steve seemed determined to know about codes in her safe.

"Never in … my desk safe," she replied, not realizing the words were coming out as more of a slurred whisper than a statement. Or, had she put them there? No, only her notes. Notes in the desk safe. Maybe notes with test codes, but not real ones. Whole damn thing far too important to trust to a physical safe that could be opened. But their bird was in the desert. No need for the codes until next week.

"So," he was articulating. "The right codes were NOT the ones we found in your desk safe?"

Why, Gail thought, would they be looking inside her desk safe?

"Not in my safe," she said again. "Codes always in … master computer."

She wanted to sleep, but he wasn't letting her, and for a moment she felt a flash of irritation.

"What happened to me?" She asked suddenly, the words far more clear than before. "Where … is this?"

Steve leaned over and talked about an accident on the way to Estes Park. Her accident. Her car. So it *wasn't* a nightmare. It had been real.

"Can I walk?" she asked, startling both Steve and someone standing by him. Maybe a nurse. No. Couldn't be a nurse. The woman wasn't wearing a white uniform, just something with bunnies on it. But did nurses wear uniforms any more?

"No paralysis! You'll make a full recovery, but you were down there in the wrecked car for days."

She tried to nod, but the effort hurt. Maybe pain was good, though as she thought about it, even more pain began to make itself known, and that wasn't fun. She wasn't into pain, as she'd been fond of telling those who wanted her to lift weights and work out more.

"Gail!"

Once again she had drifted off, and this time Steve was talking about the passwords to the master computer, and an airplane full of passengers somewhere in trouble, and they needed her codes. *Why would some airliner need her codes? We're an invisible black project. We don't exist. They don't need my damned codes!*

But Steve was insisting, and if it had been anyone but Steve she would have snapped at him. Couldn't he see how tired she was?

"Let me sleep," she said, her eyes closing again, trying to push away the voice which was emphatically saying something about running out of time.

Suddenly she was back in a beautiful field under a clear blue sky, motioning to a lover to hurry with the buttons he'd been undoing on her blouse, and realizing with a surge of pleasure that it was Steve.

Building 4-104, Peterson Air Force Base, Colorado Springs (10:32 p.m. / 0432 Zulu)

"That's *all*? That's all you guys can come up with?"

Dana Baumgartner searched the eyes of the hastily assembled team of engineers pulled from their homes to find a way to do what they had labored to prevent: Physically disconnect the airborne unit that was the entire focus of the black project they were legally required to protect.

"Those were the specifications, Colonel!" one of them said in a pleading voice. "We worked long and hard to think up every way some desperate hijacker could try to disconnect us and thwart all of them."

"Yeah," an owlish-looking engineer interjected. "Like burying the relays for the flight controls where no one could reach them, or … or …"

"I get it, guys," Dana replied. "But we've got less than an hour, and if we can't get the disconnect code, we've got to tell those pilots how to disable the system."

"Sir, it can't be done!"

"You can't cut power to the box, even?" Dana asked.

"Especially not that, sir. It could be catastrophic because of the different relays, sequences, and power source changes that would result."

"I want you to stay here and keep thinking, keep working on it, just in case. Don't approach it from the position that it's impossible. Approach it from the idea that you left out something … left a backdoor, a way to knock it off. I refuse to hear that it's impenetrable! Just do it. We have a lot of lives at stake, as well as the efficacy of this program and your jobs."

CHAPTER FIFTY-ONE

The White House (12:40 a.m. EST / 0440 Zulu)

Safely ensconced behind bulletproof glass in the front guardhouse, the well-trained officer who had greeted Will Bronson and Jenny Reynolds after they tumbled out of their rental and fast walked the distance to his window was used to random citizens wobbling in off the street to ask—sometimes demand—to the see the president. Some were drunk, some high on God knew what, some dangerously deluded or sufficiently hostile to trigger an armed response. But seldom had he seen ID cards from NSA and DIA pushed under the window without a concurrent appointment.

Carefully matching the pictures on the IDs with the faces in front of him, the officer keyed the speaker.

"Who do you want to see, and why don't I see an appointment?"

"Because," Jenny said, as close to the microphone as she could get, "This has just emerged as something only the White House can handle. It is a matter of national security, it is extremely urgent, it involves a hijacked, American-flagged airliner about to invade Iranian airspace, and we have the codes that can stop a tragedy that could result in the deaths of everyone aboard."

"Who do you want to see?" The officer asked again, evenly, fully expecting to hear the word "president" in the answer.

"The chief of staff or the duty officer in the Situation Room, even if you have to get them out of bed. We have less than forty minutes, and this is no joke."

"Stand by, please," was the response, and within less than five minutes a man they judged to be in the Secret Service detail had arrived to escort them through a metal detector and a quick pat down, and then to a tiny office somewhere on the first floor.

"You folks remain here. Someone will be back with you."

"Wait! Wait a minute!" Jenny had sat down for a few seconds before leaping up. "That airliner will be in Iranian airspace in … if I calculate it correctly … less than thirty minutes, and something terrible is going to happen if the pilots haven't regained control."

"Ma'am, you're preaching to the wrong choir," the agent said.

"I'm trying to tell you how urgent this is! Every second counts!"

"Yes, ma'am. I get it. Stay here."

The door closed behind him, and Jenny knew instinctively someone would be standing on the other side to make sure they didn't leave unescorted.

"It's too late, Jen. We've done the best we could," Will said, his face a mask of defeat.

"If they don't get their asses in gear, I'm afraid we're going to be left in limbo until it *is* too late," Jenny said, pacing back and forth while Will stood, looking helpless.

"We don't even know if your code is right."

She turned, a finger in the air suddenly. "What do you bet the White House has a Wi-Fi system?"

"Probably. With passcodes I'm sure."

"Which I'll bet I can crack!"

She was already pulling out her laptop and firing it up, balancing it in her lap with the paper containing the unlock code on the keyboard, her finger nervously tapping the side of the machine as she anxiously waited. "Come on, come on, come on!"

CHAPTER FIFTY-TWO

Mojave, California (8:40 p.m. PST / 0440 Zulu)

Jaime Lopez, Esquire, had finally reached his personal breaking point. Getting away from Ron Barrett and his manic little group in the dusty airfield office was no longer a desire. It spelled survival. Beyond the embarrassment of a serious, senior attorney pretending to be surprised hours before, when the two federal agents couldn't locate Pangia's Airbus on their ramp, the past few hours of waiting for the next shoe to drop had been a special agony. As general counsel, his purposeful deception with the agents had been *so* beneath his dignity, if not unethical. But then, again, the whole day had been such an unmitigated disaster, it hardly mattered. A few more random indignities seemed trivial.

True, there was something very fishy about the agents' story and the speed with which they had appeared, and more than likely they were lying about being from the Transportation Safety Administration. But whoever they were, their presence spelled deep trouble.

Jaime had endured the tense atmosphere of Barrett's vigil as they monitored the media's sketchy reports on the fate of Pangia Flight 10, everyone present aware of the elephant on the table—the question of whether they would still have jobs when the smoke cleared. But for some reason, the one horrific possibility Jaime could not let go of was the idea that Carl Kanowsky, the employee who had dispatched the wrong jet, was some sort of clandestine operative. The two agents had said as much after one of them spent a half hour in another room with Kanowsky's file.

"We think," he told Jaime as they were leaving, "… that the Kanowsky name is an alias, and whoever he really is, the mission he was on required him to get hired by your company. We checked his address. It's empty desert."

There had been no time to look into the quality of the due diligence checking of Kanowsky's application, but on top of all the other worries about massive looming liability for Mojave Aircraft Storage, the thought that they could have stupidly hired a terrorist made his blood run cold.

Jaime finally made excuses and broke away from the group just before ten, leaving the rest of them glued to CNN. He sat down in an adjacent office and read every line of Kanowsky's folder and application. The overall liability of the company might well turn on the contents, but there was nothing whatever that would have waved a flag at even the most skeptical of interviewers. The agents had said the address was a vacant field, but it was suspicious that they seemed to know that almost instantly. Jaime used the map program on his iPad and carefully typed in the address that Kanowsky had given, watching with a sinking feeling as the map zoomed in on a vacant patch of desert on the eastern edge of Lancaster, just as they'd indicated.

Yet, he had an almost irresistible need to see it for himself. Despite a pounding headache, an empty stomach, and an aching thirst, Jaime climbed into his car and peeled out of the parking lot.

It took a little over twenty minutes to motor south down the Sierra Highway to the outskirts of Lancaster. The address was along East Avenue "I" in the 4000 block, several miles to the east of town, and Jaime's GPS announced he had arrived as he pulled to a halt alongside a pitch dark, featureless desert landscape.

Kanowsky's address had a "#3" added, which would indicate an apartment, but there were no buildings of any sort that he could see peering into the nighttime void.

In fact, only one light was out there, he noted, something

that looked like no more than an LED bulb, maybe a hundred yards or more to the north.

Comfortable with the desert, Jaime got out of the car and took the flashlight he always carried, playing the light ahead of him to avoid any random rattlesnakes as he picked his way carefully toward the light, skirting desert brush and tumbleweeds as well as an outcropping of barrel cactus. The land was mostly flat, but it descended suddenly into a small depression, and parked in the middle of the miniature arroyo was an ancient trailer, the smallest model Airstream had ever made, with a beat up old Ford pickup parked alongside.

The light was coming from inside, visible through a dusty window. Jaime tried to peer in, but the illumination was too weak and the window too dirty and opaque to make out anything but vague shapes inside.

He knocked on the door and waited, but there was no answer. He tried again, and was weighing the advisability of trying the door when suddenly it swung open, revealing a disheveled, coughing man in shorts and a stained t-shirt, holding a tissue, the stubble of a week-old beard on his face. Kanowsky was supposed to be sixty-two, but the unkempt man before him with sunken eyes and parchment skin looked like he'd just emerged from a sarcophagus.

"So who are *you*?" the man managed, trying several times to clear his throat, his voice clearly unused for some time.

"I'm Jaime Lopez, from Mojave Aircraft Storage. Are you Carl Kanowsky?"

The man looked up at him through sad eyes, his expression one of utter defeat.

"Yes. Am I fired?"

"For … what?"

"Missing work. I have no phone anymore. I asked my neighbor last week to let you guys know I was really, really sick, but … I guess he didn't."

"No, he didn't. We didn't know you were ill."

"Bad ill," he said, coughing again.

"How *are* you?" Jaime asked, chiding himself for what sounded like a stupid question. Obviously the man was in poor condition.

"A little better. Worst flu I've ever had. Thought I was going to die and was equally afraid I wouldn't." He negotiated another coughing spell and looked back over his shoulder. "I'd invite you in, Mr. … Lopez?"

"Yes."

"I'd invite you in, but the place looks like it's been hit by a bomb and I may still be contagious."

"No problem. You did list this address as apartment number three, by the way."

The man looked up, shaking his head as he met Jaime's eyes.

"I really didn't want anyone to know I'm living this basic, y'know? It's embarrassing."

"Don't be embarrassed. I once had a law partner who lived on a beach in a tent. He'd clean himself up each morning, put on a sharp suit, and we never knew."

"You're a lawyer?"

"Yes. I'm Mojave's general counsel."

"Why … would a big lawyer come all the way out here if it isn't to fire me?"

"Well, that's what we need to talk about."

"I was hoping to come back to work next week, Mr. Lopez. I like the job."

"I see no reason why you can't, Carl, but it's not my call."

"Then, why are you here, sir?"

"First, let me ask you, has anyone else come out here today?"

"No, sir. You're the first human I've seen in a week."

Jaime shook his head in disgust, letting a few more tumblers fall into place regarding the honesty of the two supposed TSA agents.

"Carl, our company's got a big problem, and I need to ask you a question, and I need a completely truthful answer."

"Okay. Sure. I have no reason not to be truthful."

"Is Carl Kanowsky your true name?"

Jaime saw the man's expression fall as he looked down at his feet and sighed deeply. He ambled out of the trailer door and flicked on a hanging camp light over a low wooden bench, sitting heavily. A long silence finally gave way to a ragged sigh as he answered in a low, almost inaudible voice.

"How'd you find out?"

"It's a long story."

"I suppose I'll have to go back there now, right?" he looked up with tears forming.

"Back where?"

"The looney bin. In Indiana. The psychiatric hospital. It's been thirty-five years, but I knew they were still looking for me. Every night, every day, I've expected this knock on the door. I've been terrified for thirty-five years, and now …"

"Were you … ruled criminally insane for something?"

The man's eyes flared as he looked up. "Oh, God, no! No, no, no! Nothing like that. I just, had a bad breakdown and … I had several. Actually, they committed me. They said I was schizophrenic, and I'd have to live there for life. Yet one day they left the door to that living hell open, and I … just … walked away. Then I ran, as fast as I could. I hitchhiked west. A lot of truck drivers took pity on me, I guess." He looked up pleadingly at Jaime before letting his gaze fall to the desert again. "I'd rather die than go back, Mr. Lopez." He buried his face in his hands.

"What's your real name?"

It took almost a minute for Kanowsky to compose himself and look up again.

"Vic Stevens. Victor. But you already knew that."

"No, I didn't, and I don't care that you were once committed somewhere if it wasn't a criminal matter. Even if they are still looking for you, I doubt they'd spend a penny to bring you back, and we have no interest in turning you in. I checked your record with us, Carl … ah, Vic. You've been a good employee. If you want to still be known as Carl, no problem with me."

"I do. I like Carl."

"It's a good name."

"But they're still looking for me! I just know it. They'll never stop."

"Carl, times have changed drastically. People aren't locked up like that anymore. Not even when they need to be."

Yet the assurance was not about to counter three and a half decades of visceral fear.

"You're really from Mojave Aircraft?"

"Yes. Yes, I am, and I'm here because you apparently sent the wrong aircraft back to Tulsa last week."

In an instant the man's expression morphed from despair to complete alarm and he seemed to rise from the old wooden bench like a balloon re-inflating, eyes flaring in concern.

"I did *what*?"

CHAPTER FIFTY-THREE

Aboard Pangia 10 (0440 Zulu)

After almost a half hour of pulling relay cubes and trying unsuccessfully to find the key to restoring the flight controls, Dan had scrambled back out of the electronics bay to find Josh Begich still sitting in the copilot's seat, out of ideas, and looking to anyone for hope. The glow of impending daylight was illuminating the cockpit, but they were in a solid cloud deck.

"Josh, let me sit there for a few minutes," Dan said, prompting a flurry of activity as the teen quickly motored the seat back on its rails and jumped out.

Dan sat down sideways, facing Jerry. Carol, Bill Breem, and Tom Wilson had also remained in the cockpit. There was no question this was the final briefing before the battle, and two of the other flight attendants were standing in the door as Moishe Lavi came up behind them, listening. Carol considered asking him to return to his seat, but the gesture seemed futile, and she said nothing.

"What's our status, Dan?" Jerry asked, his voice betraying the disappointment he knew the copilot was bringing.

"Our status is this. We've yanked damn near everything I can find to pull, with the exception of the relay that nearly turned us over, and we powered up a few things, but nothing on the flight controls. There is a bank of relays back there in the lower rear of the cabinet I just can't reach. Just no friggin' way to get to them, even if I didn't mind being electrocuted."

"Dan," Jerry said, stopping him. "We're over the Iranian border in sixteen minutes. Do we have any options?"

Dan sighed and nodded, parsing his words.

"Okay, option one is to pull that same relay that nearly

turned us over and buy a 360 turn, or two, or three. By the third one we'll probably flame out the first engine, and God only knows what the airplane will do then. But at least we'd crash in Iraq instead of Iran."

"Is there a second option?"

"Yes. That's what I was getting to. It's pure desperation, Jerry, but Frank and I have identified the main power lead to that hellish box, and although we can't find a way to disconnect it in civil fashion, we have a crash axe and I can cut the damned thing."

"And it would let go of us?"

"Yes. But we have no idea whether the relays would return to normal position and repower our controls, or if we'd be sitting in a dead cockpit with an unpowered airplane we couldn't control."

"Those fighters are armed, Dan," Jerry said quietly.

"I know it. I would never expect an Israeli fighter to *not* be armed. What's your point?"

"They could hold off Iranian fighters, maybe, but all it would take is a lucky shot by an oncoming Iranian jet or a ground surface-to-air missile and we're Malaysia 17."

Dan sighed again, shaking his head. "We're going to flame out just over the border in any event, if my calculations are right."

"We got all the displays back, including fuel quantity. I have to agree."

"What do we have, Jerry?"

"Sixteen minutes, and we're as slow as I dare go without flight controls."

"Okay. So, here's the deal. Frank and I will keep trying individual relays until we're five minutes out. At that point, on your order, I'll cut the power lead with an axe, and we'll just have to pray a lot."

"If that's all we've got ..."

"That's all I can see. Whoever built this infernal thing did a really professional job. They may not have been planning for someone to disable it, but they effectively created the same result. I wish I could know for sure who turned the damned thing on!"

Only Carol noticed the former prime minister of Israel turning back to the cabin.

First class cabin, Pangia 10

Carefully maintaining a virtually unreadable expression, Moishe Lavi sat down and opened the laptop Ashira had returned, bringing up the document he had been working on hours before. He made a few corrections and additions, pulled in a copy of his signature, and plugged a small interface cable in between his handheld satellite phone and the computer. With the crew regaining the use of their radios, he doubted anyone would notice the sat phone, but he took care to keep it out of view nonetheless, nudging it up against the window for a better lock-on obscured by a small blanket.

At long last the connection flashed green, and he entered the appropriate keystrokes to send the carefully parsed message to the inbox of a journalist he had always trusted. There would be no doubt that within hours, if not minutes, the whole world would be reading his words, and hopefully understand, even if they did not approve.

Moishe Lavi shut down the computer and sat back, resigned to whatever the next twenty minutes would bring.

CHAPTER FIFTY-FOUR

St. Paul's Hospital, Denver, Colorado (10:50 p.m. MST / 0450 Zulu)

Pulling the chief attending trauma surgeon away from an ER full of patients had required a level of insistence and, basically, rudeness that Steve Reagan hated in others. But there had been no choice, and now a miffed doctor was standing before him in a small alcove demanding to know what the problem was, his voice low and not unkind, but decidedly irritated.

"I need you to give my wife something to wake her up enough to answer some critical questions."

"You're joking, right?"

"No, doctor, I am far from joking."

"You beat up my nurses to get me over here because you want to question your wife? Man, you're lucky she's alive! She's got to rest, for Chrissake!"

"Doctor, I can't explain too much to you, but this is a matter of national security."

"Yeah, right!" He started to turn away, and Steve grabbed the sleeve of his scrubs. The physician whirled on him.

"Get your hands off of me!"

"Doctor, is it dangerous to wake her up?"

"That's not the point. I won't allow it."

"Doctor, at this moment, there is a commercial airliner about to run out of fuel because the pilots cannot regain control of their aircraft. I am not at liberty to tell you how I know this, but I can tell you that Gail … my, my wife in there … has in her head the … the numbers for want of a better word … that will give control back. Almost 300 people will die if we don't wake her up enough to get that sequence."

"Who the hell are you?" the doctor demanded.

"I'm Steve Reagan, and I … work for the air force."

"Yeah? Well, Mr. Reagan, so happens I am a flight surgeon and a major in the Air Force Reserve, and we don't have people like you running around without IDs. So cough it up or get out of my face."

"I'll do better than that. Please wait a second." Steve pulled his phone to eye level and punched redial on the last number connected.

"General? Steve Reagan. I have a physician here who refuses to wake Gail up and who doesn't believe me. He's also an air force doctor, a major. Dr. Mark Wellsley. Yes, sir, I thought you'd say that."

Steve held out the phone. "Lieutenant General Paul Wriggle is on the other end. He's speaking from the White House."

Uncertainty now crossed the face of the doctor as he reluctantly took the phone, listening and responding in guarded fashion before asking the key question Steve knew had to come.

"How the hell do I know you are who you say you are?" The doctor looked back at Reagan, eyes flaring with distaste as he agreed to hang up and find the main number of the White House switchboard on his own and call in.

He handed the phone back to Steve as if it were contaminated and moved to a desk phone at the nurses' station, punching up information and then dialing the number, obviously astounded when he was recognized and connected immediately.

"Okay, yes, I'm satisfied. What the hell is going on general?"

A few more words were spoken before the doctor replaced the receiver and turned to Steve.

"Okay. We can do this safely, but you'll only have a few minutes, because I'm not going to let you wear her out."

CHAPTER FIFTY-FIVE

The White House (1:00 a.m. EST / 0500 Zulu)

"Will? I'm in!"

"What? To the Internet?"

"Yes! And I'm cueing up that transponder again. I think I know how to get through the firewall."

The sound of the door opening filled the room as the same Secret Service agent who had ushered them in returned, his face an unreadable mask.

"Come with me please."

Jenny looked up at him, startled.

"I need a minute."

"No, ma'am. Close the computer."

"But I ..."

"Now, ma'am."

Only a few seconds' hesitation was needed to study the man's face and know it wasn't a request. Jenny carefully lowered the lid and gathered up the power supply as she fell in behind Will, who was already moving out of the door.

"We were about to give up on you," Will said, trying not to sound too disparaging but equally aware that the man leading them was impervious.

Another agent picked up the lead and escorted them through several hallways and into an ornate conference room Jenny recognized from pictures as the Cabinet Room.

General Paul Wriggle knew he was grasping at straws, so the sudden appearance of someone claiming to have codes relating to Flight 10 was deserving of an immediate response.

Introductions were short and urgent, and Paul looked at both IDs, fixing Will Bronson with a steady gaze to make a quick assessment of his response.

"Are your leaders looking for you, Bronson?"

"Yes, sir. Everywhere, I'm sure. I think I've stumbled onto an illicit operation, which is why I sought out Jenny, here, and why I refused to come in."

"An illicit operation? By Defense Intelligence?"

"Yes, sir. It will take some explaining."

"I would think. Your boss is downstairs right now in the Sit Room and, fortunately, the duty officer didn't inform him you were here before informing the president."

"I don't want to talk to him, sir, until I talk to you, or the president."

"No time for that. Who has the codes?"

"I do, I think," Jenny replied, filling him in as quickly and succinctly as possible on reversing the sequence, using a version of a code she wrote.

"Do either of you have any idea what's going on with that aircraft, other than the pilots are locked out?"

"No, sir," Jenny answered. "We just know something turned on a … I guess, circuit or device aboard that plane that won't let the pilots control it, and I think the sequence I have … which is just eight numbers representing a reverse algorithm … will undo it. I'm just guessing, of course."

"Is there an Israeli operation behind this?"

Will and Jenny exchanged startled glances, before Will replied.

"I … honestly don't know, sir. I just know DIA, and I think some faction of NSA is involved. It could be an Israeli op."

The door opened, and the president himself came in.

"Paul?"

"Meet our missing DIA man, Will Bronson, and his NSA compatriot, Jenny Reynolds. Apparently he's not William Piper. Face is completely different."

The president nodded at both of them as he turned to

Paul.

"Your assessment, Paul?"

"Neither of these people has any idea about the basics of how this happened, therefore there can be no realistic chance that the code she's offering is meant to sabotage a disconnect. I vote we use it as fast as possible."

The president was nodding. "You're my final authority. Okay. Do it. Jenny is it?"

"Yes, Mr. President."

"Give General Wriggle the code. He'll make the calls from here. Then … stay here. Both of you. It may be a few hours but we'll want to debrief."

"Okay." She slid a folded piece of paper across the highly polished table she'd seen in countless presidential photographs, and the general opened it and studied the contents.

"This is it?"

"As best I can figure. Do you want me to tell you why I think so? The code that apparently caused the original lockout …"

The general had his hand up to stop her. "Won't be necessary. I read 62993178."

"Yes, sir."

Paul Wriggle turned to one of the deskset phones and pulled the receiver to his ear as he dialed. Colonel Dana Baumgartner answered immediately.

"Paul here, Dana. Any word from Denver since I spoke to the doctor?"

"No, sir. She's slowly coming around. She did confirm what we already know that the numbers we got from her desk safe were not the codes."

"Dana, I'm going to read you a set of numbers. The question is this: If this is the code that the unit would take if it received the appropriate satellite broadcast, would it also work if typed in or sent by UHF relay?"

"No need, Paul. The code is the same regardless of how it's delivered. Of course the MDCU entry method takes more preparation, but they're in essence all the same, a string of numbers."

"All I needed to know."

With an ashen-faced Will Bronson and Jenny Reynolds watching, Paul Wriggle checked his watch, catching their eyes as he punched up the White House operator.

"Connect me again with the Israeli Air Force Command Post in Tel Aviv. This is an emergency."

"How long do they have, General?" Will asked.

Paul Wriggle put his hand over the mouthpiece and turned to him as he glanced at the wall clock.

"Ten minutes, if that."

CHAPTER FIFTY-SIX

St. Paul's Hospital, Denver, Colorado (10:15 p.m. MST / 0515 Zulu)

"Mrs. Reagan, can you hear me?" Dr. Wellsley asked, leaning over Gail.

"She … uses her professional name. Hunt. Gail Hunt."

The doctor glanced at Steve Reagan with a tiny flash of suspicion which paled instantly in the face of everything surrounding this patient.

"Gail Hunt? I need you to talk to me now. This is your doctor."

From Gail's point of view, there was another face hovering somehow in the sky overhead, above the meadow she'd been enjoying. She tried to make her mouth work, but as before, the lips moved without sound and she tried to clear her throat.

"Okay …" she said, taking a deep breath, the last of the dream state gone. She could feel herself being jolted awake, and the pain began to reassert itself.

"Gail, your husband, Steve, needs to speak with you urgently. Please concentrate and help him out, and then we'll let you get back to sleep."

Steve's face joined the doctor's, and she smiled back at him through the confusion.

My husband? Aw-w! We're MARRIED! Why don't I remember ...

"Gail? Honey? I need you to help me get the latest codes you wrote that will release the control unit. You said they were in the central computer. I have my laptop here connected to our server. Can you guide me in?"

"We're married?" she asked, smiling.

"Yes, sweetheart," he answered, trying not to look stricken at the fact he was lying to her at a vulnerable moment, playing on her loyalties to get the information they needed, and about being married no less!

" Why don't I remember? You know how long I've wanted you? I've wanted you to make love to me for ages!"

Steve Reagan felt his facc flushing a deep red, and for a few seconds the entire reason for the marital ruse got lost in a completely unexpected kaleidoscope of images.

He yanked himself back to the present and nodded quickly at the doctor.

"Gail, we've got a lot to talk about, but right now, General Wriggle needs you."

"Is he here, too?"

"No, just me. Now, darling, please concentrate."

CHAPTER FIFTY-SEVEN

The Kirya, Tel Aviv, Israel (7:20 a.m. local / 0520 Zulu)

The military leaders of Israel had gathered in their war room for a real-time update. Prime Minister Zamir was acutely aware of the possibility that he would soon have to make a split-second decision based on little more than guesswork, intelligence, and reports from their pilots. The moment was almost upon him.

"Proceed, please, General," Gershorn said as he sipped a seriously strong cup of coffee.

"Here's the tactical situation. We have six F-15s in formation with Flight 10, and they're eight minutes from Iranian airspace. They're in a solid cloud deck up to 38,000 feet, but it's now daylight. The Pangia crew is aware of only two fighters. We did not want to frighten them. We have sixteen more fighters in stealth mode on the deck, largely below Iranian radar, ready to pop up as necessary. The crew still does not have control of their aircraft, and they have almost no fuel remaining."

"And the Iranians?"

"Eight fighters in the air flying combat air patrol just on the other side, all, we're sure, ready to engage."

"Engage who?"

"Flight 10, although our six F-15s at 38,000 feet aren't necessarily invisible."

"And we believe they're prepared to shoot down this jetliner?"

"Yes sir."

"If I don't decide to do it for them."

Silence greeted the rhetorical question.

"And the strategic picture with their ballistic force?"

"At least six ballistic missiles in four Iranian locations fueled and on their respective pads. We have real-time monitoring by satellite … the Americans are locking arms with us on this … and we believe that only one of the missiles is nuclear equipped, but the others may be biological."

"What is the rhetoric from Tehran?"

"Shrill to hysterical, all because of Moishe Lavi's presence."

"Is anyone still in charge in Tehran?"

"We can't confirm that control has been shifted to the field. We do think that if Flight 10 was to get more than a few miles inside the border, whoever *is* in charge is going to be hard pressed not to fire because the presumption would be that, as idiotic as it sounds, our friend Lavi is riding a nuclear bomb meant for them."

Gershorn referenced the main digital clock at the end of the room.

"Very well, bring up the live connection with our lead pilot."

An aide scrambled to punch up the connections as someone else handed a receiver to the prime minister.

"The White House, sir."

Gershorn looked at him in puzzlement but wasted no time saying hello.

"Mr. Prime Minister, this is General Paul Wriggle calling for the president. I know we have only a few minutes, but we now have what we think is the correct release code for that airliner, and we need your pilot to try again. Can you patch me to that pilot?"

The White House

Paul Wriggle waited for the connection with the Israeli

fighter pilot flying formation with the imperiled Airbus A330 and re-read the code sequence Jenny had handed him: 62993178. How anyone could figure out something that arcane from an encrypted satellite message he did not understand, but in lieu of any word from Gail Hunt's bedside, it was their best shot.

"We have a problem, General," the Prime Minister was saying, jolting Wriggle back to the moment.

"What is it?"

"Our pilots are already being radar locked by Iranian fighters and they've got to defend themselves. They may not have time to transmit the code again."

"This is a different code, sir. This will solve the problem if we can get the code transmitted on UHF."

"I'll do my best, General. We all will. Stay on the line with my aide. We passed the code to our pilot."

Airborne, 38,000 feet, approaching the Iraq/Iran border

Patyish 21, the call sign of the Israeli major leading the flight of six F-15s accompanying the Pangia A330, saw his tactical radar register the hostile intentions of the Iranian fighters long before they could be in visual range. Against his better judgment and instincts, he took the few seconds to jot down the eight-number sequence before ordering his wingmen into the appropriate formation for engagement. There was no time to explain to the Pangia crew what was happening, but presumably the airliner's captain had seen him pull away.

"Engaging enemy fighters," was all he had time to say, and that was probably too much, especially since he couldn't now recall with adrenaline levels rising whether he'd said it in Hebrew or English.

" Patyish 21 engaged, bearing zero-eight, fifty out," was followed by the pulsating cursor on his heads up display as he walked the pipper to the left and locked up the oncoming target who had gone "to tone," locking up his F-15 as well.

"Patyish 21, Fox Two," he said on tactical channel as he pickled off two of his air-to-air missiles. The bright plumes of their rocket motors disappearing into the indistinct clouds was startling enough to a veteran fighter pilot, but to the adjacent commercial airline crew, they had to look terrifying.

Normally he would have ordered his wingman to climb and join him in a tight left turn while dispensing chaff to throw off the incoming missile the Iranian pilot had probably fired, but that would leave the Airbus a sitting duck, and he lit his burners and pushed ahead of the Airbus into a tight right turn instead, launching two flares to pull any incoming missiles off of both of them.

The tactical channel was now full of his wingmen's voices and their clipped, cryptic reports as one by one they locked up and engaged various members of the oncoming Iranian formation, preparing to fight a high-speed battle with an enemy still thirty miles distant. The larger Israeli force below shot skyward now to join the battle, throwing overwhelming numbers at the oncoming Iranian pilots who were undoubtedly not expecting to see their tactical radar screens break out in Israeli warplanes.

Light years from Hollywood's concept of a World War II aerial dogfight, the radar-based battle revolved around digital images on the heads up displays, and whatever was about to happen would be over in minutes, without either side actually ever seeing the other.

A large explosion in the distance marked the apparent end of one of the enemy fighters as one of the radar returns fragmented and disappeared from the Israeli scopes. The major's radar picture showed the Iranian pilots breaking formation, which was expected, but what type of fighter was flying toward them was a mystery. With the rag-tag roster of single-seat aircraft Iran still flew, he wouldn't have been terribly surprised to find himself in mortal combat with the one ancient American F-14 from pre-revolution days that Iran still tried to keep operational.

The major studied his radar picture once more, expecting to see a second wave of Iranian aircraft backing up the first, and as expected, the images now moved onto his screen. The eight digits he was supposed to transmit to the airliner were still on his kneeboard but there was no time to pull back in position with a screen full of oncoming enemy, yet …

He handed off command to his number two wingman and lit his afterburner for a few seconds to get back on the left wing of the Airbus, matching speeds before pulling out his personal cellphone again to go through the cumbersome task of typing in the numeric string with his oxygen mask off, pressing the phone's little speaker against the microphone, all the while maintaining formation at 460 knots.

An explosion to his left told the tale of an Iranian warhead that had barely missed one of his men, but the fact that the enemy had succeeded in pickling one in the middle of his formation to begin with was very disturbing.

The sounds of the battle were picking up in the exchanges among his men.

"Patyish 23, engaged, bandit ten o'clock, six, Fox Two."

"Patyish 24, supporting."

"Dyan 12 is in, engaged, tally on bandit at two o clock, six miles."

"Dyan 11, break left, break left, flare. Bandit on your six with lockup!"

Digit by digit he kept his jet steady as he punched the numbers in, forcing himself not to react to the intense tactical exchanges of his pilots or the new chirping of a ground anti-aircraft missile battery that had acquired them as they continued to deal with the oncoming Iranians. Somewhere just behind him was the border, and they were now streaking into heavily defended enemy airspace.

The White House

The call from St. Paul's Hospital in Denver and Steve Reagan had come right on the heels of passing Jenny Reynold's code to the prime minister.

"Paul, we've got it! We've got the code! Ready to copy?"

"Go ahead," he said, not wanting to reward what had to have been Herculean effort with the news that it was undoubtedly too late.

He wrote the numbers down as Steve intoned them.

"Stand by," Paul Wriggle said, feeling a rush of adrenaline as he pulled the other note containing the Reynold's code across the table and placed it side-by-side with the numbers he'd just inscribed, reading them with the care of a potential lottery winner making certain his wishful thinking was not overriding reality.

My God! Paul thought to himself, confirming one more time. *They're the same!*

He forced himself to take a deep breath, the urgency suddenly gone.

"How is Gail?" he asked.

"She'll be okay."

"Thank her deeply for me."

"She's still pretty balmy. She thinks we're married, sir," Steve Reagan said with what sounded like a nervous chuckle. "I'll have to let her down easily."

"Or, you could just marry the girl! I always thought you two made a great team."

"Yes, sir."

"I have to go."

Jenny Reynolds and Will Bronson were both watching him carefully from halfway down the conference table as the general turned to them, the shadow of a smile playing around the edges of his mouth.

"Well, Miss Reynolds."

"Sir?"

"It seems you cracked the code. Your numbers were correct. That *was* the unlock sequence."

She came forward slightly, eyes wide. "Really? How do you know? Did it work?"

"We don't know if they got it in time, and I can't tell you how I know, but …" he said, aware that he was stumbling linguistically, his mind's eye a half world away with a civilian airliner flying into combat unarmed with anything more than a string of digits in the night.

He yanked himself back to the Cabinet Room. "I'm impressed that you figured it out, and, I assume, Mr. Bronson, that your efforts led to getting it here. Thank you. In fact … if it worked … I am deeply in your debt."

"When will we know, General?" Will asked.

"Soon. Very soon."

The Kirya, Tel Aviv, Israel (7:40 a.m. / 0540 Zulu)

Clearly, Gershorn Zamir thought, *this is the moment.*

An aerial battle just over the Iraq/Iran border was raging, and both he and whoever was in charge in Iran had their fingers poised over respective nuclear buttons.

"Four splashed for certain, perhaps a fifth kill," the air force chief was intoning as he monitored several radio channels with a phone to each ear. A widescreen depiction of the battle zone was before them on the latest technology screen, along with each of the potential Iranian ballistic launch sites deeper into Iran. The airliner had lumbered through Jordanian and Iraqi airspace with the respective countries either unaware of the Israeli fighter escort, or unwilling to get involved. Despite their public rhetoric to the contrary, every responsible government in the Middle East was secretly hoping the Israelis would disregard American advice and go for Iran's throat.

Gershorn glanced around the room, recounting the advice of his fellow civilian leaders who were nervously standing by to sign off on any doomsday launch decision.

Surprising, he thought, that no one was pounding on him for a preemptive strike. With all the logic of that terrible move and Moishe Lavi's suspected orchestration of this opportunity, he had expected a full court press. Yet only one of the generals and one of the Knesset members had taken him aside for the hard sell, and even they seemed tepid in their support for the nuclear option.

In truth, he was on the fence, teetering on a knife edge of indecision with his country's fate in the balance. Everything he'd ever read or studied about great men making great decisions made him feel small and terrified in the face of such awesome responsibility. He was no John Kennedy facing down Nikita Khrushchev, yet … hadn't even Kennedy waffled back and forth with agonizing indecision as his generals begged him to have it out?

"Gershorn," the air force chief was addressing him.

"Yes?"

"This is the last chance to consider shooting Flight 10 down ourselves."

"Are you recommending that we do so?" he asked, as evenly as possible.

"No, but … we must decide. That … would eliminate the

provocation to Iran without question."

"I understand that."

"We've ordered our lead pilot to make one last attempt at transmitting that disconnect code, then they are to fall back into firing position awaiting your orders if the pilots don't regain control and turn back."

"Only if I give the order, understood?"

"Understood."

So the challenge was joined, he thought. Pangia 10 was over the border, an air battle was already underway, and he could either eliminate the provocation of the Iranians by shooting down the Airbus and killing hundreds of innocent people, or let the flight continue, permitting the Iranians to do the hideous deed of murdering everyone aboard.

And, he thought, there would never be a better moment, a more justified moment, than this. Iranian fighters were essentially attacking a civilian airliner, and hundreds of miles ahead Iranian ballistic missiles had been erected, fueled, armed, and clearly targeted at Israel, at least one of them carrying a nuclear weapon. He had every reason and every right to push the metaphorical button as fast and as hard as he could and launch the very preemptive strike Lavi had proposed so passionately. Yes, the world would be outraged, and Israel would be hamstrung with sanctions pushed mainly by the Russians and Chinese. And yes, oil prices would go through the roof, and the planet could end up in an unprecedented economic depression.

But, Iran's nuclear program would be back to the stone age, especially since the Iranians had no idea how much Israel knew—how vulnerable they had been to human intelligence, and how successful Mossad's efforts had been. At a great cost, of course, measured in the lives of seven Mossad agents—some barbarically tortured before being killed—Israel knew where the fissionable material was and how to destroy it. Information not even fully shared with Washington.

Now, indeed, was the moment, and why not launch? Didn't the mullahs want to slaughter every man, woman, and child in Israel? Wasn't radical Islam's hatred and lethal intent just another version of Hitler's final solution? Wasn't he dealing with mad dogs who did not deserve the consideration afforded fellow humans?

Gershorn took a deep breath, registering in the back of his mind the fact that an Israeli jet had been hit, the pilot trying to limp back to the west with considerable damage. He looked into a sea of faces all belonging to serious and experienced men and women, and all of them looking to him for a decision.

CHAPTER FIFTY-EIGHT

Aboard Pangia 10 (0535 Zulu)

Ten minutes before the Iranian border, the digital fuel readouts indicated the engines were seconds from flameout. Jerry asked Josh Begich to return to his seat, touching his arm as he climbed out of the copilot's chair.

"Josh?"

"Yes, sir?"

"I want to apologize for my conduct hours ago in yelling at you and scaring you."

"That's okay. I understand."

"You've really helped us up here. I won't forget that."

"Thanks. What's … going to happen now?"

"I'm not sure, Josh, but go back and strap in, grab that little girl's hand you're sitting next to and say a few prayers. Carol told me you were trying to impress her, and now's your chance."

"I will," he answered, his face suddenly ashen.

Bill Breem had come off the jumpseat and moved the short distance to Jerry's side, putting a firm hand on his shoulder.

"Is there anything I can do to assist?" he asked.

Surprised, Jerry shifted as far around as he possibly could.

"No, Captain, other than watch carefully and let me know if I'm missing something."

"You haven't so far, Jerry. I …" He was searching for words that didn't come easily, but there was no time to indulge in an apology.

"Thanks. Okay, everyone strap in."

With Carol once again on her knees by the hatch, Dan

was poised below waiting for the order to cut the power lead, his gloved hands holding the wooden handle of the crash axe. Frank had been sent back to his seat as well, since the time for analysis was long past. This was their last chance, and both men knew it.

What appeared to be a flash of an explosion to the left in the distance with the Israeli fighters apparently engaging an unseen enemy ahead would have unnerved Jerry, if he wasn't already so numb. Without the ability to hear the tactical channel the Israeli pilots were using, his imagination was being fueled by his own experiences as a navy fighter pilot trying to imagine what was going on: radar lockups, missiles fired, possibility of being engaged by a ground-to-air battery, and basically flying through their own little war with no munitions, no defenses, no chaff, no flares, little visibility even at dawn, and no options. The whole thing would only last a few minutes. He assumed the unseen enemies were Iranian fighters determined to shoot them down. Who else would they be? And against a sky full of armed fighters, Pangia 10 was a fat, sitting duck.

Jerry hadn't noticed the Israeli F-15 sliding back alongside his left wing, and he had not even imagined the possibility that another Israeli pilot was in trail formation, the targeting icon on his tactical screen locked on Flight 10 as he awaited orders from Tel Aviv.

He caught himself wondering what the last conscious seconds were like for the pilots of Malaysia 17 when they were blasted out of a clear blue Ukrainian sky by a surface-to-air missile. Blessedly, they had had no warning, he thought. But here we are waiting for the end. The cold certainty of death began to enfold him, and despite the determination to fight, somewhere inside he was already letting go.

CHAPTER FIFTY-NINE

The Kirya, Tel Aviv, Israel (7:42 a.m. local / 0542 Zulu)

With one all-consuming thought demanding his attention, the Israeli prime minister closed his eyes to meet it head on. What, exactly, was going through the diseased minds in Tehran? Were all of them nothing but murderous bastards to whom infidel humanity was no more sacrosanct than insects?

Or were the *Iranians* the insects, and Gershorn the appointed exterminator?

The confidence level was high, he had just been told that control of the nuclear weaponry had not been shifted to outlying commanders. At least, not yet. Was it one of the religious mafia in Tehran hesitating or merely a professional military man using logic and not religious hysteria?

Or could there be, in the midst of that cultish insanity, someone like him, even at this moment weighing the moral as well as the strategic consequences of taking the next step? The mere thought seemed heresy, and with Hamas or ISIS and any other insane collection of genocidal maniacs it would be. But maybe, just maybe, someone in Tehran could still understand the concept, if not the benefits, of restraint.

He glanced again at the screen. No movement at the various missile sites, and especially none at the launch site Mossad had identified as most likely to be carrying what was perhaps their only nuke.

To defuse it, all he had to do was order the missiles off the rails of the fighter trailing Pangia 10. If there was no inbound airliner with Moishe Lavi aboard, there was no reason for launching against Tel Aviv, and no reason for Israel to incinerate Iran.

Airborne, in trail of Pangia 10

The pilot flying Patyish 26 assigned to trail the Pangia Airbus with missiles ready to fire had maintained the radar lock for what seemed an eternity, waiting for an order one way or another. The massive internal battle between the obligation to follow orders and the nightmarish possibility of committing mass murder, even as an instrument of his government, tore at his soul. The thirty-four-year-old father of two was not entirely sure he could squeeze the trigger if given the command.

"Patyish 26, stand by for orders."

"Roger," was the correct reply, and all he could manage as he tensed for what was coming next. A cold chill had already enveloped him, and he could hear his heart pounding in his ears as he strained at the silence on the channel.

Pangia 10

"Tell Dan to get ready," Jerry said.

"He says 'on your command,' Captain."

Jerry glanced at the moving map display. Was there any point in waiting further? Mere minutes of fuel remained.

Jerry reached up and grabbed his sidestick controller perhaps for one last comforting moment of pretense that all was normal and this had been just a nightmare.

He deflected the stick to the right, reacting in absolute disbelief as the big aircraft rolled to the right, obeying his command as if nothing had ever been wrong.

What the hell?

Carol's voice from just behind his seat partially filtered through his disbelief.

"Captain, Dan says to tell you there was a large noise down here and a lot of relays clicked. Are you ready for him to cut it?"

Jerry looked at the sidestick controller in his left hand as if it had materialized out of the either. For hours it had defied him, and now, suddenly, when it was probably far too late, it decides to work? What the hell?

Her words finally coalesced. Dan was ready to bring an axe down on the power cable below. He forced his body to swivel around as far as he could to make sure Carol heard him. "NO! Tell him do NOT cut it! Do NOT cut it! We have control again somehow! Tell Dan to get up here."

Jerry could hear Carol getting up from the floor as Dan all but levitated through the hatch, barely believing Carol's words.

"You have *control* Jerry?"

"Yes! Get back in the seat."

"Jesus, yes!" Dan scrambled past Carol, patting her on the butt as he passed in some unconscious form of celebration as he all but leapt in the copilot's seat.

"How'd you do it, Dan?"

"I didn't! I have no idea why it let go!"

The Kirya, Tel Aviv, Israel

The generals, and especially the air force chief, were feeding in an almost three-dimensional picture of the aerial battle, and as expected, Iran was doing very poorly, even as the second wave of fighters closed in. That would hasten Tehran's decision. If they couldn't shoot the airliner down …

"How long a delay in seconds between a ballistic missile launch and when our board here would show it?" Gershorn asked no one in particular.

Two members of the general staff turned to answer. "No more than five seconds, sir. This is an amalgam of real-time satellite sensors and imagery."

He nodded thanks, his mind racing. The order to intercept any launched missile in boost phase was already signed. The order to launch the nuclear preemptive strike would take a maximum of two minutes consultation.

"One more question," Gershorn asked evenly, consciously hanging on to his emotions. "What are the expected civilian casualties if we go for preemption?"

The room quieted immediately, as if a judge had asked a defendant at the start of a trial which prison he'd prefer.

"Between … 7,000 and 20,000, sir, in primary and secondary casualties in the communities in which they've tried to hide the enrichment facilities."

"And our fighter is in place for a shootdown?"

"Awaiting your order, sir."

"How long would it take Tehran to understand the threat was gone?"

"They would see the target break up and disappear. But, they might not know who shot them."

"In other words, they might still push the button based on the assumption that we were attacking?"

The generals in the room were all glancing at each other as if forming an unspoken collective resolve over what to say. The prime minister was clearly teetering on a razor edge. The wrong phrase, the wrong word, might push him in the wrong—or the right—direction.

The final tumbler suddenly dropped into place in Gershorn's mind, unlocking his resolve.

And somehow, in Tehran, he knew his counterpart had also reached an equally historic decision.

CHAPTER SIXTY

Aboard Pangia 10 (0542 Zulu)

"I tried to tell the fighters, but they're not responding," Jerry said as Dan pulled on his headset and triggered the radio the Israeli had been using. "I'm starting a turn."

"Patyish Lead, this is Pangia 10! We have regained control! Repeat, we have regained control and are reversing course back to Iraq."

There was no response, yet another explosion in the distance off to the east announced the fact that the engagement wasn't over.

"Where are we?" Dan asked.

"Just inside their airspace. Baghdad is right behind us. See if you can punch up the airport in case we need it."

"Absolutely we're going to …"

The rest of the answer was drowned out by a thunderous explosion on the right side of the Airbus and they could feel the big bird stagger and yaw to the right. Emergency warnings, beeps and horns and messages began flooding the ECAM computer screens.

"Jesus God!"

"What the hell was *that*?" Jerry demanded.

"Something exploded!"

"No shit, Sherlock! But what?"

"I don't know … maybe a missile. We've lost number two engine, I think."

Dan jerked his head back forward, quickly scanning the cascading readouts on the screen. "Yes, number two engine is down!"

"We have a fire light?" Jerry asked.

"What? Y*es*, dammit!"

"Run the ECAM procedure."

"Roger. Engine fire number two, I have the fire switch for number two, confirm?"

The procedure intimately familiar from training scenarios, Jerry reached his right hand up and touched the same fire switch Dan was pointing to.

"Roger, number two confirmed."

"Pulling two, continuing checklist. Shutting off number two start switch."

The sudden feeling of deceleration superimposed itself over all their other senses as Jerry looked with feral intensity toward his copilot.

"No, No, Dan! Number TWO! Not number ONE!"

"I pulled two!"

"We just lost number one! Confirm the fire switch is in and try a restart …"

"Jerry!"

"… we can get her back! Quickly!"

"JERRY!"

"What?"

Dan was pointing to the forward panel and the depiction of the fuel tanks.

"We're out of gas, Jere!"

"What?"

"We've run out of fuel. I've got all the pumps on."

Dan leaned left to get closer to the fuel readouts, confirming it. No useable fuel in number one main tank, and essentially none in number two.

"We're zeroed, Jerry."

"Oh, fuck! But what happened to two?"

"They shot us."

"Who? Who is they? Who shot us?"

"Man, I don't know, but it had to be the Iranians."

"But I'd just started the turn! We were nose on to them."

"I don't know …"

"Couldn't be a surface-to-air, we'd be in pieces."

"Okay, look, we need to maintain control here."

"I know it!"

"Is she still responding?" Dan asked

"Yes. Sluggish but responding."

"I'm deploying the RAT. And … we're depressurizing, Jerry. Oxygen masks on, confirm 100 percent."

Jerry let go of the sidestick long enough to sweep on his oxygen mask, checking the 100 percent position on the selector before resuming his death grip on the stick.

"Comm check, Dan. How copy?" Jerry asked, his voice sounding strange in the oxygen mask microphone.

"Loud and clear. How me?"

"Good. Run the depress checklist, but we cannot do an emergency descent."

"Hell, no. I got that. We don't want to anyway. We don't know the damage."

"Jump seat on," Bill Breem reported, followed by a quick confirmation from Tom Wilson.

"Obviously it punched our fuselage," Jerry added. "Do you suppose we've lost anyone back there?"

The question was in cadence with the rapid fire back and forth of the previous thirty seconds but the reality of it stopped both men cold. The memory of the gaping hole that had swallowed nine of United Airlines Flight 811 passengers in 1989 replayed in their heads as clearly as if there had been an HD screen on the glareshield.

"No," Dan answered suddenly. "No, not possible. The pressure loss was slow and steady, not explosive."

The electrical power flickered and stabilized with a reduced number of instruments, as Dan reached up to start the auxiliary power unit.

"The APU isn't going to do us much good without fuel,

Dan," Jerry managed, trying his best to grin at him.

"I forgot," Dan replied, shaking his head at the oversight.

"Is there an airport we can reach?"

"Yes. Baghdad International! Eighty-five miles, heading two-eight-zero. We're at 37,000 feet ... we have enough energy to glide 120 miles, Jerry. So we can do this."

"You think it was a sidewinder or something?"

"Yeah, a missile, I'll bet anything. But you're the fighter jock."

"We've got to get on the ground before someone comes back to finish us off!"

"Agreed."

"That had to be a heat seeker or we'd be toast. Had to be Iranian."

"Probably," Dan said, another possibility nipping at the back of his mind.

"I imagine our Israeli friends are still holding them off."

"Let's just concentrate on getting down, Jerry," Dan replied, trying to force his thoughts back to the myriad of tasks at hand. "Lemme dial up Baghdad tower. I have no idea if they're clear or socked in down there."

"Dan?" Jerry's voice was suddenly tentative, puzzled, almost indignant, as if the scenario was going significantly off script and there had been no approval for such a deviation.

"Yes?"

"I'm ... having control problems here, Dan."

"What do you mean, control problems?"

"I mean ... she's sluggish on roll to the left, and the vibrations ... feel that?"

"Yeah. No time to go back and look, but the right wing's probably damaged."

"Bet it ripped open our fuel tank."

"Not that it matters!" Dan chuckled, in spite of the all-consuming tension.

They had one shot at landing with no power, limited instruments, only the force of the slipstream turning the ram air turbine and batteries providing instrument power, and a totally unknown situation on landing gear and flaps.

"We can do this, Dan!"

"That's what I said. Damn right! You're in direct law. What can I do to help?"

"Make the radio calls, call my altitude, keep calculating energy status, and make sure we don't forget any emergency checklists."

"We're eighty miles out." With the iPad on his lap and Baghdad's main airport punched up, Dan located and dialed in the tower frequency and hit the transmit button for number one radio.

"Baghdad tower, Pangia Flight 10, declaring an emergency. All engines out. Eighty miles to the east, we'll be making a no-engine approach and landing. Please acknowledge and say current winds and … ah … ah … ceiling."

Seconds ticked by before the very American voice of a contract controller came back to them.

"Roger, Pangia 10. Runway Three-Three-Left is the active, 13,100 feet available, current winds three-two-zero at five knots, visibility unlimited. State fuel and souls on board."

"Fuel is zero, and we have … I don't know … several hundred souls on board. We will need the equipment and would recommend a few ambulances … we don't know the situation in the back."

"Please explain, Ten."

"We've been hit by an Iranian air-to-air missile. We were attacked by the Iranians."

"Dan … Dan she's vibrating even more. Something's coming loose out there!"

"Can you control her?"

"I've gotta slow down more … Jesus, it takes full left deflection to hold her level."

"Want me to run back and look?"

"I … think we'd better! I need to know what we've got."

An interphone call chime rang, and Dan punched up the channel. .

"Cockpit!"

"This is Lucy at Four-Right. We're on fire!" The voice was as strained and frightened as he imagined he sounded.

"What are you seeing, Lucy?"

"Outside on the right wing, we're trailing a sheet of flame!"

"Okay. One of us is coming back," Dan said, pushing the receiver back in its cradle, as he quickly briefed Jerry and reached for the glareshield, his hand searching for the engine fire switch and the button for the fire extinguishing bottles.

"You already fired one, right?" Jerry asked.

"Yes. The ECAM's saying to fire the second now. I'm shooting number two."

"Go ahead!"

Tom Wilson had thrown off his seatbelt. "I'll go back and take a look, guys."

"Please!" Jerry affirmed.

Inside two minutes, Tom Wilson was on the interphone.

"Okay, guys, we ARE on fire. It's not just whatever remains of number two engine, but it looks like we're trailing flame off the middle of the right wing. How, I don't know, since there's no fuel left …"

"Could it be the metal of the wing burning?"

"God I hope not! But it's pretty intense."

"That's probably hydraulic fluid, too, which means we could lose all the right side controls."

"No wonder she's sluggish!"

"I need to dive, Dan," Jerry was saying. "I need to blow the flames out!"

"We have some extra altitude, but if you go down too fast, we won't make the airport!"

"And if we don't, it could burn through the wing."

"She may not be able to structurally handle too much speed!"

"Gotta try! Increasing speed to barber pole," Jerry said.

Patyish 21

The major flying the lead F-15 had seen the explosion on the right wing of the lumbering Airbus just before it turned back and headed out of Iranian airspace, but the air battle was still too engaged to give chase until they confirmed the Iranians were bugging out east and the Israeli force acknowledged his "knock it off" call.

Now he ordered the remainder of his flight to reform on Patyish 22 as he plugged in afterburner and dove to the west to join up on Pangia 10.

He had not monitored the special command channel Patyish 26 had been ordered to contact, and he'd restrained himself from asking about 26's remaining ordinance when they were "safeing up" their weapons for the return. The possibility that the explosion he'd seen came from an Israeli missile was nauseating, but at least Pangia was still in the air.

The target of the huge Airbus flared clearly ahead of him as he pushed past Mach 1.8 in chase, closing the fifteen-mile gap easily before coming out of burner and timing his arrival alongside the stricken commercial liner.

Aboard Pangia 10

Carol had reached forward to grab the PA handset and

both pilots registered the fact that she was making the announcement they wished they had time to give.

"Everyone check your seatbelts tightly fastened and keep your oxygen masks on! Stay down, lean as far forward as you can. We're making an emergency descent and will be making a no engine emergency landing in Baghdad."

"I'll keep calculating the lowest altitude you can descend to and still make Baghdad, Jerry."

"How far out are we?"

"Sixty-two miles on the GPS. That means no diving lower than 24,000."

"And we're still at 31,000."

"She's shaking pretty badly, Jerry!"

"I know it!"

"I didn't see any obvious damage to the cabin, but somehow we've got a hole in us. You're coming through 30,000 now."

"That's as fast as I dare."

"Agreed. Twenty-nine, five … twenty-nine … twenty-eight, five …"

"Is someone watching back there?"

"Yes."

"Wish we could talk to the passengers, too, but no time."

"Twenty-eight, now Jerry, twenty-seven, five … this shaking is really worrying me!"

"Distance to Baghdad?"

"Fifty-four miles. We need 21,000, we're descending through twenty-seven."

"Call her, Dan!"

"Got it," he replied, yanking the handset back out of its cradle and punching the button for 4R.

"Tom … status?"

He hunched over the phone, nodding and acknowledging before hanging up and turning back to the captain.

"He says the flames are less now, but it's still burning, and every few seconds something else seems to fall off and blow away."

"Like … parts of the wing?"

"Jerry, he said each piece is glowing hot or flaming when it falls away! We gotta get down man … we're coming apart."

CHAPTER SIXTY-ONE

Situation Room, The White House (1:47 a.m. EST / 0547 Zulu)

"Who fired that missile?"

The president had reappeared in the Situation Room without warning and was standing at the far end of the table, waiting for a response.

The air force colonel who had been handling the real-time connections with Tel Aviv realized no one else was going to reply. "We're not sure, Mr. President. They apparently took an air-to-air missile up the tailpipe of their right engine just before they regained control and began to turn around."

"Before anyone *knew* they'd regained control?"

"Yes, sir," the colonel confirmed.

"Have we asked Tel Aviv that question? Who fired?"

"Not yet, sir."

"Do it, please."

The president was chewing his lip in thought, weighing the probabilities that Gershorn Zamir had issued the shootdown order, and how to keep a lid on it.

"Status of the aircraft?" the president asked.

"Out of fuel, having control problems, about thirty miles east of Baghdad and trying to make it to the airport."

"And the Iranian fighters?"

"The Iranians have lost five fighters, sir. Casualties are uncertain. Israel has had two F-15s hit, but one is limping back to base. The pilot of the other one ejected in Iraqi territory and is being picked up. The remaining Iranians have bugged out."

"Any ground launches?"

"If you mean surface to air, no sir … not that we've

detected."

"I mean ballistic. 'Wipe Israel off the map' launches."

"No, sir. At least five missiles are fueled and ready on their respective launch pads, but the Iranian command channels are deathly quiet. Of course, they could issue a launch order at any second. "

"As can Israel, I imagine."

Aboard Pangia 10

"What's the situation, Tom?"

Dan asked the question with his eyes unconsciously closed, as if waiting for a final exam score he just knew would be rotten. And indeed there was a long and worrisome hesitation measured in milliseconds from the back before the copilot's voice returned to his ear, but a slight tone of excitement sounded an up note.

"It's better, he said. "*Much* better! I can still see sparks coming off, but the flame front … if that's what you call it … it's gone. I'm coming back forward."

"Keep watching. Call if there's a change."

"Dan? Status?' Jerry asked.

Dan summarized Tom's report, adding the distance and altitude left to the Baghdad runway. "Thirty-three miles to go, Jerry! Energy's good. We're descending through 18,000, and that means we can glide no wind about fifty miles."

"You ever dead stick the simulator?" Jerry asked, his voice low and urgent, the question anything but casual. The term was all but archaic, "dead stick" being the traditional term-of-art for landing a powered aircraft without power, a maneuver for which you had one chance alone.

"Yes. In a 737, and once in this beast."

"How'd it work out?"

Caution lights blared at him from his personal mental dashboard, another aviating embarrassment he'd rather forget.

"You keep the numbers under control, it's a piece of cake," Dan answered, hoping the captain wouldn't ask more.

"I hate that phrase! Piece of friggin' cake indeed."

"So do I, now that I think about it."

"I'm full left deflection, Danny. I don't have anything more."

The words shattered what had been a fragile growing confidence. Slower speed would mean the need for more roll control, more aileron deflection, wouldn't it? What else could they use?

"Are you hitting the rudder as well?"

"Is the Pope Catholic?" Jerry shot back.

"We can't split the flaps …"

"We can't even *get* the flaps, what with the fire on the right wing!"

"You're still wings level, though," Dan said. "Speed's 260 knots. Is she getting worse as you slow?"

"What's our altitude?" Jerry demanded.

"Ah … coming through sixteen now, thirty miles out."

"I'm slowing. The control pressure to the left wasn't as great when I was diving. Now it's full."

"Want me to try mine?"

"I doubt there's anything wrong with the stick on my side, Dan."

"Jerry, nothing else has worked right in this airplane for the past six hours, and God knows what we screwed up downstairs trying to regain control."

He could see his partner take a deep breath and decide.

"Okay … take it and go immediately full left aileron. Hit the priority button just in case. If it's the same as what I've got, I'll take her back."

Dan positioned himself in the copilot's seat and wrapped his right hand around the sidestick controller and pressed the top button.

"Priority right," the female computer voice intoned as he immediately deflected the stick full left, not quite believing it when the big Airbus obeyed with a sudden roll to the left.

"Jesus! Level the wings, Dan!"

"Already ... doing it!"

"Holy moly ... you were right!"

"That sometimes happens," Dan replied through the shock that wasn't wearing off fast enough.

"What happens? That the sticks are mismatched?"

"No, that I'm right."

"Well, you've got her now, partner, for better or worse. How's she flying?"

"Reasonably steady. I can't believe it!"

"Okay, lemme get oriented here. I'll talk you in."

"Roger that. At least this time I can't screw up the autothrottles," Dan said, unprepared for the belly laugh from the left seat.

"Okay, we're down to 12,500, and twenty-four miles from the runway," Jerry reported. "We'll probably have the gear, depending on how much damage there was to the right side, but we'll have no flaps and no reverse, of course, and only raw brakes."

"We need to run the checklist."

"Yeah. That's right." Jerry reached forward to trigger the appropriate page on the ECAM, but the number of failure items and pages scrolling across the screen was beyond overwhelming.

Tom Wilson re-entered the cockpit and slipped back into the jump seat behind Dan.

"Too much here!" Jerry was saying. "I'll have to do it from memory. We'll add thirty knots for no flaps. We'll be faster than hell, Dan."

"I know it."

"The runway is more than two miles long and with a desert to overrun into, but we can't get too slow on final or too high."

"I know how to slip a bird, Jerry."

"We may have to, but we're going to run out of hydraulic pressure when we get too slow. We've got one windmilling engine and the RAT providing the hydraulic pressure."

"Got it."

"Of course the brakes have an accumulator."

"Rog."

"We're coming through 10,000 now, Dan. Speed is 220 knots, eighteen miles. I can see the runway ahead."

"Can we get an ILS up for the glide slope?"

"I … no. Not needed, Dan. We'll be a light year above the glide slope anyway."

"Oh. Yeah, I get that."

"Keep her at 220."

"Jerry, shouldn't we allow for aerodynamic damage out there?"

"What do you mean?"

"Stall speeds could have increased. We're essentially test pilots right now."

The captain hesitated, grimacing as he took it in. "You could be right. We were really shaking."

"Still are. Maybe we should test the touchdown speed while we've got excess altitude," Dan said.

"You're joking?"

"No … really, I'm not. If we're going to touchdown at 220, we need to make sure that's not stall speed, right? Let's slow briefly to 200 and make sure she's still controllable."

"Then speed up?"

"Absolutely."

"Seventeen miles out. I've got some ground contact out there. Okay, slow her up, but the second we start getting an excessive descent rate …"

"I'll dump the nose. Don't worry."

Dan held enough back pressure to let the airspeed bleed away, feeling the aircraft as best he could as she decelerated through 210 knots and then 205, aware of a sudden buffeting that was shaking the flight deck with alarming force.

"Speed up!" Jerry called as Dan forced the stick forward, accelerating the aircraft again to 220 knots. "What the hell was that?"

"Precisely what I was worried about," Dan said. "We've got serious damage out there. The buffeting was from the right side."

"We're sixteen miles out. You have the airport visual?"

"I...think so. Coming through 8,000 at 1,500 feet per minute descent."

"Not enough, Dan! Drop her to 2,000 feet per minute descent rate. We'll take the additional airspeed."

"I'd suggest gear down one mile out, Jerry."

"Right. No more."

"Maybe more if we're over 240! Our speed brakes work?"

"Yes, but do NOT use them! Keep it on this glide angle and keep the speed under 230 without them,"

"Roger. But I will use them for landing."

"Got it. We're at 7,000 feet, fourteen miles out."

"We're too high."

"No we're not."

"Yes we are, Jerry. Too high and too fast. I'm gonna 'S' turn us."

"Okay, but … don't go too far in either direction."

"Call the distance and altitude. I want to be at 1,000 feet three miles out at 220 knots. That's the needle I need to thread—the 'Gate.'"

"Okay … ah, ten miles to go to that gate, and we're coming through 6,500, so …"

"Lose 5,500 feet in ten miles and we're going four miles per minute."

"Right. That's—"

"That's 2,200 feet per minute down, or a couple of good 'S' turns."

"Okay."

"Everyone ready in the back?"

"What? Yeah, I guess."

"Yes, they are," Bill Breem replied from the back of the cockpit.

"Not too much, Dan! Just a few shallow turns."

"Got it."

"We're 240 knots now, down 2,000."

"Altitude?"

"Ah … ah … coming down through 4,000, six miles from the gate we want."

"That's about right. Coming back to centerline," Dan said, shocked that his voice sounded so unreasonably calm. "I can see the airport ahead."

"We've got one shot at this, Danny!"

"Yeah … no pressure, right?"

"Right. You're at 240 knots, 2,100 down, through 3,000 above the ground, 2,000 above the gate, a bit over four miles from the gate."

"Got it. I'm going be twenty knots too fast. Wanna drop the gear?"

"What will it do to us?"

"Slow us down. Maybe too much. But we're way too fast."

"Hold on, just … hold on. You're steady on 240, slowing a hair, on descent rate, three miles from the gate, ahead of the descent rate, a bit over a thousand to lose."

"I'll pull the nose up a bit and slow. Jerry, to recap, the Landing Gear Gravity Extend lever is below the landing gear lever and remember it has to be pulled out toward you before moving it down."

"I know."

"Just wanna make sure."

"Got it." Jerry watched the numbers winding down, trying to stay ahead of the unfolding scenario but feeling like he was somewhere behind, chasing the bird.

"We're 230 and slowing."

"Distance?"

"Two from the gate, 500 above."

"Just … a … little more."

"We're 225, Dan. One mile to go, just a hair above 1,000 feet."

"I've got the runway. Are we cleared to land?"

"Who the hell cares? But yes, we are."

"On speed?"

"Yes! Yes, you're doing it right: 220, through the gate at 950 feet, a hair less than three miles out."

"Don't drop the gear yet."

"I won't. We'll plan for a mile out."

"Pray it works."

"Already in progress. Two miles to go, 600 feet."

"Roger."

"Hold her, man. We'll have a large nose up angle on touchdown with zero flaps."

"Got it. Gear down, Jerry!"

"Roger, gear down," the captain replied, reaching to the copilot's side to reach the Landing Gear Gravity Extension selector, opening the safety door and moving it down . The sound of the unlocks on the nose landing gear releasing the nose gear into the slipstream combined with the feeling of deceleration as the main gear became speed brakes, pitching them up slightly before latching into place just as a loud metallic report reached them from the right side..

"JESUS!" Dan yelped, fighting the sudden roll to the right.

"We … lost something out there! Hold her!"

"I'm trying!"

"Half mile, 200 feet, 210 knots," Jerry called.

"It'll be a sudden flare. I'm full left stick and some left rudder … and she's shaking again!"

"One hundred feet, Dan. Hang on! Start your flare."

"Not yet."

"NOW, dammit! We could be losing hydraulics!"

"Hold it … .okay, now." Dan's hand pulsed backward on the sidestick, causing the huge panels on the jet's horizontal stabilizer to pulse upward using the last of the uninhibited hydraulic pressure, the nose of the Airbus rising rapidly as they traded speed for lift and slowed the descent rate, the deck angle becoming almost frightening. In the left seat Jerry internally braced himself for impact, but the nose continued to rise along with the onset of the same heavy buffeting they'd felt minutes before. There was nothing to do but hang on, and the fact that the four wheels per side on the main gear had just kissed the runway at almost a zero descent rate was slow to dawn until Jerry realized Dan was releasing the backpressure slowly, lowering the nosewheel to the runway and carefully bringing in the brakes to absorb the massive inertia of an Airbus at 200 knots.

"Speed brakes!" Dan called as Jerry lunged for the handle and snapped it aft.

"Careful on the brakes, Dan!"

"I know. Call my speed."

"We're 180 … 180 … 170 …we've got 7,000 feet left."

Dan let his feet feel the feedback pressure. Once the

accumulated hydraulic pressure was gone, the brakes would be nil. He couldn't fan them, just keep careful steady pressure. Too much and they'd lock with no anti-skid, blowing all the tires and guaranteeing a high speed departure from the far end of the runway. Too little and they'd meet the same fate.

"At 150, Dan; 140 now, 5,000 feet remaining; 130."

Another runway distance loomed on the right in the copilot's window with a large "4."

"We're 125, coming up on 4,000 left."

"Increasing pressure slightly," Dan said, knowing the brakes were probably already red hot.

"We'll need an emergency evac, Jerry."

"At 110 … slowing better now, 3,000 coming up. One hundred … almost ninety …"

The "3" moved past at a slower pace and he pressed harder, backing off at 1,500 remaining with the sound of a muffled explosion from the back as he felt the big jet swerve.

"We blew a tire!"

"Coming down through seventy, Dan! Careful!"

"They're fading, Jerry! I'm bringing them to the binders."

"Sixty-five … almost sixty … fifty …"

"We're not gonna make this … I've got a thousand left," Dan intoned

"Forty!"

"They're fading big time! I'm full forward on the pedals!"

"Thirty. End of the runway coming up."

"I'm steering to the right to miss that barrier."

"More, Dan! More right!"

"Working on it!"

"Fifteen and slowing. We're off the end but slowing."

The sudden transition from smooth concrete to rough sand felt like a pot-holed road as the red lights marking the end disappeared under the nose of the Airbus and Dan watched the barrier at the end come closer, slow, and stop, mere feet in front of his window.

The realization that they were in fact safely on the ground and actually at a dead stop took what felt like an eternity to fully comprehend.

"We made it!" Dan said, his tone beyond amazement.

"Yeah … we're on the ground and stopped and alive," Jerry echoed, breathing rapidly. "Holy crap!"

Smoke was already billowing from both main gear, flashing red lights reflecting off the interior of the cockpit as a squadron of fire trucks roared in to fight what they assumed would be flames.

"Let's get the hell out of this cockpit," Jerry said, feeling as if he'd been working through a completely unreal simulation. Surely there would be a quiet simulator bay beyond the cockpit door. None of this could be real.

Jerry punched up the PA before pulling off his headset to order an emergency evacuation.

"This is the captain. Evacuate the airplane! Follow the instructions of your flight attendants. When you're out of the airplane, remain clear of the wings and the main landing gear!"

The shoulder straps and seatbelts of the two jumpseats were snapping off as Bill Breem and Tom Wilson stood and disappeared into the forward cabin to take control of the emergency evacuation. Jerry was already out of his seat before realizing that Dan hadn't moved. He stopped and grabbed his left shoulder.

"You okay? Let's go!"

Dan looked up at him in momentary disbelief before snapping back into action, clawing at his seatbelt release and clambering out to follow the captain.

"Roger that!"

CHAPTER SIXTY-TWO

Baghdad International Airport (8:10 a.m. local / 0610 Zulu)

After fanning out and racing down both aisles of the passenger cabin to make sure no one had been left aboard, both pilots converged at the front left entry and stood together momentarily in an air of mutual disbelief, watching the sea of humanity they'd skippered for the last ten hours being herded away from the smoking aircraft.

Dan started to move toward the exit slide, but Jerry caught his sleeve.

"I wasn't sure we could pull this off, you know? So I want to … to thank you …"

There was a haunted look to the captain's face, the suspicion of inadequacy casting deep shadows on the glow of success, and Dan recognized it all too well from his own deep well of personal experience.

"But we *did* pull it off, Jerry! That's what counts." Dan replied, extending his hand to the captain who took it, covering it with his other hand as he looked Dan in the eye.

"*You* saved us, Danny! You did it, man! I choked …" the words trailed off.

Dan Horneman interrupted him quickly, before the word "choked" could lead to something more emotional.

"No. You didn't choke. You hung in there and led a good team. *We* did it. All of us."

"Yeah, but …"

"Hey!" Dan said sharply, smiling as broadly as he could manage. "Where do you get off thinking you cornered the market on being scared shitless?"

"I was that."

"So was I. But what say we get out of this crate before

we burn to death congratulating each other! Okay?"

"Okay."

Dan stepped out and jumped onto the slide for the quick trip to the bottom with Jerry right behind. They got to their feet as Carol waved them to follow the passengers she'd been marshalling aggressively off to the west side of the runway and clear of the fire trucks that were still spraying down the smoking main landing gear.

"I don't know if the whole plane's going to go up or not," she said. "Come on, you two. Hurry!"

"The brakes are carbon, Carol. They don't burn."

"Yeah? But they smoke pretty well."

It was Dan who thought to fish out his cell phone, turn it on, and try to punch up the direct number to Chicago, shocked when it rang without hesitation. He reached out and stopped the captain.

"Jerry, I've got Chicago on the line. I asked for Rick Hastings. You should talk to him."

Jerry took the phone somewhat reluctantly.

"Captain, Rick Hastings here. Congratulations, sir. I have a room full of people here in Chicago who haven't taken a breath in ten minutes! We are in your debt."

Situation Room, The White House

Strange, Walter Randolph thought to himself as the smiles and congratulatory handshakes ran their course. *This is a subdued response compared with other successes we've shared in this room. Of course, we were hardly in charge of anything.*

The fate of everyone aboard Pangia 10 was just one scene in an unfolding play. Much was left in motion: an Israeli pilot still evading in the Iraq desert waiting for rescue, a lethal set of ballistic missiles still standing, fueled, and ready on several would-be launch sites deep inside Iran, and he could just imagine the tension in the Hole in Tel Aviv. The president had already diverted two airborne US Air Force C-17s to Baghdad to pick up the passengers and crew within the next hour, and no one seemed to know the precise reason for his also ordering a Special Forces team in to secure and guard the airliner. What was clear to everyone in the Situation Room, however, was that something was aboard the Airbus that must not be allowed to fall into unaffiliated hands. It was unspoken common knowledge that both DIA and CIA were nearly desperate to examine the mysterious electronics, as well as find out how Lavi had pulled it off.

The president had paused minutes before leaving the room, then turned to both Walter and his DIA counterpart with a chilling request for a meeting and a post mortem in two days. Clearly the chief executive was not happy with the performance of his intelligence community, and that posed a major problem.

Walter Randolph sighed internally. The next two days would be exhausting as they tried to build a defense for every conclusion, every action, and every opinion the CIA had rendered, and DIA would be doing the same. The worst part, he thought, was that neither agency yet knew precisely what the hell had just happened, or why.

Or, for that matter, *how*.

He pulled out his pen and made a quick note regarding the mysterious William Piper. The company's conclusion in the heat of the battle had been that Piper was, in fact, the missing employee at Mojave who dispatched the wrong jet and the former Mossad agent was even supposed to be in Washington masquerading as a DIA operative. The president had been insistent on getting to the bottom of that. But then, on return to the Situation Room, the president had surprisingly appeared to lose interest.

Why? Walter wrote, underlining the word four times.

Baghdad International Airport

Ashira Dyan needed no briefing about the dangers to an Israeli agent who found herself suddenly in Iraq, even in post-Saddam Iraq. Being alive and on the ground was a positive thing, but the ground they were on was anything but good for an Israeli. That was especially true when you were in the company of the one Israeli official the Muslim world hated above all others.

As soon as Ashira's feet had hit the ground, she was struggling with her satellite phone for a connection to Tel Aviv and some sort of plan. Casually blending in with the passengers to wait for alternate transportation would be unthinkable, and perhaps lethal, on a host of levels.

Moishe Lavi was equally aware of the dangers, but the urgency of the call *he* was struggling to connect took precedence even over the sudden sweating and pain in his left arm, both of which had come out of nowhere after he slid down the exit chute.

A male voice, heavy with sleep, answered from somewhere in London, but the fact that he had picked up at all triggered a quiet flood of relief in Moishe.

"I'm alive, it turns out," Moishe said in Hebrew.

"So I hear. There is no war, you know."

"You mean, tonight?"

"Of course, tonight. Your letter … you said …"

"I know what I said. It was all for nothing. Please destroy it. Forget it. Please."

There was a tired sigh on the other end, and he understood completely. What might have been one of the major scoops of the decade had just evaporated in the journalist's hands. But Moishe knew he would keep his word.

"Very well," the man replied. "It would not make a lot of sense now anyway, would it?"

"Next time I'm in London, we'll get together, okay?"

"Certainly. Until next time, shalom. And, by the way, old chap?"

"Yes?"

"I am truly glad you're still among us."

"Thank you."

Moishe punched off the phone, angry at the rising pain and the shortness of breath he was experiencing and concerned that Ashira would notice. He stood for a moment, forcing the pain to subside and composing himself, then motioned her over to him as his mind raced through the tasks he would now have to accomplish.

"First, we have to evaporate from here. You know this, yes?"

"Of course," Ashira replied. "I am working on it."

"Very well."

"Are you all right?" she asked, studying his face in the subdued lights of the airport.

"Certainly. Just a bit fatigued."

"You look very pale, and you're perspiring. Let me find a place for you to sit …"

"No!" He had his hand out, palm up, fending her off. "Do nothing to attract attention to me, or you, for that matter. I will be fine."

The White House

The air force chief of staff had been asked to walk with the president back toward the Oval, but the chief executive stopped short of the door and turned.

"General, I don't care what you have to send in to do it, but get Lavi and his entourage out of there immediately."

"Yes, sir. We've got the transports en route …"

"No, I mean sooner. Do we have a diplomatic mission in Baghdad with an aircraft? One of our 89th Squadron birds? A charter? A business jet? Anything?"

"I … don't know, sir, but we'll get on it immediately."

"Coordinate with Tel Aviv, but get them out of there. The Iraqis must not know Lavi is there until he's long gone, if then."

Kathy Swanson, the press secretary, was waiting with the chief of staff as the president swept back into the Oval and leaned wearily against his desk.

"Where are we with the media?" he asked her. "How much do they know?"

"They know that Pangia 10 was hijacked … that's the word they're using … by its own electronics, but so far no one is openly speculating about sabotage or external control. They know the aircraft did a U-turn over the Atlantic and headed back to Tel Aviv and then turned toward Iraq and Iran. They know the aircraft has made an emergency landing in Baghdad, and that it was out of fuel. They do not know, as yet, about the explosion on the right engine or the Iranian attack."

"And they know that Lavi was aboard, right?"

"To my utter shock, not yet!"

"Really? Are any of them hinting at an Israeli-Iranian faceoff?"

"Reuters threw that into the air four hours ago, but no one else saluted it. ABC has been asking the question, but refrained from open speculation."

"And the thundering herd here?"

"Our White House press corps know something big is

afoot beyond a distressed airliner, but what I'm hearing from them is just their own speculation about what happens if an American flight originating in Israel ends up at an airport in Iran with Jewish passengers aboard."

The president's phone rang, and he scooped it up, spoke a few words, and replaced the receiver, turning back to the group.

"Seems the Israelis have already launched a business jet to Baghdad to get Lavi and his lady out of there, and he's supposed to be on the ramp in twenty minutes."

He looked back at the press secretary, who was holding up a cautionary finger.

"Go ahead, Kathy."

"It's going to accelerate, sir. The aggressive speculation we've had so far will flow into any available pathway for an explanation. Most of it at the moment revolves around what might go wrong with flight computers and complex avionics on highly automated Airbus airplanes, and we can expect the usual round of broadcast analysts chewing over the subject on the morning shows. From there, they will eventually realize this can't be explained by a malfunctioning autopilot."

The president nodded. "But Lavi's name might not surface?"

"No way to tell."

"Kathy, keep me informed regardless of the hour if speculation on the why and how begins to turn toward anything domestic, including us."

He could see her seize on the word "us," the look in her eyes betraying the realization that there was something important she did not know, and in the interest of plausible deniability as press secretary, she needed to keep it that way.

He waited until she had gone and the door had closed behind her before turning to his chief of staff.

"Walk with me. We've got two whistle-blowing

government employees sitting with Paul Wriggle in the Cabinet Room and I'm going to have to risk filling them in on what this whole project was really about."

"You may have to fill in more than them, sir. This could come unraveled."

"I know it. It's all or nothing. But if we do start down the mea culpa slide, we tell it all."

CHAPTER SIXTY-THREE

Baghdad International Airport (8:40 a.m. local / 0640 Zulu)

Every minute on the ground, Ashira Dyan reminded herself, was a minute closer to a diplomatic nightmare. Making matters worse was the very real possibility that the former prime minister was in serious medical trouble. Even with his steadfast denials and iron-jawed attempts to pretend nothing was wrong, his breathing was labored and he was increasingly rubbing his left arm and sweating profusely in the relatively cool air of the desert night.

A large black Suburban belonging to the American Embassy had plucked them off the ramp just minutes after they had jumped out of Pangia's Airbus, but for the last half hour the presumably-loyal Iraqi driver had hovered in the lee of the terminal, keeping clear of customs and the local police and waiting to ferry them safely to whatever aircraft could be found for what they all understood was an emergency exfiltration—a quick and clandestine flight away from Iraq. Moishe's medical situation was getting worse, but he angrily refused to discuss it, and after all, Ashira thought, what can we do? Even if he had a hangnail, Moishe Lavi's prospects of surviving a trip to an Iraqi emergency room would be nil.

Word that a Gulfstream 5 belonging to a European oil company had been chartered out of Tel Aviv made complete sense, until the plane had come to a stop on the ramp and the Suburban had pulled alongside. Ashira recognized the jet, and despite the Dutch registration number on the tail, she knew well it was one of Mossad's many tools for rapid extraction. The pilots appeared quickly at the top of the airstairs, both of them completing the image of two Dutch nationals wholly unconnected with Tel Aviv in their professional pilot shirts complete with epaulets. But they, too, were Mossad's men.

Ashira followed, as they shepherded Moishe Lavi into the Gulfstream. Two flight attendants greeted the former prime minister with appropriate deference as the pilots quickly started the engines and began taxiing, but the relief at leaving the ground and turning toward Israel was tempered for Ashira by her deepening concern that Moishe was deteriorating toward a full blown coronary. Quietly, she briefed the lead flight attendant, who positioned the aircraft's first aid kit at hand and placed a charged defibrillator behind his seat. There would be nothing more they could do aside from arranging for the best paramedics possible to be waiting at Ben Gurion airport.

And that was more than an hour away.

Building 4-104, Peterson Air Force Base, Colorado Springs

Richard Duncan sat nervously across from the desk of his supervisor, his face a study in apprehension. A retired navy chief with a top secret clearance, he'd been approved years before for a job no one else wanted: housekeeper in the main offices of a black project that officially didn't exist. Not even his wife knew where he went every evening, other than the fact that he cleaned offices to supplement their retirement income. Fifty-six, slightly overweight, and normally jovial, he had been summoned upstairs and escorted to his boss's office.

His supervisor was fifteen years his junior in age and a genuinely nice person, Richard had always felt, but she was clearly under pressure as she entered the office now and closed the door.

"Richard, we may have a problem," she began. "I need complete candor from you, okay?"

"Of course. Always."

"You were the only person with access to the server room night before last, and we've been trying to track down a very unusual occurrence we now think may have involved one of the servers. Was anyone else down there with you?"

"No, ma'am. I'm always careful to make sure no one follows me in without clearance. I was alone."

"Very well, then, this is the key question I have to ask you. Did anything out of the ordinary happen while you were in there by yourself?"

"Yes."

Cabinet Room, The White House

Being unable to join the others in the Situation Room who had been watching the real time information flow had been difficult for Paul Wriggle, but the president had arranged a steady stream of relayed messages to keep him informed, while he waited with Jenny Reynolds and Will Bronson. It was especially important for internal military politics, Paul Wriggle suggested, that a mere two star such as he not be seen hanging out with the president of the United States, especially when the four star general who was the air force chief of staff was in the building.

News that the Airbus A330 had successfully landed in Baghdad with the tattered remains of number two engine on the right wing immediately raised the question of how to get the jumbo jet repaired and back in the air toward the US. Paul had been on the phone almost continuously with Dana Baumgartner back in Colorado Springs as they started to pull together an aircraft-on-the-ground team, chase down a replacement engine, and work on getting someone into Baghdad to inspect the damage. More than an hour passed before word came that a Special Forces team had already arrived at Baghdad airport to secure the A330, but that was merely step one.

The general glanced at the door again, expecting it to open at any time with the president inbound. Working so diligently while suffused with a deep sense of gloom was emotionally exhausting, but he had no choice. He replaced the receiver and met the gaze of the other two people in the room as the president and chief of staff walked in the door, sitting quickly at the table across from Jenny and Will.

"I owe you two an explanation," the president began, "but I can explain only part of what has happened tonight. The biggest part of the mystery remains. What role might have Mr. Lavi played in all this, if he played any at all; and to that end, I wish the hell I could have teleported to Baghdad a while ago and shaken it out of him."

"Would there be an opportunity to speak with him later, sir?" Will asked, puzzled that the president was shaking his head sadly.

"Not in this life, Will. The jet that plucked him out of Baghdad a little more than an hour ago just landed in Tel Aviv. Moishe Lavi had a massive coronary in flight and was dead on arrival."

Jenny and Will exchanged startled glances as the president continued.

"That doesn't mean we won't get to the bottom of it. I'm convinced this was his doing, and a faction of the Israeli intelligence apparatus is probably responsible, but what I want to make sure of is that what you suspected, Will, is not true. The mere thought that the DIA might have been assisting Lavi is intolerable, and if it turned out to be true, I would have to deal with it harshly."

"But, sir," Jenny began, "… what about the aircraft? How could it lock out its pilots?"

The president glanced at Paul Wriggle and arched a thumb in his direction. "Partially because this fellow did what I asked him to do," the president began. "No, I didn't ask him to imperil the Pangia flight, but I did ask him to build a system that could disconnect a cockpit in flight." The president turned to General Wriggle. "Paul? Do you want to narrate the details, or should I?"

"Your choice, Mr. President."

"Okay, I'll do it." He turned back to Jenny and Will. "Do the two of you remember when President G.W. Bush promised, just after 9/11, that we'd be able to take control of airliners in the future from the ground and prevent hijackers from flying into buildings?"

"Yes," Jenny said. "I recall he was at Chicago O'Hare at the time. It was a planeside news conference."

"That's correct, it was. And it was a result of incredibly negligent staff work. The airline community was agape if not outraged. No one had such a system designed, and no one thought it could work. But even though President Bush's announcement was a grossly premature declaration, one of my later predecessors rekindled the idea as Project Skyhook, and while you don't need to know all the gory details, when the science looked shaky, that president decided he was going to terminate the program but announce to the world that we'd *already* equipped every US flagged airliner with such a system, even though it didn't really exist. It was kind of a brilliant idea to deter al Qaida, but at the last minute, a seismic shift in the intelligence picture scrubbed the public disinformation campaign and the project was shoved to the back burner. Actually, it was shelved because it would have been terribly expensive, and because there were a lot of experts cautioning that an accidental takeover from the ground with such a system could create havoc. Worse, President Bush had said air traffic controllers would do the recovery flying of a hijacked airliner, but most air traffic controllers are not qualified heavy jet pilots, so an entire cadre of standby drone pilots would be needed. Anyway, when I came into office the following year and was briefed on this, I decided to change the name of the project but keep a deep black project team working on it, just in case the idea might prove more viable with better technology."

Will and Jenny exchanged glances.

"And the 'it' you're talking about … that's a black project, sir?" Will asked.

"Yes. You don't need to know the official name, but I wanted a pilot project … no pun intended … for a foolproof way of taking control of a hijacked or compromised airliner from the ground. I wanted to see if the thing was ever going to be feasible, partly because I also knew that our radical Islamic enemies were never going to let go of their burning desire to hijack airliners and use them in their murderous schemes. I still think I'm right to do so. Even if we never deploy the system, we'll learn a great deal about the art of the possible. So, I've kept it going as a deep black air force project, headed by General Wriggle here. Everyone had to sign a legal loyalty contract that would slap them in Leavenworth if they ever revealed any associated classified information. Of course, I'm well aware that you two haven't signed such a contract, but I'm going to ask you to do so."

Jenny had leaned forward to say something but the president raised his hand to stop her. "You need to hear the rest of it. Somehow the top secret test airplane, the A330 Paul's people bought to experiment with got out of his hands last week and ended up being flown as a regular flight by Pangia Airways, and in the middle of the flight, this test bed electronics package suddenly activated. The activation signal came from NSA's transmitters but was supposed to be triggered only from the project's headquarters in Colorado

Springs. No such test signal was scheduled. Am I right, Paul?"

"That's correct."

"Okay, so this is why we think we're dealing with sabotage. That and the presence of the former Israeli PM, of course. Somehow, someone found out about the project and bent it to his purpose, and that someone had to be our old friend Lavi. I'd bet the next election on it. Lavi, Mossad, and a galaxy of very clever people are undoubtedly involved, and your suspicion, Will, that DIA was somehow involved is not outlandish, although it would be sad, if that were true."

"And all of this to start a war, sir?" Jenny asked.

"I personally think so. Not start a war so much as end the chance of one, in Lavi's view. But I'm convinced it was the late Mr. Lavi's last ditch effort to create an excuse to preemptively strike Iran's nuclear capabilities, which is what he openly expressed that he wanted to do. If so, thank God he failed. And he failed because you two refused to stay silent. Do I understand it right that you, Jenny, discovered the strange radio signals and called in Mr. Bronson here?"

"Yes, sir, but at the direction of my boss, Seth Ziegler."

The president leaned forward slightly, his eyes boring into Jenny's. "I understand, but it was *your* vigilance that placed it before him. So, I have to ask you, Jenny Reynolds, how does it feel?"

"How does what feel, Mr. President?"

"How does it feel to have very likely prevented a nuclear war?"

She met the president's gaze, noting a kindly smile behind the question before the answer formed on her lips.

"Surreal, sir. Very surreal."

An aide had quietly entered the room with a note for the president, who read it and nodded, folding it again before looking at General Wriggle.

"Well, Paul …" the president began, sighing, "I think our concerns about getting that Airbus flyable and out of there are over as well."

Paul Wriggle came forward in his seat with a startled expression. "Why, sir?"

The President slid the note across the table to him. "Because, according to this, there was a smoldering fire in the electronics bay they didn't find until it exploded in open flames. Our security team sounded the alarm when they discovered it, but it was too late. The aircraft is in ashes."

CHAPTER SIXTY-FOUR

Four days later

National Security Agency, Ft. Meade, Maryland (9:30 a.m. EST)

Jenny Reynolds stepped into the NSA, somewhat surprised that her security badge was still valid. She was still in a fog of emotions. Seth had relayed word to take the rest of the week off, but her world had shifted, and she was off balance. Work was to be her anchor to normalcy.

Seth was waiting when the elevator opened, scooping her into a full body embrace that he would have never dared just a week before.

"We're so glad you're okay, and so very proud of you!"

When it was apparent he didn't know when to let go, she gently unfolded his lanky arms from around her, knowing her smile was too thin and uncertain to properly thank him, but trying nonetheless.

"I just want to get back to work, Seth," she managed, finally.

"You will."

"And I'm so glad you … I mean, that there was no involvement …"

He nodded back, rolling his eyes. "I didn't know for awhile there whether you had gone rogue, or I had, or the agency, or what. It was all terribly confusing."

"God, was it ever!" she echoed, following him side by side at a slow walk toward the double doors leading to her section. "Is there any word on Will?"

"How do you mean, Jenny?" Seth asked, nudging her along.

"I got the impression he was in big trouble with his

bosses, but he hasn't contacted me since that night."

"After what you two pulled off, I seriously doubt he's in trouble. Politics may be rancid, but when the president is singing your praises, the intelligence community is all ears. Not that we aren't anyway," he said with a smirk.

Seth opened the double doors for her, and Jenny stepped in, stunned to see the whole extended team in the large room standing and looking at her, and even more dumbstruck when they started clapping and cheering. She had to suppress the urge to run, or at least to turn to see if there was someone else they were applauding.

Seth motioned for quiet and raised his voice, addressing the group and rambling through a brief speech about their pride in her perseverance and the number of people who probably owed their lives to her—a sentiment she didn't share. After all, it had been her old code the air force general's people had used. All she'd done was try to defuse the bomb they'd built with her unwitting participation. And, she thought, *it was mainly Will who wouldn't give up.*

Her face visibly reddened from the embarrassing attention, she smiled as broadly as she could manage and mouthed a thank you as she waved to her colleagues and followed Seth into his office.

"That was very moving, Seth. Thank you!"

"Hey, everyone was involved. There's even a cake for later."

"No!"

"It's a small one. We're government, after all." He looked at her quizzically. "What's wrong, Jenny?"

"Frankly?"

"Yes. No holds barred."

"I'm scared, Seth! All this attention—I'm afraid this has raised the bar so high for me I can never jump over it again."

"No one expects you to defuse an international incident

every week, Jen!"

He could see there were tears gathering in the corner of her eyes. "The president of the United States asked me … *ME* … how it felt to have stopped a nuclear war. Where do I go from there, Seth?"

"Maybe that was your moon landing."

"Sorry?"

"All the astronauts who walked on the moon—and especially the first ones, Buzz Aldrin in particular—wondered the same thing. How do you top that? Talk about raising the bar on yourself."

"So how did *they* handle it?"

"As a beginning, not an end. What you did was a milestone that showed the world what Jenny Reynolds is made of. The incident simply showed us the real you. It didn't define you. Make sense?"

"A little. I'm sorry." she said, dabbing at an errant tear. "I just want to get back to work and convince myself the world isn't a hall of mirrors with nothing as it seems."

"Well-l-l, to a certain extent it is, but I anticipated that you'd feel this way, so …" he reached over to the corner of his desk and picked up an intimidating stack of papers and binders. "This is your assignment for the next week or so. I need intercepted electronic intelligence traffic out of southern China carefully analyzed and compared to determine whether we are seeing a substantive shift in the encoding routines used in snap-on transmissions—especially important given their island building activities."

She shuddered as he placed the stack in her lap. "Really? Is this a thinly-disguised re-entry program?"

"Maybe a little, but I really do need your expert analysis. When you're ready, I'll get you briefed on the background political reasons."

"Okay."

"Why don't you stay in here for a few minutes until you're ready to go plow through all the adoring fans out there. I'm going upstairs for a meeting."

"Seth, one question."

"Sure," he said, standing.

"Do we, does anyone know, whether Moishe Lavi was behind all this?"

Seth pursed his lips and nodded slightly. "We're all suspicious, and what I pick up from those way above my pay grade is that this just couldn't have been a wild coincidence. But do I either know, or have a need to know, what undoubtedly the president now knows? In a word, no."

"You'd tell me if you knew?"

"Not if I'm told not to. Of course, I might wink at you and stomp the floor a few times, but, no need to know equals no formal information for Jenny."

"Okay."

"My guess? Not having enough info?"

"Yes, I trust your guesses," Jenny said.

"So, my guess, based on the fact that Mr. Lavi had access to the best intelligence operatives in the world and was determined to have it out with Iran, my guess is that his last act was a magnum masterpiece of deception, and only a brilliant and intrepid southern gal who doesn't think she has an accent got in his way. That's what I think."

"Thanks, Seth."

"Oh, one more thing. Pick up my desk phone and punch '3.'"

"Seth, not another accolade, I hope."

"Naw. Just someone who wants a word with you."

She lifted the receiver as he closed the door behind him, and an instantly familiar voice filled her ear.

"Will! How *are* you?"

"Actually, pretty good, Jenny. They stopped shooting people over here before they got to me."

She hesitated, and he jumped in.

"Just kidding! We weren't guilty, it seems, and for some reason they think I saved the world. I told them it was you, but they doubted a female could pull it off."

"What?"

"Okay, that's a joke, too."

"You're in rare form this morning."

"And I'll be in rarer form this evening, depending on you. Where are you?"

"I think you know. I'm in my boss's office."

"Yeah, and that was the wrong question. I was going to drop into a Barry White voice and ask what you're wearing."

"What I'm *wearing*?"

"Don't answer that. Just meet me at the same place in the same shopping center at the same time tonight. And *this* time we'll really do dinner and a movie."

"Really?"

"To start."

"Pretty bold, Bubba, thinking I'd automatically accept putting myself in peril with you again," she laughed.

"Didn't you, somewhere in that safe house, say, 'Coffee now, seduction later'?"

"I guess I did."

"Well, did I not deliver on the coffee?"

"You did."

"So, do we have a date?"

"Very well, I will agree to dinner and a movie, and I will agree to listen to you plead your case. Beyond that, no guarantees."

"Cool."

"Same time, same place, and two more requirements."

"Shoot."

"This time, no sneaking up on me and no idling black SUVs mysteriously waiting in a loading dock."

"Promise."

CHAPTER SIXTY-FIVE

One week later

Tel Aviv, Israel (11:15 a.m. local)

Two men walking slowly through Tel Aviv's Yarkon Park in deep conversation in late morning had attracted no one's attention, save for the security detail protecting the prime minister of Israel and trying to keep a discreet distance.

Gershorn Zamir gestured to a park bench and they settled onto it, the prime minister sitting slightly sideways as his slender, six-foot-two companion leaned back and sighed, his words spoken with an Oxfordian British accent.

"Thank you, old chap. My back has been giving me a bloody run for it these past few months. I could blame it on rugby, but in truth it's too much mucking around at home lifting heavy things the wrong way."

"I completely sympathize. I'm too heavy for much exercising, but just walking takes its toll these days after too many hours at a desk."

"Or at the head of a crisis center table, I expect."

"Yes. So, tell me, please, what you trundled here all the way from London to impart."

The man looked over and smiled slightly, then straightened up and looked around carefully, before continuing.

"The letter, or more properly stated, the email that Moishe asked me to destroy after he sent it in flight didn't mention how, just why."

"I would expect that."

"And, you understand, there's nothing new in the 'why': the same old fact that the mullahs would happily die and go collect their virgins if the loss of their country was accompanied by the vaporization of Israel; their first strike on Israel was anywhere from hours to days away; how he had a duty to make sure their ability to attack was destroyed, et cetera, et cetera. But the key was the statement I mentioned. The statement that he had commandeered a commercial airliner full of innocent people only because he had no other method of showing the world Iran's murderous intent. He said he regretted the impending loss of civilian lives, but that they, too, were dying for a great cause."

"Commandeered was the word?"

"Yes."

"Are you planning to publish the letter?"

"To what end, Gershorn? Even if I hadn't been on Israel's side my entire life, what would such a revelation do? I don't particularly care about Lavi's legacy, but it would stir up anger and distrust of anything Israel says or does regarding Iran, and put them in the role of victim of Zionist aggression."

"I appreciate your decision, especially since I know you're giving up a coup."

"Not really. I might be giving up an opportunity to sabotage the very interests I want to help. More than anything, I'd be driving a stake through your political heart if I revealed that letter."

"I don't understand."

"There were a few people thanked in a veiled way in Lavi's verbiage, Gershorn, and based on who they might be and the positions potentially involved, it would not take a Sherlock Holmes to discern the presence of a host of confederates in Mossad, IDF, your government, and a couple of very key people in the US."

"He *named* them?"

"No, no. Only implied. He was a master at espionage and subtlety even if he was also the proverbial bull in the china shop. But from those implied confederates come inescapable conclusions."

The PM looked away for a few moments, letting his mind run through the thicket of possible reactions from the world.

"You realize I have to search for these turncoats," Gershorn replied quietly.

"Are they turncoats? If they even exist, in their minds, they're patriots. Far be it for an obscure little journalist to advise the prime minister of Israel, but if you launch a witch hunt—as the Yanks call it—you will split your government down the middle. And, keep in mind that Moishe may have been setting up completely innocent people, whether to settle old scores or otherwise we'll never know.

"Who in the States?"

"He implied he had someone buried deep, but … he was only tossed out of office last month. There simply wasn't enough time to send over a mole and get things set up for an electronic hijacking."

"Then why did he try to take credit?"

"Because our old friend was first and foremost a master opportunist. I have no trouble believing that he found himself on an electronically locked out airliner maybe heading toward Tehran and decided to take full advantage of it."

"But, could he have done it?"

"We can never know."

"I must let it lie, in other words? Here and there?"

"Precisely what I would say if I were advising you, yes. Fortunately, I am a mere and meager journalist and not in that position, so it is well within my discretion to speak freely and as unaccountably as possible."

"And … you will destroy all copies of that communique from Moishe?"

The journalist looked over at Gershorn again and raised a bushy eyebrow.

"What communique?"

CHAPTER SIXTY-SIX

Two weeks later

Chicago (7:40 p.m. CST)

The fact that there always seemed to be a gale whipping the canyons of downtown Chicago had impressed Dan Horneman, and this evening was no exception: While dashing into the posh steakhouse, a wild gust inverted the umbrella he'd raised against a light rain.

His date had fared no better.

Laura Snyder hadn't quite repaired the serious tousling the wind had given her impressive mane of auburn hair. She had an almost feral look, he thought, as he watched her across the table. Wild and exciting, and hopefully eager for change.

Of course, whether she was his date tonight, or merely his curious ex, was yet to be determined.

Laura tossed her hair back and took a sip of Cabernet, her eyes finally boring into his with a familiar intensity.

"So, let's get to it, flyboy. I figure there's only one possible reason that you could have asked to see me tonight, since you know how I detest globetrotting men." She stopped, noting his lecherous expression. "A reason other than wanting sex."

"It has been a long time!" he laughed. "At least for us."

"Yes, it has, and therefore I assume you've decided to abandon being a gypsy at long last in order to resume chasing me."

"What?"

"In other words, you've invited me here to announce that you're resigning from Pangia to lead a normal life. Right?"

"Wrong."

"Wrong? Then, why did you call me?"

"Well, why did you come?" he replied. "Fact is, I never thought a scorched-earth resignation was a condition precedent for your affections."

"Then you weren't paying attention," she said, smiling back at him ruefully.

She slowly placed the wine glass on the tablecloth, letting a few seconds elapse before replying.

"I came, Danny, because I care about you, and I guess I remain curious about when you're going to stop chasing what you already have."

"You mean, the money?"

"No! Not the money. Your own immense worth to the world. To yourself. Maybe even to me. Have you proven everything you wanted to prove? Is the quest over?"

It was his turn to pause, his eyes studying the base of his wine glass as he twirled it slightly, nodding.

"I think I'm done apologizing, if that's what you mean."

"What, to *me?* You certainly don't need to."

"No. To the world in general, as well as all my fellow airline pilots. Apologizing for the money, for not staying and making more, for the steep learning curve as a pilot, all of it. Apologizing, as you say, for trying to prove something."

"So, what changed? I mean, I know about the flight from hell, of course, and your incredible landing in Baghdad. Everyone knows."

"Did you know they just offered me an early upgrade to captain, jumping the seniority list, as a training captain?"

Her expression fell slightly. "Really?"

"Yes. Just this morning!"

"So, we're here to celebrate?"

"The CEO made the offer. Apparently the stuffed-shirt captain who was with us that night, name of Bill Breem, joined Jerry Tollefson, the flight captain, in recommending the upgrade. And believe me, Tollefson was no fan of mine, at least not before that flight."

She nodded and forced a smile. "Then, clearly, congratulations are in order, Captain. I'm sure you'll be very happy."

"I turned them down, Laura."

She looked up at him then, head slightly cocked, memories flooding back of her childhood as the daughter of an airline pilot.

"You turned down an early captain upgrade?" she asked, incredulously. "Isn't that bordering on insanity?"

"Some will think so."

"Why, if you're not quitting?"

"I may. Quit, that is. Later, when I'm ready. But this is where I want to be for the moment, and, well …"

She nodded suddenly, knowingly, and smiled. "Aha! And, for the first time, you feel like you belong. Am I right?"

His smile broadened. "Yes."

"Was *that* what it was all about? Years of flight training and knocking around like a pimply-faced twenty-something living out of a bag? All of it just to be accepted?"

He took his finger and traced the rim of his wine glass, studying it before looking up to meet her rock-steady gaze.

"I've learned, Laura, that when great wealth comes too easily, it forces a man to question his own self-worth."

"That's eloquent, Dan."

"You asked why I called you? Because I could always depend on you to cut to the heart of the matter."

"Okay, I'm not a diplomat."

"No," he chuckled, "You definitely are *not* a diplomat! But, you *are* one of those rare people who will tell the brutal truth."

"And you're sidestepping my question."

"No," he interrupted, a finger in the air, "I'm not. I'm getting there. It was more than being accepted. It was a burning need to earn at least a modicum of respect, not for how much money I might have been lucky enough to make, but for something difficult I accomplished that can't be measured by bank balances, something I had to do myself."

"And that was flying?"

"Yes. I've always wanted to fly, but this…this involved invading a fraternity, and a tough one at that. Gaining their respect has proven very challenging, and without that hellish flight, I doubt I'd have it yet."

"In my view, Dan, it was unnecessary, but I'm not you. I already know what I'm good at, and what I'm not so good at, and I still respect me."

"I respect you, too."

She waved the compliment away.

"So, I get it, Danny. You needed to challenge yourself. I felt the same in law school. I had to be number one in my law class to prove to myself that when I concentrate on something, there are no barriers I can't jump over."

"Yes! Same thing. And you succeeded."

"No, I didn't. I came out number two, but it was okay. As for your quest, what have you learned?"

He smiled and nodded slowly. "That I can be a good leader as well as a team player, and good pilot. I was just trying to be a good pilot."

"And now you plan to keep on flying, just in order to keep validating that finding, over and over and over?"

"Not much longer. Truth is, after thinking my way through some of the more dismal moments on that flight—when I wasn't sure how we had a chance at salvation—I realized I have other priorities more important to me than flying or even making captain. He stopped and smiled slowly as he met her eyes. "In fact, one priority in particular."

"Which priority is that?"

"You."

CHAPTER SIXTY-SEVEN

Two months later

Camp David, Maryland (4:10 p.m. EST)

Normally, CIA Director James Bergen and Deputy Director Walter Randolph would have been delighted to be summoned to Camp David for a private conversation with the president, but this trip was to receive a formal ass-kicking along with their DIA counterparts. The meeting had been brutal, with an angry president determined to end once and for all the interdepartmental rivalries of his intelligence community.

Fat chance! Walter thought to himself, very glad his thoughts couldn't yet be discerned either from his taciturn expression or through some electronic gadget.

The Defense Intelligence team had departed immediately afterwards by helicopter, their metaphorical tails firmly between their legs, while the CIA team was to be driven back to Langley. But one of the president's aides caught Bergen and Randolph at the door and ushered them back into a small den. POTUS entered the room almost as rapidly.

"Jim? Walt? I'm still unclear on a key element of what happened to Pangia. Was Lavi controlling the airplane or not? Did he set this up?"

Walter Randolph shook his head. "We don't believe there is any way Lavi could have been controlling the airplane through a computer from his first class seat. And we don't believe there was any way he could have manipulated so many coincidences, including the accidental triggering of the lockout system."

"No moles on our shore, in other words?" the president said, leaning, arms folded, against the side of a sofa.

"It is always possible that there could have been a

confederate over here, but we seriously doubt it."

"DIA? NSA?"

"No, sir. Definitely not one of us. If a mole existed at all, if someone had been buried deep in Pangia or the black project or both, he would be a civilian, and a brilliant one at that. But it just doesn't figure."

"If it did, I was going to order you guys to find that mole at all costs."

"We'd be chasing a ghost, Mr. President."

"Very well. That was unclear from your joint briefing. Of course, I was too busy kicking your collective parochial asses to listen well." He looked at his watch. "I have to go. Have a safe trip back to the Beltway, gentlemen."

Three hours and a half dozen meetings later, the president of the United States settled comfortably in one of the wide wicker chairs on the veranda after handing Paul Wriggle a glass of Scotch.

"Oban, Paul. My favorite. I'm half Scottish, so these are home squeezin's."

"Thank you, sir. I've always loved a good single malt."

The president gestured to the starfield overhead, iridescent in a crystal clear night sky. "I'll always regret not getting out there. How about you, Paul? Ever want to join NASA?"

"I just wanted to fly. Anywhere. Space, atmosphere, you know."

"Yep, I do know. I felt the same, just … other interests got in the way of being a professional birdman." He turned to the general and smiled. "Now let's talk about you. What's all this retirement stuff?"

"It's time."

"I could tell you no. I could have you promoted to four star, Paul, rather than let you retire," the president said, swishing the liquor in the crystal snifter he was holding.

Paul Wriggle shook his head ruefully as he nursed his own glass. “Promotion is for those who don’t let their commander in chief down, Mr. President. Besides, that would trigger an absolute tsunami of resentment at the Pentagon.”

“I don’t think you’ve let me down, Paul. I know you’ve been terribly hard on yourself and the final assessment of things, but … you ran a very tight ship and sometimes shit happens.”

“Yeah, like a bank of computers I should have had programmed better.”

“Paul, seriously, you said yourself there had to be an extraordinary number of one-off failures to get to what happened. Who knew the test program your lady was running hadn’t been properly shut down weeks earlier? *She* didn’t even know. Who knew it would activate itself if the server was rebooted, and then start broadcasting through NSA all over the planet looking for your black box? Who knew the janitor would accidentally turn off the only computer containing that program, and then not understand he couldn’t just snap it back on? For that matter, who knew that the little chip in that computer was defective and it would re-start itself despite being programed not to? I fail to see how all of that’s your fault.”

“Because I was in command, sir.”

“Yeah, I know the protocol. I respect you for that attitude. But I’m still not even completely convinced this was all coincidental.”

Paul Wriggle leaned forward slightly, searching the president’s face for a smirk or other indication he was being kidded.

“Mr. President, you can’t think Lavi is still in the woodwork somewhere? We’ve disproved all that.”

“Oh, I know. William Piper never left Haifa. The guy who sent the wrong airplane really did exist and wasn’t a spy, and our CIA guys were incredibly sloppy in deciding otherwise. And your lady who had the accident certainly wasn't working for Lavi. How is she, by the way?"

"Fully recovered and newly engaged to the coworker who found her … saved her life, in fact."

"Good. Anyway, aside from the fact that earlier today I had to read the riot and sedition act to both the Company and the DIA for a whole laundry list of sins, including gross overreaction and leaping to conclusions, I'm not entirely sure in my gut we've got the whole story."

"Why, may I ask?"

"Too coincidental. I'm even thinking someone helped Moishe's heart attack to conclusion, or, hell, maybe he did *himself*."

"Aren't you chasing shadows under the bed, sir?"

"Maybe. Oh, we'll never know, of course. Lavi's gone, the war didn't happen, Gershorn proved himself under excruciating pressure, and Mossad will never talk. But I'm still suspicious."

"I guess I'm not."

"I'm sorry about Lockout, Paul."

"You had no choice but to shut it down, sir. I just can't believe the media never sniffed it out."

"If the aircraft hadn't gone up in smoke, they might have. Course, Airbus is still frantic to convince the world their airplane wasn't the cause. Frankly I feel sorry for them. I wish I could help them, but … not possible. Good thing our Special Forces guys were there to validate what happened with that fire, don't you think, Paul?" the president said with a wink.

Once more, Paul Wriggle looked at the president, studying his face, noting a sly smile.

"Yes, sir. That was a $200 million investment, though."

"More like a billion-dollar liability. How are your people,

Paul? Get everyone new jobs?”

“Yes, sir. All but the janitor, our retired navy chief. He was deeply upset by his role and didn’t want to go anywhere.”

“One switch. One … flick of the hand. Completely random, or … completely brilliant.”

“Sir?” Paul said, looking alarmed, and all the more so as the president smiled and nodded as he sat back.

“I’m just sayin’ …”

EPILOGUE

Colorado Springs, Colorado (9:20 a.m. MST)

Are you sure you want to deactivate this account? the screen queried.

He glanced around his small home office, listening carefully to make sure he was alone, before returning his attention to the screen. The connection with an outside Wi-Fi signal he'd hacked into was tenuous but steady, and the server hundreds of miles away in Chicago had no clue it was responding to an unauthorized source.

He highlighted the "Yes" box and hesitated a few seconds over the enter button before pushing it with a smile he couldn't quite suppress.

There was a small "click" as the screen shifted to black, and a white notification box popped up in the center:

XL@Pangiawordlair.com erased

Ironic, he thought to himself as he glanced at the box of personal belongings he'd brought home from the tiny office he'd occupied for years. The item he most prized was a paperweight, a personal gift from Moishe Lavi from many years back. He stared for a minute at the swirls of blue and six-pointed stars. No one ever noticed that the stars had six points instead of five. The fact that the paperweight had always been so blatantly obvious on his desktop, yet still invisible, had amused him throughout the years. Probably because it was just like him: There, but essentially invisible.

He could hear his wife moving around in the kitchen at a distance, and he thought about her worried reaction two days before when he'd announced he was quitting the job he never spoke about. She knew why, of course. It was demeaning for an ex-navy chief to end up pushing a broom. He never complained, but she had been embarrassed that they needed the cash, and he could tell by her worried expression, she was already calculating the impact.

"Did … something happen you're not telling me about? Were you fired?" she'd asked.

He'd put his hands on her shoulders then. "No, baby! Nothing like that. I just … well, I caught myself cleaning the same hallway twice and realized I was so distracted thinking about how I'd much rather be here with you, I didn't even realize it."

"I'm glad, to tell the truth. You've been a trooper, but you're not a janitor."

"That didn't matter," he smiled, kissing her. "I can swab heads with the best of them. No shame in it."

"How much have we got in the retirement accounts, then?" she'd asked.

"Enough," he said, mentally toting up the ones he was willing to show her, and the offshore account he wasn't. "We'll be great, babe. We're secure. We're *free*!"

Richard Duncan's attention returned to the laptop and what he had programmed as the last act. He pulled up the internal program he'd written and initiated it, watching with satisfaction as the laptop's hard drive consumed itself, completely destroying every vestige of data.

An account erased, and a life rebooted, he thought.

ACKNOWLEDGEMENTS

When you yank back the curtain on the classic but apocryphal image of an author in "countless" hours of solitary confinement with a laptop, the true story encompasses a writer on a mission leaning on countless people for answers to endless questions and urgent requests for manuscript readings. The convoluted track to finishing LOCKOUT has traversed the same territory, so a lot of thank you's are in order, beginning with my industrial strength appreciation for everything my wife and fellow author **Kathleen Bartholomew** did to help – including use an entire Cabo vacation to tighten the book and weather my pained protests that I couldn't cut another word! Great appreciation also to **Patricia Davenport** who has so ably edited most of my novels over the years, including this one, and to **Dave and Bianca Vanderwal**, **Bill and Katia Robinson**, and **Shari and Harold Harrison** for comprehensive help and support for the developing work. Thank you most specifically to fellow author and airline **Captain Karlene Petitt** (Flight for Control, Flight for Safety, Flight for Survival) for all the technical expertise and connection to many other pilots flying the Airbus A-330. Thank you as well to friend, colleague and fellow military aircraft commander **Spence Byrum**, and to fellow airline captain, first cousin, and world-class sculptor **James J. Nance**. And my appreciation to fellow Alaska Airlines **Captain Mark Alger** for a valuable 11th hour read. Heartfelt thanks for **Arna Robbins**, and a sincere thank you as well to **Bart Bartholomew, Arthur Ferrara, Curt Epperson,** and **Doctors Paul Abson** and **Diana Abson** for giving me precisely what every author needs: unvarnished feedback, not just what I might want to hear, all of which strengthened the story.

And to my new publisher, WildBlue Press, and specifically **Steve Jackson and Michael Cordova**: Gentlemen, that great line from Bogie in Casablanca applies: “Louis, I think this is the beginning of a beautiful friendship.”

OTHER BOOKS BY JOHN J. NANCE

Fiction:

Orbit
Saving Cascadia
Fire Flight
Skyhook
Headwind
Turbulence
Blackout
The Last Hostage
Medusa's Child
Pandora's Clock
Phoenix Rising
Scorpion Strike
Final Approach

Non-Fiction:

Charting the Course (with Kathleen Bartholomew)
Why Hospitals Should Fly
Golden Boy
What Goes Up
On Shaky Ground
Blind Trust
Splash of Colors

For More Information About John Nance:

https://www.amazon.com/John-J.-Nance/e/B000API14C

Use this link to sign up for advance notice
of John J. Nance's Next Book:
http://wildbluepress.com/AdvanceNotice

Word-of-mouth is critical to an author's long-term success.
If you appreciated this book please leave a review on the
Amazon sales page:
http://wbp.bz/loreviews

When a boat and its grisly cargo are found adrift off Fort Lauderdale, the investigation leads to more than "just" murder. In fact, the evidence points to a connection with an "accident" that downed Patriot Airlines Flight 63 in Bermuda with fatal consequences for all on board.

As head of the pilots' union, Captain Hart Lindy will find himself reluctantly drawn into the National Transportation Safety Board's inquiry only to discover that someone is going to great lengths that include murder and kidnapping to prevent the facts from being exposed. But who? And why?

These are the dangerous questions Lindy will need to answer in order to get at the truth about what really happened to Flight 63. His task is complicated by his own personal demons, including the horrors of past airline crash investigations, as well as having to walk a diplomatic tightrope with an eccentric FBI special agent who is barely tolerating NTSB protocol, and an ambitious female NTSB investigator with eyes for Hart.

Written by veteran airline pilot and aviation analyst, Les Abend, PAPER WINGS will keep you up in the air and on the edge of your seat in first class. You'll want to keep your belts fastened while in flight!

Les Abend is a 32-year veteran airline pilot with a writing habit. He has been a 15-year contributing editor and monthly columnist for FLYING MAGAZINE. Les has also been a contributor to CNN Op-Ed and is an on-camera Aviation Analyst, most notably offering insight regarding the disappearance of MH 370.

Check out the book here: **http://wbp.bz/pw**

WILDBLUE
PRESS

THE NEW YORK TIMES BESTSELLER
IDENTITY CRISIS
DEBBI MACK

PITFALL
CAMERON BANE

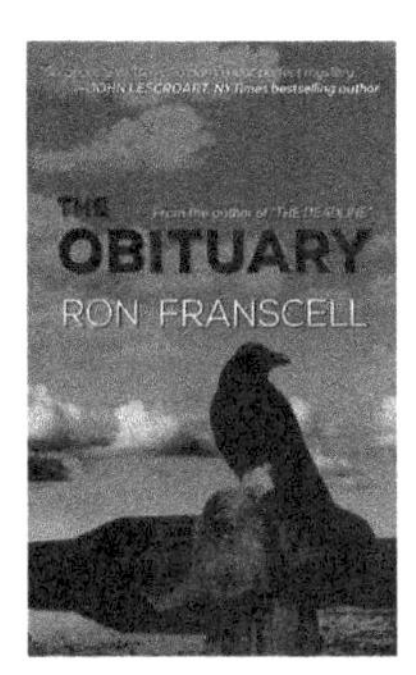
THE OBITUARY
RON FRANSCELL